ZERO POINT

NEAL ASHER

ZERO POINT

An Owner novel

TOR

First published 2012 by Tor
an imprint of Pan Macmillan, a division of Macmillan Publishers Limited
Pan Macmillan, 20 New Wharf Road, London N1 9RR
Basingstoke and Oxford
Associated companies throughout the world
www.panmacmillan.com

ISBN 978-0-230-75070-8 HB
ISBN 978-0-230-75226-9 TPB

1 3 5 7 9 8 6 4 2

A CIP catalogue record for this book is available from
the British Library.

Typeset by SetSystems Ltd, Saffron Walden, Essex
Printed and bound by CPI Group (UK) Ltd, Croydon, CR0 4YY

Visit **www.panmacmillan.com** to read more about all our books
and to buy them. You will also find features, author interviews and
news of any author events, and you can sign up for e-newsletters
so that you're always first to hear about our new releases.

To all you steady researchers and developers of our technology,
for recognizing the optimistic road to the future,
rather than seeing a slippery slope to doom.

Acknowledgements

As always, many thanks to all those who have helped bring this book to your shelves, Kindle, iPad, fancy phone, computer screen or whatever. At Macmillan these include Julie Crisp, Bella Pagan, Chloe Healy, Louise Buckley, Amy Lines, Catherine Richards, Ali Blackburn, Eli Dryden, Neil Lang, James Long and others whose names I simply don't know. Thanks also to Jon Sullivan for his consistently weird cover pictures capturing the spirit of the books and to Peter Lavery for his consistently meticulous editing. And always, thank you, Caroline.

I also have to mention all those fans whose comments, criticisms and accolades help maintain my enthusiasm for what I'm doing. Of course, on many levels, I couldn't do it without you. Thanks also to all those unpaid keepers of websites and message boards, and the contributors both to them and the social networks, who have invigorated debate on all subjects under the sun, and who are steadily cutting the ground away from underneath moribund and tribal media organizations. With the excellent tool that is the Internet they have truly taken things back to 'grass roots' and we are certainly seeing their effect in the world today.

For this book I also have to thank all those who have written on zero-point energy, possible space drives and weird energy sources. It's good to know that some are prepared to think outside the box, even if they are falling off the far side of weird.

1

Power to the People!

The rebellion was doomed to failure, even had its ostensible leader General Malden succeeded in his plan to drop the Argus Station on the largest bureaucratic conclave of the Committee, which was then located in Brussels (originally the centre of the old European Union). Malden, like so many would-be rebels of the time, was under the illusion – which the Committee promulgated – that the world government actually possessed a heart that could be cut out. In reality the Brussels governmental sprawl was just a larger and more wasteful version of the old European Parliament – real decisions weren't made there at all, but during teleconferences between Committee delegates generally residing like old-time kings in their regional palaces which, along with the Inspectorate HQs, were the real centres of power. Alan Saul's attack proved more surgical, destroying many of those HQs, and thus killing a large portion of the Committee Executive and annihilating much of the infrastructure of control. However, the government of Earth was like a hydra and, even though Saul cut off a number of its heads, they soon began to grow back. It could also be argued that he cut off many diseased heads, and the lesser number that grew back had sharper eyes and all their teeth.

Zero Minus Ten Days – Earth

It seemed somebody had left food on a barbecue for too long; the rich saliva-inducing smell like that of cooking belly pork was overwhelmed by the stench of charred fat and burning meat. Delegate Serene Galahad's stomach rumbled inappropriately and, trying to ignore the fact that she had wet herself, she checked various computer channels through her fone and linked implants. Everything was down; the worst-case scenario had occurred, and the Chestrekon Protocol had been applied. As a result, trillions of specially designed computer chips all across Earth had dismembered Govnet. WiFi was down, because optics, cable, simple fone-lines and satellite channels had been electrically unplugged. Bluetooth was now black.

Shakily, Serene uncapped her water bottle, took a swill and spat it out to get the dust out of her mouth, then finally took a swallow. She had been right about that – about the necessity of the Protocol – as she had been right about so many things. Certainly she had been right about the danger inherent in the requirement for every citizen of Earth to have an ID implant. For those in the higher echelons of government – like Committee delegates such as herself – should not be thus encumbered or so easy to track down. This could be turned against them by terrorists and subversives, just as it seemed it had now been, though on a scale unforeseen.

Recapping her water bottle, Serene gazed out from under her desk – past where her bodyguard Jimbo lay face down, a gaping hole in his back where the first two readergun bullets had struck; most of his head missing where the final one had slammed home. At the edge of the spreading pool of his blood lay her watch. This contained her ID implant, which responded to electronic queries as if it was actually where it should be – inside her forearm. She had pulled it off her wrist and cast it away the moment the readergun, fixed up on the conference-room wall, had flashed into life to set the Sectoring Consultancy team jerking about in their seats, and spraying chunks of them across the wide teak desk before them.

She expected to feel sick, but just felt numb. Perhaps it was shock, so maybe some stronger reaction would occur later.

But the carnage was over now and it was probably safe for her to come out. Certainly it wasn't safe for her to stay here – that noxious smell told her there was a fire inside the Dome's conference chamber, burning up what was left of all those frightened idiots who had come here to the Straven Conference to debate further their unimaginative solutions to Earth's population problem. The anger and the contempt that had driven her here in the first place quickly banished her current numbness, and now impelled her out into the open. She stood up, placed her water bottle down on the gritty surface of her desk, pulled a wad of perfumed tissues from her personal dispenser to clean her hands, then tried to brush some of the debris from her tight grey jacket and skirt. Annoyingly, bits of Jimbo smeared to leave streaks of blood and brain. She took another wad of tissues to clean her hands again, and finally surveyed her surroundings.

The blast had taken out one entire side of the Millennium Dome, even while the readerguns were turning the Straven Conference attendees into broken meat. Through the smoke the new opening gave a view across the Thames, over what looked like the mangled remains of the nose of a scramjet. The same view showed that the Gull developments and sectored areas of Blackwall looked undamaged, yet to their left, on the other side of the West India Canal that divided Canary Island from the main city, and where Committee tower blocks and cubic Civil Service arcologies clustered, pillars of smoke rose into the sky amid numerous massive collapses.

Ridiculous, absolutely ridiculous. Serene should never have been here.

The conference had just been getting under way when a nuke took out Inspectorate HQ London. Yet, while it had been mooted that they should suspend the conference for the interim, Messina had issued orders for them to continue – business as usual. When Serene subsequently learned that one space plane had been crashed in Minsk spaceport even while another was being stolen, and that a hundred and fifty Committee delegates had been slaughtered in a terrorist outrage in Leuven, she had realized that the expected rebellion had begun. But still Messina would not shut down the conference. Meanwhile he and many of his pet delegates had disappeared – all further orders received from him coming by sat-link. Even as terrorists continued their concerted attack on the state all across Earth, Serene had to stay here discussing decidedly un-radical plans for population control.

She turned back to scan the rest of the conference chamber. Those here would no longer be discussing the continued sectoring-out and controlled starvation of the Earth's zero-asset population. The only sign of movement left here was the flames still rising from where some lump of hot wreckage had smashed into the lower-tier horseshoe table. The five Committee delegates who had been sitting there, and their PAs, bodyguards and other support staff, were strewn on the floor, bloody meat. Delegate Schubert lay across the same table. The readergun shot that finished him must have hit him in the back of his neck, for his head was nowhere in evidence. The upper-tier tables had been similarly depopulated. It was, very literally, a bloody mess.

Time, Serene felt, for her to leave and put into motion her own plans, whether Messina agreed or not. She should see today's chaos as an opportunity for her to demonstrate the effectiveness of her own population-control plan, to take leadership away from the present incompetents in government, including Chairman Messina himself. She just needed to get back to the Aldeburgh Complex, and there get ready for when the Chestrekon Protocol ran its timed course and Govnet would begin its secure start-up.

Clutching her briefcase, slim laptop inside, water bottle tucked into its special waterproof compartment beside it, tissue-wrapped watch in the other and a disabler clutched in her right hand, Serene made her way past burning wreckage and shattered human beings towards the conference-hall exit. As she walked out into the outer halls of the Dome, she felt a surge of euphoria. She had been right and, because of that, had survived, and would not now succumb to shock because she was too much of a realist. After stepping into an executive toilet, she removed her knickers and tights, and upon finding the water and power were off, wiped herself clean with tissues. Wetting herself had been a purely physical reaction to danger; just one situation for her to deal with in a whole series of them.

The outer halls of this part of the Dome were structurally undamaged, but the readerguns had been at work. This area hadn't been as crowded as the conference hall itself, but still she sometimes had to walk through pools of blood. Finally she reached the elevator doors, waited for a moment, then swore at her own stupidity. The power was off – she would have to use the stairs.

The main exit from the Dome was surprisingly clear of corpses; just a bullet-riddled guard booth evidenced that the readerguns had been in action here. As she walked out into the stink of burning plastic and began heading towards the executive car park, it seemed she was the only living human in the vicinity. Then she saw that she wasn't.

There was no way she could mistake these people for anyone she might demand assistance from. Even from this distance she recognized their generic attire, their slouching fearful attitude, their poverty, for zero assets were here. Of course sector-fence readerguns were offline and, from the devastation she had seen, probably many of the sector fences had even been destroyed. She picked up her pace along pathways through the Millennium-Plus-One Garden – a sad attempt, she felt, to bring some green to this place – and finally reached the open gate into the executive car park. Here she paused, noting by the spatter patterns from some of the corpses that they had been shot not by the fence readerguns but by those mounted on some of the aeros parked here, perhaps even the one she had arrived in. There was a chance that whatever had penetrated Govnet – and these aeros – was still in operation. Then she dismissed the idea. The range of the aero guns was well beyond the compass of the car-park fence, so if they were still operating she would have been dead by now.

A hundred more slightly unsteady paces brought her to her own aero, whose doors refused to open automatically in response to the ID implant in her watch. She uncapped the manual handle, opened the door and hauled herself up inside, closing and then locking the door behind her.

She had come to the conference aboard this vehicle with four Inspectorate executives along with their complement of bodyguards and PAs. A couple of them she had known vaguely, but she felt no regret at their loss. Seating herself in the pilot's seat, she first strapped herself in, then began checking the controls. Other executives did not familiarize themselves with such systems, feeling it beneath them to do so. Again she felt a sense of satisfaction because again she had been proved right. All the aero's components were functional, it was fuelled and powered, but the main computer was down – its hard drive wiped and all exterior communications shut down by the Chestrekon chip.

Serene popped a cover concealing console electronics, found the chip and extracted it, replacing it with a spare chip clipped inside the cover. The console went live, with three LCD screens coming on to display code prompts. Selecting one of them Serene ordered a selective reboot, ensuring exterior com remained inoperative because there was always the chance that whatever had attacked Govnet remained active. Even as she did this, her fone signalled to her that an exterior channel had become available to it. She hurriedly shut it down, worried that her rebooting of the aero computer might have activated something else, then checked carefully: general independent fone network, voice only, no data packets and no computer linkage. Still cautious, she kept her fone shut down and selected that particular channel through the aero console, then used the wholly archaic method of tapping in a fone number. No response, just the beeping to tell her she had reached the fone she was after but no one was answering. It could be that this fone remained intact in whatever remained of its owner's head.

After half an hour of the computer rebooting, Serene saw that the ZAs had drawn closer. They were searching the dead, checking dropped bags, but had yet to summon up the nerve to enter the Dome itself. However, about twenty of them were gathering by the gate to the executive car park. They were looking for food, as always, and certainly knew that some of the vehicles here would contain it.

She paused the reboot and ran checks on the weapons system, consigning one screen before her to manual targeting. She had plenty of ammo, since it hadn't taken many bullets to kill those within her aero's vicinity. Using a console ball control, she brought a target frame over the one who seemed to be the leader of the ZAs at the gate, and poised a finger over the ball. If she waited too long they would enter the car park and then disperse, becoming more difficult to hit, and once inside the car park they would, without a doubt, be a danger to her. No one above a certain level in government went anywhere near ZAs without a great deal of protection – since their gratitude for the minimal dole they received was . . . somewhat lacking. Why was she hesitating? This was such a small thing compared to her overall plan. She clicked the ball control down then moved it gently from side to side. The guns, underneath the aero, made a sound like a compressor starting up, and Serene turned to watch their effect through the side window.

Full automatic: two machine guns, each firing at a rate of two thousand rounds a minute. The crowd disintegrated, flew apart in a mass of body parts and ragged clothing, a bloody mist boiling out behind it. Another click on the ball control and the guns shut down. Serene studied what she had done. She had expected some to survive, to be running away now, but it looked as if every one of them had been put through a mincer. No movement at all. She felt something like awe then, and a tight hard excitement. Just a few finger movements had done that. Now here was power. She tried to dispel the feeling, for what she had just done had been entirely necessary. Somewhat shakily, she returned her attention to the reboot and, long before anyone else ventured near the car park, she started up the aero's fans and took it off the ground.

Then, as her view of London expanded and she saw the sheer extent of the devastation, the steady beeping from the console interrupted her inspection and a tired, familiar voice spoke out against a raucous crackling.

'I should not be surprised that you survived, ma'am.'

'Nor should I be surprised that you survived too, Simeon,' Serene replied curtly, though mildly pleased that her security director, Simeon Anderson, was still alive. 'Why am I getting so much interference?'

'Well, Govnet being down doesn't help, ma'am, but it's not only that,' he replied. 'I'm told we're building up to a humdinger of a solar storm – seems almost to have poetic timing.'

'Yes, whatever,' she said. 'How many of the team survived?'

'Hard to say,' he replied. 'We lost seventeen here, but fifty-four were either at home or outside the Complex for other reasons, and I've been unable to contact any of them.'

Serene grimaced. Readerguns had come as a standard fitting when the Aldeburgh Complex had been built but, as she took charge there and made the place her own domain, she had deactivated them.

'What killed the seventeen?' she asked.

'Aero guns – they just opened up on anyone within range.'

That figured. 'How many of you there now?'

'Twenty-four.'

'Keep trying to contact the rest. I'll be with you within an hour.'

'What happened, ma'am? What the hell happened?'

This was the closest she had heard her security director come to voicing emotion and she paused for a moment, gazing out of the screen as she considered her reply. Everywhere she looked, smoke was rising into the sky. She had just passed over a long scar cutting through the urban sprawl where it seemed likely another scramjet had come down, and to her right a massive smoke cloud marked the spot where she knew the Northeast Inspectorate HQ was located.

'We got hit hard. What data are you getting now?'

'Nothing from the satellites, which might be due to the storm, and Govnet won't secure-start at least for another hour. I foned whoever I could get through to – Breckon in North America, Mouheed in China, Rocheur in Germany – and the same story from them: readerguns, spiderguns, razorbirds and shepherds all turning on government employees, all air traffic dropping out of the sky. And Breckon, who has access to the Kansas radio telescope array, tells me that, despite the solar interference, he can see that the Argus Network is gone.'

'Gone?'

'Dropped out of the sky . . . I saw a few fire trails but I didn't make the connection until I spoke to him. Apparently it was quite a show, night-side.'

The whole network? Serene just did not know what to say, but she incorporated this fact into her calculations. More than ever now, her plan seemed the right one.

'Not just that,' Anderson continued, 'Argus itself is currently beyond the orbit of the Moon and heading away.'

'I see,' said Serene, trying to keep her voice in keeping with her name. 'So Breckon, Mouheed and Rocheur weren't at their respective Inspectorate HQs when this went down?'

'All of them at home.'

Serene considered all that had been happening prior to her diving under her desk at the conference. The rebels had penetrated Govnet at an unheard-of level, and taken control of all of Earth's military resources. She now suspected she knew what that fire over to her right might be. Clearly, the rebels had dropped the Argus Network satellites on Inspectorate HQs all across Earth, and that smoke cloud rose from HQ Northeast. It seemed the rebels had also either stolen Argus Station, or dispatched it off into the Solar System.

'Keep gathering data and be sure we have as much capacity as possible for when Govnet comes back online,' she said. 'You've checked our system for comlife?'

'Comlife . . . yeah, had to be. Our system was visited, and a lot scrambled – someone knew every damned access code. We're now fully hard-system; I've changed all the codes and closed doorways it left behind.'

'Okay . . . do you still have outside power there?'

'No, the Sizewell fusion reactors did a safe shutdown. We're using the wind turbines.'

'Good enough,' she replied.

She didn't need a great deal of electrical power for what she intended. The signal would transmit virally through Govnet, to be rebroadcast from any available radio transmitter. Not too many of them would be needed either, because those ID implants it reached would then rebroadcast it again, and it would spread, like a plague.

Argus

The scanning helmet completely covered Saul's head and face. Usually this would not have been disconcerting for him, for he could have kept watch through the cams pointing down from the ceiling, or through any nearby robots like the spider-gun squatting over by the door into the laboratory. However, after his attack on Committee rule on Earth, it seemed almost as if the sun itself had registered its protest at the destruction he had wrought.

Just hours after Argus Station swung around the Moon in a low-fuel course change, then fired up the Traveller VI to begin its non-conjunction course for Mars, the solar storm had begun. The last sight Saul had of the sun was a flare arcing out and back down – forming a bridge large enough to roll entire worlds around – then it had been necessary to put up the station's EM field to prevent those inside being roasted by the sleet of radiation. Only the optical telescopes still functioned, and their images weren't the best. But this also meant that right now he could not, without plugging an optic directly into his skull, access the station's computer system and thereby any cams or robots.

'Your synaptic density is about twice that of a normal human being,' said Hannah.

'Do you have all the data you need?' he asked.

'You don't like being blind,' she remarked.

'I do not.'

'Yes, you can take off the helmet.'

Saul quickly lifted it from his head and gazed across to where Hannah had ensconced herself before an array of screens. Did she look unwell? Did she still hate him for the task he had given her? It was difficult to tell. He swung his gaze across all the equipment occupying her laboratory, to the viewing window into her adjoining surgical theatre. He'd known from the moment he came in here that she had been preparing for that ghoulish chore.

Arcoplex One, which was one of the three cylinder worlds extending like thick spokes from the centre of Argus Station to the outer ring, contained seventy delegates, along with Chairman Messina. They were all guilty of murder, whether personally guilty or having issued orders for mass exterminations. They had been given a choice of life or death, though in order to live they must have their minds erased. None had chosen to die, and Hannah must now carry out the chore of implanting specially designed biochips that changed neurochem, zapped synapses and made new connections – wiping a human brain like a magnet drawn across an old magnetic tape. Of course, mindless humans were a resource drain they could not afford here, so Hannah intended to make the wipe quite specific, so that a lot of what had been inculcated into them as children and as teenagers would not be erased. They wouldn't lose their toilet training, for example, or the ability to communicate, or much of their early education. Saul supposed they would end up much like children, though like children with little urge to play.

He now swung his attention to the screens ranged before her.

Here were pictures of his brain, energy statistics, data-flow diagnostics and much about the medical side of what had happened to him. One screen showed the bio interface as a blur at the centre of the neurons it had grown. Since those neurons and the synaptic connections they made were based on his own genetic blueprint, they weren't distinct under resonance scan until Hannah ran a computer program to utilize data that had been stored in the hardware in his skull. This provided the scan image of his brain *before* she had installed the interface and its related hardware and, now able to make the distinction, the program coloured new growth in a vibrant green. The interface looked like the core of an epiphyte, its branches spreading throughout his skull and even penetrating down into his spine.

Mistletoe in my head, Saul thought, but then remembered that plant was poisonous so decided to drop this analogy.

'It grew too fast – there are imbalances,' she said.

'Inevitable – since it responded to mental pressure, and I was under a lot of it. The epiphyte underwent forced growth. What are the dangers?'

She sat back from her consoles, wiping a hand down her face. 'Epiphyte, yes, quite . . .' she said, and then continued, 'The blood supply in your skull is struggling to keep up. You're growing new capillaries, and the old ones are expanding, but still demand is outstripping supply . . . You're going to need supplements.' She stood up and walked over to a cupboard, took out an electrical pill dispenser and began inserting tubes of pills. 'You're eating?'

'There hasn't been much time to, but, yes, every opportunity I get. I'm always hungry.'

'To be expected,' she said. 'I would say you are near the limit of what your body can handle without further assistance and, frankly, what it's handling is already beyond the limit of a normal human body. You should be dead by now.' She was referring to the things he had done to himself before Smith wiped out his original mind. Using nano-machines and tailored viruses, he had upgraded what nature had given him.

As a result he healed faster now, adapted faster, his immune system was boosted.

'Any further growth and any increase in processing will put you in danger of embolism. You are also at the point of diminishing returns, due to cell starvation.' She finished filling the dispenser and now began programming it.

'So what can we do?'

'We can install carotid valves to control the blood pressure in your skull. There are ways of upping your red-corpuscle count, and I can run nutrients straight into your bloodstream. However, the best option would be for you to shunt some of that processing outside yourself.'

'Which I already do – since a lot of me is now in the computer systems of this station.' But, of course, he knew that wasn't what she was talking about.

'But you're disconnected from it right now.' She shook her head. 'That's beside the point, anyway. You do run processing outside yourself, but you mirror and map a lot of it inside your organic brain, because you're translating from machine code to organic processes. Though what you can do outside yourself is becoming increasingly complex, your organic brain is still the control centre.' She paused, losing her doleful expression to a glint of maniacal enthusiasm, as she always did when venturing to the cutting edge of her research.

'Exolocation,' he said, unable to resist second-guessing her.

She turned towards him. 'Of course, you already know that.'

'How would you go about it?' he asked.

'Do you need to ask?'

'Yes, because I've decided to give you the opportunity to tell me about it.'

'Big of you.' She handed over the dispenser.

'Do go on.'

'I would take samples of your brain tissue, place them in nutrient-infused aerogel matrices and, through carbon microtubules, feed in oxygen and further nutrients.'

'How would you take out the waste?'

'With simplified leucocytes and biomechanical kidneys.'

'And this would work?'

'There would be failures, which is why I'd first grow maybe three or four samples.'

Saul smiled. It was a thoroughly fascinating prospect: organic extensions to his brain, extra brain mass grown from his own brain tissue and maintained in portable units. He hesitated. There was so much still to do and he now wanted to get back to his room in Tech Central, plug an optic into his skull and get on with it. However, he understood himself well enough to know that his anxiousness to leave stemmed from how vulnerable he felt when unable to connect into the systems around him.

He relaxed, sat back. 'Take your samples.'

Earth

During World War Two the British government had developed radar here and, during the ensuing cold war, atomic weapons research had been sited here. Throughout World Wars One and Two, and until the nuclear age, a huge amount of bomb development had been conducted here too. Serene felt that her own work here was thoroughly in keeping with this place's history.

Orford Ness extended parallel to the coast, from what

had once been the town of Aldeburgh, but was now one of the big coastal cities incorporating Orford and Leiston on either side. Over the previous century the spit of land had grown, tidal action heaping up more shingle, while concrete rafts and docks were built out to sea to support first the maintenance of the wind farms, then the spread of fish farms. Upon all this, the Complex itself had been built, also bridging inwards to the land.

Serene took her aero over Aldeburgh itself and sucked in a sharp breath at the extent of the devastation, and again resisted the temptation to seek data from Govnet, which, only ten minutes previously, had begun its secure start-up. She would wait until she was within the Complex and able to ensure that any precautions that could be taken were made.

The city's population had mostly consisted of government employees running the sub Northeast administration, but now it seemed that the only movement visible down there was flocks of ragged gulls scavenging in the bloody streets, or fires eating through the office blocks. However, there would be more movement some time hence. She had already seen hordes of zero assets, from the massive sectors of the Cambridge sprawl, slowly tramping about in the previously forbidden agricultural lands of Mid-Suffolk. She had also seen much similar movement across Essex.

Though there was some damage in the Complex, it wasn't anywhere near as bad as the inward city. She noted people gathering on the landward side of the Ness channel, and she wondered if at least some of them might be her missing staff. Certainly, even if they weren't, she would be needing recruits.

Beyond the Complex, the sea was chequered with decaying fish farms extending all the way out to the ragged towers of wind turbines, for most of which there had been neither the funds nor the inclination to repair. However, five turbines were now working again, powering her Complex now that the Sizewell reactor was down – another precaution she had taken earlier and further affirmation of what now seemed to be her destiny.

Coming in over the aero-port, she circled for a moment while deciding where to land. She could see bloodstains on the carbocrete and, parked off to one side, a forklift with its tines loaded with corpses stacked like logs. Then, as she began her descent, she saw Anderson striding out with two uniformed security staff behind him. For a second she didn't like that, didn't like to see him accompanied by armed men. But in the end she must trust, at least to a limited extent, someone. She took her aero down and landed, shut down its engines and headed for the door.

'You're gathering data?' she said as he held out a hand to assist her down from the aero.

'As we speak,' he said, looking grim and slightly distracted – probably by a feed issuing from his fones and the implants in his skull. 'Chairman Messina is gone, along with most of his pet delegates.'

'What?'

'We're still trying to get the story clear . . .' Anderson paused, and seemed slightly stunned. 'You said we were hit hard, but I wonder if you know just how hard.' Once she was down on the carbocrete he gestured inland. 'All across Earth, it's the same as what you probably saw over there. We estimate that over two-thirds of the upper Committee Administration, Military, Executive . . . everything . . . dead.'

She had suspected something like this, had seen some sign of it during her flight here, made her calculations on that basis, but now actually being told she was right jerked her to a halt. For a second she just wasn't sure what to say next, then, 'Zero assets and societal assets, people outside of the Administration?'

'Mostly untouched – massive casualties from aero and scramjet crashes and infrastructure collapse, of course, but generally the zero-asset death rate is down on the previous quarter, while our programs predict that societal assets will show a greater propensity for survival now.'

She gazed at him assessingly. 'Then we must ensure that the former don't swamp us, as that stupid sectoring idea will have turned them more hostile than before.'

He nodded, understanding perfectly.

'So, now tell me about Messina,' Serene asked, as they began to head towards the Complex's entrance.

'The rebellion was widespread and damaging, but had no chance of success, and was just a distraction while rebels seized Argus Station. When that space plane crashed at Minsk, another was in the process of being stolen—'

'Yes, I know that,' Serene interrupted. 'Who exactly are – or were – they?'

'It's a little confused at the moment.' Anderson pushed the door open ahead of Serene and held it for her. 'Initially we have reports that the leader of this group, this "Revolutionary Council" was someone called Malden, who escaped IHQ London.'

'Seems plausible, since IHQ London was nuked.' She strode ahead down the corridor, glancing through one door into a big clean-assembly room. Ahead lay the chip-etching plants and the biochip division, all self-contained, run on robotics controlled from the Oversight Room. Her operation here had been very efficient. Her future – and much larger – operation would be more efficient still.

'Yes, but it seems this Malden died during the attempt to seize Argus Station, and Station Director Smith had regained control. This did not stop Messina summoning his delegates and taking an assault fleet from the Australian Outback spaceport.'

Serene smiled nastily. 'Messina wanted an excuse to take Smith down anyway, and he wanted to shift his powerbase offworld.' She paused, suddenly confused. 'So Messina controls Argus now?'

Anderson shook his head. 'The last we heard was from assault-force communications. It seems someone else seized control of part of the station, and started up the Mars Traveller Engine at just the right time to wipe out most of Messina's force. It seems likely that it was this man who brought down the satellite network and turned our own guns against us.'

'Do we have a name?'

'We do – he's called Alan Saul.'

'Any data on him?'

'Just a fragment from IHQ London: a disposal order sending him to the Calais incinerator.'

Serene wasn't sure why that got to her. She shivered.

Soon they reached the armoured doors leading into Oversight, which slid open ahead of her at some unheard command from Anderson. She walked inside and surveyed all those personnel sitting gathering data at the various consoles.

'Administration survivors – anything useful?' she asked abruptly.

'North Region survivors with available transport are heading to the enclaves on the Isle of Mull, though some are making for Inspectorate HQ Glasgow – one of the few to remain untouched. Those in the Midlands are heading to those places as well, or to the offshore algae farms. The same pattern is being repeated all across Earth – Committee survivors with access to transport are trying to put water between them and the zero-asset hordes.'

'A sensible move, but one of limited duration. Have you managed to contact any European delegates?'

'None at all.'

'Then I have authority over the European Region, so summon those on Mull and elsewhere here.' She paused to strip off her jacket and sit at her own console. 'We've got some organizing to do.' She glanced over at the door leading into her apartment, telling herself she would head there sometime soon, clean up, then pause and ready herself for what she must do next. However, it would be ten days before she passed through that door for anything more than short power naps, to use the toilet or to gulp down another handful of stimulants.

Mars

The news from Earth was now completely non-existent, but even the dismal picture they had obtained, before the solar storm blew up, lacked impact, especially since they had been on the very knife edge here, where, for survival, even air had been rationed. For five days after Varalia Delex blew out the windows of Hex Three at Antares Base on Mars, it had been necessary to divert a large portion of the reactor's output to melting Martian ice and electrolysing the water for its oxygen. It had also been necessary to cut all non-essential power usage, even to cut heating in all non-vital areas. During those five days a total of eighty-two personnel were confined to their cabins with the instruction to stay in bed and breathe

21

shallowly – to remain as inactive as possible without being dead. It had been close, and luckily no one had actually achieved that state of total inactivity. Now they had power to spare again, and they were using it.

Var walked slowly ahead of her two companions along the roof of the wing adjoining Hex Four, finally coming to a halt at the edge of the building. The construction robots, newly fired up, were dipping and weaving inside and outside the hex like a flock of iron swans. Gazing at this activity, she allowed herself to feel hope, perhaps for the first time since the Committee had sentenced them to death. In deciding to scrap the Traveller spacecraft through the bubblemetal plants of Argus, to shut down further Traveller construction and thus abandon the personnel here on Mars, the Committee had expected the eventual demise of her and her fellows to be almost certain. To push that demise to complete certainty, it had instructed the political officer here to thin out the population, ostensibly because this would enable the remainder to survive, but really because the resulting loss of expertise would ensure that those left behind didn't live. But Political Officer Ricard and his staff were all dead, because Var had killed them all.

'So run through it for me,' she said. 'How far along are we?'

Martinez, chief of construction and buildings maintenance – which, in this environment, was a very important task – gazed at the work in progress. 'We're finishing the upper section of the block-work wall and cementing in the ties for the dome. The furnaces are up to speed, I'm told, but best to ask Lopomac about that.' He gestured to the other man accompanying them.

Lopomac, who had been one of those who had helped her

dispose of Ricard and his crew, nodded sagely. 'The furnaces are now running and we're processing the silica sand. We should be able to start pouring the glass panes soon.'

'That's a lot of power we're burning,' she commented. 'I really hope Gunther knows what he's talking about.'

'He's the expert,' said Lopomac. 'Relying on experts, as has become quite evident, is how we're managing to stay alive.'

Lopomac was referring to another near-disaster when the reactor started to fail. Among the staff here they had managed to find a specialist in powder-cast ceramics who had been mis-assigned, in a typical Committee screw-up, to work in construction under Martinez – epoxy-bonding regolith into building blocks. That man had managed to work out a method of making the reactor components the Committee had perpetually failed to send them. Notable, Var felt, how that same man had been on Ricard's kill list as a non-essential.

Var nodded agreement, but her mind started to stray to other concerns. The Argus Station was still on course to reach Mars in just over two years, but whoever was aboard it had not responded to their earlier attempts at communication. Also, she had been unable to find out whether Messina's *Alexander* was still under construction, though she did find out that other Earth-orbit stations were still functioning. Another concern was why both Martinez and Lopomac had been keen for them to come out here. She now switched her suit radio to a private band they had selected while suiting up.

'So now we're out here, let's talk,' she said.

'It's come to our notice that there are those here who are a little unhappy with the power structure,' said Lopomac. He glanced at Martinez. 'They've been attempting to recruit others who might not be completely loyal to you.'

'I wasn't aware of that, but I still don't see why it was necessary for us to come out here.'

'Simple answer,' Lopomac responded. 'They're mostly in Mars Science, and we've suspicions that they've hacked into Ricard's security system.'

'Rhone?'

'As far as we know, not him. Delaware and Christen seem to be the ringleaders. They are contending that we should run things here under a scientific meritocratic democracy – the strength of voting being proportional to IQ, which of course would mean more power for Delaware and Christen. It would also mean, Delaware feels, that he would be in with a chance of running this place, since his IQ is only a few points below your own.'

'And yet,' Var noted, 'despite such high intelligence, he's too stupid to realize how any squabbling now has a very high chance of being fatal for us all.'

'What do you want us to do?' asked Martinez – that question implying much.

Var considered the first option. Those two scientists could have some unfortunate accident. However, she felt there was no one here they could afford to lose – two first-class minds least of all. So what to do about them?

'Actually, we do have a form of "meritocratic democracy", in which my chiefs of staff have their say, though of course no vote. I will therefore delegate this to one of those chiefs. Tell Rhone what's going on and leave it for him to deal with.' She paused in thought for a moment, recollecting her history class and the phrase, 'Will no one rid me of this troublesome priest?' and added, 'Though you should ensure he is aware that we really cannot afford to lose any personnel at all.'

'Will do,' said Martinez. 'They tried to recruit me, too, so it's best coming from me.'

'Any other business?' she asked.

'Not really,' said Lopomac.

As they turned and began heading back towards the central hex, Var felt a sudden surge of disappointment. Humans in adversity could be at their best, but take the pressure off just a little and they resorted to type: squabbling for notice, clawing for power, security, comfort, luxury. She remembered something her brother Alan had once said.

'We are a disappointing species,' he had noted in his usual flat uninflected tone. She had thoroughly agreed with him but wondered, as ever, if that species included Alan Saul himself.

2

ID Implants

The first large-scale ID implant trial was conducted by one of the forerunners of All Health, EHS (the European Health Service), in an attempt to overcome the difficulties inherent in the highly politicized and unwieldy computer system used for keeping the health records of citizens. The idea was that you could walk into a doctor's surgery, or be stretchered into a hospital, and implant-readers would immediately update the doctors with all they needed to know about you. The trial was a failure for two reasons: because the data the implants held was just copied from the computer records, so medical fact was difficult to separate from political jargon even when it was correct and uncorrupted, and because of a severe outbreak of MDRSA3 (third-generation multidrug resistant staphylococcus aureus) in the hospitals doing the implants – an outbreak kept under a news blackout – and half of those receiving the implants dying. However, since the political motivation behind the trial remained and politicians are never in a hurry to abandon a bad idea, further trials were conducted and, over a period of twenty years, 'medplants' were forced on the population of Europe as a precursor to the ID implant we know today. It is estimated that between two and five million people died during these next trials, but news blackouts were no longer required to suppress the story, since by then no independent media existed.

Zero Minus Five Days – Argus

The spidergun crammed itself in the airlock cylinder first, with its oddly shaped limbs raised up and pressed against the walls to make space for Saul. He stepped in, then turned and palmed the control to close the door behind him and activate the elevator. The cylinder entered the central spindle, then travelled down through its curved transport tube to the floor of Arcoplex Two, the spin of the arcoplex impinging more and more to give him the illusion of weight.

For some days now Saul had not ventured out of his cabin, other than mentally. He had run the station from there, with an optic plugged into his skull as he oversaw the complete reorganization of the hierarchy and set his people and his robots to clear up the mess and make the endless repairs. He had made calculations that extended into highly esoteric maths on how they might survive with the resources they had. As a result of these calculations, he had issued orders that might have seemed nonsensical to some, but which he knew would yield good results later on. Now, he felt, the station was running well and, though reluctant to leave his room in Tech Central, fascination at what had recently been found in Arcoplex Two had lured him out.

The cylinder airlock doors opened onto a long corridor running through one of the many buildings that crammed Arcoplex Two. The spidergun slid out first, its movements uncannily lifelike and fluid now as, like all the robots aboard Argus, it operated under his new programming. He stepped out after it and studied the reception committee.

Hannah looked careworn; with the steady destruction of human minds she was performing obviously taking its toll.

'Hannah . . .' he said, pausing to find the correct words, 'are you good?' Being too solicitous was not the way; better to acknowledge that he knew she was experiencing emotional pain, but expect business as usual from her.

'I've been better,' she replied, rubbing at the dressing on her arm where, like many on the station, she'd had her ID implant removed. 'And I've been worse.'

He dipped his head once, then swung his attention to the others waiting.

Brigitta and Angela Saberhagen also appeared tired, but seemed to have lost that blank indifference in their ex-pressions: the result of a state of mind that alone enabled many to survive under Committee rule. They, too, had dress-ings on their arms where their implants had been removed. The station doctors had been very busy for some time: station staff forming queues outside the doctors' surgeries during their free time. Just over ten per cent of the people here were now without ID implants, including Saul himself, who had had five implants removed from his forearm.

'You have everything ready for me?' he enquired. He knew precisely what they had to show him – had known for three days – but had realized that his omniscience tended to defuse the enthusiasm of those who worked for him.

'We're ready. You'll find the Committee had some inter-esting projects running here,' said Brigitta. Angela grimaced, as aware as Brigitta that he had already peered into every nook and cranny of Robotics and knew precisely what was here.

Langstrom, a wiry black man who was now Saul's police commander, and Peach, a tall Nordic blonde woman who was one of his officers, also waited here.

'No problems?' Saul asked.

'None at all,' said Langstrom warily.

'Then let's go.' Saul gestured down the corridor.

The spidergun went first, now sufficiently independent to need no mental prod from Saul, and he followed. Hannah fell in beside him, and the twins came next, Langstrom and Peach coming up last. There wasn't really much need for the last two – they were only here because they felt they had to be, and Saul had not ordered them *not* to be here. He had already checked out any possible dangers in the arcoplex, and his robots were installed all around him.

'What about you?' Hannah asked.

'I'm good,' Saul replied.

He could explain to her about the quantities of information he was able to process. He could explain how he could now individually control hundreds of robots, how he now created programs with a thought, some of them almost operating like independent intelligences. But how to explain the synergy arising from the biological interface she had implanted in his skull? How to explain not so much the growth in his abilities as that implant spread its neural network, but the integration? Then again, perhaps he *could* explain to Hannah, for she was the one most likely to be able to understand.

Numerous successive corridors brought them to an elevator which took them up, in two parties, to the robotics factory near to the arcoplex spindle. They stepped out onto a glass-panelled floor, walking lightly and bouncing in the lower spin. Saul peered down at the assembly floor visible below. It was a combination of production line and specialist workshop. Raw components were transported up by cargo elevators from floors below, three partially assembled carcases of construction robots lay directly below him, while a fourth, all but finished, was undergoing trials in a test rig. Twenty people worked on this floor, but most of the assembly directly below was being conducted by the brethren of these robots – the three humans Saul could see working on specialization of the basic construction robot. In the next area various maintenance robots were being put together. Beyond this lay Large Component Construction, where the parts for the bigger station robots were made.

Brigitta, who had moved up beside him the moment he walked out onto this floor, began a hesitant commentary, with the implication of, *of course you know all this*, until, from behind, Langstrom interrupted, 'What about the military stuff?'

Brigitta had glanced at Saul as if seeking permission and, when he nodded, replied, 'It was never made here – always transported up from Earth. We've got some packaged razorbirds and shepherds, but I've no idea why. Shepherds are just too big and the razorbirds would need substantial reprogramming to fly in zero gravity. And the only spiderguns here are those Messina brought with him.' Thereafter Brigitta continued her commentary with more enthusiasm now she had a more congenial audience.

During a pause, Saul said, 'Of course, this is not what I've come to see.'

'We go to the end, then down a couple of floors,' explained Brigitta. 'I'm not quite sure what the aim was.'

'A police force of unquestioning loyalty, I suspect,' said Saul, glancing round at Langstrom.

The man frowned, seemed about to wipe this expression from his face, then stubbornly retained it. He said, 'It was because of people not asking questions that Earth is like it is today.'

'Precisely,' said Saul, as he stepped, after his spidergun, into the end elevator.

The chief of Humanoid Unit Development had been one of the casualties of the recent station conflict. He had not been here in Arcoplex Two when Messina's forces attacked, but in his executive quarters in the Political Office. He hadn't been involved in the fighting, but stray rounds had punched through a small section of the PO, including his quarters, and vacuum decompression had killed him some minutes later. That was a loss, for he had been a brilliant man. However, had he survived he would have been considered one of those 'difficult' cases: a valuable mind in the skull of a multiple murderer who had experimented on human beings, not because he was forced to by the Committee but because he delighted in it. And here, in the HUD, he had applied some of the results from his research.

'Are they fucking alive?' asked Langstrom.

Ten of them stood in a line against one wall, frames supporting them, all sorts of umbilical pipes and cables plugged in. Each stood over two metres tall – big leathery-skinned humanoids, male in body shape but without sexual organs.

'They're machines,' Brigitta informed him. 'The skin is semi-organic and they contain many cross-tech components – quite a lot of what's inside them being based on human tissue – but these things were assembled, not grown.' She paused for a moment, forehead wrinkling in a frown. Perhaps such distinctions were not so easy to make in this case.

'Why?' Langstrom asked. 'I thought the multi-task idea had gone out the window.'

For many years it had been the contention among roboticists that the best shape for a robot would be a humanoid one, since the human world had been built to fit humans. However, that was before factories became wholly robotic, and before the reality of specialized robots became apparent. If you wanted to repair a pipe under the sea, for example, better to send a robot with integral welder, with no need to breathe and no likelihood of suffering from the bends. The few humanoid robots still in existence on Earth were kept as quaint affectations of the very rich – which generally meant Committee delegates.

'A result of Chairman Messina's growing paranoia,' explained Saul. 'He wanted to be able to depend completely on his bodyguard.'

'His paranoia is no longer a problem for him,' said Hannah.

Saul gazed at her but could not read her expression. Messina himself had been the first to go under her micro-surgery, and was now slowly recovering in Arcoplex One. Already, even after this short time, station personnel had a name for people like Messina. They were being called 'repros' – the reprogrammed.

Hannah steadily returned his gaze. 'What are you going to do with them?'

'These?' He waved a hand at the racked androids.

'Yes, them.'

Considering the atrocities committed in the development of these androids, Saul had thought about having them destroyed. But they were just a spit away from being put online, and he was reluctant to waste what could prove valuable assets. When he probed earlier, from Tech Central, he had found a route through to some minds that were complex and strange, ticking over like high-performance cars caught in traffic. They could do things the other station robots could do, and more, and they contained technology the like of which he had never seen before. And, if he was being totally honest, they fascinated him, for he saw potential in their semi-biological brains that no other station robots possessed.

'I'm going to use them,' he decided. 'Another pair of hands is still another pair of hands.'

'You don't need any more bodyguards,' protested Langstrom.

'No, perhaps not.' Saul turned to Brigitta. 'You know what's left to do?'

Brigitta looked puzzled for a moment, but Angela replied, '*I* know.'

'Do it, then. Get them commissioned and tested.' He turned away.

Year Zero – Earth

Serene closed the door firmly behind her and walked over to her mirror, gazing at her face. She looked as tired as she felt. Ten days of organization, ten days of trying to maximize her resources, gain control, and now this. She'd just returned to Oversight after an inspection tour of the growing town of Administration survivors, and had known, by Anderson's expression, that something had gone badly wrong.

Without preamble he had announced, 'We've lost Glasgow HQ – it's been overrun. Only twenty survivors got out.'

'What?'

'Seems the ZAs are getting organized.'

'They had readerguns at Glasgow,' she said. 'There were four thousand of them there.' Then she managed to get herself under control. 'Our perimeter readerguns?'

'I did shut down radio access to them five days ago, but now we have direct fibre-optic control from here.' He paused, grimacing. 'They won't be enough, though. Glasgow had no problem with their readerguns; they just ran out of bullets.'

'Then it's time,' she said. 'It's time.'

She realized that, despite her apparent self-assurance and despite her hardness of purpose, she had been procrastinating. She had allowed herself to sink into bureaucratic time-wasting; pursuing detail and ignoring the central problem. She had not taken charge, and now it was time to. Glasgow was a wake-up call that brought home to her the necessity of what she must do. The face in the mirror returned to her a slow nod. She turned away, methodically stripped off her wrinkled suit, and went to take a shower. Then, just as methodically, she changed her appearance, and hardened her mind.

Finally, clad in an Inspectorate uniform of light blue slacks, shirt, tie and jacket, her weapon holstered at her hip, Serene again studied herself in her mirror, then carefully applied some make-up. Yes, this was the right choice. For too long now she had been making do, running herself ragged and not really taking control. During a time of emergency she needed to project an air of military efficiency, and of strength. No bureaucratic power suit now, with its associations of Committee fudges and paper shuffling. After a moment she donned the cap, studied it for a moment, then discarded it. No, instead she unpinned her hair and shook it loose, tied it in a ponytail, then clipped a palmtop and a disabler to her belt, finishing the ensemble with a brooch depicting the United Earth logo on her lapel. Yes, just right.

Next she turned from the mirror and walked over to her

display cabinet and peered inside. Various examples of the hardware manufactured here were laid out on white velvet. Four generations of ID implants sat in a row. Three chips, the size of hundred-Euro coins, were the minds of respectively a razorbird, a shepherd and a spidergun. A fourth chip of the same size sat at the centre of an array of sub-chips smaller even than ID implants. These depicted the control hub and subsets of a readergun net. Under glass domes sat some of the biochips manufactured here for research organizations all across the Earth, and seven of these were even now being installed in seven somewhat reluctant 'volunteers' who would be deployed on Govnet as a counter to Alan Saul.

She suffered a sudden cold sweat at the thought. Govnet was still very vulnerable, but as yet there had been no attack from Saul. Almost certainly that was due to the solar storm and, when it finished, he would once again be able to reach back to Earth from Argus. She needed to secure Govnet before that happened. She needed her seven 'comlifers' up and running – and soon. However, there was something more urgent that needed dealing with first.

Many of the chips were too small to study easily with the naked eye, so magnifying screens had been inset in the upper sheet of the display case. She reached out and touched the glass just above one of the chips, starting up the screen so it showed her a clear image of a cube just ten microns across. Five of the faces of this item were studded with gold electrodes, while on the sixth face was a small rectangle – the biological component of the small biochip. Here, at the Complex, they had made the blueprint for this device, also the prototypes, and still made the biological component; fifteen billion of the finished item had since been manufactured in a further three hundred automated factories all across Earth.

They were a part of the standard ID implant. Ostensibly –
with their biological component facing out into the human
body – they were able to read DNA and detect whether the
implant had been removed and placed in another body.
Apparently they were a failure, because the circuitry was easy
to bypass. They were considered a black mark against Serene
herself – a failure many of her Committee opponents relished
too much to study too closely.

However, here, only two other people other than her knew
that, upon receipt of certain computer codes, these chips
would activate and carry out their true purpose. What the
other two didn't know, what had been known to a team of
four development engineers who were *mistakenly* arrested and
executed by the Inspectorate three years ago, was that these
chips were in *all* ID implants, including those of Committee
delegates, and not just in those of the ZA citizens they were
supposedly intended for.

Serene turned away, strode to the door.

'Anything new?' she asked Anderson, as she stepped back
out into Oversight.

He turned towards her, looking even more tired and
hassled. 'The twenty survivors from Glasgow are heading
here. Another fifteen of our staff have reported in, and I've
allowed them to come across from the mainland. Sheila's gone
over there to meet them.'

When she arrived back here ten days ago, Serene had
hoped that Sheila Trondheim might be one of the casualties.
'Your idea?' she asked.

'Yes.'

Good, because right now she didn't want Sheila around
with her large, self-indulgent and thoroughly inappropriate
conscience. 'Anything else?'

He paused, obviously reluctant to tell her the next thing, then said, 'The total of known surviving delegates on Earth is now up to twenty-four. Delegate Angone of Region SE Africa has just made his presence known.'

Annoying – that now made three delegates in total with authority ranking over hers. 'He's been keeping his head down,' she noted. Probably consolidating gains, making sure of his power base.

Anderson still looked grave. 'As soon as he announced his presence, he claimed to assume top authority for the "interim of Chairman Messina's absence", and is organizing a teleconference for 20.00 GMT tonight. You are instructed to attend.'

Serene grimaced. She'd known it wouldn't take long for the survivors to crawl out of the woodwork and start competing for the top job, but she had hoped to have known about them all by now.

'Nevertheless . . .' she said, pausing to take a slow breath, 'we now have work to do in Comtrans One.'

His expression became even grimmer. He'd known this was coming, ever since she returned. This knowledge had been implicit between them, but perhaps actually accepting it was difficult for him. Perhaps not as difficult as for Sheila Trondheim, who was the other person here who knew, but still difficult enough. Serene would have to deal with this problem. When she carried through her next plan, three people would know precisely what she had done – and that was two people too many.

He nodded, detached the eye-screen extension to his fone and placed it down on a nearby console, then stood ready and waiting. She surveyed the room, noting that Clay Ruger, Anderson's lieutenant, was on shift today. Clay was an ambitious and capable man with weaknesses that could be exploited. He was a sociopath but also a coward, like so many in high position, and quite simple to understand and manipulate.

'Let's go,' she said.

Outside the door, Anderson signalled for the two guards to follow them.

'No,' said Serene, without looking round, 'they stay here.'

'We're still not as secure here as I would like,' Anderson warned.

'Nevertheless,' Serene replied, leading the way from Oversight.

Comtrans One was where they kept all the communications hardware: the signal boosters and other devices connected to the aerials and satellite dishes on the roof, the coders for laser transmissions, and the Govnet sub-servers and modems. Anderson entered first, halting in the middle of the room while he gazed steadily at the main console there.

'You know I'm with you all the way on this,' he said.

Obviously her dismissal of the guards had worried him. She noted how he casually rested one hand on the butt of his holstered pistol. 'I know you are,' she replied. 'If you weren't you would have done something about it before now. I know you well enough, Simeon, to understand that.'

'They have to go.' He turned towards her. 'It's the only way we can survive – we know that now . . . after Glasgow.'

She strode past him to the console, unhooking her palmtop from her belt. She placed this down on the table to the right of the console and opened it, then gestured to the seat. 'Set us up for transmission. We want a local burst first, to secure things here, then the full Govnet transmission.'

He took the seat and quickly keyed in the required instructions, the screen now showing the main aerial and microwave array online, followed by subsections giving admission to other networks across the world, including readerguns, the transponders in all robots, and radio modems and servers. After that first burst, the signal would go viral. Serene Bluetoothed to the console here, sorted through her secure files and found the program required: the one that added just two digits to every zero-asset implant code on Earth. She readied it, then found two individual implant codes additional to that, and cued them up too.

'We're ready?' she asked, linkage established and her finger hovering over the return key.

He had to clear his throat first, then after a nod managed a strangled, 'We're ready, ma'am.'

This then was the moment – so much like when she had pressed down the ball control to activate the guns on the aero she had flown here a seeming age ago, yet so much more.

'I'm reminded of some historical context,' she said, the politician in her insisting some words be said now. 'When I press this button it's like a reset for the whole human race. It's like the "Year Zero" proclamation made by some of the worst and most genocidal dictators of our past, yet here and now it is utterly necessary.'

'I know it's necessary, ma'am, but it isn't easy,' said Anderson.

There, that itchy niggling of conscience which could grow into something inconvenient – the risk she just could not take. Nothing could stand in the way of what she intended to do now, and nothing must stand in the way of her future plans. She pressed her finger down on the return button, watched the loading bar appear and begin filling. There, it had started, just like that – easy. It wouldn't get every zero asset on Earth, since not all had the new implants – just eight billion of them.

'I did this with you. It wasn't just you,' he said.

Of course, he'd expected her to kill him here and now. He thought she'd dismissed the guards just so she could privately dispose of someone who knew too much.

'Yes, we did this together,' she replied. 'And now I want you to head out to Sheila, ostensibly to help her with the selection process out there, but mainly to get her reaction. We need her to keep her mouth shut.'

'Understood,' he said grimly, again resting his hand on the butt of his sidearm.

He thought he understood, but he didn't yet. In about an hour's time he would begin to feel the effects of the biochip now active in his implant. By the time he realized what was going on, it would be too late for him. He might try to get back to Serene to exact some vengeance, but the chances of him achieving the quarter-hour journey from the perimeter back to here were remote.

Once activated, the biochips would release, from that sixth face on the cube, a potent cybervirus to multiply and spread through the recipient's body, moving as fast as the beat of a heart. But it released more than just one mass of this thing, half virus and half nanomachine, for it acted as a template for further copies, continuously feeding them into the bloodstream for as long as the body's bioelectrics kept the ID implant powered up. It was nasty, and fast. Based on the Ebola virus as the safest base agent to cut down on the possibility of air transmission, it also possessed a nano-mechanical component that made a nerve-toxin similar to Novichok agents. It took effect in an hour, whereupon loss of physical control was quickly followed by paralysis. During tests it had been a toss-up between whether paralysis of the heart or massive bleeding in the lungs killed the recipient first.

In her own mind Serene had named it 'the Scour' but, within days, as the signal retransmitted all around Earth, it would become a name familiar to all. She would ensure that her own personal signature became adhered to what she had created.

Mars

Var stepped into the agricultural laboratory and gazed at the equipment all around her, some salvaged from the old base, much of it put together from parts scavenged here. *Screw you, Ricard,* she thought. Switching her gaze downwards to the soil troughs, she considered how Ricard and his enforcers were now themselves components of the new soil used here.

Gunther, now chief of Hydroponics and Agriculture since Kaskan had sacrificed himself to destroy one of Ricard's shepherds, gazed pensively at the green shoots spearing up from some of the troughs. He seemed to have developed a nervous tic, which became more pronounced when he coughed into his fist. He then rubbed at his chest, as if it was troubling him.

'We received no seed stock from Earth, obviously,' he said. 'But we found that we actually had some stock here.'

'Yes, I know about that,' Var replied. 'I wouldn't have approved the work on Hex Four otherwise.'

Hex Four had been designated an arboretum right from the start, but completion of its construction had stayed on hold while the Committee constantly failed to send the required seed stock. However, after Var shot Ricard and gained approval from other heads of departments for her assumption of leadership here, she had ordered an intensive survey of the resources immediately available, including all the personal possessions, even those in storage belonging to personnel who had returned to Earth. And it was these last that had made possible what she was seeing here. She had not expected much, since the allowable weight of personal effects wasn't much more than could be fitted into a wallet. However, for political staff like the enforcers and Ricard himself, things had obviously been different.

Ricard had actually possessed a small jar of olives, and Gunther's staff, working non-stop in shifts, had been able to resurrect some of the stones. One of the enforcers had kept an apple carefully stored away in a vacuum-sealed cool box for some special occasion, and Gunther had removed viable pips from that. But the mother lode had been the stored effects of one Tina Bream, who had worked in what was now Gunther's department and who had returned to Earth four years previously. She had brought in her own small quantity of seeds in very small containers: seeds for blackberries, raspberries, gooseberries and redcurrants, and even two plum stones and two cherry stones. She had also obviously been collecting seed from the empty plates of the political staff too: here some orange, lemon and pear pips, there some peach, nectarine and avocado stones.

'Okay.' Gunther flinched as if ducking a blow – a reaction to her that seemed all too common, and unjustified. Yes, she had been ruthless, but necessarily so. The reaction of some people to her now she felt stemmed from them being so thoroughly accustomed to Committee rule, to leaders who could have someone dragged off for torture or execution almost on a whim. Gunther gestured to the troughs with one shaky hand. 'We've had no failures at all yet . . . though not everything has been planted. After the dome goes up on Hex Four, we're going to have to partition it to provide the various environments. My suggestion is that we divide it concentrically: the hottest climate at the centre, then progressively cooler out towards the edge.'

'That seems sensible, as it should make temperature control less wasteful.' She gestured to the plants already growing from the troughs. 'What are these?'

'Bream's own stock – the seeds and stones had all been carefully treated, freed of any fungal or other infections and primed for immediate germination, so they were ready for planting quickly. All the other stuff we have is being carefully nurtured in my clean-room.' He gestured again, jerkily, towards an airtight door at the far end of the laboratory. 'What we have here,' he stabbed a quivering finger at the seedlings before them, 'are from various berries, and one quince pip I didn't spot the first time round, along with two plum and two cherry stones.' He gazed at the plants with something approaching awe, and certainly that would be the reaction of many others here at Antares Base.

Unlike most of them, Var was herself the daughter of parents high up in the Committee Executive, so she had eaten blackberries, raspberries, plums . . . in fact she could think of nothing Gunther was growing here in his laboratory that she hadn't tried at one time or another. It was only when her parents were dead, and her status dropped to that of a valuable societal asset rather than an asset with *connections*, that Var found out just how luxurious her earlier life had been. Thereafter, like most people on Earth, she had necessarily become accustomed to highly processed foods, tank-grown carbs and proteins artificially flavoured, black-market sausages containing meat you didn't really want to know about, GM beans with odd physical effects and bread that was more wood pulp than anything else – all flavoured by such occasional luxuries as much-diluted mercury-laden fish paste from one of the offshore fish farms, or the odd gull's or crow's egg.

'I understand that you've had some other successes too?' She felt it necessary to keep this conversation running; necessary for her personnel to know she appreciated what they were doing; that she enjoyed their successes and commiserated with their failures.

'After finding those seeds, we decided to have a brainstorming session to see if we could come up with other places to search. We found a large collection of fungal spores in some of the air filters, from which I'm now growing some edible mushrooms.' He paused to scrub at his unshaven face, then gazed about himself in bewilderment.

'Gunther,' said Var, 'you need to get some sleep. You're no use to me if you start making mistakes.'

He nodded in full and complete agreement, took one step forward and steadied himself with one hand resting on the edge of a trough. 'Not been feeling so . . .' he started, then he clutched at his chest, leaned forward and vomited blood all over his precious plants.

He was the first.

Earth

When the readerguns turned on the guards along the South Cray sector fence, the zero-asset population held back. Only when an aero crash demolished a section of that fence did they finally react. Chingly had been in the middle of the crowd that poured out into the adjacent government district, where he and his fellows had found the world utterly changed. They had found freedom first, and now they found possibility. So much blood and so much death, and Chingly instantly recognized those who had lived high on the hog while his own kind starved, if not by their clothing then by the thickness of the flesh on their bones.

The orgy of looting that followed seemed part nightmare, part wet dream. He found it difficult to accept what he had found in some of their homes, and his stomach ache reminded him of what he had found in various kitchens, cupboards and warming refrigerators. He and his twenty or so companions had separated from the main crowds, made their looting more methodical, and dubbed themselves the Cray Zees. They ate whatever would spoil, and all now carried heavy rucksacks full of food that could last. They'd taken weapons, too, from dead Inspectorate guards and soldiers, and in one case torn a readergun from its mounting. But they had used these guns to do no more than scare other ZAs away from their pickings. When they found any surviving Inspectorate or other government employees, they used other methods.

'Cray Zee!' Chingly bellowed, trying to be comfortable with the horrible images in his mind. The rest of the gang, sprawled around the fire over which they had previously been roasting an odd papery-tasting sweetcorn, responded in kind. They were all as drunk as him on the stash of raw spirit they'd found in containers alongside a still in one of the houses they'd recently broken into.

Chingly tried to accept that what they had done to the government employees they had found was well deserved, but still remained uncomfortable with his own actions. After filling his belly, he had found his libido returning in full force, and it seemed right to butt-fuck that stuck-up bitch wearing her grey power suit. He preferred that method, since the rest of her had already been well used by the other Cray Zees, and she was bleeding quite badly. She'd stopped bleeding about an hour later; about ten minutes after Denk slit open her guts.

Man, that corn was rough. Chingly rubbed his stomach, which felt tight and a little painful. He tossed away his roll-up and moved back a bit from the fire, because the smoke seemed to be bothering him now. His lungs felt raw.

'Fucking shit!' said Mills, tossing spirit into the fire so it flared. 'I feel like shit.'

Maybe that was the cause – just a rough stash of bootleg liquor. It was certainly potent because Chingly felt numb, couldn't even feel his feet, and now his hands were shaking. He put his own drink aside and tried to stand. *Very drunk.* Then, as he finally gained his feet, he felt a niggling in his chest. He coughed up something warm and salty into his mouth and spat it out, then gazed in bemused dread at the red phlegm spattered across the crushed-down corn, before abruptly falling on his backside. Shit, one of the new TBs! He needed to enjoy what he could now, before he died like so many in the sector, drowning in phlegm and blood.

'Hey, Mills, wassup?'

Mills was lying on his back now, convulsing, a bloody foam about his mouth.

'Y'know, I don't feel so good,' said someone behind Chingly, but his neck felt suddenly stiff and sore and he didn't want to turn to look. A pain began growing behind his eyes and his right cheek started shivering as if just that portion of his body had grown cold. Across the fire, he saw Denk stand up and lurch forward.

'Where is it?' he shouted, then fell into the fire. He started screaming, but just lay there burning.

'Help . . .' Chingly began, then coughed violently, bringing up a great gobbet of bloody phlegm. But that didn't seem to clear it. He was wheezing and bubbling now, coughs erupting as often as Mills's convulsions. On the other side of the fire someone else stood up, and then just went down again. The screaming continued, and the smell of burning flesh permeated the air.

'Bad . . . corn,' Chingly managed. He tried to stand again, but found himself lying on his side, unable to get enough oxygen into his lungs while staring into a burning face. Beyond the face, and beyond the flames, he could see no one standing – all of them felled like . . . like the corn. Blackness edged his vision, just for a second, then it swamped him completely.

The first reports arrived with the passengers of the next fleet of aeros to land. Serene expressed horrified surprise, and then shed a brief tear on subsequently learning that the plague that seemed to be spreading across the world had also taken Simeon Anderson and Sheila Trondheim. But she was evidently far too busy to let it affect her much.

'Apart from some tragic exceptions, this malady seems to be killing off zero-asset citizens,' she told her Oversight staff and, via intercom, the small town of Administration survivors at the Complex. 'It seems likely to be some form of super-flu, against the like of which many societal assets and government staff members have been inoculated.' She had already run a search on that – to select a few million SA and Administration

ID-implant codes in those whose inoculations were not up to date, and activated the biochips in those implants, just to make casualties less specific. 'It seems that the rebels and subversives that attacked us are quite mad, and that this Alan Saul, their leader, is not just a revolutionary but a nihilist.'

Such power resided in her palmtop, still linked as it was to Comtrans One . . . but further killing to make the casualty list less specific was absolutely necessary, since it helped conceal the physical source of the Scour, and thus its ultimate source: herself. She could not allow her involvement to be known, for it would turn people against her, interfere with her plans, and she just knew that no one else possessed such a clear vision of how the future should be.

'I have information,' she added, 'that these people were running a germ-warfare research base on mainland Europe, where they developed this affliction which, in an expression of their nihilism, they named the Scour.'

She paused to study the expressions of those immediately around her and saw fear, anger and grief, but no disbelief. So conditioned were these people to accepting what they were told that, even if they did disbelieve her, they would never show it. The reaction would be somewhat different amongst the surviving delegates, and some others in the hierarchy immediately below them, which was why, one and a half hours ago, she had transmitted the codes for every delegate listed, whether still surviving or not. Those immediately below them she was holding off on: no point killing people who might be useful once those they owed loyalty to were dead. She did not waste lives.

She continued, 'A terrible blow has been struck against the lawful authority of the government of Earth and, though we can grieve and rage, we must also work hard to re-establish order. This is why I am gathering together personnel and dispatching Inspectorate teams to all the power stations in Europe. First we must turn on the power itself and then we must restart the machinery of our civilization.'

The prospect excited her. Though billions had died, and were still dying, so much of Earth's infrastructure was automated. The vast population of zero assets had been sustained by this automation, but it was this same automation that would make it possible to restart everything. There would be no dearth of resources, now that there would be no vast unproductive population to both feed and control. In fact, Alan Saul had effectively done her a favour, too, by wiping out millions of bureaucrats. They would not be needed in the sleek government Serene was creating, and she fully expected herself to be ruling over a completely functional civilization within a year. First, however, she needed to establish her authority. She checked her watch: five minutes to eight. It was time for some privacy so she could take part in what seemed likely to be a very interesting teleconference.

'Clay,' she said, turning to Anderson's lieutenant, 'you are now my executive officer, so keep the pressure on. I want lawful authority re-established fast but, more important than that, I want production and transport back online, so tell our teams to go easy on the SAs they recruit. Also, do we have control of Tactical Excision in Belgium?' The European launch site for tactical atomics was certainly something she might need, and soon.

'We have control.' He nodded tightly. 'European Administration and Inspectorate survivors are somewhat more organized than here, and will accept your authority until told otherwise. TEB was one of the first places they ensured was under control and available – they used two tacticals against the ZA horde moving coastwards from the Frankfurt sectors.'

'Good – and the rest?'

He continued. 'We've probably got more than enough food stocks available now, and the auto-trucks are all ready to run. Our secondaries are also implementing population centralization. Also, all the east-coast power stations are undergoing start-up testing.'

That seemed surprisingly fast, but Serene nodded as if she had expected no less, and headed for her private quarters. At the door she hesitated, turned back, 'What off-Earth facilities are still available?'

Clay answered without pause, 'Most of the communication satellites are still available, as none of them was brought down. The Hubble Project is still running, and we have two space planes there. The old space stations, Cores One and Two, are still functional – all staff surviving. Also the Mars Traveller factory complex hasn't been fully decommissioned.'

'Space planes on Earth?'

'Twelve planes at Outback Spaceport and sixteen at various other smaller facilities across the world are all operational. Twenty-three are in for overhaul, and SPP – Space Plane Production – has a further twelve near to completion, though production has halted for the present due to a scramjet crashing into part of the main factory.'

Serene nodded again, feeling slightly numb. She needed to enquire further into all she had set in motion, for it felt almost as if it was careening out of her control. Surely, despite her optimism, it couldn't be this easy to restart a planet after so much death and destruction?

She stepped through into her apartment, took a steadying breath, then headed over to her big-screen console and sat down before it. One minute to eight, and the screen was already dividing up as delegates came online. And some, it seemed, had come online and gone off again – the screen segments they had occupied now just displaying a United Earth logo. Next, one of the segments expanded, pushing others to the border, and a stern-looking Asian face became clearly visible.

'It seems, despite the seriousness of the situation, some delegates have not seen fit to attend,' said Delegate Angone of Region SE Africa.

Serene kept her expression bland, even as one of the smaller screen sections turned a blurry red. It seemed one of the delegates had just coughed blood all over his webcam.

'I would first like to speak to you all individually, then I'll permit half an hour of open discussion through me, as the chair of this meeting,' he said.

A screen segment expanded, cramming Angone to one side. Serene recognized Yinnister from New Zealand, whom she had known was one of the twenty-four surviving delegates but whose presence she had not originally expected. Yinnister had been close to Messina, and Serene had assumed Messina had taken all those loyal to him up to Argus.

'I would like to know,' Yinnister said, pausing to cough into a handkerchief, 'what makes you think you can claim the authority to chair this meeting.'

Another screen division and Delegate Sinegal added, 'Yes, I too would like to know that.'

It seemed that three delegates who, under the previous regime, had authority over Serene were still alive, though Yinnister didn't look too good.

51

'My position in the hierarchy is not open to question,' Angone stated.

'A hierarchy that effectively no longer exists,' said Sinegal, over Yinnister's coughing. 'Messina is gone and, as far as we can gather, is either dead or a captive. Here and now we must establish a new world order.'

Serene couldn't agree more, but suspected it would not include Yinnister or Sinegal, since now Sinegal seemed to have developed a pronounced tic, and there appeared to be a tear of blood at the corner of his eye. Also, of the eighteen screen segments that had appeared, yet more had flicked over to the United Earth holding logo so that, apart from her and the conversing three, only five more delegates were present.

'You are arguing against yourself, Delegate Sinegal,' said Angone, still looking stubbornly healthy. Perhaps, like Serene, he had decided keep his ID implant separate from his body. She opened her palmtop and started running a signal trace, quickly locating Angone not in Southeast Africa as expected, but in Egypt, in the newly rebuilt Red Sea resort of Sharm-El-Sheikh – a place where many delegates took their vacations.

'If a new world order is to be established, who's to say *any* of us Committee delegates should have *anything* to do with it? Our hierarchy therefore stands since, by dint of our positions, we are rightly placed to take up the reins of power, and my status over you all puts me in the prime position to assume the chairmanship.' He paused, obviously staring at his screen. 'What is the matter with you, Delegate Sinegal?'

Sinegal's head was down on his desk, but he raised it for a second to say, 'I am unwell.' Then his screen segment also switched to the icon.

'This is ridiculous,' said Angone, as three more segments also switched to icons. 'What is going on here?'

Serene resisted the temptation to tell him, as she wanted no recorded proof of her guilt. Better to let this Alan Saul take the blame – he was far enough away now to be beyond being caught and questioned. Angone went to holding. Was he, too, starting to feel the effects of the virus? Serene sat back and waited patiently, her fingers interlaced below her breasts. After a moment Angone reappeared, looking very worried.

'It appears that this Scour presently sweeping our world is not confined to the zero-asset population.' He paused as the last screen segments blinked out, leaving only him and Serene. 'Delegate Galahad, I see that it is now just you and me.' Again that pause. 'It's somewhat coincidental that it was you who identified the source of this Scour.'

Obviously the alarm bells were ringing in his head. She needed to deal with him before he tried to assert authority in Europe.

He continued, 'I need you to send me details of this rebel biowarfare laboratory your people found. We'll reconvene tomorrow at the same time.' His screen segment blinked out.

Serene was out of her seat in a second and into Oversight, standing over Clay. She hesitated for just a moment. The human cost was irrelevant, but the Red Sea was on the endangered list . . . No, this had to be done. She said, 'I want a launch from TEB immediately. Here are the coordinates.'

She put her palmtop down beside him, it showing only the numbers her signal search had found. He keyed them in, a map coming up on his screen showing a location on the Red Sea coast.

'Why there?' he asked.

'It is not for you to question my authority,' she told him. 'However, just this once I will reply. A large contingent of the African Inspectorate military wing has occupied the city and is disobeying direct orders from Delegate Angone. It seems someone is intent on carving out their own kingdom, and this cannot be allowed.'

The firing order was now up on the screen.

'I'll need confirmation of the order.' Clay's expression was bland as he slid a palm-reader across to her. He didn't believe a word of what she had just said, but that didn't matter just so long as he obeyed. Serene pressed her hand down against the reader and then instinctively stooped forward, even though the retinal scanner and pulse transmitter inset in his screen would easily find both her eye and the ID implant contained in her watch.

A beep of acceptance followed, then a screen segment opened to show a cam view of part of the launch facility. A pan-pipes missile rack rose into view from some underground silo, and one of the four-tonne cruise missiles blasted into the sky. The thing, which would go SCRAM shortly after going airborne, would arrive at its target very quickly.

'Give me the map,' she instructed.

He punched a couple of keys and it appeared: Europe, North and Northeast Africa, the missile's route showing as a dotted line, the missile itself as an amber light travelling along that, joining up the dots, slowly at first then accelerating as it went into SCRAM. The thing was now accelerating at a rate not allowed with passenger scramjets, since though the occupants would certainly arrive, most of them would be dead. Still, it would take at least another ten minutes for it to reach its target and, if he realized his danger, Angone could abort the thing. Serene watched the timer up in the corner of the screen, herself remaining a still point with all the activity in Oversight swirling around her. Finally, when the missile was joining up the last few dots, she stepped back, reached up to her temple for the control for her fone, called up a visual cortex menu and quickly found Angone's number.

'I said not until tomorrow,' was Angone's immediate response. Obviously he wore one of the newer fones that could link to local webcams, for his image appeared in her visual cortex. He looked distracted, angry. Doubtless he was busy learning about the terrible toll the Scour was taking on the surviving delegates.

'I am contacting you to confirm,' said Serene, deliberately vague.

'Well, you'll have your confirmation: tomorrow at 20.00 GMT. Incidentally, I still haven't received your report on this biowarfare lab. You do have a report, don't you?'

'In fact, that's the other reason I've contacted you. As you can imagine, things have been rather chaotic here, so I've had little time to file it. The laboratory itself was mostly destroyed by the assault team, and we only learned what they were making there after our interrogation of a captive.'

'So there must be a vid file of that interrogation?'

'Certainly: I should be able to transmit it to you within the next few minutes. You need it immediately?'

'You're damned sure I need— What?' He turned, obviously being addressed by a shady figure behind him. 'What!'

'Very well,' she said calmly, 'I'll send it to you shortly.'

'Get me TEB!' he shrieked, moving out of the webcam frame as he shot up out of his seat, cam tracking jerking as it followed him up. The scene whited out for a moment, Angone transformed into a charcoal silhouette, then blinked out completely. The moving light on Clay's screen abruptly expanded and the words 'objective achieved' briefly appeared before the screen switched to whatever Clay had been dealing with before.

A tone chimed in Serene's head: current number unobtainable.

3

Dig up the Foundations

Back in the twenty-first century, a technological singularity did not just seem possible, it seemed inevitable; but those booting up their computer models of human technological development neglected one critical force: the power of human stupidity. For technology to develop so fast that it goes beyond the ability of humans to model it, the underlying bedrock of science must be rigorous and stable. Yet, even in that century, science was becoming unduly influenced by political thought and execrable creations like post-normal science. Science itself began to break down when Karl Popper's dictum of falsifiability was abandoned in favour of faith, and when funding for it became wholly controlled by political expediency. Scientific thought stagnated when the scientists themselves became frightened to pursue lines of research that led them away from whatever consensus happened to be the love child of the politicians who controlled the funding. They became merely puppets producing the results required of them, distorting their research to fit, taking their thirty pieces of silver and crying in their laboratories; dwarfs scuttling away from the shadows of giants like Feynman and Dyson.

Zero Plus One Month – Argus

'You're done?' Saul said, gazing at Hannah steadily.

She felt a tightness growing in her stomach with the return of her fraudulent friend, her panic attacks. With the pressure off, it seemed it was stirring from slumber. She clamped down on it as best she could and surveyed the gleaming surfaces around her.

It had taken her some hours beyond what she had considered her shift to set the surgical equipment in her operating theatre back to a general-purpose mode, clear away all the additional equipment she had been using over the last month, and return her laboratory to order – return it to a place for research rather than production-line surgery. No more would station police be bringing her yet another heavily sedated Committee delegate, facilitator or executive who had remained blithely indifferent while signing orders for mass murder. No longer would she be destroying memories and adjusting minds down to a base template – a mostly blank slate. Now she could get back to her real work. But he knew that, of course he knew.

'Yes, I'm done,' she agreed.

It should have taken her longer but a sickness spreading through Arcoplex One, probably from the decaying corpses there, had shortened the duration of her chore to a month by killing off twenty-two delegates. She wasn't sure whether to be glad about that or not.

Her gaze now slid to one of her work tables, on which stood three half-metre-square brushed-aluminium boxes. Even after tidying everything up, she had continued working: bringing these boxes out of her clean-room to ensure that the samples from Saul's brain were still growing in their aerogel matrices, that the nutrients remained balanced and the waste was being properly extracted. She had even connected them up to her computers here and studied the waveforms – the shapeless thoughts already being generated in the growing brain matter. Now exhaustion was catching up with her, and she was too tired for the panic attack to get a firm grip on her.

'And you're okay?' he prompted.

He thought she was burdened with guilt, beating herself up about erasing the minds of erstwhile Committee delegates, and styling herself no better than them because of what she had done. Or did he really think that? Considering how Hannah had reacted to violence of any kind, a normal human being would perhaps surmise that what he had driven her to do was reason for her to be miserable. But Alan Saul had never been a normal human being, even before Director Smith had tortured him to the point of extinction, before his strange resurrection, before the advanced implants in his skull and before he melded his mind with the artificial intelligence, Janus. Perhaps he could see through her, and knew that Hannah's problem was that she felt no guilt at all.

'Why are you here?' she asked. 'I got the impression you were staying in Tech Central until we can turn off the EM field.' She glanced towards the spidergun crouching just inside the door. Doubtless the usual horde of robots would also be scattered throughout Arcoplex Two, though she didn't think that was about cowardice but about control.

'I've come to speak with Professor Jasper Rhine,' he said.

Before she could stop herself, Hannah emitted a snort of disbelief.

'You have some opinion?' he enquired.

Hannah tried to read his expression. Was he amused,

angry or indifferent? It was difficult to tell. His eyes were still a dark pink – something initially due to blood-pressure imbalances in his skull, but now due to she knew not what.

'It's interesting work,' she said tentatively, 'but I would rather rely on fusion, and I would rather not waste time and energy speculating about the transubstantiation of human souls into the fourth dimension, and the connection between the human "energy field" and holistic healing.'

'But is that all his work is about?' he asked.

She conceded to herself that it wasn't. 'I'm not completely dismissive,' she said, formulating her opinion on the spot. 'There are the possibilities inherent in Casimir batteries, rectifier convertors and the tangle communicator . . .'

'All theorized and tested a century ago.'

'So what's your interest?'

He swung his gaze around her laboratory, it coming to rest on the three brushed-aluminium boxes. Hannah turned and noticed one of her nearby screens suddenly running streams of code. He was taking a look at it, in his own inimitable way.

'We should be so much further ahead than we are now,' he opined. 'The Committee put human endeavour back a century at least. So much of the technology we have now is last century's news.'

Despite her weariness, Hannah felt her curiosity stirring. 'We should have entered the technological singularity by now?'

He shook his head. 'Difficult to know where we are on the exponential curve, when you don't know what the exponents are. No, I'm simply stating that, by subjecting the best minds in the world to the strongest political control, the Committee shut down free thought, hampered creativity and suppressed anything outside the box.' He began heading to the door, then paused and turned back. 'Do you want to come?'

He'd done it again. When he entered her laboratory, all she had wanted was sleep. Now she knew she had to go with him. She stripped off her lab jacket and tossed it over the back of a nearby chair.

'So you're saying that what Rhine is doing is creative . . . outside the box?' she asked.

'No, on the surface he is doing precisely the opposite.'

'If you could elaborate?'

The spidergun rose up onto its legs and exited ahead of him. He stepped out too, and Hannah hurried to catch up.

'At the start of the twenty-first century, the whole issue of zero-point energy was hijacked by pseudo-scientists,' he lectured. 'Like electricity and magnetism of two centuries before, it was associated with the supernatural, the miraculous. General scientific opinion gradually hardened against it and then, with the rise of the Committee, the whole issue petrified. There's been very little real research into zero-point energy for over a hundred years.'

'Which hardly explains Jasper Rhine's function here, does it?'

'Messina,' explained Saul, stabbing a finger upwards, in the general direction of Robotics. 'Just as with those androids the Saberhagens are working on, Jasper Rhine's so-called research was another pet project of Messina's. Rhine was instructed to investigate the interaction of the zero-point field with the human energy field. To put that into simpler terms: there have always been those who fear death so much they want to believe that something exists beyond it.'

Hannah suddenly got it. 'Messina wanted proof that the human soul exists?'

'On the button.'

'So you're visiting Jasper to tell him he'll henceforth be working in Hydroponics?'

'Certainly not.'

Jasper Rhine stood just inside the door to his huge laboratory. Thin and exceedingly tall, he had developed a constant stoop to make himself look smaller. His hair was blond and ragged, as if he had impatiently taken the scissors to it himself within recent days. His eyes were like black buttons and his narrow face bore the wrinkles of one who had suffered a great deal of pain. Just noticeable on his face and the backs of his hands was a web-work of narrow white scars.

Computers packed this place, jury-rigged in ways Hannah, during her few brief visits here, had been unable to fathom. Various experiments were also running. A complex tangle of glass tubes, through which clear fluid flowed, emitted bluish glows from within its midst. A framework supported a torus five metres across, this wrapped in electromagnets to which heavy cables snaked across the floor. Other machines here, within enclosed booths, Hannah knew to contain the tools for chip-etching and nano-machining. It seemed such a waste to have all this stuff here for the research of nonsense. What on earth did Saul intend?

Rhine looked terrified, and well he might, for here was someone who would be able to see through all his bullshit. He could babble all he liked about sono-luminescence, vacuum fluctuations and the ground state of hydrogen, and Saul would be baffled by none of it. However, Hannah remembered that he had looked terrified when last she saw him, and others who had met him had commented on this too. It seemed he spent his life in a constant state of fear.

'You received my instructions precisely two weeks ago,' Saul stated.

Rhine gave a sharp nod, and shivered. Hannah noticed that he seemed more tired and somewhat less clean than he had appeared last time she saw him. 'You told me . . .' he choked to a stop for a moment, took a deep breath, then continued, 'to abandon a lot of research projects.'

Saul gave a slow nod. 'Nothing will be lost, since memory storage has never been a problem, and some of the data from those projects might be useful.'

'Chairman Messina considered it all . . . useful and of prime importance,' Rhine managed.

'Yes, but I've read all your submissions to him: *Vacuum Fluctuations at the Point of Death*, *Zero-Point Initiation of Human Thought* and *Kirlian Aural Interaction with the Zero-point Field* were the ones that told me all I needed to know, however.'

'You've read them all?' Rhine looked devastated. Perhaps he wasn't used to people actually reading his papers.

'All of them are post-normal science; all are based on statistical artefacts, wishful thinking and what I can only describe as an attempt to create a scientific basis for religious faith,' said Saul. 'Your last paper, on the underlying universal mind, is the one most blatant about it.'

'So you dismiss it all? You're shutting me down?' The man looked as if he was about to cry.

'Not all of it, just the pseudo-science rubbish you fed Messina so as to keep your resource allocation, and to have enough projects running under which to bury your real research – the research I now want you to focus on completely.' Saul stared at him for a long moment. 'There will be no more razorbirds or inducement cells in your future, Jasper Rhine. You will give me the truth even if you think

63

I'll find it unpalatable. All hypotheses will require empirical proof before they can be submitted as theories, and will thereafter undergo every possible test to disprove them.' He paused again, allowed himself a rare smile. 'The spirit of Karl Popper is going to be on your back henceforth.'

Rhine not only straightened up, but brushed his hair from his forehead, then inspected his fingernails with something approaching disgust. Saul had done it again: he had judged this man perfectly, used the right words just so, and reached into Rhine's skull to flip over a few switches. But what was that about razorbirds and inducement? It didn't take much thought for Hannah to realize that perhaps Rhine had once not been very cooperative with Messina. Here stood a man who had been broken and forced into submission. This whole station was full of people just like him.

Saul scanned the room. 'You have the prototype power cells here?'

Rhine made a jerky gesture to a nearby bench, then after a pause led the way over to it. He pointed at a small stack of plain grey objects, like dominoes, amidst the other equipment.

'Pick one up,' he said.

Hannah glanced at him, and noticed his face had lost some of its stress. There was a hint of excitement there, a ghost of the boyish enthusiasm seared out of him in an inducement cell. His eyes, she now realized, were dark brown, and not black.

Saul reached out and took up one of the objects, held it for a moment, then passed it to Hannah. She almost dropped the thing.

'Very cold,' she said, then reached out to touch the bench. It wasn't cold at all.

Saul turned back to Rhine. 'What percentages are we talking about here?'

'Nano-rectification of nearly eighty per cent of all external EM radiation and the same for heat. The ZPE accounts for a debatable five per cent of the power output.'

'What can they sustain?'

'Seventy watts constantly, unless in quantum vacuum.'

'What is this, Saul?' Hannah interrupted.

He glanced round at her. 'It's cold because the heat from your hand is being rectified into electricity and stored. In fact every electromagnetic radiation in this room is being converted into electricity through folded nano-films of rectifiers inside it. They rectify a small amount of electricity direct from the zero-point field too.' He swung back to Rhine. 'I want these in production as fast as you can, because we'll need to cut down on the energy debt as soon as possible.'

'They're batteries?' asked Hannah, not quite wanting to admit what she was holding.

Still gazing at Rhine, Saul replied, 'Batteries that recharge themselves constantly from their environment, batteries that theoretically can output energy even when surrounded by only quantum vacuum.' He shook his head and reached out to pick up another one of the objects. 'The paradigm changed a hundred years ago, but then the research dropped into a cul-de-sac where increasingly complex methods were proposed to extract free energy from the zero-point field – while ignoring the other possibilities.'

'It seemed as if Messina didn't ignore them,' said Hannah.

Saul waved a dismissive hand. 'I'm talking about the realities, not the fantasy. I'm talking about the real research conducted here . . . aren't I, Jasper?'

'You may be,' said Rhine, non-committal.

'But you think it's possible . . . or something like it, don't you?'

Hannah gazed at Rhine's expression. Maybe this was something he had spent so long keeping covered that he was finding it difficult to speak about it now – whatever 'it' was. Eventually he struggled to get the words out.

'If you are talking about the Alcubierre Drive then, yes, something like it is very possible indeed.'

'I am unfamiliar with the name,' Hannah interjected.

'How?' Saul asked Rhine, ignoring her remark.

'Polarize the quantum foam . . . then collapsing the ZPF ahead induces expansion behind.'

'I thought there would be a requirement for exotic matter, negative-mass structures and Bose–Einstein condensates?'

Rhine shook his head and allowed himself a superior smile. The man would now explain something that Saul quite obviously already knew, and would feel more confident, boosted, and thus be more enthusiastic about producing what Saul required of him.

'Exotic energy,' he explained. 'The apparent effects of exotic matter can be generated by the interaction of EM radiation fields with tensioned space-time.' Rhine gestured about himself to indicate all of Argus Station. 'Our EM radiation shield could supply half the equation. All we would then need is the tensioning device, which, the moment the interactions begin, would become a vortex generator.'

'Speed?'

'Of the tensioning mass?' Rhine shrugged. 'Overall spin would be . . . three-quarters c, with the spiral eddy currents taking us as close as it gets.'

'Very high energy requirements to get it up to that speed,' Saul observed.

Rhine waved a dismissive hand. 'If you believe Einstein.'

Saul allowed himself a private smile, then continued, 'Anyway, I meant, what is the overall speed of the space-time bubble. Theories on that haven't changed much in centuries, and they put it at twenty-five per cent.'

'No, it's governed only by how fast you can collapse the field.'

'Then I want plans and I want evidence. I want you to work out how we build it and, if you convince me it will work, we'll start construction of your tensioning . . . of your vortex generator directly after we've finished enclosing the station.'

'It will work,' said Rhine, 'and I can prove it.'

Saul nodded and turned to Hannah. 'A theorized warp drive is what he means. We're talking about inertia-less flight, faster-than-light travel, and everything that entails.'

Zero Plus One Month – Earth

The sun was shining on massive activity within the Aldeburgh Complex. Aeros were taking off and landing, personnel were disembarking or boarding. A couple of big heavy-lifter aeros were delivering a fusion reactor and, even as Serene stood there taking it all in, a scramjet shot overhead. There was no indication at all of the grim horror that lay just a few kilometres inland, except the smell.

Serene took the nasal spray out of her pocket, gave herself a shot up each nostril, and the putrid smell went away. Right at that moment, factories in Britain, Germany and Portugal which previously manufactured nasal inhalers for a particularly virulent herpes sinus infection, were mass-producing these devices. Even so, supply was struggling to keep up with demand, especially from those working the in-field clear-up teams. Serene turned to gaze at a distant pillar of black smoke: the pyre taking in the dead from Aldeburgh and from the hordes of zero assets lying beyond. It had been burning for ten days now.

Serene grimaced then headed towards her own aero, Clay walking beside her and the rest of her security staff and her PAs following behind. When she arrived, two guards boarded ahead of her, one turning to help her up the steps. She entered and went through to sit in the pilot's chair, Clay coming through next to occupy the chair beside her.

'We have a pilot on hand,' Clay noted.

'I like to keep in practice,' she replied, strapping herself in then starting up the engines. 'A lack of self-reliance can kill.' She took the vessel up into the sky and tilted it nose-down towards that pillar of smoke.

As they flew over Aldeburgh, she noted the huge activity in the streets. The only people visible down there were the in-field clear-up teams clad in bright yellow hazmat suits as they collected bodies that the heavy machinery swarming below couldn't reach. The motorways in both directions were also crammed with convoys of trucks.

'The cargo-rail networks?' she asked.

'They'll be up and running tomorrow.'

She nodded. This was a microcosm of what was happening all across Earth, though in some regions they were using different methods of transport and disposal. One example immediately sprang to mind: in South Africa they had built ramps down to the sea and were using telefactored bulldozers to shove the corpses into the waves. Apparently the sea along that coast was alive with surviving sharks drawn in from the deep; even two killer whales, thought to be extinct for over twenty years, had been spotted.

'What's that?' Serene asked, noticing something below, in the zero-asset sector beyond the city's centre, and bringing her aero lower.

'The river Alde,' Clay replied, his voice neutral.

Only its movement showed that water ran between the carbocrete banks and under the enclosed walkways penetrating the rust-stained concrete wall to the rear of a megaplex. Its snail-pace crust consisted of corpses, to which the flow seemed to impart the illusion of life: here an arm flopping over, there a boot kicking defiantly at the sky, there a head jutting up with eyes white and tongue protruding cheekily. Serene could think of no explanation for why so many of the dead had ended up in the river. Perhaps something about the Scour drove them to water, or perhaps this was part of that same instinctive drive that had originally impelled so many zero assets towards the sea. She took the aero back into the sky, and continued towards the smoke.

From the residential perimeter of the city, factory complexes extended for ten kilometres to tall security fences. Again there was movement but little of it from living human beings. Here auto-trucks were being loaded and unloaded, while occasional chimneys belched smoke or steam. Not so much of a corpse problem here, since this area was mostly automated, and the problem only became evident in the agricultural land beyond the fence. As soon as the aero cleared the factory complex Serene gazed in numb awe at what she had wrought, then abruptly decided to land the aero. When he realized what she was doing, Clay reached for his nasal spray and took a couple of hits. Serene could hear the others behind doing the same.

Serene landed, the aero's feet settling with a soggy crunching audible to all inside, and she shut down the engines. After a moment she checked her instruments, for it sounded as if something was still running, then she realized the noise was coming from outside. It penetrated as a droning massive din, as if from some ancient computer room with its switching of relays and hum of transformers.

Certainly there was movement here, what with the filthy seagulls and a scattering of crows, but they only complemented the sound. The view also didn't seem clear, as if there were smudges on Serene's sunglasses. She slid a pack of wipes from her top pocket, took off her sunglasses to wipe them, then realized the haze obscuring the view before her was not due to them. Both haze and noise had one source and it was flies: trillions of flies swarming in great foggy clouds over the hectares of corpses.

Good, she thought. *At last.*

'They dropped even while they were on the move,' said Clay. 'It's weird.'

The scene reminded her of pictures she had seen of the Tunguska meteorite impact, where trees had been felled evenly in one direction by the blast wave. Or perhaps a better analogy might be the passing of a harvester of GM bamboo, neatly cutting down and laying out the stems ready for the big collectors that conveyed the harvest directly to a nearby biofuel power station. A wheat crop lay before her, trampled flat by the advancing horde, all heading in one direction; and then the largest proportion of the horde felled while stubbornly refusing to change direction. All of them collapsing, all of them lying with their heads pointing towards the sea which, even though almost devoid of life, could be glimpsed sparkling merrily in the sunshine, between the tower blocks of Aldeburgh City.

'We were thinking it would be better to use one of the big automated ploughs here,' said Clay, then pointed: 'we are already doing some clearing at the perimeter.'

In the distance a massive dozer was heaping up corpses, then scooping them onto the back of a long flatbed agricultural trailer.

'They're going to the fire?' Serene indicated the pillar of smoke, which was considerably nearer now.

'To the fire, yes.'

'When will that all be finished?' she enquired.

'It will need to burn for three months,' Clay replied.

'What about burial?'

'Every piece of earth-moving equipment available is at work, even the old ones that require drivers. All the biofuel power stations on Earth are currently running on zero-asset corpses. And every five kilometres, along all coasts, we're making ramps to push the mounds of corpses into the sea – just like in Africa. The estimate is that we'll manage to dispose of just ten per cent of the dead before the remainder are only bones.'

'Surely we have more efficient methods?'

'When we've finished security-checking Govnet, and can start running the robots, things should improve for the in-field teams as regards moving the dead.' He shrugged. 'But where do we move the corpses to?'

'Our agricultural land is no longer at a premium, therefore much of it can be used.'

71

'As we are doing,' replied Clay.

'It's a short-term problem which nature will eventually solve for us,' Serene stated.

'Nature already is solving it for us,' said Clay, indicating with a nod the masses of flies settling on the aero's windscreen.

Serene smiled briefly, and resisted the temptation to apprise him of a reality recently detailed to her by a taphonomist – a man whose discipline was the study of decomposition. A hundred years ago such masses of corpses would have been much further along in decay after one month. That so many of them were still intact here after so long was due both to a severe lack of all the microbes and insects that had served as Earth's undertakers, and to the sheer number of corpses they now needed to deal with. That was perhaps one of the best indications of the present state of Earth's biosphere she had heard.

Serene was glad to see the flies.

Zero Plus Three Months – Argus

As he stepped out of the elevator airlock at the end of Arcoplex Two, and then paced along one of the walkways running past the cylinder world's massive end bearing, Saul looked up at the 'roof' gradually being constructed out from below the watchtower windows of Tech Central, perched atop the asteroid. They would need to get all the reactors out of storage to keep up the work rate, and he calculated that enclosure would be completed a month hence.

He smiled to himself – a perfectly human response both to what he saw here, and what he felt had been another interest-

ing visit to Arcoplex Two. The progress of the twins in
Robotics had been slow but sure, and Rhine's work was
opening up whole new horizons of possibility. Moreover, the
samples of his own brain grown to maturity in two of those
boxes in Hannah's clean-room – the other of the original
samples had died – made it quite possible he would arrive
successfully at those horizons and venture beyond them. The
effect from them – the echoes in his head – he had considered
removing, but the echoes seemed a perfect representation of
being in the mansion of large empty rooms that some part of
him now wandered. But Saul knew that his present ebullient
mood had little to do with any of those three projects.

I was blind, he thought, *but now I can see again.*

The solar storm was dying at last and, though it still
interfered with signals to and from Earth, things weren't so
bad inside the station. Now, but for a few small interruptions,
he could remain permanently linked into *all* of himself.

Over the last three months it had been difficult to take
himself out of his room in Tech Central, and each time he left
he did so only after thoroughly checking the area he was
heading to and swarming it with his robots. Now they no
longer seemed necessary, because he could gaze through every
available camera, through the eyes of his numerous robots:
now he could taste and smell through thousands of sensors,
even touch with specially sensitized robotic limbs; now, in
fact, the station itself had returned to being his entire body.
He was the ruler here too, he was the Owner, and it seemed
necessary for him to begin showing his face to the human
population again so as to establish firm personal control –
to remind them to whom they owed their lives, and who
could take away those lives in an instant. He also did not like
that his manifest implements of power here were exactly the

same as they had been for the Committee: the readerguns, spiderguns and other robots, and the distant impersonal instructions.

Such things he now considered before he died.

A human being, facing fatal danger, charges up with adrenalin and slows his perception of time to a crawl. Alan Saul, who some might not have considered human even before his brain implants turned him into something more, experienced the same surge of adrenalin. Already operating at super-cooled computer speed, his mind accelerated, and time slowed for him to the passing of aeons.

In a nanosecond he recognized the danger. That figure, suspended on one of the new bubblemetal beams extending out to the enclosure framework, was no robot but a human being in a spacesuit. Whoever it was should not be there, according to all work rosters, which Saul checked in that nanosecond. The figure also wore a vacuum combat suit, and a glimpse through a cam much nearer to it revealed it levelling an assault rifle. Saul threw himself sideways, simultaneously spurring his spidergun into action, its weaponized limbs coming up and targeting just as the distant muzzle flash impinged.

Perhaps it was an illusion, an artefact of death, but Saul was sure he saw the ceramic-tipped bullets descending on him like angry hornets, and he was sure he saw the clouds of depleted uranium beads hurtling up from the spidergun. The first bullet hit him in the right-hand side of his chest, the second punched into the right-hand side of his gut. He felt every sensation: the first bullet penetrating between his ribs, ripping his lung, fragmenting, and those fragments smashing several back ribs out from his spine; the second bullet thumping home, spewing a wrecked kidney out of his back. Perhaps he could have survived these. Hannah Neumann possessed the technology and skill to repair even more severe damage, and his spacesuit's breach-sealant circuit would stop the holes and prevent him boiling his blood away into vacuum. However, the third bullet punched into the back of his space helmet and, broken into three pieces, it shattered his skull as it entered, shards of ceramic and bone tearing into delicate brain tissue as well as the new dense growth of artificially generated neurons and synapses.

The damage stopped his heart, stopped his breathing, blood and brain boiled out into space until a great gobbet of yellow breach sealant plugged the hole, incidentally filling one side of his helmet.

This Alan Saul died.

'I see you've found them,' Hannah had said.

The connections had been there, waiting invitingly. Had he wanted to go there? Had he wanted to take himself even further away from the original human he had been? Of course he had, because, given the opportunity, any 'original human' would choose greater intelligence, greater power. That desire was wired in. In an instant he had connected to one of the units and, at once, it was just as it had been when he amalgamated with Janus: a sudden expansion of his mental horizons – but this fitted him comfortably; there had been no resistance. It had been like submerging himself in a still, cool pool of clarity. He held the connection open, felt the mental pressure draining from his skull, then from the first unit opened a connection to the second. Using an analogy with old computing methods, he had decided to call this last unit his D drive. He had begun copying across . . . everything he was.

'I am making a backup,' he had said.

She'd turned to him, startled. Hadn't she realized the possibilities in what she had made? Here she had done something that had been speculated on for centuries: she had made it possible to copy an entire human mind. Here, essentially, was a form of immortality.

'I also want you to make more of these units,' he'd added, 'for yourself first, and for others here later. Rhine must be the next in the queue after you.'

Dislocation.

The extent of Saul's world collapsed, instantly, down into something dark and limited and primitive. He had never expected to use this so soon, and it wasn't really ready. To his secondary backup he'd copied across the entirety of what he was down on Earth, before the bio-interface began growing in his skull, but no more. The primary extension to his mind held spillover, just something to relieve the pressure, and the connections of both of them were via the new growth in his skull – growth that was now damaged and malfunctioning. He was merely human, a damaged human no longer even occupying a human body, but with the attention and capacity of the same.

Through the spidergun's sensors, he saw the distant figure come apart in a cloud of flesh, vaporizing blood and tatters of spacesuit. The spidergun hesitated to obey his new orders, his grip on it slipping, its mind a bright and shiny complexity he couldn't quite grasp. But its sensitivity to him now lay beyond the simple computer code it had once used and, after running some checks of its own, it sprang into action. It was fortunate that it had become a more complex machine than before, because the detail of its movements lay beyond him. It snagged his body, pulled it back down to the walkway he had been drifting away from, enfolded him in two limbs and headed for the airlock elevator, to take them back down into Arcoplex Two.

Alan Saul, linked to his cerebral hardware, and what remained of his brain and organic augmentations, tried to comprehend the damage from a dark vastness. Consciousness was a hazy concept to him, just as was his conception of himself and his location. Very little would be recoverable from that damaged being without oxygenated blood flooding its wrecked brain; unfortunately that blood would rapidly fill up his lungs and gut and also pour out of the holes there. Luckily, the breach foam in his helmet had sealed both helmet and skull, but still there would be numerous bleeds.

So, thought the Alan Saul struggling for coherence, *is what remains of that Alan Saul worth saving?* He realized it was possible; some part of him now making cold calculations. The blood might preserve a good portion of the brain throughout the time it would take the spidergun to get the corpse to Hannah, and then throughout the time it would take her to set to work on the damage. He decided it was worth it. There was a lot there that might be recoverable and, in the consciousness he had become, he discovered an old-fashioned attachment to owning a physical organic body. Via the hardware and undamaged portions of the body's neural network, he struggled to find and identify what he wanted, his perception of the Argus Station diminishing as he applied himself to the complex task of dealing with his body's autonomic nervous system. Eventually he restarted the heart, but the task drained him, reality stuttered . . . a whole minute gone, the spidergun now nearly at Hannah's laboratory. He needed to locate her. From a place full of shadows, he struggled to visualize and map Arcoplex Two, laboured to link into the cams. He found her still in her laboratory, just paces away from what had now become his true self, residing in those two boxes, and managed to speak to her through her fone.

'Hannah . . . I . . . I have been shot,' he told her.

'What . . . Alan?'

'Just . . . listen,' he said, 'Right lung . . . lower torso . . . my head. I am dead.'

'I . . .'

'Surgery . . . right now – my spidergun brings me.'

She was sensible enough to ask no further questions, just head at full speed to the surgery adjoining her laboratory. Blackness, again, and more time lost. Now he was in the laboratory, his blood leaking out on the floor.

Things to do.

'I have been shot' – the words saved in a mini-file.

'What do you want me to do?' Langstrom asked, and Saul didn't even know he had been talking to the man.

It required massive concentration to string the words together, to lose the hesitation. He lined them up first, open to his inspection, before sending them. 'Retrieve what you can of the assassin and find out what you can from him. Start a section-by-section search of the entire station, missing nothing and ensuring no one can get past you.'

'Will do.' Langstrom paused. 'How bad are you hurt?'

'I'll survive,' Saul replied as he faded, not knowing.

Hannah took one look at what was now effectively a corpse, as the robot loaded it on to the clean-lock gurney, then she swung round to gaze at the blurring readouts on two of her screens – the two that were connected to the two metal boxes in her clean-room. She felt cold fingers drawing down her spine as she realized why he had been able to speak to her; that it wasn't what lay on that gurney actually speaking. She abruptly turned away, overrode the lock into her surgery to take him straight through. Two of her staff arrived and donned surgical gowns, quickly following her inside.

'Strip off the spacesuit,' she instructed them, as she prepared her instruments.

Blood poured out as they first disconnected all the seals on the suit. They tried to take off the helmet, but with no success.

'Quickly!' Hannah barked.

One of the men stepped over to a nearby equipment cabinet and took out a small electric circular saw and quickly affixed to it a diamond wheel, while the other took from the same cabinet a set of bolt croppers. In very short order, Saul's suit lay in a soggy heap on the floor, the helmet in two halves. Rather than bother with any of the lifting equipment available, they manually shifted him to the surgical table, strapped him down, tweaked the position of the table to bring his head up high, and shortly after that were attaching feeds for artificial blood. Using an external cardio-stimulator that injected a series of hair-thin titanium wires to provide current where required, they restarted his heart, which had failed again, and the blood filled his veins – then came out of the various holes in his body almost as quickly as it went in, pouring over the floor. Under Hannah's instruction, one of the men pulled over a surgical unit, and it began simultaneously injecting surgical snakes into his two body wounds, quickly sealing the worst bleeds. Meanwhile, Hannah, after slicing away breach foam to expose the wound to his head, pulled over her specialized combined micro- and macro-surgery and set to work.

As he gazed at all this, Saul understood the detail, but only as a distant spectator. Nothing seemed real; he drifted in a dream, in some half-conscious state. Then, maybe because of some repair she had just made in his skull, everything momentarily slid into proper focus.

'Must remove all . . . damaged matter,' he told her via the intercom, causing her to jerk and quickly withdraw her hands from the telefactor gloves. He was only aware of having spoken after the fact, and wasn't entirely sure of how he had accessed the intercom. The two men looked up in amazement, and some horror, for they were being spoken to by the mess on the surgical table before them.

'I think I know what I'm doing,' Hannah replied, returning her hands to her telefactor gloves, and her attention to the screen images the optics were providing.

'Repair . . . then use tissue stores from the failed unit, rebuild and . . . regrowth.' Why did he say that? He didn't know. Time passed; images on a screen, but no emotional content.

She had shaved and then lifted his scalp to remove a hemisphere of skull from the back of his head. His brain had pulsed blood as she pulled out pieces of shattered bone and ceramic bullet, and injected numerous probes and other instruments. She was now cutting out lumps of tissue killed by the impact shock and depositing them in a kidney dish, then micro-cauterizing and repairing veins, so that the bleeding became less. She had also begun putting in struts and discs of collagen foam for support, for without these his brain would deflate like a speeded-up film of a rotting orange.

'You'll be on life-support for six months before I can even restore your autonomic nervous system – if I even can.'

'I can guide regrowth,' he replied. 'I can run my body . . . through the implants. My body will . . . restore . . . I will . . .'

She paused, absorbing that.

'You'll control regrowth, just as you control your robots?'

'Yes.'

And the truth? The truth was that it was taking a substantial portion of his erratic mental function to keep his body running. His perception of the station had crashed, and his control of the machines within it was now minimal. Maybe he could fully control one spidergun, but definitely not two. His cam vision had dropped back to something wholly human – for he could only manage to look through one cam at a time without becoming confused. But, worse than all this, his perception of himself seemed to have faded, as had his perception of time and place.

He felt adrift in a dream that was Argus Station.

4

The Reaper's Blunt Scythe

Before doctors and medical technology came along to queer the pitch, death was a quite easily definable state. If your breathing and your heart stopped, you had achieved that state and little else was considered. This, in its time, could lead to some unfortunate results when the person checking the death failed to make absolutely sure, as fingernail marks on the insides of lids of ancient coffins attest. As time progressed, it became possible to restart the heart, restart the breathing and then to maintain both. Brain death due to the total necrosis of cerebral neurons then became the point of no recovery, but even that was a movable feast and a hunting ground for lawyers. This line was then blurred when the necrosis became a matter of degree, when cerebral matter could be regrown or replaced, and then became almost invisible when it became possible to programme new neural tissue. The new line was then the death of the personality, but even that became a moot point and was not necessarily connected to the death of the human body concerned. Combine the fact that we can now clone human beings with the seeming likelihood that we will soon be able to record most of the information a brain contains, and the meaning of death moves into the territory of philosophers – a place where ancient certainties themselves go to die.

Argus

Damn, she didn't need this now. She wanted to stay with Saul, to be ready if anything went wrong, to be ready to ensure that he lived. But the implications of what Le Roque had told her, and the images she had seen, could not be denied. Her expertise was required, and essential. Not only that: her refusing to come would hint to Le Roque, and others, the extent of Saul's injuries, which was something she hadn't broadcast. She would see this through and get back to him just as fast as she could.

Twenty-two people had died, all within an hour of each other, all of them repros and erstwhile delegates. Others had conducted the initial autopsies and revealed some derivative of Ebola, but now, factoring in those pictures from Earth and the fact that the deaths occurred shortly after the EM shield had been shut down . . .

Arcoplex One, where most of the deaths had occurred, was quarantined, as were the quarters outside the arcoplex which the victims had occupied, but there were no further deaths, and subsequent blood tests, both within the arcoplex and through- out the station, had revealed no further spread. The corpses had been consigned to the outer ring, to storage in rooms open to vacuum, along with the numerous other corpses that were a product of this station's recent history. It was a puzzle Hannah had not been involved in because of her focus on Saul, and it was one to which she suspected little effort had been applied in solving since, in the end, the victims had been Committee delegates. Now she was involved because of what was happening on Earth; because, according to some recent data intercepted, people had been dying back there of something similar.

'Keep me apprised of what you learn,' Saul whispered to her through her fone.

These words sounded rehearsed to Hannah, as if he had readied them for this moment.

'Why? You'll probably know before I do.' She pulled on her spacesuit helmet and it automatically dogged down.

'I did not tell you . . . as others were listening,' he said, 'I am . . . much less . . .'

'What?' Hannah paused at the airlock, cold fingers drawing down her spine.

'The copy of me, which is speaking to you now, did not fully load before I was shot. I've lost everything I gained through melding with Janus. I'm not even as functional as Malden was. This will change as your tissue implants in my original skull grow and as the neural net reconnects, but right now I can watch through only one cam and maybe control just one robot.'

Pre-compiled, every word; something prepared for this moment. He was still on the surgical table in her private surgery, her two assistants finessing the major repairs to his body. He was, however, now controlling the beat of his own heart along with a few other heretofore autonomous functions. Hannah stepped into the airlock, suddenly frightened. Alan Saul was the glue that held this station together and, if anyone discovered the extent of his debilitation, it could all fall apart. It was significant that the only one he trusted with this knowledge was herself.

The elevator took her out to the endcap, where she departed the airlock, past the massive end bearing, and made her way up to Tech Central. She stepped into one of the new walkway tubes and very shortly reached the temporary airlock inside – put there until the walkway had been built outwards and connected to Arcoplex Two.

Within minutes she had reached the lower corridors of Tech Central, propelling herself along by grab handles in zero gravity. Only when she took a cageway up to the floor Medical was located on, and saw Technical Director Le Roque awaiting her, did she remember to remove her space helmet.

'You've got some of them here?' she asked.

Le Roque gestured towards the door into Medical. 'Four of them – and another is on its way and should be here within minutes.' He appeared puzzled. 'I'm not sure how they relate to what we're seeing on Earth.'

'Timing,' said Hannah. 'They all died within an hour of each other and just after we shut down the EM shield and – in my estimation from that video feed you sent me – from the same disease as killed those back on Earth.'

'I see,' said Le Roque, still appearing puzzled.

Hannah entered the room ahead of him and, once inside, began stripping off her spacesuit. Three corpses were strapped on gurneys outside the surgery, while a fourth was inside, undergoing a second autopsy conducted by one of the military doctors, Yanis Raiman. She strode up to the glass to study the corpse, which lay open like a gutted fish. Raiman had obviously been struggling at it, for the corpse had vacuum-dried like old leather.

'What have you got so far?' she asked.

Raiman looked up. 'The massive internal haemorrhages I picked up on before, but I'm also finding a lot of nerve damage that was previously missed.'

Only now did Hannah note that he wore a full medical hazmat suit. She glanced round at the other corpses on their gurneys. All of them were contained in sterile body bags. If she was right, there was no need for such precautions, but the chance of her being wrong meant they still had to be taken. She turned to watch as the door opened and two security staff towed in the last gurney and pushed it down to the floor so its gecko feet could stick.

'The virus . . . nanoscope,' Saul whispered in her ear.

As the two security staff departed, Hannah went over to a nearby console, and linked up to the surgery nanoscope into which Raiman had placed a number of samples. An image came clear, reams of data scrolling up beside it. Hannah ignored the image but studied the data intently, looking for clues, looking for confirmation.

'Manufactured,' she concluded at once.

'What makes you think that?' asked Raiman, studying the surgery screen.

'Easy to mistake it for Ebola, since it is based on that virus. Ebola is a favourite for biological warfare – always has been. But this one has a cybernetic component to produce a nerve toxin. Check the chemical stats – because you don't find iron molybdenum and platinum catalysts in anything natural.'

'Ah, I see,' Raiman replied, quite obviously *not* seeing.

'But how did it get here?' Le Roque asked.

'It was here already,' said Hannah. 'What we need to know is how it was activated.'

She turned away from the screen and from a nearby cupboard removed a medical hazmat suit and donned it, then proceeded through the clean lock. In a moment she was standing over the corpse, noting where it had bled, checking the desiccated organs in glass bottles on a nearby work surface, then rolling closer a mobile ultrasound scanner.

Meanwhile Raiman had stepped back, quite prepared to let her take over.

'I'll set the scan to the viral signature,' she said. 'I want to locate its vector.'

It took five minutes' scanning. The concentration of the virus was all too plain.

'His right arm,' she noted, not exactly pleased to have been right.

'Did not have . . . ID implants removed,' Saul whispered through her fone.

Hannah nodded; that was it, of course. The twenty-two victims were those delegates who had not had their ID implants removed before the EM shield shut down. She picked up a scalpel, ran a finger down the corpse's arm until she felt a slight lump, made an incision and, using a pair of forceps, removed the implant and took it over to the nanoscope.

'Le Roque,' said Saul from the intercom. 'I want you to return to the control centre and get a team busy analysing that data from Earth further and collating anything else they find of relevance.'

Tick-tock – another prepared order.

'I see,' said the technical director.

As she stood beside the nanoscope, Hannah turned and glanced back at Le Roque through the glass. He looked pale and grim as he headed away. Did he hear it? Did he notice the disconnection between Saul's words and Saul himself? Or was that just her imagination working overtime? She returned her attention to the implant and dropped it into a sample tube, which she then inserted into the nanoscope. She concentrated fully on what she was doing but, even so, the implication of Saul's instruction nagged at her. The video feed she had seen might be only a very small part of the whole story. The implications hit home fully when she studied the implant, checked the hardware that interfaced with the body it occupied and found the biochip. It was saturated with the virus and its surface structures clearly indicated that, when active, it had actually been in the process of generating the thing.

'Earth was hit first,' she said leadenly, 'then the signal got through once our EM shield went down.'

'What's that?' asked Raiman, moving over to stand beside her. He had not seen the video feed; wasn't entirely sure what this was all about.

'Check implants already removed . . . if they . . . still available,' Saul said to her through her fone, then out loud, 'Yes, Earth.'

He had to hang on in: there was too much to do, too many preparations to make. He drifted about the station, sometimes watching ghostlike through cams, sometimes wholly occupying virtual worlds. He felt weary, utterly drained and at the limit.

Must concentrate.

A view opened into Langstrom's office, where the soldier sat at his desk gazing at a video file on his screen. It was a transmission picked up from a camera on an aero back on Earth, and the horrifying scene it showed was thoroughly familiar to Saul.

'You have a report for me,' he said, speaking from the intercom, his cam reception breaking up even with that small effort.

Langstrom jerked and looked around at the door, then up at the nearest cam. He nodded and cleared his throat. 'I do.'

'Make it.'

The soldier cleared his throat again, and stood up. 'The shooter might have been one of Messina's troops, because we're getting no DNA match with anyone we know of in the station. During our search of the outer ring, one of my teams was fired on, and two of my men killed. We returned fire, then went in pursuit and saw two people fleeing.' He paused, obviously uneasy. 'We had them backed up against one of the ring sections, where new supports are going in for the enclosure, but they escaped across it and lost themselves somewhere in the next two kilometres of ring.'

Langstrom had relied on Saul's omniscience; expecting the two shooters to be unable to cross an area swarming with robots, expecting these people to be caught or killed. Here, then, was definite proof of Saul's debility.

'Keep searching . . . I want them found,' he said, unable to put together a plausible explanation for the inaction of his robots in the time he had to talk.

'We've still got them confined to the outer—' Langstrom began.

'Later,' Saul snapped, then set pre-recorded words running. 'You need to go to Tech Central now. You need to see this . . . I've ordered all high-level staff there for the same reason, then afterwards, once they are apprised, we'll broadcast it throughout the station.' He hadn't given the order – he'd relayed it through Le Roque. With luck, the likes of the technical director would see this as Saul merely attempting not to humiliate his underlings by knowing everything and attempting to micromanage everything.

'To see what?' Langstrom asked.

'What . . . you will see. Go.'

Rather than trying to find his own way through virtual space to Tech Central, Saul simply followed Langstrom, using a tracking program through the cam system. He saw Hannah join the soldier, looking very worried about what she had recently learned of the events on Earth, and probably by her knowledge of Saul's real condition. The two finally arrived in the main control room of Tech Central, where all the other lead staff in the station had gathered. Included in this crowd were Le Roque, Girondel Chang, the Saberhagen twins and other appointees new and old.

'You are all here,' said Saul through the intercom.

Le Roque peered up at a nearby cam then, as previously instructed, turned and stabbed a finger down onto his console, turning on a big screen above it. Again the man had not questioned why he should be doing this, which was good – better for him not to know that it represented one too many tasks for Saul to handle mentally. Now it was time for his rehearsed speech, and his prepared answers to expected questions.

'As some of you will know, twenty-two repros recently died from what looked like Ebola,' he began, the first image appearing on the screen to show a satellite view of the South American peninsula. 'After quarantine, sterilization of relevant areas and blood tests, no further infection was found and the issue was shelved. However, new information has now become available, with the consequence that further autopsies have needed to be conducted. I'll let Hannah explain.'

Hannah dipped her head in acknowledgement towards the nearest cam, then reluctantly stepped forward.

'The virus is based on Ebola but is an artificial construct with a cybernetic component,' she said, then paused to close her eyes and rub at her forehead with her forefinger. 'In the victims I examined, I traced its source and found it to be a biochip within their ID implants.'

A muttered response arose to that, probably, Saul reckoned, from those who had yet to have their implants removed, though he did not now have the resources to check on that.

Hannah continued, 'I've since tested all the ID implants previously removed aboard this station, along with those kept in stock. I found only one that was without the biochip and that came from Technical Director Le Roque, and it was the only ID implant more than fifty years old. This discovery is why, I hasten to add, we've speeded up the implant removal programme and now made it compulsory.'

'What activated the biochips in this way?' asked Girondel Chang.

'Good question. They were activated by a signal code specific to each chip.' Hannah paused. 'It was probably sent months ago but since then has continued to propagate in computer systems on Earth and throughout the solar system. It only got through to us here after we shut down the EM shield.'

'But why?' asked Brigitta Saberhagen.

'Let me . . . answer that,' said Saul, then began another prepared speech: 'From the data we've been able to obtain thus far, it seems these biochips were devised as a radical alternative to sectoring, but whoever created them has now also used them in a bid for power on Earth. All but one of the surviving delegates on Earth is now dead. Those who died here on the station were the only delegates still carrying implants. The surviving delegate on Earth, one Serene Galahad, ran the centre for implant research in Britain and the biochip industry all across Earth. She is now claiming that the massive death toll was caused by a rebel-manufactured plague called the Scour.'

'Massive death toll?' someone asked.

His tone flat, Saul said, 'All zero assets with implants, which means ninety-eight per cent of them.'

Right on cue, Le Roque magnified the picture on the screen down towards that South American coastline. In from the shore the regular structure of the sprawls now became evident, while offshore a large half-moon island became visible.

'The island,' said Saul, 'was not there three months ago, but it was not the result of volcanic activity. It is now breaking up, but was previously a floating mass five kilometres long and two wide. The pictures you will now see are from a month and a half ago. Give us that fish-farm cam image, Le Roque.'

A wall of rotting human corpses flashed into view, two metres tall, all tangled together, and crawling with flat white crabs. The view retreated to give the whole horrible panorama, seagulls circling above it like vultures.

'You're seeing just a small portion of it here. We estimate, just guessing how many were under water, that this one island consisted of fifty million corpses. There were, and still are, masses like this offshore along just about every coastline on Earth. That is one method of disposal this Serene Galahad ordered to be employed, but there's more.'

Another view now: a mountain of corpses with roads heading up the sides, up which earth-moving equipment trundled to deposit yet more corpses.

'Another old clip,' Saul noted, 'because as the corpses started to liquefy, her people started losing earth-moving equipment.'

Now a fire belching clouds of smoke into which massive grain conveyors fed a steady stream of the dead, now mostly just rags and bones.

'This is a current video. This fire has been burning for the best part of three months.' He paused for a second. 'A lot of the pyres are going out now, but the skies are still yellow all across Earth and every rainstorm is black, either from the smoke or from trillions of dead flies.'

He'd now said enough. In complete silence, the people in Tech Central had watched the parade of horrifying images. Finally someone spoke up, his voice catching.

'How many?' asked Langstrom.

'Just under eight billion,' Saul replied and wondered if, even with his mind operating to its full capacity, he could ever truly comprehend such a figure. He also wondered how Earth's history would remember him, since it seemed this Serene Galahad was claiming that he had actually caused this plague, this worldwide slaughter.

Saul now drifted away, disconnecting from the cam and from the intercom, his mind feeling like the air hollows in a nautilus's shell, reality slipping away into a dream state. *I'm dying*, he thought, as if to test the words. *I'm dying again.*

Mars

Another one, thought Var, as she quickly pulled on her clothing. The disease had hit very fast and killed eight people. Chief Medical Officer Da Vinci had the virus identified as some form of Ebola, but hadn't committed himself beyond that. In response, Var had ordered the imposition of the virus protocols established under Committee rule. That meant relevant areas were quarantined and disinfected. The personal effects of those who died were placed outside, where the Martian atmosphere would effectively sterilize them, and their bodies were buried outside too. Ultraviolet lights were left on permanently throughout the base, alcohol-based hand-cleaner units placed everywhere, teams constantly cleaning and sterilizing. The community room had been closed in order to minimize human contact, and constant blood tests and physical scans were ongoing. And yet now – after three months and just when Var was relaxing the strictures – another death.

Once dressed, Var headed out of her cabin. Perhaps she should not have considered the results from the blood tests a good enough reason to start opening things up again. Da Vinci had convinced her otherwise, however. In his estimation, the chances of the disease spreading now, after so much time, were very low, but the detrimental effects of keeping the gym closed were quickly becoming evident. The low gravity of Mars simply wasn't enough to sustain bone growth and muscle mass. Base personnel needed resistance exercises and their regular time in the spinner.

One of Martinez's men stood guard directly ahead, behind a hazard tape, while twenty metres further along another stood ready behind another tape. They were both armed, which was surprising, but not half as surprising as seeing the corridor still open and no infectious-disease protocols being immediately employed. The two should be wearing hazmat suits, the corridor should have been sealed off with sheets of plastic, and a pressure differential applied. There should have been a suit here waiting for her, too. She was about to question the guard nearest about this, but then realized she might be mistaken. When Lopomac called her he had said, 'We've got a death.' He hadn't used the word 'another', nor had he mentioned the virus.

Var ducked under the tape, headed straight over to the

door leading into the gym, opened it and entered. Amidst the various weight-training and CV machines, Martinez, Lopomac and Da Vinci stood gazing down at a body bag lying on an exercise mat, while Da Vinci's two assistants were unfolding a gurney nearby. Over to one side stood the spinner, a five-metre-diameter cylinder ten metres long, driven by big electric motors to wind it up to sufficient speed for those who had entered it to experience up to two Gs. It was standing still – all exercise suspended for today.

'What have we got here?' she asked, striding forward.

The three exchanged furtive glances, and Lopomac finally said, 'What do you think, doctor?'

Da Vinci grimaced and kept his eyes down. 'I won't give an opinion until I've done an autopsy.'

'Seems quite simple to me,' said Martinez. 'He did something stupid in the spinner and broke his neck. That doesn't require an autopsy.'

There was something odd going on here, and Var felt uneasy. She prided herself on being able to assess any situation quickly and find the right response. It seemed almost as if Martinez and Lopomac were bullying Da Vinci, and he was having none of it. The three now moved back as the two assistants stepped in and picked up the body to load it on the gurney.

'Let the doctor conduct an autopsy,' said Var. 'We should investigate this rigorously – I've never heard of anyone getting killed in a spinner accident.'

'We're all suffering bone depletion,' said Lopomac, 'so it doesn't seem that unlikely to me.'

She gazed at him for a second, finding she couldn't read his bland expression, then turned back to Da Vinci. 'Do you have suspicions?'

The doctor raised his head and gazed at her almost defiantly. 'Yes, I have my suspicions,' he said. 'I'm a little baffled as to how a man could have sustained such a severe break inside a smooth cylinder.'

'It was up to the two-G setting,' observed Lopomac.

Da Vinci rounded on him. 'It would be convenient for people to think that. Maybe someone killed him out here, then threw him into the spinner and set it on two Gs just to make it look like an accident.'

'This must be investigated,' repeated Var, 'and thoroughly.'

She stepped over to the gurney. Even though this might be murder, she was quite relieved it wasn't another Ebola death. Murderers could be found and punished and, since the number of suspects available here was extremely limited, and generally their locations were known, she didn't think this would be so difficult a case to solve. In a way she quite welcomed the distraction. She reached down and unzipped the top of the body bag, turned the head inside it to face her, then found her heart hammering in her chest as a whole new set of calculations began running inside her skull. She realized that, from the moment she had stepped in here, she had not asked them who was dead. That would look bad. She also now understood the odd reactions of those already here.

'Delaware,' she said. 'Now that's awkward.'

'Or convenient,' said Da Vinci, 'depending on your perspective.' He headed for the door, beckoning his assistants after him. One of them reached out and zipped up the bag, then they followed, heads ducked as if trying not to be noticed.

Var hesitated. Should she stop them leaving? Should she lock down on this? She knew well enough that honesty and truth would play no part in what would ensue; people tended to believe what they wanted to believe, and now everyone in Antares Base knew about the dressing-down Rhone had given Delaware and Christen – the two from Mars Science who had been plotting to unseat her. She did nothing, however, and the door closed behind the gurney.

'Who killed him?' Var asked, without turning.

'It was an accident,' said Lopomac. 'Da Vinci won't be able to prove otherwise.'

Var rounded on him. 'Did *you* kill him?'

Lopomac looked surprised and baffled, which meant he was innocent of the crime, or a very good liar.

'What about you, Martinez?' she asked.

Standing with his arms folded, the man shook his head briefly. 'If you'd asked me to make him have an accident, I wouldn't have been this sloppy. More likely one of his suit seals would have given out while he was outside.'

'Then *you* didn't kill him?' Lopomac asked her.

'No, I didn't,' Var replied. 'And if neither of you two did, then that leaves us with a problem.'

They were gazing at her doubtfully, judgement reserved, and she imagined that they were reading a similar expression on her face, too. What to do now? If she didn't investigate this, then it could poison this entire base, yet how could she spare resources for an investigation when they were still on the edge of survival? And, more importantly, if they did find out who had done it, what then? Whoever did it would have to be killed, since they could not spare the resources for imprisonment either. And she could not afford to lose either Martinez or Lopomac, if it turned out to be one of them.

'Perhaps Delaware and Christen had a falling out,' suggested Lopomac.

Now there was an option: two birds with one stone.

However, no one would believe the convenience of that, and no one would believe a diminutive woman like Christen to be capable of breaking someone's neck.

'No,' said Var firmly. 'You, Martinez, will assign one of your men to this. I want everyone located in the relevant timeframe, and I want people questioned. Meanwhile we'll see what Da Vinci comes up with. Maybe it was merely bone weakness.' It seemed a vain hope.

'Okay,' said Martinez, quickly heading for the door as if he wanted to be gone.

After it closed behind him, Lopomac asked her, 'You really didn't kill him or have him killed?'

'I'm not a savage,' said Var, well aware that many on the base wouldn't believe that.

'Then perhaps we need to consider just how inconvenient a death this is for you.'

Very true, Var felt, the image of Rhone of Mars Science coming to the forefront of her mind. But she mustn't leap to conclusions. Just maybe someone had decided to 'rid her of that troublesome priest', because too much loyalty could be a penalty of leadership too.

'And *you* didn't kill him?' she repeated, for confirmation.

Lopomac shook his head. 'I'm with Martinez on that. If I'd done it, there would have been no body to find.'

'Okay,' said Var, considering how frangible a thing loyalty could be, and how easily it could be faked.

Earth

In the three months since it struck, 'the Scour' had gained currency as an epithet all across Earth, and this particular period of time they were calling the 'Year of the Flies'. Much organization had been required to deal with its fallout, and so Serene had appointed four hundred delegates to govern the regions of the planet. However, already fifty-eight of her appointees were proving treacherous.

'I'll need confirmation sent to my palmtop within the hour,' she said, as she gazed ahead – through the high-security fences, past the readergun towers, inducer emplacements and across the minefield – towards this surviving twenty square kilometres of Tuscan countryside.

'It's on its way to you now,' Clay replied. 'They are the ones who set up the laboratory and had recent Scour victims transported there. They staffed the place with scientists kidnapped from our Nanking factories, and diverted resources to it from West China Region's disposal budget.'

Still the business of sanitizing the planet was continuing, still some fires were burning, and still the befouled earth-movers were dumping their loads in the sea or carrying them to mass graves extending kilometres across. In cold regions the corpses were still intact, in hot and damp regions they were little but bones and clothing, and in desert areas they were dried-out husks. But they all had to go because now they were causing death tolls among the surviving population: thirty million from cholera when a large portion of the North American water table became contaminated; fifty million from Ebola – a cross between the manufactured version and the old original; another twenty million from a resurrected form of the Black Death spread by fleas on the backs of rats, whose populations were so vast now that they swarmed like locusts all across Africa; and a further total of over a hundred and fifty million from other diseases too numerous to count. These tolls were in addition to the deaths caused by the crashed infrastructure; or regional conflicts where Serene had not been able to establish her control quickly enough, and often where the revolutionary council was trying to establish a foothold; besides regional conflicts she ended by tactical nuke. But this was all good, she felt, since, for her purposes, the human population needed to be much smaller – the only irritation being that some useful people were dying, too.

She checked her palmtop as the file came through, and immediately fed it to a program that would check it against other reports she had received from sources other than Clay and his people. Then she looked up at the two armoured vehicles and security van ahead of her limousine as they drove through the gates into Alessandro Messina's private estate, and her driver followed them.

'The laboratory?' she enquired of Clay.

'When they knew we were closing in, they locked the staff inside and used an incendiary, but by then we'd already got into their computers and copied their files. The evidence is secondary – since none of the fifty-eight would put their name to anything – but it's firm.'

'So they were trying to isolate the Scour and turn it into a bioweapon?' she said.

'So it would seem,' Clay replied carefully.

Had she detected something in his voice? Did he know the real aim of that laboratory? When she had first received the report, it was obvious to her that the delegates concerned had been trying to nail down exactly what the Scour was and where it had come from. This she simply could not allow.

Soon her limousine, with its protection team ahead, its motorcycle outriders, and two armoured buses of her staff and then two more armoured cars behind, was motoring down a road seeming transplanted from another century. Maybe, just maybe, even more of Earth could be returned to a similar state. Already she was receiving reports of the benefits resulting from the Scour's massive death toll.

The seas of the world that were not dead, or in the process of dying, at first extended their coastal dead zones by between ten and twenty kilometres, after having four billion corpses dumped into them. Now they seemed to have picked up after that large protein injection, and then benefited from a massive reduction in the flow of effluent, chemical fertilizers, industrial waste and, apparently, from an increase in sunlight and thus in temperature. Even though some pyres were still burning, because of the eighty per cent reduction in industrial and transport pollution, the world's air was cleaner than before.

Serene herself had gazed in wonder at videos of enormous shoals of crustaceans like shrimps and krill, then only a few months later at ten square kilometres of sea boiling with squid. She had been told that already plankton levels were higher than they had been in fifty years and that fish stocks, breeding from those escaped from the fish farms, were on the increase. Unfortunately, only a genetic laboratory might be able to bring back now extinct species like the tuna or the grey whale.

'Keep me apprised of any further developments,' she told Clay, and cut the connection.

Other benefits were becoming evident on land. With the world population now standing at only about nine and a half billion, with vast areas of sprawl unoccupied and agricultural output scaled back, large swathes of land were blooming. Whole fields, tens of kilometres across, had been left fallow and were sprouting weeds, in some places biofuel crops were growing beyond the point where the harvesters could harvest them, and forests of bamboo and willow were stretching for the sky. In the sprawls, tough GM beans and soya were starting to crack through the carbocrete and thus give access to sunlight to other less hardy wild varieties. In one such sprawl, in the East European Region, someone had even reported seeing a roe deer, though that had yet to be confirmed. Upon learning of all this, Serene had ordered the planting of Gene Bank seed stocks of wild plants, and in Britain the first oaks for a hundred years were starting to grow. However, only after doing this did she learn that while some seed stock was still available, the bulk of the genetic stocks were gone, along with the Gene Bank database. They had been transported to Argus Station not long before that station departed Earth.

Finally, amidst groves of olive, orange and lemon trees, Messina's mansion came into sight. Her car and its large retinue finally pulled up in the garden-enclosed parking area before a huge sprawling mansion vaguely in the style of a Tuscan farmhouse but constructed of modern materials and with all the modern facilities inside. Though impatient to get inside for a look around, she waited until her security network had been fully established, which took only ten minutes since they were only checking two cam black spots unavailable to them previously.

Gazing through one of the car's windows she observed a couple of shepherds striding through the grounds, while up on the roof of the mansion a spidergun gleamed in the hot sunlight. She smiled to herself, then looked down as her palmtop beeped for attention. Yes, Clay had neglected to mention the incompetence of the commander of the assault team sent against the laboratory – and that this incompetence had resulted in a destructive fire. However, the man had been punished, and it was an understandable omission on Clay's part for she was too busy for such details. She regretted that the commander had been executed by Clay's enforcers, but at least the man would now be unable to say anything about the orders he had received from her directly. She flipped to another program page, where fifty-eight ID implant codes were queued up, and didn't hesitate for a second as she hit send. By the time she'd entered this house, the fifty-eight would already be dying.

Finally receiving the security all-clear through her fone, she tapped on the glass separating her from her driver and personal bodyguard. They both immediately exited the car, and her new bodyguard, Sack, came round to open the door for her. She stepped out, using her nasal spray, because there was still nowhere outside that was not heavy with the stink of decay. Ten paces from the car, all her personal assistants had quickly fallen in behind her. The constant hiss of nasal sprays accompanied her towards the house until drowned out by a whirring and clattering from above, as five razorbirds swooped into attendance over her head. These amounted to unnecessary security, but the recording they were to make was one she felt wholly desirable. After some touching up and editing, she would later broadcast it across the planet.

'Motivation,' she said. 'The people of Earth have always required motivation, and they have received it.'

The expected question arrived from the head of Global Statistics. 'To what motivation do you refer, ma'am?'

She came to a halt, her right foot on the first rough stone step leading up to the oak and metal-studded front door of the mansion, which now stood open. 'Vengeance is a great driver of human endeavour,' she pontificated, then with one hand made a circular motion above her head, 'and of course out there live nine billion people who would like some payback.'

She had used a program to make a particular calculation and now knew that over ninety-eight per cent of the survivors would have lost someone close during Alan Saul's attack upon the Committee Administration or to the Scour. There wasn't one person in her staff here, or in her now three hundred and forty-two delegates, who had not lost someone similarly, and that's just how she wanted to keep it.

'I could say that now the people of Earth must live and work towards the goal of bringing to justice the greatest mass murderer in human history.' She paused in deep reflection. 'But we cannot resurrect the billions who have died, so what is the point of vengeance?' She climbed up onto the steps and turned to face them all. 'We must have something stronger than vengeance to drive us, and we have that too. This Alan Saul has not only murdered billions, but he has also stolen the genetic heritage of Earth. Most Gene Bank samples and most genetic files of the extinct species of Earth are currently aboard Argus Station. And we must get them back.'

The first space planes were already launching, the two Core stations were changing staff, and materials and resources were once again being relocated offworld. These she would use to recover the genetic heritage of Earth, so she could create Paradise here and – because Paradise always had a ruler – herself rule over it. It was also necessary to establish humanity more firmly offworld, so as to take the pressure off Earth itself. She abruptly turned away from them, climbed the steps and entered the mansion's front door. Ignoring the line of house staff waiting to greet her, she located the door leading into Messina's main office and headed straight for it.

'Kelly Shimbaum only.' She gestured peremptorily to her entourage, then opened the door and stepped inside.

As expected, the ex-chairman's office was opulent, supplied with every luxury and every technology available. Serene rounded a massive ebony desk and plumped herself down in the soft-upholstered chair behind it, placed her palmtop on the expanse of wood before her. The desk itself, of course, was otherwise utterly devoid of paperwork and visible hardware. She sat back, fiddling with the controls on the chair arm, then after a suitable delay raised her gaze to the short and tubby Vietnamese man standing before the desk, sweat beading on his forehead.

'So,' she said, 'tell me about the *Alexander*.'

5

Slice 'n' Dice

In the beginning, military unmanned surveillance drones were bulky things that had to fly high, away from enemy fire. New materials gradually reduced their size, and better motors and computer control brought them closer to their targets. As materials technology progressed and high-density power storage became available, the machines were made smaller and new methods of locomotion were devised. The next generation of drones looked like birds: flocks of geese, swans, hawks, eagles and often, where appropriate, vultures. But one strand of their development diverged when special forces found additional uses for them. The troops realized that the hard high-tensile ceramics, graphine and glass that their birds were constructed from could be sharpened, and that additional software could be written to act on recognition software. These were especially effective at night, and the troops soon found they could gut an enemy without even drawing a commando knife. Thus the razorbird was born – never quite as effective as a missile or a gun, but always inspiring more terror.

Mars

Var felt exhausted as she stepped into Hex Four to gaze up at the new triple-skinned geodesic dome, then around at the completed walls. She considered the work they had finished over the last three months, and regretted how eight of those who had survived Ricard would never see this. That was a crying shame because now, really, she felt all of them had a good chance of survival here. She even wished Delaware had lived to see this, and not just because of the huge headache his death had caused.

The investigation, meanwhile, dragged on. Da Vinci had confirmed that Delaware's broken neck was not accidental, since someone had obviously tried to twist his head off like a bottle lid. There were also traces of powder from surgical gloves, but no traces capable of nailing the murderer. Two people had been exercising in the gym just before Delaware, but had left before the spinner was turned on. Martinez and his chief investigator had decided to break out some of Ricard's supplies and used a brain-function monitor while questioning those two, merely confirming their story. According to all systems in the base, no one else had entered the gym within the time frame of Delaware's death. Whoever had done this had somehow managed to alter system records without leaving a trace.

Martinez now wanted to work his way through every other person on the base, questioning them under brain-function monitor, too. Var had even submitted herself – with witnesses – but it seemed that few believed her results, having lived too long under the Committee to believe any claims made by authority. Now Var was considering stopping the investigation, since the atmosphere in the base had become poisonous, with resentments arising and already leading to a couple of fights. And it seemed pointless to waste resources in catching a killer and then having no one believe that the one caught was guilty.

While she gazed at the tall seedlings transported from

Gunther's erstwhile laboratory, Var was feeling a growing disappointment with all those around her, when the call came.

'Var, you need to get to Mars Science One, asap,' Rhone urged her.

'What's up, Rhone?' she said lightly, but immediately suspicious.

After being told of their perfidy, Rhone's dressing-down of Delaware and Christen in front of her had seemed real enough, but some instinct told her he wasn't as sincere as he appeared. She had always experienced this feeling about him – that he was on the edge of betrayal – then was always surprised when he next supported her. It was irrational, with no basis in the logical world she always tried to inhabit, but she still could not dismiss her suspicions.

'It's complicated. Do you know about the tangle box?'

'I know a little about it – the instantaneous communicator that cost the budget of a major urban sprawl but never worked?'

'That's the thing. Well, it's working now.'

Var felt something creeping up her spine. She knew more about the tangle box than she cared to admit; knew it was cutting-edge science, almost fantasy science; that it should be actually working probably promised more for the human race than anything invented in the last couple of centuries. The possibilities Rhone had just opened up with those few words were . . . numinous.

'I'm coming right now,' she said, turning to the bulkhead door.

Only when she was through the door did she pause and consider. Rhone probably knew that news like this would bring her running – that she might come running without taking any precautions. So she took them now.

'Lopomac?' She queried through her fone.

'I'm on my way – I take it you just got the news?' he replied.

So it wasn't just herself being summoned into some sort of trap. 'Who else has been informed?'

'All the chiefs of staff, and I'm also bringing a few of Martinez's guys . . .'

That was shorthand for those personnel – generally from Construction and Maintenance – who were now the de facto police force here. They would be armed, of course. Perhaps this should have comforted her but, the way things had been since Delaware's murder, she had become increasingly doubtful about those she had considered loyal.

'Good, I'll see you there.'

Maybe it was true. Maybe the communicator, containing carbon nanotubes whose atoms were quantum-entangled with those of similar atoms in a twinned box in some zero-point energy-research establishment on Earth, was really working. Maybe instant communication was now a reality, and causality had just received a terminal wound.

Quite a crowd had gathered in Mars Science Lab One, and Var allowed herself to relax a little. The atmosphere was almost party-like with its excited chatter and speculation. But, as soon as she entered the room the chatter subsided and the party atmosphere dissolved. She paused, a sudden resentment welling up inside her as she gazed at those present. Given the option now, she would have been happy to just leave, let them make their own way in future, but there was nowhere for her to go. She briefly considered stepping down and letting someone else take over, but realized, in that instant, that she would then become the object of a witch hunt. These people now felt the need to blame someone for their problems, and she was much closer to them than the Committee, if it even existed now at all.

Var stepped forward and the crowd parted to let her straight through to where Rhone sat at a console, with Christen beside him, the oval screen above them not entirely necessary but lending the whole set-up a futuristic air. Rhone turned to her, grinning wildly. Why did she doubt him, for his expression seemed sincere? Christen spared Var a blank glance, then concentrated again on her instruments, her back turning suddenly rigid.

'What have we got?' Var asked.

'Data,' Rhone replied enthusiastically. 'Real fucking data. We're establishing parameters at the moment, have received a text message and are preparing to go to full video and sound in a few minutes.'

'Show me the text,' she demanded.

Christen hit a button on her keyboard and some words appeared on the screen: PREPARE FOR COM AT 1.05 GMT – RHINE.

'Why do I know that name?' Var asked.

'I'm surprised you do, because Messina has been sitting on him for years,' said Rhone. 'I only learned about him because of the usual Committee screw-up, when some bureaucrat confused us with each other.'

'Who is he?' asked Martinez, from just behind Var's shoulder, where he was clearly watching her back.

'Messina's pet zero-point energy researcher,' Rhone explained.

Martinez grunted dismissively.

'So this is Earth calling to deliver instructions from whoever is now in charge of that mess back there?' Var suggested.

Rhone shook his head. 'No, Rhine's laboratory was aboard Argus. And this is Argus calling.'

'After all this time,' Var noted.

'They couldn't call before because of the solar storm, which is still interfering badly with radio communications.'

'It doesn't interfere with this?'

'Theoretically, no.' Rhone shrugged, then glanced back at the oval screen, eyeing a counter there. He stood up and gestured to his chair. 'I think this one is for you, Base Director Var.'

Var studied the faces surrounding her, then decisively took the vacated seat. She glanced at Christen. 'Make sure you're recording all of this.'

The woman nodded. 'Of course . . . background too, any data we can get.' Her voice was utterly controlled and utterly cold. As well as being her co-conspirator, Delaware had been her lover. Martinez had ensured that Christen was being watched, which Var didn't like much because that seemed too much like something the Inspectorate would do.

Now a face appeared on the screen; slightly distorted for a second, then adjusting. For a moment Var thought the adjustment was still a bit off, for the man's face was thin and seemed etched with too many wrinkles and the white lines of scars.

'That's him,' said Rhone from behind her.

Jasper Rhine smiled delightedly. 'It works!' he exclaimed, then turned aside to adjust something, his arm apparently spearing out on one side of the screen.

Var jerked back.

'3D,' said Christen, her tone superior.

Var leaned forward. 'I'm speaking to Jasper Rhine?'

He focused on her as if surprised. 'Who are you?'

'I am Varalia Delex, Director of Antares Base on Mars. I am also anxious to know what the hell is going on with Argus Station.' She ran out of words. She wanted to know so much – such as who was responsible for trashing a large part of the Committee infrastructure on Earth by dropping the Argus satellite network on it – small things like that.

'We're independent now,' said Rhine, waving a dismissive hand while still concentrating on something out of view.

'What do you mean "independent"?'

He focused on her again. 'The Owner runs the show here, but we're free.' He paused, momentarily puzzled, then shrugged. 'Free as can be.'

'First com in a month, and we get a direct line to the asylum,' Martinez muttered.

'So many thought I was crazy,' Rhine snapped back, obviously having overheard. '*He* doesn't, though. We'll be constructing the generator directly after enclosure, then they'll see.' He nodded to someone out of view, the screen flickered and now a woman gazed out directly at Var.

'Sorry about that,' she said. 'Jasper is a bit twitchy at the best of times. My name is Hannah Neumann.'

Var noted the sharp intake of breath from both Rhone and Christen. They knew – or knew of – this woman. Could this be the person who controlled Argus? No, Rhine had referred to an 'Owner' who was male?

'Understandably the state of Jasper Rhine's mind interests me rather less than the Argus network dropping on Earth, and the Argus Station now being on a non-conjunction route towards us,' said Var. 'Perhaps you can tell us something about that.'

'In good time,' said Neumann. 'First I need to know who is *fully* in charge there. We have only just learned that Antares

Base has undergone a . . . change in overall leadership. You'll have to excuse our tardiness, but the solar storm is only waning now and we're just starting to pick up data from Earth.'

'We no longer have a political director,' Var declared.

'Why?'

'Because I shot him.'

Neumann just stared at her for a long moment, before bowing her head in acknowledgement. 'So you are now as independent as we are?'

'I don't actually know how independent *you* are. I am in charge merely because that was easiest, and because leadership contests aren't a good idea when you're fighting for survival.' She glanced at Christen, who flinched. 'But certainly we don't have an "Owner" here.'

Neumann said, 'He styles himself the Owner because it's a title not completely degraded by its misuse on Earth. He now *owns* this station because its computers are part of his mind, and all its robots and cams are just extensions of his hands and eyes.'

'Biochips, comlife,' interjected Rhone. Var glanced round at him and he stabbed a finger at the screen. 'Her . . . that's the sort of stuff she was talking about – human minds interfaced with computers.'

Var absorbed that information, not entirely sure of the detail but pretty sure of the results. She turned back to the screen.

'It still sounds arrogant,' she said to Neumann, trying to keep her voice level.

Neumann shrugged. 'He dropped the Argus satellite network on Inspectorate HQs all across Earth, and turned all the robots of Earth against the Committee. He wiped out something like two-thirds of the upper Committee administration and military and most of the Committee itself, including Messina, who is now . . . our prisoner. So I think I'll allow him his arrogance.' She paused for a second, then went on, 'But you've got more immediate problems. Have you had deaths there, within the last three months, from something you may have identified as Ebola?'

Var nodded numbly. How did this woman know that?

Neumann continued, 'Right, the signal must have got through despite the solar storm. The deaths we had here only happened after we turned off the EM shield.' She paused for a second, contemplatively, then continued, 'They were caused by a cybernetic virus emitted by biochips integral to your ID implants. That means you need to get all your implants removed, and fast. The woman who now styles herself the ruler of Earth, one Serene Galahad, seems to have the power to activate that virus in any implant she chooses, and she might just decide that independents on Mars are not something she wants.'

'Jesus, that was it!' exclaimed chief medical officer Da Vinci.

'Galahad has no scruples in this area,' Neumann added. 'You've seen recent images from Earth?'

'Some sort of plague,' said Var. 'We're not getting much.'

'It's the same thing, and it killed just about every zero asset on Earth within one day – eight billion of them. It then went on to kill the remaining twenty-four delegates on Earth, except Galahad herself. And it tends to affect anyone who in any way questions Galahad's authority.'

'Eight billion,' Martinez repeated numbly, others behind him echoing his words.

Var suddenly found a reason for hope. Maybe this news

would be enough to dispel some of the bitterness in the atmosphere of the base. Then she pulled back from the thought, suddenly feeling very selfish as the true import of this woman's words impacted. *Eight billion.*

'You need to get on with removing your implants now,' Neumann insisted. 'We'll talk again in twenty hours precisely. There's no hurry, as we've got plenty of talk time before we meet face to face.'

The screen darkened. Var whirled around to Da Vinci, her stomach feeling like a knot of lead. 'That's true?'

He was distracted for a moment, still mulling over the horrifying news, then after another moment her words impinged. 'Almost certainly.' He nodded. 'In every case the infection was concentrated in the arm, around the implant. And I thought that maybe, due to sloppy aseptic procedures . . .'

'Move fast, then, to get all remaining implants removed.' Her own was gone, so she had no worries for herself, but she could ill afford to lose any more personnel. 'Come on, let's get moving.' She stood up. Best to keep people busy and distracted, and not let them think about this revelation too much.

'Wait,' said Rhone, nodding towards the screen.

There was an image there again, highly distorted and really creepy because the face there seemed to possess pink eyes.

'Why . . . do I know you?' whispered a voice that sent chills down her spine.

'Who is this?' she asked.

'I am . . . I am the Owner.' He faded away, and the screen turned white.

The voice sounded almost as if it hadn't issued from a human being, so why, oh why did it seem so familiar to her?

Earth

Kelly Shimbaum nervously proffered a squat little ten-terabyte memory stick. Serene eyed it for a moment, then took it and set it down with an emphatic click on the desk beside her palmtop.

'I asked you to tell me about the *Alexander*,' she said quietly. 'So tell me.'

Shimbaum gestured at the stick. 'The Chairman . . .' he began, then realized his danger and changed that. 'Messina liked me to make a video presentation of the latest status update.'

Serene glanced towards one wall of the office, which presently looked just like a huge window offering a view across the extensive and lush gardens surrounding the house. The entire wall was in fact a high-resolution screen on which she could view the presentation Shimbaum had handed her. She contemplated the screen for a long moment then shifted her gaze along the adjacent wall to a short column on which perched a sculpture looking something like the by-blow of a hawk and a praying mantis rendered in heat-coloured iron.

'That's all very well, Kelly . . . I can call you Kelly?' The nervous little man gave a stiff nod as Serene swung her gaze back to him. She supposed she could call him anything she liked and he would have to grin and like it. 'Good. Now, what you have to understand, Kelly, is that until about twenty hours ago I wasn't even aware of this project, so updating me on something I know nothing about might result in some confusion, you understand?'

'Yes, ma'am.'

'So I repeat: tell me about the *Alexander*.'

'Messina started the project twenty years ago,' he began, his face now sheened with sweat, some of which had already soaked into his collar. 'He wanted a big stick to wield out there because of the danger of the stations or Mars slipping out of his control.'

That made perfect sense. The problem with off-Earth environments was that only intelligent and highly trained personnel could work satisfactorily in them, and such people were not as easy to control as the average zero asset. Antares Base on Mars seemed a case in point that needed to be investigated: despite Serene ordering communications with the base to be opened once again, there had been no reply from its political staff. This could be due to solar interference, which was still high, but it had also been mooted that they, along with everyone else there, were now dead – which had been the intention. However, Hubble images showed the base still powered up and some signs of activity about it. Perhaps the radio transmitter had been destroyed during Political Officer Ricard's thinning-out of the population? Serene shook her head in irritation and got back to the point.

'How come so few in the Committee knew about this project?' She did not know who had known about it, only that she hadn't.

'I didn't question his instructions.'

Serene repressed her irritation at that response and continued, 'So, after twenty years . . . how far along are you? What are the *Alexander*'s capabilities, and how big is it?'

'The *Alexander* is the first ever space battleship. It was built around the engine taken from Mars Traveller IV.' He paused, then added, 'Documentation detailing the smelting of that engine on Argus was falsified.'

'Do go on.'

'The ship is two kilometres long, and four hundred metres in diameter at its widest point. Eight further fusion engines fixed in rings of four at two points along its body enable it to turn very quickly. It's carrying seven hundred tactical atomic cruise missiles, with yields ranging from one kiloton to one megaton. These can be launched by its railgun or can launch under their own power from its ports. That same railgun is also supplied with case-hardened iron slugs that can be accelerated beyond scramjet missile speeds to deliver a cold yield of nearly half a kiloton. Additionally it possesses twelve antimissile lasers and a not-yet functional long-range maser. The crew complement is one hundred, with quarters for two thousand vacuum-penetration troops, and below the main bridge turret are Messina's extensive quarters – currently being fitted out.'

'Of course,' said Serene, feeling as if her guts were trying to crawl out through her throat. *Such power.* 'So it is ready to fly?'

He shook his head. 'Unfortunately not, ma'am. Messina wanted to take it to Argus Station with him, after that place was seized, but its construction scaffolds are still in place and all internal systems have yet to be connected up and tested.'

Serene just stared at him. His tone had turned slightly patronizing for a moment – the superior technical director of the *Alexander* Project having to apprise a mere politician of physical engineering realities. She picked up the memory stick, touched a control on her chair arm, and a panel in the desk's surface slid aside to reveal various ports and controls. She inserted the stick and routed its contents to her screen wall.

'It seems odd to me that construction scaffolds remain in place when all that remains to be done is internal systems work.' She gestured to two bamboo seats on either side of an occasional table set against one wall of the room. 'You can now take a seat while I watch your status report.'

He walked over woodenly, slightly more afraid than when he had first entered the room. Perhaps he was remembering that she was a physicist by training, who had then branched out into nanotechnology, long before her distaste of the political inefficiencies all around her had driven her into a new career. What he didn't know was that she had already obtained information over and above what he was currently presenting her with, because she had her own source on the *Alexander* itself.

The presentation was as glossy and as slick as she expected. The video of the *Alexander* in its station seemed grainier, less impressive, less real than a science-fiction CGI. However, noticing someone space-walking on the station gave her more of a sense of its scale and she began to *know* this was for real.

The narrative wasn't delivered by the technical director, but by someone obviously recruited for his assured verbal delivery, but the words had certainly been carefully drafted by Shimbaum himself. Serene easily read the subtext and quickly confirmed much of what her source had told her. There was absolutely no reason for the construction scaffold still to be in place; it was in fact a hindrance to systems testing and the impending engine and weapons testing. She opened her palm-top and rescanned various reports she had read during the scramjet flight here to Italy. So long as the ship remained confined within that station, Shimbaum retained his power-base. Meanwhile, the highly trained crewmen and Captain Scotonis were obliged to sit on their hands or repeat virtual weapons drills and emergency procedures.

The presentation ended, with various credits – listing

names she would be sure to have investigated. She gestured to the space immediately before her desk and Shimbaum headed back over to stand like a naughty pupil before his headmistress.

'The rather extreme reduction in Earth's population,' she said, 'has freed up many resources, Kelly. Yet still our population is too high, and the one resource we have in excess is people.' She gazed down at the controls exposed in the desk before her. Among them lay a miniature screen which, when tapped with her forefinger, displayed a simple menu selection.

'I don't understand,' he said, jerking his head slightly so that a droplet of sweat fell from his nose onto the floor.

Serene gazed down at the spot where it had fallen. The white carpet was one of those that rotated its fibres into combs in the underlay, cleaning out all dust, dirt and spillages, which were then conveyed away through a network of microtubules. She returned her gaze to his face.

'Earth requires vengeance,' she said, 'and it requires the genetic database and samples currently aboard Argus Station. What it doesn't require is little empire builders like you undermining the efficiency of its projects so as to retain personal power and status.'

'I've done the best I can. The Chairman has been more than pleased with my—'

'Not good enough,' she interrupted, touching her finger to one menu selection and sitting back.

Atop its short pillar, the sculpture opened out its two scythe-like wings and fantail before it launched, the wings blurring into motion with a sound like a clapped-out petrol engine starting. It rose to a hover even as Shimbaum turned towards it, his mouth dropping open. The razorbird unfolded two chicken limbs below, each terminating in a long glass hook. Then, the sound of it turning to a high, ear-piercing whine, it shot towards the terrified man.

'I—' he managed, then the thing was on him with a noise like a hatchet chopping into a watermelon. He staggered as it clattered away from him and then turned smoothly to head back to its perch. Blood gouted from his neck, from his nose, and from the widening line dividing his head from forehead to chin. His skull fell in half as he collapsed, pumping blood across the self-cleaning carpet.

'Sack,' instructed Serene through her fone, 'in here now.'

Her personal bodyguard was through the door in a moment, gazing down at the corpse on the floor with something approaching disappointment. She eyed him for a second, suddenly attracted by the sheer physical presence of the big man, but then, knowing the ultimate reason behind the sexual frisson she was feeling, she dismissed it – at least for now.

'Take that mess away,' she said. Eyeing the spatters of blood on her desk and the long spray of red up one wall, she added, 'Oh, and get some of the cleaning staff in here, too.'

A team of four house staff arrived to wipe down her desk and clean the spray off the wall, then bag up and cart off Shimbaum's remains, by which time the pool of blood had been reduced to a pinkish stain by the self-cleaning carpet. Meanwhile Serene manipulated further controls on the desk, opening a communications link through the screen wall and, just as the staff were about to depart, the person she wanted to speak to was gazing at her from the screen.

'Captain Scotonis,' she said, smiling. 'You are now in charge of the entire *Alexander* Project. I want that ship commissioned within . . .' she paused to recheck some statistics, '. . . within four mouths. Don't let me down.'

Scotonis, a heavy-set Asian with narrow moustache and

tuft of hair just below his bottom lip, lowered his gaze for a second, doubtless studying the bloodstain on the carpet. He had been in com long enough to have witnessed Shimbaum going into the body bag.

'Certainly, ma'am. We'll be ready for you.'

The bloodstain was completely gone by the time Serene began studying a report concerning effluent pollution of the American Great Lakes, gathering statistics on the remaining population surrounding them – in what had once been the state of Michigan – and considering what degree of thinning-out there might be required.

Argus

Hannah's surgery seemed just another place in his head, it being easy, if he allowed it, for his focus to become unstuck from time. If he allowed the waves of weariness assailing him to triumph, if he released his rigid control for just a second, he could just as easily be talking to Rhine in his laboratory, or walking towards the ruination caused by the nuclear blast at Inspectorate HQ London, or even lying again in that crate that had conveyed him to the Calais incinerator. Only a firm intellectual knowledge of his position in time allowed him to keep hold of things. Only sheer strength of will kept him together. But this was just part of his malaise, for his sense of self had no location, and the physically real was no more immediate than some processing space either in his damaged skull, that brain tissue in a container in the clean-room adjoining Hannah's laboratory, or some silicon within the station itself.

Saul opened his eyes but, because of the bullet damage to

his visual cortex, his body was blind. Closing his eyes did not shut down vision; only stopping the program he was running through surrounding cams could do that. His perception of this body of his was no more than that possessed by the spidergun presently waiting in a corridor outside. Yet, he did feel weary, and sleep – which he had forgone for so long – beckoned to him.

'Shall I sleep?' he asked himself, not sure if he had spoken the words out loud, and as if his physical being was making an appeal to some other.

The coldly functional part of him opined that sleep might be a good idea, since it would help with the healing of this physical body and the brain it contained. So he began flicking over mental switches, allowing that purely human function to take over; parts of his mind comfortably sinking into a place where he could release control, relinquishing . . . everything. Then, on the border of oblivion, he felt a sudden panic, because the whole process seemed to be going into cascade. This was coma, so how could he wake up again? He was allowing himself to slide into normal human sleep without a chemical timer, without the neural safeguards to bring him out again, and he now seemed unable to stop the process.

He fought to stay conscious, but found the only way to retain some grip on the conscious world was by driving down mental partitions; separating away parts of his mind both here and in the container in Hannah's clean-room. He fought to retain control and realized, very quickly, that his complete self could not do so. Only a part of him could do that – just one of those partitions. But to what end? What was the best course to follow?

Seemingly without volition, he found himself gazing through a single cam into Jasper Rhine's laboratory. The man was working on a schematic of some massive engine, something Saul seemed to recognize almost at once. Here it was, a design loosely based on the theorized Alcubierre warp drive. Saul instantly copied the schematic to his mind, lost himself in its possibilities, nearly dismissed it because of its physical simplicity, but then knew that it was right.

Approved.

It went into the system queue, but there was something missing, something else needed. He visualized Argus Station's present non-conjunction class route towards Mars. He felt himself fading as he encompassed it, the effort to stay conscious a Sisyphean labour. He riffled through astronomical maps and surveys and at last found what he wanted, then sent his instruction to the station's steering thrusters and to the Traveller VI engine. The core of Argus Station would be, albeit briefly in astronomical terms, returning to its original home.

Must see this through . . .

Who could he trust?

Hannah . . . He managed to utter, just that one word through her fone.

But she was powerless without him, unless . . . His instruction spread virally, leaping from robotic mind to robotic mind within the station. Further panic then as that viral spread also included odd semi-organic minds in HUD. But the panic faded, as did Saul.

Then he was gone, mostly.

As she headed back towards her laboratory, Hannah tried to dismiss her growing feeling of panic while recognizing that it was the real thing, the certainty that things were getting out of control and not just one of her panic attacks. She should have stayed with Saul; she should have monitored him more closely. But events seemed to be conspiring against her. First that damned implant virus, then Rhine's demand for attention. Then that call from *him* – just her name – and now no coherent response from him.

'Saul?' she tried again, through her fone, and again got a strange muttering response. Had his physical body died and sent his secondary neural tissue into shock? It seemed highly likely. The monitor in her laboratory showed a general lack of coherence of the synaptic firings in that secondary tissue. It seemed to have descended into a fugue, a dream state.

She reached the corridor leading to her laboratory and noted the spidergun dutifully on station, turning one sensor limb to observe her. It then abruptly pointed two limbs at her – behaviour she hadn't seen before, unless the robot was assessing a threat. She halted. Was Saul looking at her through those sensors? That seemed unlikely to her now. Instead, the thing was just continuing to run on his programming: a new kind of life set in motion by him before . . . no, she must not think like that.

'Hannah,' called Brigitta from the other end of the corridor, as she and her sister came hurrying in response to Hannah's earlier summons.

The spidergun now turned towards them, and they halted. Then, after a moment, it decided none of them was a threat and it dropped its two raised limbs back to the floor and slowly closed itself up into a big steel fist. Still eyeing the weapon, the three women advanced cautiously to converge at the laboratory door.

'Hey, it's good they survived,' said Brigitta, still eyeing the spidergun. She was talking about Mars.

Hannah paused, then decided to run with this, felt she

needed a breathing space before entering her laboratory, then the surgery, and thus finding whatever it was she would find there. 'There are some good minds out there,' she replied, referring to Mars. 'They would have known at once that they'd been abandoned and known that they couldn't afford any political staff.' Even as she spoke, she tried to accept the cold realism that must have been involved. Varalia Delex had stated quite simply that she had shot the political director. She had not appeared defensive or challenging – it was the same kind of unemotional murderousness Hannah had witnessed from Saul.

'And that tangle communicator,' Brigitta was obviously awed by the new technology, knowing that they stood in a moment of history. 'We all know how that changes things.'

'Something of an understatement, certainly,' Hannah replied. 'Rhine has proved again that he's not the lunatic everyone supposed.'

'There's the other stuff he's working on, too,' interjected Angela, obviously impressed enough to break her usual silence.

'Yes, there is,' said Hannah, but her interest was now waning. She needed to go through that door. She didn't want to talk about hypothetical space drives right now. The tangle communicator was one thing, mostly covered by quantum physics, but actually screwing with relativity on anything larger than the quantum scale seemed like fantasy. With some trepidation she reached out and palmed the reader beside the door, then ducked to accommodate the flash of a retinal scan. She entered, the twins following her, then headed straight for the clean lock leading into her surgery.

'That communication with Mars was not why I got you here,' she announced. 'We may have trouble.'

Providence appeared to back her up right at that moment, as hollow booms echoed throughout the station. Brigitta stepped over to a console and called up station data.

'The smelter plants just retracted,' she said. 'What the hell is he doing?'

Hannah held off on replying that his pulling in of those plants was probably no more than a nerve reaction, impulses from a severely disrupted or dying brain. But she still clung on to hope, and said nothing at all.

It seemed to take forever to strip off, shower and pull on some disposeralls, but finally she was inside the surgery gazing down at Saul. He still lay tubed and wired to the machines, and all the displays indicated that he was still alive. However, she walked over to him, held the back of her hand over his mouth, and felt the soft whisper of breath through her surgical gloves. She felt some relief, of course, but realized it could be false. He had run some sort of mental program in the hardware within his skull to control that autonomic function. The program would continue running even if the rest of his organic brain was dead. Checking pupil response was useless, since most of his visual cortex lay in a kidney dish in her laboratory fridge. Pinching him was pointless too, since it seemed he had shut down his sensitivity to pain just to enable himself to function.

'What's going on, Hannah?' asked Brigitta, through the surgery intercom.

'I'm getting nothing from him,' Hannah replied. 'No response.' She took hold of his shoulder and shook him. 'Saul?' No reaction: in fact his body was locked rigid. She turned on her fone and spoke his name again: 'Saul?' All that came through was that odd muttering sound, as if from a distant spectre in some haunted house.

'This is the trouble you were talking about?' Brigitta asked.

'It is.'

Saul had been shot and was now in a coma – she dared not think any other way – so who was now in charge? Obviously he wasn't capable of making decisions. The debates and the demands for proof of Saul's competence would soon begin, and Hannah reckoned the division into power bases and the infighting would surely ensue. Doubtless there would be those who wanted the station turned round and heading back to Earth immediately . . . and then there would be blood in the air supply.

'Is he dead?' asked Brigitta.

Hannah gazed down at the figure on the bed, then abruptly staggered and had to reach out to steady herself against the bed. A moment of disorientation ensued and she wondered if she had been pushing herself too hard, then she saw that the two sisters had also been put off balance, Angela righting herself with a hand pressed against the partition glass.

'Steering thrusters,' said Brigitta, looking puzzled. 'So he's not dead, is he?'

'No,' said Hannah. 'I don't think so.'

'Can he die?' asked Angela. She rarely spoke, this Saberhagen twin – but when she did it was directly to the point.

Earth

The monorail journey to Rome had been fast and comfortable, and Serene had hated it. Despite the line being bordered by a no-man's-land packed with readerguns and genetically modified mastiffs, despite the escort of aero gunships and the elevated security all down the length of Italy, it just didn't feel safe. When the train ran at ground level, it could not help but be overlooked by sprawl arcologies or government tower blocks, many of which were empty of life, admittedly, but contained just too much ground for her security teams to cover, and too much space in which a sniper could hide. And when the train track ran above these, on pillars a kilometre high, she felt even more exposed. Just one missile and it would all be over for her.

'I'll be taking an aero back,' she told Clay huffily. 'And I'll be flying it myself.'

'Yes, ma'am,' he replied obediently.

The Centre for Advanced Medicine – established sixty years ago in the Vatican City by Pope Michael the Last, as Govnet media had dubbed him – had grown until it occupied the City entire. Of course, it had been necessary to move out a lot of art treasures to accommodate it, whereupon they had ended up spread across the world, decorating the homes of those delegates who had been overseeing the slow dismantling of the Roman Catholic Church. Serene stepped through a door held open for her by Sack, and into a corridor whose modern appearance gave no hint of the ancient stonework surrounding it. Her entourage, excepting Clay, remained in the reception room as instructed.

'So bring me up to speed,' she instructed as she strode ahead. She was, of course, already completely up to speed, but she had found that pretending ignorance tended to reveal any underlying agenda on the part of whoever was answering her enquiry.

'We had to recruit more "volunteers",' he told her. 'Two of the original seven died under surgery, and another three died a few hours after they woke up. They just shut themselves down and there was nothing we could do about it.'

'Why did they do that?'

'Apparently, in their elevated state, they saw no purpose in continuing to exist.'

'But now you have replaced them and have seven ready for me who do see a purpose in continuing to exist?'

'Apparently – though we do have safeguards,' Clay told her, as they finally reached the door at the end of the long corridor. 'We've surgically denied them control over their own nervous systems, immobilized them, and have them working under inducer. If they disobey, or try to take control of more than we allow them, like trying to access readerguns or robots, we can shut them down in a second.'

The door opened into what had been, until a few weeks previously, an amphitheatre in which modern surgical techniques could be demonstrated to an audience of students. Much of the seating had now been torn out to make way for computer equipment, and power cables and optics were routed all around the area like lianas growing on the wreck of an ancient civilization. A circle of seven couches occupied the centre of the amphitheatre – all facing inwards. At the centre of these stood a column, scaled with screens and surmounted by an inducer array. Various technicians were working in the immediate area, one of whom, Serene noted, was giving a couched figure a sponge bath.

'But how will they perform, should Alan Saul launch another attack against us?' Serene asked, as she made her way down towards them. 'They might choose that moment to self-destruct.'

'Conditioning,' Clay replied. 'The biological interfaces in their skulls are highly advanced, and when they melded with their comlife elements they were completely distanced from the real world. However, disconnected as they are from any influence over their nervous systems, they can't shut anything down, and agony has a way of bringing them back down to earth. It will take maybe a further three or four weeks, but by the end of that time they'll be utterly unable to disobey.'

Finally reaching the floor of the amphitheatre, Serene walked over to stand beside the pillar and looked around at the seven lying on the couches. All of them were naked, five of them men and two women. They had been electro-depilated for reasons of hygiene, and the scars on their skulls had healed into a cross-hatching of white lines, but the scars on other parts of their bodies were new. Optical plugs in their skulls trailed cables linked to free-standing servers. Other optics ran from their torsos to various machines attached to the sides of their individual couches. As Serene understood it, only the cables leading from their heads were required for them to access Govnet – any radio option being denied them – while the other optics extending from their bodies were for control over their nervous systems. They could not now shut down their own hearts, nor could they suppress their pain response.

'So Alan Saul has hardware in his head just like these.' She gestured at them dismissively.

'Unfortunately not,' said Clay.

'Explain,' she instructed.

'The biological interfaces and internal computers we are using here are the product of Hannah Neumann's research undertaken two years ago. The database of her recent research was trashed, we think by Saul himself, and all physical results of it were either destroyed when IHQ London was nuked, or were stolen by Salem Smith when he worked there, before taking on the directorship of Argus Station.'

'So how much more advanced than this is the stuff in Saul's head?'

Clay gazed at her expressionlessly. 'As far as I can gather, by having access to Messina's private files you would know that better than me, ma'am.'

He knew what she knew, so she wouldn't catch him out in any half-truths or outright lies. She nodded soberly to herself, then turned abruptly as a woman lying on one of the couches began to shriek repetitively. Serene had heard that sound before, knew the rhythm of the agony an inducer supplied. She glanced back to Clay, who had his fingers up against his fone.

'She recognized you,' he explained after a moment, 'and tried to gain access to the readerguns outside, for when we leave here.'

'An assassination attempt?' Serene swung back to look at the woman as her screams dropped in register to a steady groaning. 'Have her killed and replaced.'

'No, ma'am,' said Clay. 'She was completely aware that she had no chance of success, but was hoping for precisely the reaction you have given. It was a suicide attempt.'

Serene grunted in contempt and turned back towards the stairs. 'Okay, ensure she stays alive, then. Now show me the rest.'

Serene did not like having to use these 'comlifers', as they had been dubbed, but they were a precaution she needed to take. Clay was correct: she did know more about 'the stuff in Saul's head'. One year and four months ago, the erstwhile Chairman decided that the bio-interfaces Neumann had developed were sufficiently advanced for installation in himself and in his core delegates, so had them transported to Argus Station. Those interfaces were much in advance of what was being used here now. However, Neumann had continued working towards producing something of an order of magnitude yet more advanced; something Messina had decided he wanted just for himself. But he wasn't quick enough. Inspectorate HQ London was destroyed and Argus taken over before he could get his hands on the new interface.

It had taken Serene a while to piece things together from various reports. The forensic investigation of the slaughter at IHQ London, before the nuke was detonated, detailed how an exec called Avram Coran had removed a crate of physical objects from Hannah Neumann's laboratory. Yet that same Avram Coran had apparently died in an aero accident over the English Channel some thirty-six hours earlier, just after he had visited a gene bank whose computer systems were trashed shortly after his visit. A stolen All Health trailer bus had been seized, and a forensic investigation revealed evidence that Hannah Neumann had been inside it and had used the sophisticated surgery therein. Someone else had been there too – someone whose genetic fingerprint just could not be identified.

Serene very much suspected that the genetic fingerprint was Alan Saul's, and that right now he had some of the most advanced bioware ever developed sitting inside his head.

6

Comlifers

Over a century ago the phrase 'computer life' described computer programs that mimicked life. In other words, they grew and bred and evolved. However, over the ensuing years it became a catch-all term not only for programs that modelled living creatures and ecologies, but also for those that mimicked the function of the human brain. Towards the end of that century, the term became restricted to describing brain modelling, and to a limited extent displaced the old term 'artificial intelligence', which itself was applied to expert systems that often possessed no human characteristics of thinking at all. In the time of Alan Saul, it became completely confined to describing computer reconstructions of a functioning human brain that could effectively be used as a software interface between a living human brain and a computer. In that time, under Serene Galahad, those people who thus interfaced with computers were called comlifers, with its intimation too of them serving a life sentence.

Argus

The voice speaking over the station intercom was Saul's, sounding utterly reassuring and utterly in control, yet Hannah knew he lay apparently comatose in her surgery. This only made sense if she considered that all of Saul did not reside in his physical body's organic brain.

'Prepare for a course correction,' he said. 'The Mars Traveller engine will be firing at 7.00 a.m. station time.'

Another prepared statement maybe? And how long ago had it been prepared? What the hell, exactly, was guiding this station?

Le Roque issued his instructions calmly, no more aware of Saul's condition than anyone else aboard, except Hannah and the Saberhagen twins. Preparations were made and, after the big Traveller engine fired up, ran for two weeks without anyone being hurt, people soon returned to their usual tasks. Le Roque, however, wanted to talk.

'He's not answering me,' said the technical director.

Hannah shrugged. 'What am I supposed to do about that?'

'You're closer to him.' Le Roque glanced up at a nearby cam, obviously anxious. 'What the hell is he doing? This route change is taking us off course for Mars and swinging us out into the edge of the Asteroid Belt. That could kill us.'

'The Asteroid Belt is not the same as the one you see in space-war interactives,' Hannah lectured him snootily. 'They're not very close together.'

'No, what we define as asteroids are in fact not very close together, but that definition fails to take into account small rocks capable of vaporizing large chunks of this station at the speed we're now going,' said Le Roque. 'Do you have any idea what a chunk of rock the size of a pea could do at twenty thousand kilometres per hour?'

'Yes, I'm not entirely—'

'And we're heading straight for the disruption zone,' Le Roque interrupted.

Hannah was suddenly annoyed, though she knew herself

well enough to understand that was because she didn't really know what the director was talking about.

'Disruption zone?' she enquired.

'It's where the asteroid below us came from,' he replied. 'Think of it: millions of asteroids and what were previously thought of as asteroids but have turned out to be loose accumulations of rubble, dust, fragments – all barely stable after billions of years – then we come in and snatch the Argus asteroid away, meanwhile sending the remains of the Traveller VI tumbling into the belt. That destabilized the immediate area, and the disruption spread, so that now nearly two million kilometres of the belt is a mess.'

'The objects in the belt are still very far apart, so we should be fine,' said Hannah, further annoyed with herself the moment she said it, because she considered herself quite capable of admitting to her own errors.

'Maybe, but Argus station presents one hell of a big profile.'

'Best you take it up with him, then,' Hannah replied, then quickly left Tech Central.

For over a month Saul just lay there, apparently with rigor mortis set in, but for the fact his heart kept beating and he kept breathing. He was still healing, though, the brain tissue she had used steadily growing and making connections; the organic net from his bio-interface unwaveringly repairing itself and reinstating connections. As he lay there, she'd tried to guide the process, to make it adhere to the maps she had of his mind as it was before, but had only been partially successful. The problem was that it grew with reference to the two masses of other brain tissue sitting in two one-metre-square boxes in her clean-room, and also seemed to be making partial connections to certain parts of his brain that he seemed to have partitioned off in some way. Yes, he was healing, but would he ever wake up and, if so, would what then woke up even be defined as a *person*?

Connections from his brain also remained open into the entire Argus computer system, and it seemed that, through that system, windows opened into his dreaming mind. She'd heard complaints from technical staff about strange strings of code propagating in their computers, like worms, then just transferring away, also disturbing images appeared in screensavers and visual coms, and nonsensical messages and spine-crawling sounds issued from speakers. The whole station seemed to have turned into a haunted house. People spoke in whispers, jerked nervously at unexpected sounds, and checked the shadows in the corridors. All this created an air of gloom, as well as a fear difficult to nail down.

There were ways she could force things with Saul, but she was in entirely uncharted territory here and might do irreparable damage. She had so far ascertained that he had allowed himself to sleep but without putting in place the processes that would wake him up. He was in a coma, and it seemed she had stepped a hundred years into the past with him, to a time when people woke up from comas for no real discernible reason, or woke not at all.

'Le Roque called me up to Tech Central again,' said James, her lab assistant.

He had only just returned with some downloads obtained directly from a construction robot, all of which type were still working on the station enclosure – in fact getting near to completing it. Saul remained connected to them, too, via some of those mental partitions, and she hoped to get some data on what was happening with him. James's approach to a spidergun for the same reason had been unsuccessful – they wouldn't let anyone near.

'What does he want now?' she asked.

'He wants to talk to you personally, and he wants to know why you're not answering your fone.'

Hannah checked her visual-cortex menu and noted eight unanswered calls from Le Roque, twenty from Langstrom, five from Rhine and a recent one from Brigitta.

'Tell him that I'll speak to him when I've got something to report,' she said, then opened up the channel to the last of these. 'Brigitta?'

'How is he now?' asked the more talkative Saberhagen twin.

'Healing, slowly, but still not conscious,' she said. Then, with some irritation, 'I said I'd let you know.'

'That's not really why I called. I need your input.'

'On what?' Didn't Brigitta realize just how bad things could get? Hannah couldn't leave Saul now while he was so vulnerable. How long before either Le Roque or Langstrom decided to take full charge of the station? How long after that before they decided that maybe they would like to stay in control, and that maybe it was time for Saul's coma to end, permanently?

'I'm in HUD with Angela . . . you need to come and see this.'

'I do have my own problems here,' Hannah replied.

'This may be related . . . we're getting the same data-exchange processes here that you're seeing between Saul and the robots. We think he's loaded something to them.'

'Them?'

'The androids.'

Hannah felt a chill. She turned to gaze at the body lying

in her clean surgery, almost lost among the feeding tubes, optics and wires she'd plugged into him.

'What are you doing?' she whispered to him, and stood up. 'Keep an eye on things here,' she instructed James. 'No one is to have access unless I say so, understood?'

He nodded. 'I doubt anyone will try.' He pointed towards the laboratory door.

'Yes, quite,' she replied, heading that way.

Stepping outside, she turned to study the spidergun still installed outside her laboratory. The constant presence of machines like this was probably why both Le Roque and Langstrom weren't being as demanding as she might have expected. Neither of them was entirely sure what the situation was with Saul; and neither of them wanted to become the focus of his attention by doing anything . . . hasty.

It took her a few minutes to reach Humanoid Unit Development, during which time she ignored a call each from Langstrom and Le Roque. The Saberhagen twins were waiting for her outside the door leading into the unit. The two were smoking hand-rolled cigarettes – a new affectation among some on the station since a patch of mature tobacco plants had been found growing in the Arboretum. The smoke would be unlikely to have caused any problems in HUD, so it looked to Hannah as if they had come outside for a break, for an escape from whatever seemed to be stressing them out. Even they were not unaffected by the present odd atmosphere aboard the station.

'So, what's this about?' Hannah asked.

Brigitta drew on her cigarette, then ground it out in a little hinged box she was holding, snapping it shut before she reached to palm the door lock. 'Come and see,' she said, pushing the door open and entering.

Hannah followed her, glancing at Angela, who remained leaning back against the wall, smoke trailing from her mouth and with her eyes closed.

'Over the last month we've been building some basic programming and frankly struggling, as nothing seemed to stick. Two days ago something dumped those programs and took over,' she said. 'It just closed us out. While Angela worked on trying to continue programming them as planned, but failing, I've been tracing the source of the interference, and it came through the computers we were using for programming, via the station network, from your lab. I then managed to shut it out, but that's made no difference. They're all interlinked and when I try to wipe it out in one of them, it immediately starts recording back across from the others.'

'Viral?'

'Call it a virus, call it a worm, whatever – it's programming that perpetually recreates itself and it's very, very complex.'

'Comlife.'

'Yeah,' Brigitta agreed.

Hannah turned to study the androids. They had been fascinating before, even when they were immobile, for the leathery-skinned manikins stood over two metres tall and looked as tough as old oak. They were sexless things that possessed practically featureless heads, without ears or eyes, just a visor of the same leathery material as their skin and the harsh slit of a mouth, and big, long-fingered hands.

Now, however, they were on the move. Even as she entered the room behind Brigitta, ten eyeless visages turned towards her. The one nearest her tilted its head like a curious child that had spotted something of interest. Further down the row, one of them had an arm free of the frame and the nylon webbing straps which had previously supported it and still bound it. It was holding up the same hand for inspection, clenching and unclenching it slowly.

'Let me see,' Hannah said, walking over to one of the consoles.

Brigitta followed, tapped in a command and data began scrolling. Hannah studied it for a long moment, then sat down and pulled up her sleeves and set to work. She began opening files, inspecting packets, linking to the computers in her lab and opening analysis and diagnostic programs, trying to ignore her immediate snap assessment but only finding confirmation of it. After a while she sat back, her heart thudding hard in her chest, her mouth slightly dry.

'Well,' she said finally.

'Well what?' asked Brigitta.

'They're alive,' declared Angela, who had just returned.

Hannah swung round in her chair and regarded the pair of them. These two were brilliant, their education and knowledge extending across numerous disciplines, but they simply were not familiar with the things Hannah herself knew.

'Comlife is largely a copy of the synaptic neural processes we see in life, but running on, at its basis, binary programming,' she lectured. 'That's what made it possible for living human beings like Saul, Malden and Smith to interface with computers. There's a gap to bridge, because of translation difficulties, and a heavy reliance on modelling.'

'Then this is comlife,' said Brigitta.

Hannah shook her head, not quite sure how to reply. She closed her eyes for a moment, feeling her way. 'Saul loaded an AI called Janus to the hardware and bioware in his own skull. It was a comlife copy of Saul's mind, with a binary base that allowed him access to computer systems. It was, if you like, his guide and translator, though much more closely interlinked.

The core of Saul is mainly human, organic, synaptic, even though much augmented, operating through silicon binary hardware. These,' she gestured to the row of androids, 'are the reverse. They're mainly binary AI with a smaller organic synaptic component. Yes, I guess what's running inside their heads can be called comlife, but of a kind we've not seen before.'

Hannah stood up, not knowing what more to add.

'Release us,' said the first android in the row, the resonance in its voice sending a shiver down her spine. 'Instruct us,' it added.

Hannah stared at the thing. The sound of that voice meant nothing to her. A complete psychopath could reside inside that body, even if such a typically human description could be applied. It occurred to her that the same reasoning might now apply to Saul.

'That's a new one,' remarked Brigitta. 'So far it's mainly just been asking to be released.'

Hannah gestured to the door and they trooped outside, closing it behind them. Once outside, Angela began rolling herself another cigarette, spilling tobacco from her shaking hands.

'What are they capable of?' Hannah asked.

'They're strong and fast,' Brigitta replied. 'And they have defences.'

'How strong? How fast?'

'Their bones are made of concentric microlaminations of carbon fibre and steel, all with bearing surfaces, which means they are flexible but practically unbreakable. They're packed with artificial muscle sustained with oxygen and nutrients through microtubules and tensioned electrically. That makes them about five times stronger than a human being and they can act and react faster than any human nerve impulses. The stepper motors at their joints increase that same strength to something equivalent to that of a construction robot.'

'Dangerous, then,' said Hannah contemplatively, realizing something that maybe the twins had missed.

'That isn't all of it,' said Angela, puffing out a cloud of smoke as she spoke.

'Tell me.'

Angela reluctantly continued, 'Their skin is another laminate. You'd be able to penetrate it only with an armour piercer, and then the chances are that you'd encounter another layer of armour underneath. Even if you get through that as well, your chances of hitting something vital are remote. Everything inside them is distributed: mind, power supply, nutrient supplies and stored oxygen.' She tapped her skull. 'The brain isn't only in here, it's everywhere. Even their senses aren't completely located in their heads, as they have receptors for light, sound and smell located all over their skins.'

'Hard to kill,' Hannah observed. 'You're scared of them.'

'Yes,' said Brigitta. 'Shouldn't we be?'

'Anything else?' Hannah asked.

'An electromagnetic field is generated through the skin – so EM weapons won't work against them and, to a certain extent, they'll deflect coherent radiations,' Brigitta said. 'That's about it, I think, but it's enough.'

'No,' corrected Angela. 'Remember the internals.'

'That's right,' said Brigitta. 'They've got internal nanomachines that they can consciously control, which means they can repair any damage. I don't know yet if they can also be used as a weapon. That's it now, I think.' She glanced at her sister, who merely shrugged and drew on her cigarette.

'One point you neglected,' said Hannah. 'If they can consciously control those nanomachines, that means they can grow and change. Already they are growing mentally, as is obvious from the readouts, which are very like some I saw from Saul as he expanded his new neural net.'

'Enough reason to be afraid,' said Brigitta.

'When you feel you are ready,' said Hannah, 'you should then decide whether or not to release them.'

'What?' Angela exclaimed.

Hannah studied the two of them. They had analysed and understood so much and, like so many brilliant minds, they'd missed seeing the wood for the trees. In fact they'd missed something blatantly obvious. This was why sometimes scientists needed prosaic minds around them, to slap them across the backs of their heads and point out the elephant in the room.

'They're as strong as construction robots, you told me,' she explained. 'So do you think that, if they wanted to break free, those nylon webbing straps would be enough prevent them?' She watched them gape at her, then added, 'Maybe they're just making a polite request?' The twins still had nothing to say to that. 'I have to get back to Saul,' she said, and headed away.

As she walked back to her laboratory, Hannah tried to ignore her conscience, which at that moment was telling her she was being a coward. The twins had wanted someone there in charge, someone else to be responsible, to tell them what to do. She had simply pointed out something obvious, and then run away. It was like the situation with her and Saul regarding the mind-wipe she had conducted on the Committee prisoners aboard the station. She had not wanted the responsibility, and had only accepted it when he forced it upon her. She now felt uneasy and slightly disgusted with herself.

Such thoughts occupied her wholly, to the extent that she did not realize an escort had fallen in behind her as she entered the corridor leading to her laboratory. She halted abruptly when she saw what lay directly ahead. The spidergun was right up against the wall, all its limbs folded inwards, clenched – and it wasn't moving. She transferred her gaze further along the corridor. Langstrom and Peach stood watching as two repros held her assistant James pinned against the wall while they cuffed him. The medic, Raiman, and two other medics from Tech Central were also present. She glanced back as two more of Langstrom's men closed in behind her.

'Dr Neumann,' said Langstrom, stepping forward, shouldering some sort of large heavy weapon with a silvered barrel ten centimetres across, a power cable leading from it to the heavy pack Peach carried on her back. Clearly he'd made one of the EM tank-busters portable, and used it on the spidergun.

'What the hell do you think you're doing?' She transferred her gaze from the EM tank-buster to his sidearm, then briefly flicked a glance over some of the weapons the others were carrying. 'I see you've armed yourselves – against the Owner's explicit instructions.'

He tapped a hand against the top of his sidearm. 'The situation requires them – there're things that must be discussed. We've called together a meeting of heads of staff, and your presence is required.'

'Like hell.'

'I'm sorry, but you have to come along,' he said.

'What are *they* here for?' she gestured at the medics.

'They are here to make an assessment of Alan Saul's condition,' Langstrom replied.

And so it starts . . .

'They will do nothing of the sort . . . he's my patient and I'm staying here.'

'Unfortunately not, Dr Neumann. Please don't make this any more difficult than it has to be.'

Hannah swung her attention back to the spidergun. Still it wasn't moving. Probably from this they had assumed that Alan Saul wasn't paying attention, might even be dead. Such an attack on one of his robots should undoubtedly have elicited a response from him.

Hannah did not make it difficult, because in the end she was an unarmed woman – and not the sleeping demigod in the room beyond.

Mars

Var was spending far too much time in her cabin, but she would have had to be a robot not to feel some resentment about the attitude of other base personnel towards her. It was as if they had lived so long under totalitarian rule that they could not accept any other condition. They seemed incapable of questioning their belief that she had killed Delaware and, beyond getting some sort of justice for the man, there seemed therefore no reason to pursue the investigation. No one would believe the results, because all of them believed she was the guilty party. She insisted the investigation continue, however, out of a stubborn belief of her own – the need to discover the truth.

Now, having finished her shower, and again fully clothed and knowing there was nothing critical she could pursue on her computer, Var hesitated at the door. What was her way out of this bind? She wanted to be pragmatic in her running of Antares Base, which required some degree of authoritarianism, but she did not want to be seen as oppressive. Yet she had noticed how the people here were now working less enthusiastically for their own survival. It was a crazy situation.

She pushed open the door and stepped into the corridor, and decisively set forth. Within a few minutes she had arrived at Da Vinci's surgery, encountering five personnel sitting outside in the corridor, awaiting their turn to have their ID implants removed.

'Good morning,' she said cheerfully.

Through the window opposite the seats they occupied along one wall, she could see dust settling after a windstorm in the night, its particles ignited in shades of rose and amethyst by the sun peeking over the horizon.

'Director,' one of them nodded in acknowledgement.

The others nodded too, but quickly returned their attention to their palmtops. She stepped over to the door and pushed it open. She found Da Vinci bending over the forearm of a patient seated in a surgical chair. He held up a cautionary hand for a moment, then abruptly stood upright, waving his patient away. The woman shot Var a wary look, then quickly headed for the door. A sterile circular plaster now covered the skin where her chip had been removed.

'How's it going?' Var asked Da Vinci.

'You saw the very last of them sitting outside as you came in, Base Director,' said the doctor. 'It's not a complicated procedure.'

'The last time you called me "Base Director" was when

147

Ricard was still in control,' said Var. 'There's no need to be so formal.'

'It seems a healthier option,' said Da Vinci.

'So you, too, believe I killed Delaware?'

He just watched her for a long moment, then said, 'Perhaps you didn't yourself, but there may be some useful idiots around you who did do it. So it seems sensible to behave in a way that lessens one's chance of becoming a target.'

The expression on his face indicated analytical interest, but Var could not help noticing the slight sheen of sweat on his forehead. He was obviously frightened of her, indeed scared to be saying such things.

'That seems the same advice that everyone else in this base has taken, and there I have a problem,' she said. 'Our personnel are all keeping their heads down, just as they did under Ricard.'

'But that is no problem, surely?'

'I'm afraid it is,' Var asserted. 'Our survival here is still not assured and we need innovation, new ideas, invention. We need clever people arguing with each other and batting around ideas. What we don't need is people sitting on useful ideas because they want to remain beneath notice.'

'And this has happened?'

'It has. On the base's message board, and only because his discovery was referred to by someone else, I found out that Haarsen of Mars Science has found a way to cut down on our heat loss by five per cent,' Var explained. 'He didn't flag his discovery or bring it to the attention of Martinez, and when I went to see him about this he was terrified, expected to be arrested. He hadn't reported it to Martinez because he thought he would get into trouble for using samples of insulating spray in his experiments. This is madness.'

'So what's the solution?' Da Vinci asked.

'You tell me,' Var replied. 'People are talking to me as if I'm Ricard. What I should do?'

Da Vinci hesitated, looking hunted. 'I'm not sure I'm the best person to ask.'

'Maybe not, but it's you I'm asking now.'

After a further hesitation he bit the bullet. 'The feeling is that you should step down, that a new base director should be voted in, and that the murder investigation be handed over to Mars Science.'

'That's what people think?'

'That's the consensus.'

A very coherent consensus of opinion, Var felt, almost like one that had been carefully nurtured. Was she paranoid to think that someone specific was working behind the scenes to unseat her? No, she wasn't, for the fact of Delaware's very inconvenient death remained. Now she had two things to consider: what was best for the base, and what was best for her. Perhaps she was being arrogant in assuming that she was the best person to lead this place but, as she well knew, those who were never accused of arrogance were also those who never succeeded at anything.

If she stepped down, the chances of this base surviving might be reduced but, then again, with the people here happier about who was in charge, the opposite might happen. But what about her? It seemed highly likely that whoever ended up in charge would turn out to be whoever had been working against her. And, though she couldn't prove it, she felt sure it was Rhone of Mars Science. If that was the case, then she could be utterly sure that any murder investigation conducted by Mars Science would not exonerate her. What then? She would certainly be executed, because this base could not afford the resources for a prison – and Rhone could not afford to have her wandering free.

'Then I will have to consider that,' she replied to Da Vinci, and turned back towards the door. He made no reply as she stepped out into the corridor, just followed her to the door and called the next patient in.

Var walked away, deep in thought, only realizing after a short time that her route was taking her towards the Mars Science laboratories. She continued to consider her options but there seemed no way out. It was not as if there was some haven she could flee to – the base was rather like the entire planet Earth in that respect. She had to stay in power here, and to do that she would probably need to be . . . harsher. Her alternative was her own death.

The sound of footsteps behind her only impinged at the last moment, as whoever was coming hurried to catch her up. She began turning, wondering what problem she was about to be presented with now, then a stab of paranoia spun her round faster. The knife speared towards her midriff but, taking a slice across her forearm, she managed to bat it aside. Christen glared at her, pulled the knife back and slashed at her face. Var stumbled back as Christen followed her, striking again and this time clipping the front of her shirt.

A whole series of calculations passed through Var's mind. She was unarmed, so perhaps her choice all those months ago not to wear a sidearm had been a foolish one. If this went on any longer, Christen was going to slice her up. If she ran, she'd likely end up with that knife in her back. She had to end this now, quickly, but how?

Christen lunged again, over-extending herself. Var evaded the stab, turning to catch hold of her attacker's wrist, desperately, in both hands. Christen drove a foot down against Var's shin and agonizingly into the top of her foot, and Var's grip began to slip. The woman was much stronger than she appeared to be. Next her fist smashed against Var's temple and everything went black etched with bright yellow veins. Var just reacted wildly. She let go of Christen's wrist with her left hand and brought her elbow back just as hard as she could, aiming for Christen's head. The woman jerked her head back at the last moment, and Var's elbow hit her hard, right in the throat.

The next thing Var knew, there were people all around, intent on separating them. Her legs gave way and she ended up with her back against the wall. A horrible choking sound issued from somewhere as a crowd of half-seen figures gathered around Christen.

'Get Da Vinci!' someone yelled.

'The knife,' Var managed, but she was ignored.

She began crawling across the floor to where she could see the knife. It was now Christen's only hope. Var had felt the cartilage break under her elbow. Christen needed to breathe or she would die, and only a tracheotomy could save her now. But someone kicked the knife away, and then a boot slammed against Var's head, bringing back the darkness and those yellow veins. She never actually lost consciousness, but events for some minutes remained unclear to her. When she finally managed to stagger to her feet Da Vinci had a tracheotomy tube in Christen's throat and was trying to revive her, but she seemed just inert meat.

Martinez and Lopomac then arrived, and Var could see the doubt in their faces – and when Rhone arrived, she could see nothing in his face at all. Everyone else looked hostile. Var walked away, dripping blood. She would wear her sidearm from now on, and the people here would do what they were damned well told, or know the consequences.

Argus

Alex felt a surge of unaccustomed delight. He was alive, Chairman Alessandro Messina was alive! Alex squatted down beside Alexandra – his communications officer and the only other surviving member of the squad – and watched the short video file as it cycled. Initially the figure it showed did not have the Chairman's face, but the program Alexandra was using had soon decoded the plastic surgery and revealed his true underlying features. There he was, Messina himself, clad in overalls as he walked along beside a hydroponics tank, stopping periodically to use a pipette to take a sample of tank nutrient and place it in one of a series of numbered sample bottles.

Only after the initial euphoria had passed did Alex start to get angry. They were making the ruler of Earth carry out the work of a robot, a slave, a zero asset. They'd humiliated him by forcing him to wear the clothing of a menial. This, if nothing else, confirmed for him just how petty and vindictive were the terrorists who had taken control of the Argus Station. However, most of Alex's anger was directed towards himself. He reached up, as he often did in moments of stress like this, to rub at the fine web-work of scars at his temple and extending up into his cap of black hair – which was distinguished from that of his dead brothers only by a tuft of grey over one slightly larger scar located there.

'We allowed ourselves to succumb to despair, Alexandra,'

he said, noting her glance at him in brief puzzlement upon hearing her true name. 'We did not sufficiently check the data, and now our task is even more difficult.'

They should have tried for job reallocation and ensured they ended up out on Smelter Two, where the Chairman and numerous other repro delegates had been moved after the first assaults. They could have protected him from the final assault that put him in hospital, from which the news surfaced that he had died, when in fact he had undergone facial reconstruction. No . . . Alex shook his head in irritation.

'So, beyond vengeance, we return to our primary objective,' he said, his voice carried from his suit to Alexandra's via an optical cable – radio wasn't a good idea here as, even when coded, it might be used to locate them.

'Just freeing the Chairman will not be sufficient,' Alexandra reminded him. 'We must continue to make meticulous preparations. We cannot afford to get ourselves killed, like Alex Two.'

The two of them paused to contemplate her words, remembering the brief scream as the fusillade from the spidergun tore Alex Two to shreds. Alex, who until a few days ago had possessed the secret name Alex One, nodded in agreement. This was precisely why they had not tried to get close to the Chairman. If they were to rescue him, they needed to find a way off this station, and that way was clearly the *Imperator* and its as yet untried hibernation chambers.

'But, really, Alex Two did not waste his life,' Alexandra contended. 'It is only because Alan Saul is dead that I was able to find this.' She gestured to the video clip. 'While he was alive, I couldn't penetrate the system as I now can.'

'If he *is* dead,' said Alex. 'That broadcast he made seemed pretty real to me.'

It seemed an age ago now since Alan Saul had spoken about the terrible disease that had swept across Earth, and displayed those horrifying images. Since then the two survivors of the squad had spent their time merely surviving, living like rats in the walls, slowly accruing resources, but aimless and depressed because they believed their prime reason for existence had died, while still unsure if their shot at vengeance had succeeded.

'Falsified,' said Alexandra confidently. 'We saw where those bullets hit and it's not possible that he could talk after that.'

It was her lack of experience that made her so sure, Alex realized. She had only ever seen people die when gunned down. She had never seen, as had Alex, shattered meat put back together again by modern surgical methods.

'Also,' she continued, 'the search for us has involved human personnel, but not robots. Consider what happened when Langstrom's troops first located us.'

Again a pause for contemplation. On that occasion they'd been cornered, backed up against an area occupied by construction robots, as the human searchers were closing in. In what he had thought was the vain hope that Alan Saul had at least been sufficiently disabled by Alex Two's assassination attempt to not be watching, Alex had made the decision to cross that occupied area. The robots had ignored them. So it was just possible that Alexandra was right, and Alan Saul was dead.

'So we must reinstate our previous plan of action,' he declared.

Alex now considered that further, because even without Saul controlling the station, their position was bad. He damned himself for acting out of despair in that assassination attempt, and for earlier procrastination. Their squad had been placed on Argus for very specific reasons: they were first of all Alessandro Messina's spies, rooting out plots against him, passing on the results to his main protection teams; and next they were his secret protection team, providing the last resort should all else fail. Concealed by false identities as diagnostics and maintenance engineers, they had been able to range about the station to this purpose, but no longer. Almost certainly their presence had been missed from the maintenance teams, and analysis of Alex Two's remains would have been carried out. So, surely inevitably, by now someone would have worked out precisely who and what they were.

Damnation! Perhaps if they had acted right at the beginning of all this, there might have been a chance, maybe a very small chance, for them to grab Messina, steal a space plane and head back to Earth. That chance had passed as the station moved beyond the Moon and began heading out towards Mars, and then they found themselves simply unable to act in a station filled with hostile robots, humans and the ever-watchful and dangerous being that had taken control here. Alex shook his head: twenty-twenty hindsight was indeed a wonderful thing.

'We need to talk to Earth,' Alexandra said abruptly.

'Why?' Alex asked, gazing at her bright-eyed naivety. 'There's no help for us back there.'

Alexandra stared at him, a flicker of disbelief crossing her expression. 'Schematics,' she explained, gesturing to the mess of jury-rigged hardware she had put together. 'Remember, our computer access is minimal out here, so I won't be able to download a station schematic without being detected.'

Alex nodded, for she had a point. 'So right now we're operating on what we remember, and otherwise we're blind,' he said. 'We first need to know where we can resupply ourselves, after Langstrom uncovered our hide. We need oxygen, food and water – and more firepower.'

'All the data on this place is back there, along with tactical planners who can help us,' said Alexandra. 'I'm sure they *will* help us when we give them this news.' She gestured at the video on the screen.

Alex could think of many reasons, however, why they would get no help. Carefully he said, 'But we saw what happened back there.'

'We saw, but we also know that Committee power is still current – so we have to try.'

Ah, the optimism of a four-year-old, thought Alex. He watched her intently. 'What can you do?'

Alexandra pointed towards the outer edge of the station. 'There'll be dishes out there,' she said. 'I should be able to hack one and get a signal out, and I'm certain *someone* will be listening, despite everything.'

He tried to cast doubt: 'I have to wonder if Delegate Serene Galahad would be prepared to help us. It seems quite likely that she won't want the Chairman back.'

Alexandra looked quite offended by the very idea. 'We have to try,' she pronounced.

He nodded and smiled, realizing that he wouldn't be able to educate her any further today.

'It seems to me,' he said, 'that even if she doesn't want Alessandro back, she certainly won't want this station to remain in the hands of terrorists and subversives. We'll have to play on that, so let's go.'

As he pushed himself away from the wall, ready to head for the nearest exit from their hideaway, Alex called up his visor display, noting he had about eight hours of air left. Since they shared air between them, that figure applied equally to Alexandra. Over their time as refugees they had resupplied themselves through dangerous forays into pressurized parts of the station, occasionally grabbing some water but otherwise reusing the water processed out of their urine packs, and very occasionally finding something to eat. If they came close to really running out of the means of survival, if all options to that end were finally closed down, as seemed to be Langstrom's aim, what then? Surrender?

In some emotionless part of his mind, Alex realized that even surrender might give them a further chance to free the Chairman, but his conditioning prevented him from contemplating it too deeply, at least for now. As he found his way out towards the edge of the station, he vaguely recollected those long sessions with his teachers, interspersed with the regular visits to surgery, followed by thumping headaches and healing cuts in his skull.

Earth

Amazing, just a month after the population reduction around the Great Lakes, and the sewage plants were already back at optimum performance, processing everything heading their way. Clean water was being pumped back into the system while well-rotted and dried human sewage was coming out of the conveyors to pour into the backs of automated trucks. These then conveyed this form of fertilizer to the maize fields further south. They now even had hydrogen fuel available for that. The only fly in the ointment was that half of the trucks had necessarily been reassigned, along with something like fifty per cent of the Great Lakes transport system, to move the bodies, and that many of the maize fields were now occupied by fresh pyres.

'You'll have more up-to-date stats than me,' she said to the figure appearing on her screen wall. It was a lie, of course, as she knew precisely what the numbers were.

'It's now gone over twenty million,' said the dead-faced woman, Gene. She was the environmental officer for Serene's new North American delegate, and a woman who had recently lost her husband and two children to the Scour. These three had died along with the previous delegate and any of his staff possessing knowledge of the report on effluent pollution of the lakes. After all, Serene did not want anyone joining up the dots.

Gene continued, now with a flash of anger, 'You're going to get him for us, ma'am. You're really going to get him. It's not all talk . . .'

Serene nodded confidently, suppressing the anger she felt at having this menial dare question her. 'Alan Saul and the rest of those rebels aboard Argus Station will pay for their crimes, for their assault against Earth and against humanity. They will pay the ultimate price. My only regret is that they cannot be made to pay it a billion times over.' Then again, the more she learned about the research and development conducted by this Hannah Neumann, the more she realized how people could die more than once. 'Something like twenty per cent of the resources of Earth are now being diverted to this end. Space-plane production has recommenced, and I'll soon be making another announcement concerning that matter. However, the business of running this planet cannot be neglected, so I would like you to continue with your report.'

'Lake Huron is dead,' Gene said, 'well, apart from the masses of anaerobic bacteria it contains. It's now just sixty thousand square kilometres of sludge, so what we're doing will make little difference in the short term.' Her image gave way to one side to show an image of the lake, divided up by the fish-farm barriers, processing plants and floating road-ways, and surrounded by sprawl heaped up like technological mountains. Processions of big tipper trucks previously used to bring in feed, along with the cargo flatbeds that used to be employed to transport out the processed fish protein, were working all across the lake. The tippers were emptying their contents into the lake; forklifts were unloading the flatbeds. The lake had thus far swallowed seven million corpses, and was now acting as a giant digester tank.

'What's left of Lake Ontario we might just as well fill in, what with the heavy metal pollution, but Superior and Michigan are doing surprisingly well, and the water-purification plants are making some headway there. We've done better with Erie because of its size, and we have short-term algae blooms and some small areas of water weed re-establishing. If things continue at the present rate, we may be able to start restocking that lake at least within five years.' Gene paused, her expression turning bitter. 'The Scour seems to have spared at least some of them.'

'I don't think that's somewhere we want to go, do you?' Serene berated her, suppressing her own delight. Now, if only she could find some excuse to start demolishing the sur-rounding sprawl, natural landscape could be exposed, trees planted . . .

'I'm sorry,' said Gene. She gazed out of the screen specu-latively. 'I'm a little distracted . . . I've been asking for reassignment.'

Why did she think Serene needed to know this?

'Really?'

'I want to go offworld and help with our projects out there, help to bring Alan Saul back . . .'

'I understand,' said Serene. 'Everybody wants vengeance and everyone who has lost someone wants to be involved. However, you must remember that you *are* involved. Everything you do to improve efficiency, rebuild infrastructure and ensure the smooth running of our planet means more resources can be diverted towards dealing with Alan Saul. With your expertise, Gene, you are better placed where you are.'

'But—'

'No buts,' Serene interrupted, her voice hardening. 'Consider yourself lucky to be alive and in a position to help, and try to remain alive in order to do so.' Serene swiftly cut the link. *The damned cheek of it!* Just because her own ruthlessness had not been overt, well – she eyed the expanse of self-cleaning carpet before her desk – outside her immediate vicinity at least, there were people who thought they could question her. Perhaps she needed to be a bit more blatantly ruthless?

'Ma'am.'

The channel was assigned Priority One through her fone, so he'd better have a damned good reason for contacting her through it.

'What is it, Clay?'

'We've got communications from Argus Station, and I felt you needed to know about this at once.'

'Alan Saul?'

'No, it seems there's a small undercover squad, one of Messina's, still free on the station. They've managed to turn a dish towards us and get in contact. Apparently they made an assassination attempt on Alan Saul, and he may well be dead, but now they're in hiding.'

Serene experienced a sudden surge of disappointment, followed briefly by anger. It annoyed her that Saul might have been killed by some means other than as a result of her own orders.

'What do they want?' she snapped.

'Data. They lost a lot of data and equipment recently. They want station schematics and access to a tactical planning team.'

'To what purpose?'

'They want to rescue Alessandro Messina, who is apparently still alive.'

'And they think I would like to help them? I hope you didn't laugh out loud.'

'Certainly not, ma'am – they're a good source of data, and are giving us some gold on the current situation aboard the station. That structural work we observed in the recent Hubble pictures is them enclosing the station disc.'

'I need to talk to them,' Serene decided.

'You can, but there's a com delay of thirty seconds and their situation, as regards their oxygen supply, is critical.'

'Okay, give them station schematics and limited tactical planning – just enough for them to resupply themselves. Then I'll speak to them.'

'Will do, ma'am.' He closed the channel.

Serene sat back in her chair, her elbows on its arms and her fingers interlaced under her chin. The *Alexander* had already test fired its railgun and was now just days away from test firing its main engine. And then, after maybe a further few months of testing and work on the internals, it would be ready to begin its pursuit of Argus. It seemed to her that she felt the hand of destiny on her shoulder.

7

Leaner Society

There can be no logical explanation for the vicious genocidal attack upon Earth and its peoples by the madman Alan Saul. It could be supposed that his hatred of the Committee was why he targeted the infrastructure of the most advanced socialist state the world has ever seen, but why did he then loose the Scour upon us? Was he motivated simply by a hatred of all humanity? Whatever his motivation, and though he succeeded in committing the most heinous crime against humanity ever known, he failed to halt the progress of civilization. It can in fact be argued that by killing nearly the entire zero-asset population and wiping out so large a portion of the bureaucracy required to control and direct it, he cleared the field for Serene Galahad's new world order. The factories of Earth were relatively untouched but, with a smaller population making demands on them, Galahad was able to build a leaner and more efficient society – which it seems likely was not his aim at all.

Argus

Who are you?

Sometimes, for a frustrating period of time that could be either hours or microseconds long, he was aware of his condition, knew he had to wake up. The rest of the time he was washed to and fro in a sea of information, some of it current, some past and some just plain fantasy.

I am Alan Saul. I am the Owner. Who are you?

Her face just hung there, untouched by those informational maelstroms. She looked like the ghost of a double exposure on old-style film, or like something indelibly etched into the underlying reality of the universe. He knew her, he knew that face, he knew her from something deep and utterly integral within himself. Yet, in what passed for consciousness, partial as it was when it arose, he knew her not at all. Merely the artefact of a damaged mind, then?

He drifted, found himself running through a crowded street, all around him people in ragged clothes watching with avid eyes, then big uniformed enforcers pushing them aside and liberally applying those new handheld inducers, called disablers. The screaming, it was his fault; he should not have endangered them like this, he should not have put them in a position where enforcers had to be sent to fetch them back. *Them?* He turned, searching all those faces. There was someone with him, someone important . . . His mind leapt away, unable to process that . . . instead found somewhere else to go.

Minds, ten of them the utter proof of how something good and right could come from something so ugly, like roses growing in pig shit. So much data, so much information . . . weaned from the most inhuman research. That man called Nelson, or Leonardo, and his ways of maintaining life making the brilliant vivisection cruelties in HUD a possibility. Even Hannah's research taken there and hammered into new and horrible shapes . . . the most advanced robotics forced into an amalgam with screaming flesh.

Ten beautiful minds – touched on in dreams that seemed an age ago now, and free at last.

Who are you?

She wouldn't go away. She was watching him, and he felt that she had always been watching him. He found himself discomfited by her gaze . . . while drifting, catching new information. Some sort of news story acting as a further illustration of the horror caused by that arch demon Alan Saul?

The image was an old one, from the North India Region, from the Brahmaputra–Ganges flood basin. Saul gazed at the boy squatting by the mast of his small boat, a cloth over his mouth and his eyes wide and black. He looked as if he was out on a fishing trip on a mountain lake. However, a closer study revealed the true picture, which, so the narrator informed the waiting public, was taken only five kilometres from where millions upon millions of corpses had been heaped, literally into mountains. The climate and the flies had ensured that the corpses were quickly bloated, rotten and seething with maggots, and a subsequent monsoon had caused the scene displayed here. The flood of billions of litres of water, maggots and fluids from dissolving corpses had completely swamped the urban sprawl that occupied the flood basin, and this boy was one of the few survivors. His boat rode on the writhing glutinous mess while the mountain behind him consisted mainly of bones to which a few stubborn fragments of flesh and gristle still clung.

'He must be punished,' continued Serene Galahad. 'And we must retrieve the Gene Bank data he stole.'

Did it seem to him then that the other woman looked on with a slight twist of contempt to her mouth? No, no, she looked just the same – and she wasn't looking there, she was looking *there* . . .

A massive ship sat in its construction station, big robots

peeling away surrounding scaffolds like a loose rind, clearly revealing the gleam of heavy armour, missile ports and a maser turret. Was this a dream? No, he knew it was real, and that ship was as imminent as a sledgehammer. He had to pull his consciousness out of this well, and back into the *real*, but the effort was too much and he felt so utterly exhausted . . .

Hannah, help me . . .

After she had suited up, she expected them to take her to Tech Central, but it soon became apparent that they were moving round the circumference of the asteroid rather than heading up on top.

'Arcoplex One?' she enquired over her suit radio.

'Yes, it seemed best, since there are conference rooms available there,' said Langstrom. He glanced round at her. 'Best place for a long sit-down discussion of our situation. It may take some time because this is *no longer* about a single individual issuing orders.'

Ah, democracy, thought Hannah, remembering Saul's opinion of such a concept in this environment – and how they might all die even while the votes were being counted.

Once they were inside Arcoplex One, Hannah studied her surroundings. She had not visited this cylinder world since first coming here with Saul when he dropped the Argus network on Earth and then issued his ultimatum to Messina and his delegates. No corpses were visible – none of the two thousand victims Messina's troops had nerve-gassed during their attack – though there were still stains visible on walls and floors, and the occasional scrap of clothing had stuck in place. All the corpses taken from here had either gone through overworked station digesters or been moved to the outer ring to be stored in cold vacuum – as a potential resource.

Just beyond the elevator doors, Langstrom and Peach divested themselves of the EM weapon, passing it on to some waiting troops, who swiftly set about remounting it on a tripod. That was a precaution, doubtless, against the arrival of a spidergun or some other kind of robot. Did this mean they were completely turning against Saul? Peach remained there with the troops, while Langstrom gestured for Hannah to follow.

It seemed to her that they were heading towards the conference room where Saul had confronted Messina and the delegates, but they soon diverged from that route to come up to a set of sliding double doors. Langstrom detached his suit glove, pressed his palm against a lock and the doors slid aside. Within lay a long conference table with people already seated, some of whom she recognized and others she didn't know. Le Roque sat at the head with Chang to his right and an empty seat to his left. Those seated two down from Chang on the other side were a woman called Dagmar, who ran Zero-Gravity Hydroponics, and an Asian man called Taffor, another agronomist, who ran the Arboretum. Next along, sat another two men who Hannah vaguely recognized as having something to do with Construction. At the further side of the table sat an unfamiliar man and woman, then came two empty seats and another empty seat at the end. Le Roque immediately stood up and gestured to the seat beside him. Hannah gazed at him for a moment, then took the seat at the far end of the table. He acknowledged that gesture with a shrug, and sat down again. Langstrom took one of the other empty seats.

'I rather resent being dragged away from my patient like that,' said Hannah. 'Why is it so important that I be here?'

'We need to know the Owner's condition,' said Le Roque. 'I've been trying to talk to you about that for some time . . .

so has Langstrom. We may be heading away from Earth but the danger the Committee represents is by no means over, and we face new trials, new dangers. We are in deep vacuum now, and it's quite possible we won't survive it. What is the Owner's condition?'

Hannah considered various answers, various lies, but in the end decided on a partial truth. 'Saul was very badly injured by the assault made on him. I've repaired most of the damage and things are looking good, but obviously going slowly. He is currently sleeping, which is perhaps best while he heals.'

'How long until he wakes?' asked Langstrom.

'How long is a piece of string?' Hannah shot back. 'Any time now, or maybe a month from now.'

'He's not conscious, then,' Langstrom affirmed, 'which means we need to get a firmer grip on station security.'

'Yes, I'm not surprised that you would suggest that,' said Hannah sarcastically.

'You have your laptop?' Le Roque asked.

Hannah unhooked it from her belt and placed it on the table before her. 'I do.'

'Check the file attached to the last email I sent you.'

Her laptop blinked on the instant she opened it, and she checked her mail. There had been a lot of it, some from eddresses she did not recognize but nevertheless had to be those of people aboard this station. She checked down until she found a message from Le Roque, with an attachment.

She read his message: 'Here is the DNA map of the individual who shot Saul. Check it against the further DNA map below, look at the name, and please get back to me.'

A cross-matching program was imbedded in the attachment. The first map corresponded to the second to within ninety-nine point nine eight per cent. That couldn't be right. Then she realized that, of course, it could. Some of the scientists alongside her in the Albanian mountain enclave, before it was broken up, had been working on such projects. She studied the name below the final DNA print, and shuddered. Really, she shouldn't feel such superstitious dread, as this surely didn't mean much.

'A clone,' she declared. 'That doesn't really make someone any more dangerous, or any less.'

'I disagree,' said Langstrom. 'I've seen these Messina clones before. They're very specialized, surgically altered, totally loyal and trained beyond anything possible with an unaltered human being. They're dangerous. That's been illustrated by the fact that the two remaining ones have evaded capture by us for as long as they have.' He paused, looking grim. 'It is also the case that they were not soldiers surviving from Messina's forces.'

'What?' Hannah asked.

'The equipment we found in their hide was all from the station – none of it brought in from outside. Also three maintenance staff have gone missing, and if you check a further email from me, you'll find that DNA traces found in the cabins of the missing three all match up with Messina's map too. And with Saul no longer in control . . .'

'But he will be back in control soon,' said the male of the two personnel Hannah did not recognize. He looked to her in appeal.

Le Roque held up a finger, pressing the fingers of his other hand against his fone. 'We should have some data on that shortly.' He leaned back and listened to whoever was talking, nodding and making single-word replies as he did so.

'Perhaps we should be introduced,' said Hannah, indicating with a smile the two unknowns at the table.

'Leeran,' said the woman, then gesturing to her partner, 'and Pike. We oversee the furnaces.'

So that was why she hadn't recognized them. They spent most of their time out on the furnaces and bubblemetal plants that currently extended outside the station.

'Pleased to meet you,' said Hannah, instinctively recognizing allies.

'So that's it,' said Le Roque, leaning forward. 'According to Raiman, Hannah has not been giving us the full truth. The Owner . . .' he paused for a second, 'Alan Saul is severely incapacitated. He's lost enough brain mass to turn any normal human being into a bedridden vegetable. There's regrowth indeed, but no indication that what will result afterwards will be any more able than one of our repros.' He gazed steadily at Hannah. 'We need to make some decisions.'

'Raiman has no idea of the true situation,' said Hannah. 'He's a military medic and his is just not the same area of specialization as mine. He doesn't understand bio interfaces or the resultant neural growth.' She paused, groping for the best way to put this. Certainly, if Le Roque, Langstrom and others here were turning against Saul, then it would be best if they did not know about Saul's backup, his 'D drive'. 'How does Raiman explain Saul speaking to you all after he was shot?'

'Did he?' asked Dagmar.

'Raiman?' asked Hannah. 'Did he what?'

Dagmar shook her head, refusing to lift her gaze from the tabletop. 'Did Alan Saul speak to us?' She began playing with a pen, tapping it against the table surface. 'What we heard

169

could quite easily have been created from recordings of his voice.' Now she looked up directly at Hannah to add, 'With someone else providing the words.'

'Are you really accusing me of that?' Hannah asked, the back of her neck feeling suddenly hot.

'I'm merely pointing out a possibility,' Dagmar replied.

An uncomfortable silence descended for a moment, broken by Le Roque clearing his throat, then continuing, 'That's as may be, but we still have decisions to make. I've kept this on ice until this meeting, and now we need to see it.' He swung his chair round, holding up a small remote which he directed at the screen on the wall behind him. Hannah felt something tightening in her chest when the United Earth logo flicked into being, then faded to show Serene Galahad standing on the carbocrete of a spaceport, a space plane looming behind her.

'It is with great pleasure that I can announce to you that vengeance is possible, as is the more important goal of retrieving the Gene Bank database and samples. It perhaps seemed to us all that the mass murderer Alan Saul had taken himself beyond our reach. However, thanks to the foresight of Chairman Alessandro Messina, this is not the case.' Serene held up her hand, above which a frame etched itself out of the air, before accelerating towards the screen to fill it with the blackness of space, liberally sprinkled with stars.

'Twenty years ago, Alessandro Messina understood the dangers of subversion, terrorism and rebellion in space, and in secret he began to make his plans. He needed something up there beyond Earth that could move fast and deliver a suitable response to those who might undermine humanity's future.'

The screen view swung round to show a massive spaceborne construction station, out of which an equally huge spaceship was currently manoeuvring. Hannah stared at this thing. It could quite easily be some CGI effect that Galahad was using for her own obscure purposes. Some sort of propaganda exercise maybe as a justification for world-resource reallocation and an excuse for resultant starvation and further death tolls. Or perhaps just a bit of media glitz to take people's attention away from just such problems . . .

'Messina named this ship the *Alexander*, but now I feel it is time for a renaming. I considered the *Vengeance*, but perhaps that is a name that has been overused. So of course, considering what Alan Saul has inflicted upon the people of Earth, there is a more appropriate name available.'

The scene changed, the ship now viewed far out from its construction station. Sounds began to impinge, a repetitive thrum like someone hitting a taut cable with a hammer. These sounds had to be added, since this view was recorded through vacuum. Perhaps they were what the crew supposedly aboard the vessel were hearing.

The station started to come apart, great pieces of it exploding away, tearing up, the whole thing splintering like the trunk of a tree under machine-gun fire. Then either something else hit it, or the projectiles had hit something vital. The station exploded, the glare blacking the screen for a second, then the next jerky image showed glowing chunks of it tumbling away. The next view, probably captured by a camera on the Moon, showed one such mass of material crashing into its surface. Then another scene: debris burning up in Earth's atmosphere, the view descending past them down towards the land surface, structures visible, then space planes neatly arrayed across a carbocrete expanse, then onto the surface itself, to Serene – a close-up of her face.

'The name of this ship is henceforth the *Scourge* – for it is the whip with which we will punish Alan Saul, and all those other traitors up there on Argus Station. I hope you are watching this up there, you people. We are coming for you now.'

Le Roque clicked his remote, blinking the screen back to the United Earth logo.

'There's more in the same vein,' he said. 'A lot about how well Earth is doing since the attack on it, how production is up, resources growing, space projects expanding and advancing faster than they ever have before.'

'Is that thing for real?' asked Taffor.

'It's real,' said Le Roque. 'It must have been concealed under some sort of EM cloak that's now been removed. We can see that damned ship from here.'

Hannah folded her arms, much of her anger at having been dragged here draining away and a cold dread settling in its place. They needed Saul more than ever now. Without him, without that demigod mind working for them, they would be defenceless.

'How quickly could that ship reach us?' she asked.

'I haven't calculated that,' said Le Roque, 'since the time it takes depends heavily on when it leaves. But what is certain is that it *will* get to us, and there's nothing we can do about that. And you saw those weapons.' He swung back to the screen again, already holding up his remote. 'Now there's this: a personal message for us.'

It was Galahad again, sitting behind a desk, looking relaxed and tapping idly on the buttons of a palmtop. 'I'm not entirely sure who I'm addressing right now,' she said. 'I'm not entirely sure who now controls Argus Station. Certainly, Alan Saul is no longer at – so to speak – the wheel.' She smiled.

'Maybe I'm talking to Technical Director Le Roque, or Captain Langstrom, or Dr Hannah Neumann – all of whom seem to have risen under the regime of someone arrogant enough to call himself the Owner.'

Le Roque paused it there and turned to address them all. 'It seems evident to me that she's letting us be aware that she knows a lot about what is going on here. I'm guessing she's in contact with Messina's clones.' He turned back and set the broadcast running again.

'Whoever it is,' Galahad waved a dismissive hand, 'I have an offer for you. I am not so foolish as to think you will turn Argus Station around and hand yourselves over to me, but there is still a way we can all get what we want. Since your inexplicable course change, you will reach the Asteroid Belt in eight months' time. There I want you to load onto a space plane the Gene Bank samples and database, along with Alan Saul, dead or alive, and moor the plane to the Asteroid which under new century listing is designated GH467. You may then swing back round towards Mars, or wherever it is you think you are going. If you do not do this, the *Scourge* will eventually catch you, and you will all die.' She paused as if in thought for a moment, looking slightly sad as she returned her gaze to her palmtop screen, then continued. 'Everything else at that distance from Earth can be faked for the satisfaction of the people of Earth. Having collected what I want, the *Scourge* will then destroy GH467. Anyone viewing that event through telescopes not government-controlled will be unable to see enough detail to know any different, and subsequently such video will be adjusted so it will seem the Argus itself was destroyed. Some story about Alan Saul's cowardly escape aboard a space plane can be fabricated.' She looked up. 'You must speak to me soon.'

Le Roque clicked off the screen and it seemed everyone remained focused on it for a long time afterwards.

'Talk to her, yeah, right,' said Pike.

'Seems to me,' said Leeran, 'that she's just trying to work out some way of getting her hands on that Gene Bank stuff without using force. That *Scourge* comes against us, and everything she wants might end up being destroyed.'

'No, I disagree,' said Le Roque. 'We've got no manoeuvrability and that thing has. It could simply take out the Mars Traveller engine, tear us up a little to ensure plenty of death and disruption, then dock and send in troops. We don't stand a chance.'

'If you give her what she wants, she'll do that anyway,' said Hannah.

'Maybe.' Le Roque nodded. 'But I really think that we've got to talk to her. We can draw out the bargaining, maybe feed her bits of Gene Bank data at a time.'

'Then we die when that runs out,' said Leeran contemptuously. 'And do you think for one moment that will hold them off from attacking the moment they reach us?'

'And Alan Saul?' asked Hannah.

Le Roque held out his hands helplessly. 'Give me alternatives. What the hell do we do?'

'We do what we can to survive,' said Langstrom. 'This was never going to be easy. The Owner knew that, too.'

Past tense already, thought Hannah, sitting back. The Saberhagen twins weren't here, which would have weighed this meeting more towards an attitude of 'Fuck you, Galahad' and 'How can we kill that ship?' She initiated her fone, found a number she wanted in her cortex menu, and called them.

'So you're at a meeting,' said Brigitta. 'Funny how Le Roque forgot to invite us.'

'Yes, funny that,' Hannah replied.

Others at the table turned towards her, realizing what she was doing. Langstrom looked suddenly suspicious and began to rise from his seat.

'You know that matter we discussed before I departed,' said Hannah.

'Yeah, I'm still thinking about it.'

'Would you take an order from me?'

'Second to Saul.'

'Release them,' Hannah told her. 'Let them go right now.'

'Ah, that kind of meeting,' said Brigitta.

'Yes, it's that—'

A voice interrupted their exchange, speaking human words that in no way issuing from a human being. 'I choose to name myself Paul,' it said. 'Instruct me, Hannah Neumann.'

Mars

They'd looked askance at her when she turned up for the latest broadcast from Argus with a gun at her hip, but then their expressions had shut down. *Fuck them.* She'd sat for a while in her cabin, binding up her arm, and then taken a rest, her head aching. She'd gone out like a light for twenty minutes, then woken up with blood soaking into her bed and realized she needed more than just dressings. All of them had seen that she'd been sliced and knocked almost unconscious, but no one had come. Belatedly Da Vinci had used wound glue to seal up the cut – along with a few staples – given her some painkillers and an analgesic cream. He hadn't asked her about the very obvious blow to her head, and had quite obviously wanted her gone.

Now there was a meeting to discuss the information Argus had supplied. The atmosphere in the community room was hostile, even poisonous. Most here were trying to keep neutral expressions, but failing. No one had asked her about the attack on her, not even Martinez and Lopomac, who looked grim. Was she being paranoid in thinking *everyone* was now against her?

'The truth,' she said, standing up once everyone was seated, 'is this. That ship could rail out a nuke right now and, though it would take some years to arrive here, the thing could drop itself on Hex Three with an accuracy measured in centimetres.'

'You seem mighty familiar with its systems,' noted Rhone. 'It occurs to me that, as the overseer of the Mars Traveller building programme, you probably always knew more about this than you're letting on.'

Var glanced at him. That seemed a comment specifically aimed to generate distrust against her. Was he now about to become more overt?

'We all saw the broadcast,' she said, 'and it doesn't take a whole lot of mental watts to work out what we're up against. And, no, I knew nothing about this.' The lie rolled off her tongue with worrying ease.

'But if it does fire on us, we'll see it coming,' noted Martinez.

'And how exactly does that help us?' asked Lopomac.

There seemed a degree of tension between the two of them. Was one of them having his doubts about her leadership, and the other in disagreement?

'That is precisely why we are sitting here,' said Var, studying each of her chiefs of staff in turn.

Carol was here – Carol, who had been at her side when she went up against Ricard. She just looked depressed now and maybe disappointed. Gunther's replacement in Hydroponics and Agriculture, Liza Strome, had joined them, too, along with Da Vinci and Leo from Stores. They were all obviously thinking about recent events, and really needed to snap out of that. Didn't they understand the danger they were in?

She continued, 'A long-range nuke is the first threat to us, followed, after a time, by nukes and high-velocity railgun slugs from orbit. Just one of either of these hits us, and we're gone.'

'Why would that ship come here?' Strome asked. 'Its designated mission is to go after Argus, which – as we understand it after that course change the station made – it's likely to intercept out at the Asteroid Belt.'

Var turned towards her, fighting the urge to be dismissive. 'First off, we've responded to none of their communications, but the Hubble will show them that we're still active. They'll be suspicious and want to check, and they'll eventually find out what has happened here. Second, we have a dictator on Earth who has wiped out a significant portion of the human race. She's also eradicated surviving Committee delegates to ensure her rule remains unchallenged. So I don't think she'll be prepared to tolerate us.' She paused as if in thought. 'Maybe she won't send the *Scourge* here after it's dealt with Argus, but are you prepared to bet your life on that? And, anyway, we've seen the activity ramping up in Earth orbit, and from that we know that she intends to establish an even stronger foothold beyond Earth than Messina did. It's not a case of *if* her forces come here, but *when*.'

'I agree,' said Rhone, yet again surprising her with his

support. 'This Serene Galahad will either stamp on us or ensure that we take a leading part in some sort of show trial, either here or on Earth. Either way we die, if we're lucky.'

'Lucky?' asked Strome.

Martinez, obviously uncomfortable with her naivety, quickly interjected, 'If Galahad doesn't have us killed, she'll have us adjusted – probably adjusted till we're drooling and in need of nappies.'

Good, they were now all starting to think about this very real danger.

'So how do we respond?' Var asked. She had some ideas of her own, but fought to keep them in check. It would be so easy to feed off the resentment she felt and become all dictatorial. Better to let them have their input first.

'I have some suggestions,' said Rhone, reaching up to touch a finger against his fone.

Var stared at him, wondering just what game he was playing now. He returned her stare. 'We have a weapons designer in Mars Science – Linden Haarsen.' He paused for a second before saying, 'Yes, get in here now.'

Haarsen came through the door rather quickly, further arousing Var's suspicions. But, then, perhaps she shouldn't relate everything that happened to herself. Rhone wasn't stupid and had probably understood the situation very quickly. She recognized Haarsen as one of the quiet individuals, usually in a lab coat, who was always hovering in the background behind Rhone. He quickly squeezed in beside Lopomac, placing a laptop on the table.

Var gazed at him. 'You have something for us?'

Haarsen looked to Rhone, who gave his permission with a brief nod. This irritated Var no end. It seemed to be a sure sign of empire-building inside Mars Science.

'We need a DEMP,' Haarsen said.

'If you could explain for the others here who might not know that acronym?'

'Directed electromagnetic pulse,' Haarsen explained. 'I could build us an EM pulse weapon within the time available – one capable of knocking out even the hardened computer systems of cruise missiles.'

'Time available?' Var enquired.

'As you said at the opening of this meeting,' said Haarsen uncomfortably, 'that ship can rail out tactical cruise nukes even from Earth orbit right now.'

Var glanced at Rhone. She'd never given any instruction that what was said within these meetings should be private, but it annoyed her that he had obviously been using his fone to broadcast from here to his own staff.

'Do go on,' she said.

'If missiles were fired off now, they would take four years to reach us. Therefore, if they intend to fire missiles, they will do so either now or in the near future.'

'Why?' asked Lopomac.

'The first reason is simple orbital mechanics. If they fired in, say, in six months, with relative planetary orbits diverging, the time it would take for them to reach us doubles to eight years. But that is supposing that they do fire from Earth orbit.'

'But that ship is coming our way,' said Strome.

Haarsen swung towards her. 'They can't fire on us while the *Scourge* is at full speed because that would ramp up the speed of the missiles to the point where they wouldn't be able to slow down enough to enter our atmosphere and subsequently manoeuvre to drop on us. Those things don't have fusion engines like Argus or the *Scourge*.'

'So, on the face of it,' said Var, 'building a DEMP seems to be a reasonable precaution to take.'

'Then what?' asked Martinez abruptly.

Var glanced at him. Perhaps he too was seeing the shape of things.

'Yes, precisely,' said Var. 'Then what?'

No one seemed to have any answer.

'I too have been checking some figures,' she continued. 'The *Scourge* will have to slow down to intercept Argus, and there'll be a delay while it deals with that station. We can assume it will strafe the station first, then dock and send in troops. Remember, Galahad doesn't want just to destroy Argus; she wants to get her hands on the Gene Bank data and samples. After that, the *Scourge* can accelerate again. I estimate, what with the big deceleration it will need on arrival here, the ship will be over us in about two years' time.'

'The DEMP will be able to knock out anything self-guided,' said Haarsen, but seemed at a loss for anything else to add.

'But would be completely ineffective against line-of-sight railgun slugs. So building a DEMP to deal with a possible threat four years hence when we're likely to be attacked in two years seems rather pointless, don't you think?'

Both Rhone and Haarsen suddenly looked peeved. This had clearly been a little power play: Rhone wheeling out his pet weapons designer to demonstrate how useful and forward-thinking he was. Quite obviously, Rhone was no synthesist, or else he would have spotted the enormous hole in his own reasoning.

'So what other options do we have?' Var asked, and waited patiently.

Rhone should have been the one to see the only real

option, but it was Martinez who now spoke up. The big bulky man leaned forward, tapping one thick calloused finger against the tabletop to emphasize each of his points. 'Atomics and railgun slugs from orbit? Seems to me the penetration capacity of both ain't great. A slug at full power probably fragments or even turns to plasma on impact. Both'll leave nothing but glass on the surface.'

'And your point is?' Var asked, perfectly aware of what his point was.

'Maybe they've got some way of dropping troops; I don't know. But even if they have, those guys will be at a big disadvantage.' He paused, stabbing his finger down again. 'We dig. We go underground.'

Var swung her attention to Rhone and waited.

'Yes,' he said reluctantly. 'There are faults down there – some big caves extending right to Coprates Chasma.' He tapped a fingertip against the table. 'We've still got all the records from the original geological survey, but still this will take a lot of work.'

'Isn't there a deep fault twenty kilometres north of here?' Var asked, feeling sure he knew about it. 'That means we probably won't even have to sink shafts.'

'I believe you're right,' he admitted.

Var swung her attention to Haarsen, who was now looking sour-faced. She flung him a bone: 'We'll be needing explosives to blast things wider over there, and we'll be needing defences. It also occurs to me that, should there be landing craft aboard the *Scourge*, then a DEMP weapon might make them rather difficult to control.'

Now he looked happier. Var sat back, feeling completely dissatisfied with this meeting. Either she had just proved that she was the best person to run this base, by showing the only course they could take to survive, or Rhone had been planning some entirely different course. It could all be in her mind, all a product of faulty paranoid reasoning, but it seemed to her that if they didn't go underground, the only options were surrender or death.

Maybe Rhone's main plan was to assume command, ensure she ended up dead, then report back to Earth that the main rebel leader had been dealt with. And perhaps, if that was his aim, he was right. They could defend themselves here, maybe for decades into the future but, beyond then, as Earth's full might came into play, they would eventually lose – and Var could see no way round that.

Earth

Clay gazed at the fine hairs on the back of Serene's neck as she studied the scene displayed on the small screen in the aero's cockpit. He wondered if she now regretted destroying the erstwhile *Alexander* construction station. It had been an overly dramatic gesture by which to demonstrate the *Scourge*'s power, and its loss had put back offworld construction, though not for long the way things were ramping up. Even so, she should have had the ship fire on the surface of the Moon – that would have been sufficient to deliver the message to Argus. It would also have sent a message to the people on Mars who, it seemed highly probable, were rebels too. It appeared unlikely that their communications equipment was so damaged that they could not rig up some method of replying to the frequent messages sent to them from Earth.

'How long?' she asked.

Clay, whom she had summoned up from the contingent

of her staff occupying the body of the craft behind, leaned forward to peer at the image, quickly trying to put his thoughts in order. He knew by now that she would stand for no bullshit and, with her scientific background and a mind like a bacon slicer, she would recognize any such at once.

'I'm told it'll take over a month to get the small smelters back online,' he said. 'But to replace everything that went into the Argus smelters and bubblemetal plants will take a further six months, presupposing this and the others of its kind still work.' He now gestured to the landscape lying beyond the cockpit screen, and specifically to the massive facility they had come here to see in the final days of this tour of hers round *her* planet.

Serene did not look up for a moment. She continued studying the various views she could get of what remained of the Mars Traveller construction project. Huge scaffolds hung in vacuum, dilapidated sun mirrors framed the ugly utility of the smelters, big factory cylinders stood open to vacuum within the scaffolding, large areas of their plating now gone. Construction robots, some of them the size of monorail carriages, clung to the scaffold like termites in the remains of a decayed tree.

He continued, 'The big smelters have been mothballed for twenty years, ever since Argus took over, those that weren't scrapped, that is, and will take a year to get up to speed. We'll need more, too, and they'll take . . . some time to build.' He leaned further forward, feeling the need to get physically closer to her. She had listened carefully to his reports when he first arrived at Messina's Italian mansion, then just dismissed him. It was only after they returned from Rome, after seeing the seven comlifers, that she'd made it quite obvious she wanted something else from him. They had fucked on Messina's huge canopied bed, but only the once. After that, nothing – he returned to being her subordinate and she asked for nothing from him but information. Had he been a disappointment to her, and had she now decided to find that sort of relief from someone trained for the purpose, as had many Committee delegates in the past?

'And how long before we can actually start building anything?' she asked.

'Some processes can start almost at once, but I'm told eight years before the first new-design Travellers can be commissioned.'

'Not good enough,' she said. 'I want more space planes, more people up there, and I want them to work *harder*.' She sat back, gazing at him, then reached out with one finger against his chest and pushed. He abruptly backed away, realizing she was uncomfortable with such proximity. He glanced round at Sack, who sat in a chair at the back of the cockpit, with his meaty arms folded and his expression blank. All it would take was a little hand signal from her, and Sack would be up on his feet, probably using his preferred technique of snapping a person's neck like a stick of celery. She had given that signal quite a few times back at the mansion after – so staff there told him – frequent use of a razorbird had permanently stained the self-cleaning carpet in her office.

'Messina screwed it up quite badly,' he said, abruptly straightening his tie and trying to look more businesslike. 'I'm not sure I understand why.'

'It's quite simple,' she replied, flicking the screen off and looking up. 'He'd lost interest in Mars and wanted both Argus and . . . his *Alexander* up and running. He was already diverting resources from the Mars Base ten years ago, but he finally started winding it down a year ago.' She paused, now staring through the aero cockpit screen. 'I didn't quite realize how big a loss Argus was until now.'

'They should be test firing within the minute.'

She glanced round at him, as he listened to the notification through his fone. She probably knew anyway. He was aware that she relied on numerous sources of information, cross-checking all the time, weeding out the liars, slackers and those stupid enough to audibly contemplate the possibility of being rid of her.

Luckily he had only lied to her once, and the three men who knew about that were all dead. Two of them had survived the incendiary fire in that laboratory she had ordered to be raided. But they had survived long enough to tell Clay exactly where the Scour had come from. The other had been the assault-team commander. After also hearing the story from the badly burned scientists, the commander had gone a little crazy, because he'd fought his own way out of ZA status, leaving a family behind him, all of whom were now dead. He told Clay about the orders he had received directly from Serene Galahad, about how the incendiary fire had been due to him and not the laboratory guards. He had talked too much, which was why Clay shot him through the head, then shot the two scientists.

'It's all set up for you,' he finished.

'Should I remain here, ma'am?' asked the pilot.

She was piloting craft less and less. Maybe she considered that one of those earlier quirks that did not sit well with her new status, or maybe it just got in the way of the workload she was dealing with hour upon hour.

'Just keep us hovering here,' she replied, and returned her attention to the view.

It had taken some hours by scramjet to get here, to the

mass driver facility. The titanic device, a cobwebby relic of a bygone age, sat towards the edge of Outback Spaceport – in fact space planes were visible in the sky either ascending or descending beyond it. Yet, on wide roads spearing off into the distance towards massive opencast mines, giant ore trucks were on the move, and smoke was boiling into the sky from the chimneys of the furnace complex, which sat like a city made for robots between them and the driver itself.

'It's the climate,' said Clay, in search of something to say.

'What?'

'It's because of the climate that this driver could be quickly made operational again. Nothing much rusts here, you see. They had to clear out some bodies and make some internal repairs, though – ZAs had set up house inside the thing. Also, barrel wear was minimal so, before any major maintenance is needed, we should be able to run it at full capacity for at least a year.'

'Yes, I see.'

Further notification came through his fone. 'Firing in one minute,' he told her.

The mass driver lay on a ramp built up at fifty degrees from the ground. The two kilometres of coils and electromagnets looked, from this distance, like a huge busy train terminus tipped upwards by some geological cataclysm.

'And what is it firing?'

'Ten-tonne iron cases, each tipped with a ceramic nose cone,' Clay explained. 'The inside they load with ingots of whatever other metals might be required up there – copper, tungsten, chromium or whatever. They also used to do special packages containing components manufactured down here, and sometimes plain water or lubricating oils. If it could fit into ten square metres and survive the huge acceleration, then it would be sent. Once, so I'm told, something was sent that couldn't survive the acceleration.'

She glanced at him. 'What?'

He had unearthed this particular story only a few hours ago, and he thought it was the kind of thing she would like to hear. 'A previous technical director who was caught using this mass driver as a means of smuggling unhealthy commodities to station staff and as a punishment was fired into orbit inside one of the cases. Nothing much left of him but sludge. Those receiving the goods at the other end were shoved out of an airlock.'

She shrugged, dismissing it. 'So what happens when they reach space? They will be moving very fast by then, surely?'

Clay felt sweat breaking out on his forehead. *Stick to the point, keep your head down and, most important, get somewhere you are less likely to be subject to the murderous whims of Earth's dictator.* 'Not so much. They lose velocity in Earth's atmosphere on the way up, finally falling into a stable orbit. The collector ship is in permanent orbit at a matched velocity, and when it has collected a full load, it decelerates to its destination.' He gestured to the screen. 'It's firing right now.'

Serene concentrated on the mass driver, waiting for the show. He watched it, too, could see nothing of note at first, then raised his gaze to a vapour trail cutting a line up into the sky. Then, as the trail began to bow under the high wind, another trail cut upwards. Shortly afterwards, even through the aero's insulation and over the sound of its fans, he detected the rumbling of multiple sonic booms, like a thunderstorm grumble that just went on and on. After a few minutes the sky was neatly banded with similar trails.

'That's all of them,' Director Rourke told him through his fone. 'Does she want to come and see the furnace complex?'

The director did not sound eager. Many people were learning what Clay had already realized: that it was better to remain below Serene Galahad's notice and just get on with your job.

'That's it,' said Clay. 'They've fired twenty projectiles and with no problems. Technical Director Rourke would like to know if you want to see the manufacturing of the cases – take a tour of the furnace complex.'

It would just be another big factory complex with its noise, its robots, its dirt and its obsequious managers. Clay noted her slightly bored expression and knew that, though she was thoroughly aware of the necessity of all this to achieve her secondary purpose of surely establishing humanity offworld, her primary interest seemed to be in restoring the wildlife and ecology of Earth – hence her determination to get back the Gene Bank data and samples. He sometimes wondered how these two aims matched up. Did she visualize a future with a low-population garden Earth, while the bulk of humanity lived in tin cans out in the solar system? She had already seen space planes on a production line ten kilometres long, scramjets too on another such line, and shown only mild complimentary interest. The one time she had become animated about any machinery was upon seeing the factories producing the giant bulldozers and macerating machines that would be used to clear unoccupied areas of sprawl, clearing them down to the hidden earth.

'I think I'll give this one a miss,' she said. 'Send my apologies to Director Rourke.'

'Yes, ma'am.' Clay paused at the door, even though he had effectively been dismissed.

She turned to regard him. 'There's something else?'

'I should get back to Aldeburgh,' he said. He would be relatively safe there and, but for these occasional tours, she seemed perfectly happy to remain in Tuscany. 'There's a lot that needs to be caught up on. It's difficult to find recruits with the right . . . attitude.'

She nodded in agreement, doubtless contemplating all those she had already found lacking and who had ended up in pieces on her self-cleaning carpet. Most of those people with the 'right attitude' had previously found their way up within the Committee Administration, which meant, after what Alan Saul had done, they were now just so much ash in the ruins of Inspectorate HQs, administrative centres or scramjet crash sites all across Earth.

'I think not,' she said.

'Why not?' Clay asked. Was it now? Did she know what he knew? Would she now give Sack that special hand signal?

'Because I have a rather longer journey in mind for you.'

He suddenly felt quite sick, both with relief and a growing fear. He knew precisely what she was talking about. She wanted someone she could trust – as much as that was possible for her – to be aboard the *Scourge*. He tried to think of some objection, some assertion that he was irreplaceable where he was, but knew there was nothing to offer. By making himself so useful to her, by working far beyond his basic remit, he'd now achieved a promotion he didn't want.

'Surely Captain Scotonis is able enough to—?'

Suddenly the cockpit filled with chunks of armour glass and a vicious swarm of metal fragments. Something slammed into his side, and for a second he thought Sack had grabbed hold of him . . . then he realized he was up against the cockpit wall. Ahead, the horizon was tilted upright, smoke boiling across the shattered screen. Behind the cockpit he could hear agonized screaming, and saw the glare of hot fire through the door into the rear section. He saw Serene reach across, hit the pilot's belt release. The man dropped from his seat, landing soggily just beside Clay, soaked in blood, one arm nearly detached and the back of his skull missing.

Serene dragged herself into the pilot's seat, wrestled with the controls, the aero's engines producing a horrible metallic clattering.

Clay closed his eyes and clung on, wondering if the impact with the ground would kill him – or the fire.

8

Dark Soldiers

It has been rumoured that secret government research has taken implant technology far beyond the point where the technological component can be properly called an implant. Rumours of hideous experiments, where terrorist prisoners are experimented on, abound in scurrilous stories on the Subnet. Such spreaders of rumour and dissention tell horrific tales of researchers casually removing the organs, limbs and bones of their subjects so that state-of-the-art implants and prosthetics can be tried out on them. There are stories, too, of victims being stripped of their nervous, lymphatic and venous systems so that technological replacements of these can be tested; of computer replacements of the brain itself being trialled; and of brains divided, reordered and combined with hardware to form new structures. But the darkest stories of all are of people rendered down by this process until almost nothing of the original remains; of dark cyborg soldiers being created in nightmare orbital laboratories that seem like some annex of Hell. But it is, in the end, all the same sort of conspiracy theory as can be found in historical files about Area 57, FTL space drives and UFOs. It is the retreat of the permanently disaffected, those who cannot accept that we live in the best of possible worlds.

Argus

Le Roque's face grew pale as he listened to his fone, then he blinked and gazed down the length of the table at Hannah. 'What have you done?'

Hannah's stomach felt tight, dreading what the android's response might have been to her instruction to protect Alan Saul, to protect the Owner. Had this Paul and its fellows gone straight to her laboratory to kill Dr Raiman and any other medics found there? Had they also killed the guards Langstrom had left behind? She wished she'd been more specific.

'One of those things the Saberhagens were working with is now in your laboratory,' confirmed Le Roque. 'Raiman and his people are out in the corridor – it won't let them near the Owner, told them to stay out.'

Some relief there, but this was by no means over. Hannah swung her attention towards Langstrom, who was listening to his own fone, his expression grim. He turned to Le Roque. 'My men opened fire on it,' he said, shaking his head. 'No effect – so I've ordered other men to break the armour piercers out of storage.'

Le Roque continued to gaze at Hannah. 'I need an explanation, Dr Neumann.'

Hannah spread her hands placatingly. 'I've simply ensured that Saul remains protected. He won't be handed over to Galahad, and he's going to remain under my care.' She glanced at Langstrom. 'You've no need of armour-piercing bullets, and they wouldn't work anyway. The androids were programmed by Saul himself and, until he is well, they will take their orders from me.'

'A police force he can trust absolutely,' remarked Langstrom bitterly.

Hannah shrugged, trying to appear confident, though unsure of her ground. 'Police for Saul only. You still police this station at large.'

'More like doctrinal police,' said Langstrom. 'Real police are real human beings who retain the ability to question, to make decisions based on reality.'

'Proctors,' said Hannah abruptly, remembering the enforcers of correct political thinking from her university days, and also remembering how, before the Committee, such proctors had kept the chaotic and undisciplined student body in line. Wasn't there an older meaning still? Yes, religious police – and that seemed appropriate since they were guarding a being who had, at least for a short time, been a demigod.

'Proctors,' said Le Roque. 'So what else do you intend to do with these proctors, Dr Neumann?'

Hannah stood up. 'I intend to ensure that we find a way out of this that doesn't involve giving up Saul or surrendering ourselves. I intend to ensure that we survive, and don't all end up shitting on the floor of an adjustment cell on Earth.' She looked around at the others seated at the table. 'We're done here now until I can pull together those staff who'll provide a more positive input. Then I suggest we discuss this matter again.'

'Langstrom,' said Le Roque. 'Take Dr Neumann into custody while we resolve this situation.'

Langstrom stood up, looking very unsure, his hand on his sidearm.

'Who do you take orders from, Langstrom?' Hannah asked.

'I take orders from the Owner,' he said. 'However, in the Owner's absence I must take orders from the next person in authority aboard this station, and that is Technical Director Le Roque.'

'You merely follow the chain of command, then, and tend not to think for yourself?'

He frowned, then abruptly dipped his head and reached up to press his fingers against his fone. He listened for a moment, then abruptly spat, 'Get out of its way – then get over to the armoury. We're going to need something a bit more substantial.'

He glanced pensively at the door before quickly moving round the table. His gun came out of its holster as he caught hold of Hannah's jacket. He pressed it into her side and dragged her away from the double doors, which at that moment abruptly slid open. One of the newly named proctors ducked inside, the top of its head only a few centimetres below the ceiling. Little pieces of blue ceramic fell off its tough skin – the remains of low-penetration station weapons. It shrugged, shedding further fragments, and a pink haze like St Elmo's fire rippled across its hide. Hannah did not know precisely how, but she recognized this as the first one that had addressed her, and as the same one that had spoken to her over her fone.

'The EM weapon couldn't stop it,' said Langstrom – his comment directed to Le Roque as he pulled Hannah closer.

'Hello, Paul,' she said.

'Hello Hannah Neumann,' the proctor replied. 'Would you like me to disarm Captain Langstrom, and render him harmless?'

'Not right now,' Hannah replied, shivering. The resonance

of the voice was completely off key and, though the proctor spoke such reasonable words, there seemed to be terrible implications behind them.

She turned to Le Roque, who, along with the others, had stood up and moved back from the table. 'So where do we go from here, Le Roque? If I order this proctor to free me, how are you going to counter that?' She paused for a second. 'And you, Langstrom. Are you going to kill me and then die shortly afterwards just so Le Roque can maintain power here?'

'Le Roque?' Langstrom enquired. Hannah could feel the dampness of his sweat through his uniform, could see it on his cheek. He was in a horrible position and knew it. What would he do next? She must not underestimate the possibility that, faced with this thing called Paul, he might not react rationally.

'Release her,' said Le Roque.

The gun retracted, a sigh escaping Langstrom as he let her go. Slightly unsteadily she walked over to stand beside the proctor, Paul. The android towered over her, completely immobile, but with a thunderstorm tension in the air all about it. Then it turned and dipped its head as if to peer down at her.

'Your instructions?' it asked.

She felt a moment of panic, and suppressed it. She should just concentrate on the words it uttered. She should not see them as a question asked by some demon she'd just summoned up from Hell. 'We go back to Arcoplex Two,' she replied, 'and we'll take it from there.' She turned towards the doors.

'Dr Neumann,' said Le Roque, 'you understand that we had no choice?'

195

Power had shifted abruptly.

She nodded an acknowledgement and stepped outside, Paul looming over her, the doors closing behind them.

'I want you to secure the station armoury,' she decided. 'I don't want Langstrom's men running around with guns and rocket launchers.'

'Already done, Hannah Neumann,' replied Paul. 'I sent a spidergun the moment Captain Langstrom dispatched Sergeant Peach there.'

'Spidergun?' said Hannah, halting abruptly.

'We have all been awaiting your command,' the proctor informed her. 'You have only to issue instructions.'

'All the station robots?' she asked, suddenly horrified.

'All that can hear you, and all the others through those.'

She hesitated, almost felt like running back to Le Roque and handing power back to him. What horrified her? That same thing Saul had shoved into her hands before, and now again: responsibility.

'This is not going to be an easy conversation to conduct, so we must both think ahead to anticipate questions we might be asked, and add the further detail our answers might require,' said the woman on the screen.

'There's a tidy-up program running alongside this image feed,' said Alexandra, pausing the broadcast from Earth.

'So this Serene Galahad is vain,' said Alex.

Chairman Messina had once met Galahad during one of his many world tours. She was a British delegate, but not as active in the administration there as others – her rank was bestowed simply because of her scientific expertise and her organization of ID-implant manufacturing. Warned of subversive elements within her vicinity, and of some doubt about her own loyalty, his protection teams had been kept on high alert. Alex One and his brothers had been ready in a fast-drop boat underneath an aero hovering above the Aldeburgh facility, just in case something happened there that the conventional protection teams down on the ground couldn't handle. This was why, out of the hundreds of other delegates he had encountered, Alex remembered her.

'I'll try to clear it up,' said Alexandra, 'so we can get a proper look at her.' She set the broadcast running again.

'You have by now seen all the data we sent and therefore understand the situation here. I am also told that the station schematic we sent has enabled you to break into some storage rooms to resupply yourselves, and that you have since found a safe hideaway. That's good.' She paused for a second in thought, one side of her face blurring and distorting as Alexandra tried to get rid of the tidy-up program. Galahad then continued, 'For the people of Earth it is essential that we retrieve the Gene Bank data and samples, and that Alan Saul – if he still lives – and the rebels with him, be brought to justice, and that the delegates aboard that station then be freed. And it is, of course, also essential that Chairman Messina be released and returned to Earth. We need his wisdom, his experience and his insight.'

Alex found himself nodding in agreement, then abruptly ceased and felt a little sickened by such a reaction. This woman had been considered a danger to the Chairman when he was still back on Earth and Alex doubted that anything had changed. The delegates had always been the most perfidious and therefore in need of the closest watching.

'Got it,' said Alexandra.

Galahad's image distorted again then resettled, now revealing a big dressing on her face, some hair missing on one side of her head and a black eye.

'Burn dressing,' Alexandra noted.

Alex shrugged. Whatever – it wasn't really relevant.

Galahad continued, 'To these ends, we are sending the *Scourge* – the ship whose images we sent to you earlier. This ship is entirely capable of destroying the Argus Station, but obviously we don't want that. The data must be recovered and Chairman Messina must be secured and rescued. So, your best function for now will be to act as our eyes and ears aboard the station. Your prime objective will be to remain concealed, while you gather tactical data and send it to us on this frequency. I know that you have located Alessandro, but you must not act on that yet. It is also essential that you locate the Gene Bank samples and data. I'll pause now to give you a chance to reply.' Her image froze.

Alex and Alexandra sat and discussed the broadcast, only briefly, because they had already gone over what they needed to know. Then they replied.

'How will the *Scourge* attack this station, and where would it be safest for us to position ourselves? Is it likely that you will fire on the station, and what are the chances of the Arboretum cylinder world being hit – that is, should we get Messina out before the attack begins? After finding this Gene Bank data, what should we do with it?' Alex paused, wondering if there was something he had missed. He couldn't think of anything.

They then waited. He kept checking his watch as the time she would have received it arrived and passed. It took a further ten minutes before they received her reply.

'The form of the attack,' she said, 'will, to a certain extent, be dependent on the tactical information you now supply. There is also a limit to the amount of information I am prepared to provide you with, since there is still a danger that you may be captured and interrogated. However, the rebels aboard will already have surmised that the station will come under disabling fire first, followed by the injection of an assault force. Most of this fire will be concentrated on installations in and about the asteroid itself, where the main population is concentrated. It will be heavy enough to cause atmosphere breaches, disable power supplies and sever communications and transport, but not so heavy as to completely wreck the computer architecture of the station, since we do not want to destroy any recording there of the Gene Bank data. We will therefore tend to avoid any server rooms and data stores. My tactical teams also tell me, you will be delighted to know, that one of the most likely storage places for the Gene Bank samples and data is the Arboretum cylinder, so we will certainly avoid inflicting any damage on that place at all.'

She smiled at them then, and the sincerity in her expression made Alex uneasy. He was one of the first clones created, and so by now, at the physical age of thirty, had learned to recognize deceit, but he could not detect any sign of it in her.

'I have to add,' she continued, 'that if you can, without any high risk of being captured, get to the Gene Bank data and transmit it to me, on this frequency, then you should do so. The Chairman himself would agree on how essential that data is for the regeneration of his beloved Earth. I could warrant that he would even be prepared to sacrifice himself in order to ensure that end. Now I will listen to one further message from you, then I must return to the administration of a planet until the Chairman returns.'

'Chairman Alessandro Messina will not sacrifice himself – nor will he be sacrificed,' was all Alex said in reply.

It took a further five minutes, on top of the signal delay, before they received her reply to that statement.

'My apologies,' she said. 'I was only talking about what I believe his opinion would be, for he values himself only as high as he does his duty. However, he is more important to you, to me and to the people of Earth than any data imaginable. Please understand my sincerity in this. Now I must leave you to attend to your duties, while I attend to mine. The leader of the tactical team assigned you will once again take over. I wish you the best of luck, Alex, and hope that in the future we can talk under better circumstances.'

Her image froze again.

'So what do you think?' Alex asked.

'She seems sincere enough,' said Alexandra. 'The Chairman would not have made her a delegate if he hadn't trusted her.'

Alex gazed at her thoughtfully, remembering a fragment of some previous mission he had been engaged on ten years before Alexandra was anything more than a blob of jelly in her amniotic tank. The memory was slightly confused by the many conditioning sessions since, but he certainly recalled, at Messina's request, torturing to death a delegate who had made an attempt on the Chairman's life. Poor Alexandra: despite her brilliance with coms she was still, at only four years out of her tank, lacking in experience. To her the world was still divided into black and white. On the one side stood the rebels, subversives and terrorists, while on the other stood Messina, his delegates and the administration of Earth. To her it wasn't at all complicated. Her naivety made him feel so very tired.

Things were better, as a brief venture into what Saul recognized as semi-consciousness gave him an overview. He felt the bandwidth of connections expanding as those units they extended from or terminated against healed, regrew, came online. He also understood that even when not fully in the world, he had influenced it and set in motion a counter-force; something to stand against that massive ship whose presence in near-Earth space felt like a hot nail being driven into his head. And Hannah had responded, too, taking the reins he had released but had failed to instruct her to hold.

Data continued flowing, and he could understand it better. He could distinguish now the difference between station computing and the events and propaganda broadcast on ETV. The demonization of Alan Saul never stopped and, motivated by the need for vengeance, the people of Earth seemed to all the more willingly wear their chains and work at a killing pace under Serene Galahad. Here another image appeared; here more damnation invoked.

One of the Gobi desert basins had been used as the Asian continent's inner dumping ground. Any surviving population had been moved out and their buildings levelled. Then the corpses had been brought in by heavy ore trucks, and dumped and dozered up to a thickness of ten metres across an area of a hundred square kilometres. Months of decay, during which the flies had clouded so thick that people venturing into the area had choked to death on them, had reduced this layer to five metres of bones. They called it 'the Plain of Bones' now. It was poetically apposite, but by no means unique. In a moment of coherence, he managed to link to Govnet and discover that there were now a hundred and four places called the Plain of Bones, plus hundreds of others with similar titles: the Ossuary, Bonefield, Field of Skulls and numerous sites that had acquired the name 'the Scourings'. That was all he managed to get before something – some shadowy force – tipped him out again.

'For this they must be punished,' declared Serene Galahad, seated in a plush office, looking all confidence and strength, her clothing plain and almost dowdy to impart the comforting image of motherhood. 'But we must bring that data back here so we can grow a new Earth in the bones of the old.'

The broadcasts contained nothing new. He could detect the joins, the words reordered, the CGI changes of scene and the changes in her appearance. She had not actually spoken live for a long time now. The ersatz Serene moved on to talk of awards, promotions and the lionization of individuals who had invented something useful, speeded up some process, increased some production figures. It seemed to Saul that the ghost of the hammer-and-sickle shimmered once more on a red background and that *Pravda* was again alive and well.

She watched, too – the woman etched into underlying reality, the one he had seen somewhere, and heard speak. She had been far away, yet also impossibly close, space seeming an agonized curve in between. Sometimes he felt that curve, and found himself howling from behind a screen in Jasper Rhine's laboratory. Other times he felt a brief twisting, distorting wrongness, and found himself gazing from the eyes of the proctor called Judd, in the outer ring. He knew, in an utterly theoretical way, what was being built there, and knew that theoretically it should work. But every time Judd tested a new section, and the machine just hinted at what it could do, he saw the working of the universe through utterly unhuman eyes, because that wrongness – that twisting – should not happen now but was a strand of a possible future stretching back to the now. It was a picture of reality that the normal human mind could not grasp.

'*Hannah*,' he somehow managed to say.

'Alan! Alan, is that you!'

'*Hannahahhahahnonono . . .*'

'Alan! You have to wake up!'

His mental grip slid away, and he glimpsed himself lying all tubed and wired on the table in her surgery, a seeming meld of corpse and machine. He glimpsed someone in a corridor with his hands clasped over his ears, gazing in horror at a public-address speaker. He saw Le Roque leaping out of his chair in Tech Central and backing away from some night-mare images on his screen. Then briefly, for just one steady instant, he saw the station entire: every image from every robot sensor, every cam, every external array and dish, and even through the human eyes of those who wore cortex-linked fones. It was numinous . . . and so seemed the blackness that followed.

Earth

It had been five hours since the broadcast, but still Serene cursed her stupidity. She had read the recently revealed reports on Messina clones, about Alexes supposedly just like those that made up that undercover squad hiding aboard Argus Station. She had read about the conditioning, the brain surgery, the inducement and the brainwashing. She had known how it produced something utterly loyal to the Committee and the administration of Earth, but only *after* a total and unquestioning loyalty to Alessandro Messina. She had also known that the Alexes were supposed to be almost childlike, socially inept and trusting. And she had got it wrong.

The Alex she had spoken to had not been quite so easy to handle, and in retrospect she realized that though the wholly naive Alexes might be used in military units they wouldn't, in any sane world, be used for undercover infiltration work. So, for her to even hint at Messina dying had been completely the wrong thing to do. She had complacently slid into error by assuming that the Alex was loyal to the office when in reality that loyalty was primarily to the man. That particular Alex must have lost any awe of Messina's administration and his subordinates. She put her error down to her present physical condition and mental state, the latter of which she intended to do something about right now.

She walked slowly and carefully into the room, every stab of pain from her damaged pelvis further feeding the cold rage inside her. Gazing about at the awaiting technicians, managers and political officers, she reached up self-consciously to touch the dressing over the burn on her face and running down the side of her neck. The doctors had told her that grafts of her own skin from her personal stock would eliminate any scarring, and that the implants in her pelvis should soon heal the damage there. She had painkillers she could take, but they blurred her round the edges, made her less sharp, and she needed to stay sharp. That was evident.

The assassination attempt had been well planned. Rounds of armour-piercing bullets were fired from the top of the mass driver and through the cockpit screen, to take out the pilot. They couldn't have known she was in the cockpit, too; if they had, the bullets would not have been concentrated on the pilot's position, but on her. Taking out the pilot, however, was not enough to bring about a crash, not enough to ensure the death of Earth's dictator, since the aero's autopilot would have taken over, to bring it down safely. Hence the subsequent two copperhead tank-busters fired from the ground. The first of them took out one engine and one entire fan, the second filled the rear compartment with vaporized copper, incinerating fifteen of the passengers. Had Serene not instantly taken the controls, the machine would have plunged straight into the ground. As it was, she felt lucky to have managed to drag herself out of the wreck.

'Have they been brought in?' she asked, turning to Clay.

'They're in,' he confirmed.

Clay had got off lightly, just a broken arm and a few cracked ribs, all now internally splinted and not hindering him in any way. Sack hadn't been so lucky. The rear compartment wall he was sitting against had heated up, melting the plastic of his seat, thus jamming his safety belt. He managed to snap the belt only when it had burned through enough to weaken it, and then follow her and Clay out through the shattered cockpit screen. Currently he occupied a room in an advanced Committee hospital in Sydney, on life support while the doctors there tried to replace his ninety per cent skin loss with some artificial concoction.

'And you're sure we got them all?'

'I got all who remained alive,' he replied. 'I had to use and lose some good contacts and close down some undercover networks but, yes, all of them.'

Now that he knew he could not use their brief sexual liaison as leverage, he was trying to assert how useful he was here on Earth, perhaps also hoping that recent events might have changed her mind about sending him to the *Scourge*. He would be disappointed.

'What do you mean by "all who remained alive"?'

'Twelve of them got forewarning, and made a visit to a Safe Departure clinic before I could get to them.'

She stared at him. They went to a suicide clinic, easily slept their way into death and then a community digester. She would have to close those clinics down. They were an anachronism the people of Earth could no longer afford. They promoted the idea that a citizen's life was his own when, in reality, it belonged to the state. They should not have the option to end it so easily. That should be the prerogative of herself and *her* government.

She refocused her attention on the people within the room, and on what she had come to see here at this Security Development Facility in Brazil. It hadn't originally been included on her tour route but, considering the fact that some societal assets felt in a position to try and assassinate her, she had changed her mind.

She could send a signal to ID implants to kill with the Scour but, since the Scour was being blamed on Alan Saul, she wanted something that was her own, some power to kill instantly that was *obviously* her own. She needed visible evidence of her ability to take any life she chose. And here they were developing just what she needed. She walked over to the table and surveyed the collection of items on display. They called these things DUs – disciplinary units.

'These are all of them?' she asked.

'Yes, ma'am.'

The developer, Santanzer, was a nervous individual who reminded her of Shimbaum. Apparently, because the director of this establishment and most of his management team had been visiting an Inspectorate HQ in Brazil when Saul decided to drop a satellite on it, this place had since been run by a disparate team of political officers and low-echelon managers. They had obviously decided that Santanzer should be the one to speak to her. She was starting to realize that her harsh reputation was causing some irresponsible staff either to absent themselves when she visited, or to pass responsibility further down the chain. In future she would ensure she spoke only to whoever made the decisions, but just for now she would let it go. She picked up a silver ring twenty centimetres across, gazed at it for a second then put it down dismissively. The item was in fact an explosive collar.

'Too dramatic,' she said, remembering her stained office carpet in Italy, 'and too messy.'

Next she picked up a rather heavier item which could inject a selection of drugs directly into the recipient's neck. This might have its uses, but it wasn't what she wanted right now. Another collar delivered electric shocks, while another was a pain inducer, and still others were varied combinations of all these things. But she liked simplicity, and finally selected a ring made of a strap of metal that seemed almost indistinguishable from a large jubilee clip, and studied the metal cylinder that the free end of the strap passed under.

'This.' She held it up to show Clay.

He nodded and turned away to speak through his fone to the guards currently standing watch over the prisoners. There were thirty SAs in all, including Technical Director Rourke from the Outback mass driver, one of her recently appointed Australian delegates, along with her advisers and bodyguards – a total of forty-eight people. Of course, the delegate and her staffs had not been involved in the incident, but that a bunch of democratically minded SAs could conduct such an assassination attempt under her watch could not go unpunished.

'Diamond filaments imbedded in the metal make it practically unbreakable,' Santanzer explained. 'Those filaments are what science-fiction writers have been dreaming about for centuries, and now we have them. They could be used to take elevators up into orbit.'

She gazed at him with slight contempt. Here was yet another *expert* trying to blind the stupid politician with science.

'Strange you should put it that way,' she observed. 'To my recollection, diamond filament was manufactured in China over eighty years ago, but since cost of production was so prohibitive, and other much cheaper options were available for the more prosaic tasks it might be used for, it was shelved.' She eyed him carefully. 'We can easily manufacture it now because of a steady improvement in furnace design over those eighty years.'

He didn't know what to say for a moment, then gulped out a, 'Yes, ma'am.'

'What I would prefer you to tell me about,' she continued, 'is this motor here and its power supply.'

'Yes, ma'am.' He seemed unable to do more than mouth those two words.

'Perhaps a practical demonstration?' she suggested nastily. 'Here and now rather than the one being prepared for us?'

He spoke all in a rush. 'The battery is a nanotube store, kept up to charge by induction through the strap itself. It discharges into a micro-conveyor, which is an array of micro-wheels on a—'

'I know what a micro-conveyor is. Please continue.' She glanced round at Clay, who nodded, then pointed to the door leading out of there. She began heading towards that door, her four new bodyguards close behind her, Clay trailing them, and all the other flunkies walking attentively but silently after him.

Santanzer stayed at her side. 'The conveyor simply closes the strap, which is prevented from being pulled back by spur hairs within the exit hole. As soon as the device receives an ID code, it checks it against the recipient's implant and, if there's a match, it can close the hoop . . . sufficiently in less than a second.'

As she reached the door, two of her bodyguards moved ahead to open it and check the area beyond. That was unnecessary, really, since the place had been swarming with Inspectorate enforcers for a week before her arrival, but this was what they were trained to do. After a moment they nodded, and she followed them through, Santanzer was still at her side, and frequently looking back towards his superiors in the vain hope that one of them would take over from him.

'But there is more than one speed setting,' she observed as she stepped out onto a platform overlooking a warehouse floor.

A racket greeted her there: the meaty thuds of rifle butts liberally applied, the shouting and begging and the screams from those feeling the touch of a disabler. Steel stairs led down to the main floor, a large area that had now been cleared of crates. Fifty Inspectorate enforcers had the prisoners all crammed together, and there seemed to be a bit of a riot going on. The prisoners, it seemed, were objecting to their new neckwear.

'It allows any setting you choose,' Santanzer replied, gazing over the rail with horrified fascination as he finally started to accept what might soon happen here.

Two bodyguards went down the stairs first, and she followed, her pelvis complaining at the extra effort. Finally down on the warehouse floor, she walked out to where a large comfortable chair had been provided for her, a small round table standing beside it, upon which sat a bottle of champagne in a cooler, and a single flute glass. She unhooked her palmtop from her belt and placed it on the table, then carefully sat down while Clay checked the secure seal on the bottle, before opening it and filling the glass for her. It was one taken from Messina's stock, specially sent over for the occasion – and specially sealed and poison-free so long as the seal remained intact. She took a sip, opened her palmtop and studied the list of ID implant numbers displayed, and the icon for the new program that had just loaded. Then, after a pause, she raised her gaze towards the prisoners.

'Bring delegate Grace Turpin and Technical Director Rourke forward,' she instructed.

Enforcers cut the two she named from the crowd, shoved them to the front and then down onto their knees. Their suits were soiled and soaking wet, and only now did Serene detect the slight smell of faeces and urine. All these people had been kept without access to toilet facilities for some days, because, after their sojourn in Inspectorate cells in Australia, they had spent most of their time in the holds of aeros or scramjets. Doubtless they were dripping wet because the enforcers here had recently hosed them down to make them at least a little more presentable for her. She eyed them for a second longer before selecting their two implant codes from the list ranged before her, then dragged them across and dropped them on the ring-shaped icon. A new menu opened to show numerous settings. The thing was of a gratifyingly simple design: she could govern the speed of strangulation, she could render

210

someone unconscious then open the collar again, and she could snap the collar closed so quickly it would decapitate whoever was wearing it in, as Santanzer had told her, less than a second.

'Chairman,' said Rourke, 'we were utterly shocked and—'

The slowest setting, she decided, but without full closure since that would make a terrible mess here. Of course, she wouldn't have to clear it up herself, but felt some sympathy for those who would. The two began making retching sounds and struggled to free their hands from the plastic ties binding their wrists behind their backs. Grace Turpin toppled over on her side, her legs kicking, her body thrashing and bucking, and shortly afterwards Rourke lay down beside her too. One and a half minutes of this was followed by a further thirty seconds of death rattles and the occasional spasmodic twitching.

Serene took another sip of champagne, then flicked her gaze back to the list. Some in the crowd of prisoners were sobbing, four had tried to run and been beaten to the floor, while one had managed to ram his head into an enforcer's gut and then deliver an excellent kick to another enforcer's head, before running. A disabler dropped him, screaming, beside a wall of crates.

However, most just remained in a kneeling position, doing nothing. She had previously noticed how, if you first selected a couple of prisoners from a crowd you intended to do away with, the rest somehow convinced themselves that they were being given an object lesson, and that they weren't going to die, too. She smiled with a feeling of peace easing the tension in her body, selected the whole of the rest of the list and dragged it to the ring icon, left the setting the same, pressed send and sat back.

The noise was abominable, and in a short time the smell was too. Serene finished her champagne, then poured herself another glass. The enforcers moved back from the thrashing, retching mass of humanity. Out of this mass crawled one woman whose collar seemed to have malfunctioned.

'Deal with her,' said Serene, pointing.

An enforcer stepped over and beat in the woman's skull with his rifle butt.

In two minutes it was all over.

'Santanzer,' Serene said next.

The man stepped over beside her chair. 'Ma'am?' He didn't look well

'You are now the technical director of this facility. How soon can you go into production?'

'Within two days, ma'am.'

'At what rate?'

'The furnaces can produce two metres of strip every hour, but motor production and assembly is slower – about five to six thousand collars every twenty-four hours,' he replied.

'Not enough and not fast enough,' she said. 'That's only a million in six months. You'll be provided with all the resources you need to increase that figure.'

'How many do you want?'

'Let's go for a nice round figure,' she said, standing up. 'If you haven't produced a billion within the first year, I'll be back here to find out why.'

She headed for the stairs feeling slightly woozy; the champagne had gone to her head.

Argus

They had food and water here in this zero-gravity hydroponics unit, and remained safe from discovery after Alexandra had managed to run a program through the local agribots so that they would ignore this apparent new staff complement. But Alex had become frustrated by the lack of action, and by all the sneaking about and spying. However, their instructions from Serene Galahad, then reaffirmed by the leader of the tactical team on Earth, had been quite explicit: no military action. Instead they were to watch and report everything they could and be ready for the arrival of the *Scourge*. Now, as Alex listened in frustration to the various sounds penetrating the surrounding walls – the clattering, the intermittent whine of a cutter and occasional deep groans and bangs – it seemed that they were trapped here, and that they were about to be found.

'What are they doing?' he asked Alexandra.

She continued studying her screen for a moment, then looked up. 'It looks as if they're dismounting the whole hydroponics unit.' She paused for a second, her expression distant. 'To isolate us?' she wondered, clearly puzzled.

Alex shook his head. 'Then why not just send in the robots? In this confined area we wouldn't stand a chance.'

'Maybe,' she suggested, 'they're worried about the damage if there's a firefight in here. Hydroponics is important, so perhaps they just intend to isolate us and wait us out.'

Good, she was starting to think a little bit more outside the box.

'I don't think so,' he opined. 'We're just in the way.'

She focused on him. 'I don't understand.'

Alex frowned for a second then continued, 'That thing

they're building in the outer ring . . . we saw how they cut straight through underneath the space dock, took out those big structural beams and repositioned them. They're building it all the way round, and this unit is standing in the way. So they're moving it.'

'Makes more sense, that. I guess if they wanted to isolate us, they just had to weld the doors shut,' she said, adding, 'Maybe we should sabotage it?'

'You heard what Tactical Analysis said,' he said. 'They can discern no military application for it, other than maybe some sort of EM defence, which the station already has. It looks more like some sort of fast transport system and, if anything, it's a good thing that they're diverting station resources into the project.'

'I still don't like it,' said Alexandra.

At that moment, the whole hydroponics unit shifted and the lights went out. Alex turned on his suit light to compensate, while Alexandra remained focused on her screen.

'Completely detached,' she said. 'We've got some big construction robots out there taking hold. I think you're right and it looks to me as if there's a place deeper in already prepared. We're only being moved about twenty metres.'

They now sat in silence, holding on tight as the unit was moved. Then it clanged to a halt, the lurch not enough to disturb the agribots still working all around them. The racket from outside could be heard again, and Alex felt his tension ease when he heard the familiar sizzling of welders. When the lights came back on, he checked his watch. It was time to record another report. He gestured to Alexandra, who moved away from the screen, pulling herself up into the overhead scaffold while he moved into position and set the screen to record.

'We have data on the other weapon, which I will transmit with this report,' he began. 'It is not, as we first supposed, a railgun, but some sort of beam weapon.' He gave a brief description that provided no more data than the pictures they would send, then continued with, 'Alexandra has managed to locate some old cargo manifests which indicate the final destination of cargos being sent here. As you surmised, the Gene Bank samples were transported directly to the Arboretum. They went there rather than to Arcoplex Two mainly because of the storage space. The data, however, is another matter. It was brought here in permanent-write carbon-crystal storage, then fed into the station system. We don't know the location of the PWCC, but copies of the data are stored throughout the station. We tried to access them, but something's happened – the whole system seems a lot more aware again, as it was when Alan Saul was still in control. We just managed to get away from the console we were using before a spidergun arrived. That's all for now.'

'What I don't understand,' said Alexandra, 'is why there aren't copies of that data all across Earth – you could get all of it on terabyte sticks.'

'It's not for us to question that,' said Alex. 'Remember, it was under the Chairman's orders that the data came here, so it was under his orders that none of it should remain on Earth.'

He watched her acquiesce and dismiss the question from her mind, but it still remained in his. With data storage so easy, it seemed ludicrous to confine something so valuable to just one location. The Chairman must have considered this data part of his power base, maybe as a hedge against the possibility of revolution on Earth while he was up on Argus. Those down below would not have been able to maintain power while

Earth's biosphere died all around them, and without the Gene Bank data they would have nothing with which to regenerate it all. All he had to do then was wait them out.

'Send the report,' he snapped, uncomfortable with where these thoughts were taking him.

Alexandra dipped her head in acknowledgement, and set to work. However, it soon became evident that she had encountered a problem.

'What's the matter?' he asked. 'Are you getting that same weird shit again?'

The images and sounds seemed to come out of nowhere, though Alexandra explained it as a kind of inductance effect on her equipment. But what could possibly induce what looked like a nightmare artistic montage of flesh, blood, bone and insectile machine? What was inducing sounds like the howling of some half-man and half-beast, or the muttering of lunatics in dank dungeons?

'Nope, it's not that, thankfully. I think it must come from that thing they're building out there,' she said. 'Every time they run another test on a section of it, it screws up com. I'm not getting the weird shit now, just weird readings. The carrier wave keeps compressing and expanding.'

'Time dilation, signal shift, Doppler effect?' Alex queried. 'There's all that stuff about relative velocities, as I recollect.'

She looked up at him, annoyed. 'We're not going fast enough for those effects to be very strong, and anyway they are constant and easily corrected for. This is something completely different.' She paused for a second to again study her screen. 'Ah, it's gone now.' She stabbed a finger down on a key and sat back with a satisfied look on her face.

'We should take another look at that station schematic,' Alex suggested, 'see if there's somewhere safer we can use.'

She briefly twitched her head. Negative. 'We're not going anywhere for a while,' she said. 'Look.' She turned the jury-rigged screen towards him.

The screen showed robot activity in two directions. The structure they were building was approaching them from either side, concentric with the outer ring. Alexandra then manipulated a ball control to focus down on something nearby. One of those big humanoid robots was in the area, too. Leaving the hydroponics unit now would be highly risky – quite possibly fatal.

9

Cloning

By the mid-twenty-first century the cloning of farm animals and domestic pets was commonplace, while the idea that anyone was cloning human beings was dismissed as just a conspiracy theory. Then came the lawsuits initiated by grown human beings who, suffering one genetic malady or another, claimed to be the results of secret Pan Europa experiments in cloning. These claims did not get far because, by then, the power of unaccountable government had grown huge, and the legal system was in the process of being fully incorporated as an arm of the state. Even though such claims were quashed, it had by then become evident that human cloning had been going on for some time. It was the territory of the rich and the thoroughly egotistical, which by then meant the elite of political and media circles – the latter having essentially given up any pretence of being anything other than a propaganda mouthpiece of government.

The *Scourge*

'Good to meet you, Captain Scotonis,' said Clay, reaching out to shake the man's hand but finding the motion put him off balance in the heavy combined acceleration- and space-suit he wore, so he had to grab for the edge of the airlock.

'So you would be Clay Ruger, our new political officer,'

said Scotonis, gazing at him with tired and reddened eyes as he reached up and touched the collar he now wore.

'You may call me Clay.' Clay reached up and tapped a finger against his own collar. 'We live in perilous times,' he added.

He certainly hadn't wanted to put it on, having witnessed Galahad take such pleasure in killing with this device, but in the end had no choice in the matter. And how much difference did it make to him personally, when he knew that Galahad could render him just as dead by merely sending a signal to his implant? How different, after all, was strangulation to choking on your own blood as the Scour ripped your body apart?

'So glad to have you aboard,' said Scotonis, a trifle bitterly, 'despite your obvious lack of space legs.' He turned and propelled himself smoothly along the corridor. 'You'll have to take care, Political Officer Clay, because here lack of experience can kill.'

Clay followed him. 'Are you threatening me?'

Scotonis halted abruptly and turned. Clay nearly barrelled straight into him, but managed to stop himself at the last moment.

'My apologies, Political Officer Clay. That did not come out right.' He paused reflectingly, his head turned away as he fought to get himself under control. 'I just lost two of the assault force to a faulty airlock seal.' He now turned to face Clay, his expression wiped blank. 'They failed to follow procedure in two ways: they didn't check their external suit pressure gauges before unsealing, and they unsealed while still inside the airlock.'

This was precisely why Clay did not want to be here: space was dangerous and it could kill you in an instant . . . a bit like Serene Galahad.

'I thought all suits and airlocks were computer controlled, with safety backups? I thought it was impossible to open a suit to vacuum?'

'All modern suits are – but most of them went off with Messina and his assault force. In a perfect world we would have been able to take pre-tested and perfectly functional vacuum combat suits. As it is, we are two hundred short, so are having to use adapted Mars external activities suits.' He continued moving along the corridor, slower this time, with Clay following.

'I do hope that is not a criticism,' said Clay.

'Certainly not,' said Scotonis. 'I understand the urgency of our mission and why waiting another two weeks could not be countenanced.'

Back on Earth, Clay could have nailed Scotonis for the subtle criticism. Unfortunately there was no immediate re-placement for the man, which was another problem with space, since people sufficiently intelligent to be trained to operate in this highly technical environment tended to have minds of their own. For this very reason, Galahad had ensured that everyone aboard this ship would be wearing one of her collars.

'Our lives are unimportant,' he said, 'but our mission, to retrieve the Gene Bank data, and to bring Alan Saul and his rebels to justice, is essential to all the peoples of Earth.'

'Yes, of course,' said Scotonis.

At first sight, the bridge of the *Scourge* appeared to be an armoured dome, but the floor they walked out on was not attached to the walls, with a large gap lying between, and it actually sat inside the top of a sphere. In suspended acceleration couches all around this sphere, members of the crew worked instruments inset in the wall. Before four chairs on the main floor stood a multi-screen – a single curved piece of transparent pixel-laminate. Two of these chairs were occupied by the pilot and the gunner. A third chair was for Captain Scotonis, while the fourth – the one Clay would occupy – had apparently been put here for Messina himself. Scotonis easily walked over and took his seat, Clay following slowly, unfamiliar with gecko boots and not wanting to make a fool of himself by ending up completely detached from the floor.

Having strapped himself in, Scotonis waited with obvious impatience for Clay to finally get to his seat and do likewise. Scotonis then tapped some control and the entire floor revolved, exposing different sections of instrument wall as well as different crewmen. Clay hadn't understood the purpose of this movable floor until it was explained. During high acceleration, those at the instrument wall would be secured and immobilized by expanding acceleration suits. Those in the command chairs wore a different kind of suit, and would be turned so that they faced the direction of acceleration, just as in conventional vessels on Earth. In this way they would be able to continue to function, and to make command decisions.

'Pilot Officer Trove and Gunnery Officer Cookson,' Scotonis introduced the other two.

For a moment the two gazed at him expressionlessly, then Trove, a thin black female with a completely shaven skull, evidently noted that he too wore a collar. She reached up and touched her own then gave him a brief nod. He had started to note a lot of this recognition amidst collar wearers. It seemed a kind of salute, a *you too*, along with the anger and the fellow feeling.

'Interesting design,' said Clay, gesturing to their surroundings.

'Designed by committee,' said Cookson flatly – another subtle critic.

'Attention, all,' said Scotonis, his voice reverberating throughout the entire ship. 'Our countdown is at T minus one hundred and ten minutes. Crewmen, you know what to do. All passengers, please check your suit data feeds for any updates to launch-safety protocols. Those without data feeds, check your portable computers and link to *Scourge* One. The code is SA1276890V and should be appearing on all public screens right now. It's all there, but to sum up: make sure all loose objects are secured, plug your suit air into the ship feed, and strap yourselves in tightly. This is going to be quite some ride.'

Clay wondered if the ship's WiFi code was in some way significant, for it sounded like an ID code for a citizen – a societal asset. He unhooked his palmtop and opened it, first linking to the ship Internet to check the safety instructions, then opening up the list of ID codes for everyone aboard, but found no match. A further search linking to a database on Earth, however, revealed the number was Thespina Scotonis's ID code, or rather it had been when she was alive. He felt a moment of worry, until he discovered that Scotonis's wife, and his children, had died from the Scour – that same terrible disease Alan Saul had inflicted on Earth.

A hundred and ten minutes ground by with glacial slowness. Scotonis and all the others were constantly checking systems, continually revolving the floor for no apparent reason and bringing up all sorts of views on the multi-screen ahead. Conversation was desultory at best. Clay would ask questions and they would be answered, and that was the end of it. He concentrated on his palmtop, calling up data, checking how things were going back on Earth, sending messages to his staff and wondering why he couldn't have spent this time in his cabin. He might only make a fool of himself by getting up and leaving now. He would wait here and pretend an interest in the technicalities all around him.

When, at T minus ten minutes, the multi-screen showed massive umbilicals detaching, he finally began to take more interest and his hands started sweating.

'I understand that the extra fuel tanks and chemical boosters haven't been tested.' he enquired genially.

'Rather difficult to test a one-burn chemical booster,' Pilot Officer Trove observed.

'They're pretty safe,' said Scotonis, glancing at him. 'This one was retrieved from the Mars Traveller project. They used to use four of them precisely as we're going to use this one, providing a big burn to fling us away from Earth before fusion-engine start-up. It'll shorten our journey time by about three weeks.'

'I see,' said Clay. 'And, as you noted, a few weeks can make all the difference.'

Scotonis gazed at him for a second, then dipped his head in acknowledgement of this point.

'Why not four boosters, then?' Clay asked. 'This ship isn't much smaller than one of the Mars Travellers.'

'There was only one available,' said Scotonis, a hint of a smile twisting his mouth. 'And, with the present state of the Traveller Project, it would take some weeks to manufacture more, and the cut in journey time would have been cancelled out by those extra weeks, so it was obviously pointless waiting round for that.'

Touché, thought Clay, realizing the lack of spacesuits could have been made up in that time.

The next ten minutes passed rather faster than Clay might

have liked. He ensured he was plugged in to the ship oxygen supply but, like the other three, kept his helmet open and breathed ambient ship air. When a robotic voice began the final one-minute countdown, second by second, he noted the others closing up their helmets and he copied them. Next, the floor locked into place with a heavy crump, and meanwhile those all around, suspended from the instrument walls, were locking the suspension arms of their cradles.

The last ten seconds arrived.

'Pray, if you believe in that shit,' said Gunnery Officer Cookson reassuringly.

'Pre-igniters on,' said Trove. 'No errors.'

'Five,' said the robotic voice. Even it seemed to be counting now with some reluctance: 'Four . . . three . . . two . . . one.'

'Hang on to your balls,' said Scotonis, just as a dragon kicked Clay in the back and roared at him.

'Ain't got no balls!' Trove shouted over the thundering.

'Lucky you!' Cookson shouted back.

Clay's suit tightened around him like a giant fist, and blackness encroached on the periphery of his vision. He didn't know whether that was due to the acceleration, or the stark terror that seemed to have crawled up his spine and wrapped itself around his brain.

Argus

As she gazed through her spacesuit visor at the new structures slanting out towards the station skin, Hannah refused to let herself get downhearted. She had to keep pushing, to keep other people from letting their own feelings defeat them, to keep people from succumbing to the horrible atmosphere aboard the station and the idea, already expressed, that they were trapped on a ghost ship sailing to Hell.

Of course, Saul's most recent venture into near-consciousness – there had been fifteen so far – had not helped matters at all. The horrific images that had been appearing on every screen in the station and the sounds issuing from the public-address system were bad enough, but this time the spiderguns went into alert mode, one of them even firing on and destroying a small construction robot, while the proctors had just frozen where they were and howled for a full three minutes, before then moving on as if nothing at all had happened. It was madness, and the only way to keep it from affecting them too deeply was to stick to the practicalities.

The structures she was studying were rather like the cageway she and her companions now stood in, but with numerous bulky objects attached, and some seriously heavy cables snaking into those from newly relocated reactors. Three months it had taken to build them, three months since that particular meeting.

Le Roque had come to it, and so had Langstrom, who was no longer wearing his sidearm and, like all station police not engaged in searching for the Messina clones, was once again carrying just an ionic taser. The two men had both seemed subdued, but had their input once they realized Hannah would not allow this meeting to degenerate into re-criminations.

'We build railguns, we ramp up the output of the collision lasers, we build beam weapons and we turn this station into a fortress,' Brigitta had asserted, at one point.

'Apposite observation,' Le Roque replied. 'We are therefore just like a fortress in that we are a totally static target.'

They had all seen the figures and could do little to gainsay him, though Pike and Leeran took the opportunity to make some barbed comments about his defeatism.

The programming was available: tactical planning for space warfare – all the modelling they required. All the modelling to cover what they could make, what they could jury-rig, and all the modelling to cover whatever the *Scourge* carried. And yet nothing worked.

A total of three railguns could be built in the time available, and plentiful iron slugs smelted from the Argus asteroid. The collision lasers were juiced up and, quite possibly, could burn up a good proportion of what the *Scourge* could throw at them. It was also the case that the station's EM field would negate the *Scourge's* EM pulse weapons. However, manoeuvrability was where it all fell down. The *Scourge* could detect and avoid railgun fusillades. Here on Argus they could certainly detect them, but could not get the station out of the way in time. Stuff would get through, the station would be stripped of its armament, then the *Scourge* would dock and spew out its thousands of troops.

According to the models.

What gave Hannah hope was the maser, for the model had discounted it as an option. However, the Saberhagens had cracked that one with some quite brilliant and original ideas, so there was still reason for hope.

Hannah continued making her way along one of the cageways leading to the station rim, a spidergun scouting out the course ahead of her – a robot that Paul now insisted should accompany her everywhere – and with Brigitta and Pike hurrying to catch up.

'So when did this happen?' Hannah asked over her suit radio.

'I've been checking program logs,' Brigitta replied. 'It started two months ago, directly after the last enclosure hull plates were welded in place, and has been going on ever since.'

'So let me get this straight,' replied Hannah. 'Every time a robot finishes a programmed task here,' she gestured to the big railguns, 'or anywhere else on the station, for that matter, rather than go somnolent, it heads out to the station rim, and you never noticed until now?'

'There's more to it than that,' interjected Pike. 'Furnace-production and factory-component stats haven't been adding up either. I thought it was all down to the damage we received out there. I didn't find out the truth until after we started going into serious solar die-off and had to start pulling more power from station reactors.'

This was one of the many problems they now faced. As they moved further away from the sun, the solar mirrors – even complemented by the additional mirrors they had man-ufactured – weren't providing as much heat as they could manage before, and so the reactors were under an increasingly heavy drain. In fact it had been necessary to take all the spares out of storage and put them online too.

'So someone or something has not only infiltrated the robots, but our metals plants as well?'

'Damned right,' said Pike. 'I started checking yesterday and found large quantities of components being delivered to various points on the outer ring. A lot of the stuff is similar to the electromagnets and superconductive wiring Brigitta is using, hence my not noticing before. But, since checking, I've seen some weirdly designed electromagnets and other stuff I haven't even been able to identify. There're also lots of sections of titanium-alloy cylinders with an internal silicon dioxide hex-chain carbon finish – as near to zero-coefficient of friction as we can get. Christ knows what they're for. I've seen nothing like them before.'

Hannah gazed ahead towards the outer ring. *Someone or something* . . . Had those clones of Messina's managed a successful and thorough penetration of the station's computer systems? It seemed highly unlikely. Was this some kind of project worked out between Langstrom and Le Roque? They had seemed to acquiesce to her leadership, but that could have just been a front. But, even then, she doubted they had the ability and resources to manage something quite like this. That just left Alan and his machines – an idea that scared her thoroughly. All the station machines, including the proctors, were still connected to Alan's sleeping mind – a mind which, from the images all had seen and the sounds all had heard from the station system, seemed to be experiencing hellish nightmares. It was a mind that dwelt within a human brain – with additions – that seemed to be taking on a shape beyond any analysis.

The cageway was attached alongside one of the ore-transport tubes that led from the asteroid to the rim, where one of the big sun smelters and factory plants extended out into space. It was along this tube that raw materials were transported out from the asteroid to the processing plants, and back along which the finished products were conveyed. Glancing back, Hannah noticed that the asteroid had grown visibly smaller, such was the material that had already gone into enclosure, the weapons and now, it seemed, whatever the robots were building in the rim. Reaching the inner face of the rim, she walked up along it on her gecko boots, as if along some massive highway curving up into a metal forest. It occurred to her, even as she walked, that the enclosure hadn't made a huge difference to the view. True, they could no longer see any stars from inside the station, but the thousands of LED lights scattered through that vast internal space did look remarkably like stars.

A wide cargo lock stood ahead of them with its two hinged doors open. Even as they approached, a construction robot scuttled out of it like some busy termite, carting in its heavy forelimbs what looked like a few tonnes of floor plates. Ignoring them completely, it launched itself into the station interior, tapped a cross-member a hundred metres out in order to alter its course, then sailed on into the distance.

'And that's another one,' Pike added.

'Another what?'

'I also found out that the amount of scrap being fed into the plants has increased substantially,' he replied. 'They're obviously ripping stuff out of here to fit this installation inside, whatever it is.'

'Is that all of it?' Hannah asked.

'There's more,' said Brigitta. 'I was going to check it out further before I said anything, but it seems some robots have been making alterations to the transformers that run our EM radiation shield. I only noted that when I found out that the system programming for the field had changed.'

'Shit!' said Hannah. 'Shit! Shit!'

'That's about all,' said Pike.

Hannah grunted acknowledgement at that, then said, 'Be careful in there. They might not be programmed against riveting us to some wall.'

They entered through the cargo lock and found a massive hole punched through the floors of the rim itself. They followed this down through three floors and soon found what they had come here to see.

229

An entire rim floor had been cut away, leaving a groove twenty metres wide extending concentrically in both directions for as far as they could see. All around this, considerably more had also been cut away to expose the main structural beams. To these had been attached further beams, which converged in towards the groove, where they supported a section of . . . *something*. A massive collection of electromagnets enwrapped a fifty-metre length of mirrored tube that was about half a metre in diameter. Even as she watched, robots were working to fit another two-metre section of tube, while a small, specially designed cylindrical robot was busy actually inside the tube simultaneously welding, grinding down and then spraying and optically polishing the latest join just after it had cooled.

'All round the station rim,' observed Brigitta.

Hannah nodded. This looked as if someone – or something – was building a particle accelerator right around the inside of the station rim – a particle accelerator fifteen kilometres long.

'So what the fuck is this?' asked Pike.

'I have absolutely no idea,' said Hannah.

'I see you have come to inspect,' said a voice through her suit radio. 'Optimum build rate would increase with less diversification.'

The proctor walked out onto the remains of the floor that had been mostly cut away, something other than gecko boots keeping it in place. It wore a suit made of some kind of shiny material that covered it entirely, and it carried in its right hand a long metal staff.

'What the hell are you talking about?' demanded Brigitta. Obviously they were all hearing this exchange over their radios.

'But work rate should increase once your weapons are done,' it continued.

This proctor wasn't Paul, but the one that had named itself Judd. She recognized it only because of the staff it had taken to carrying – a titanium scaffolding tube packed with esoteric electronics. Paul had called Judd 'the builder', but offered no further explanation. However, at that time, Hannah had seen how, now they were free, the proctors were changing quite rapidly, and all of them in different ways. She had also begun to notice, now that she had overcome her initial reaction of stark terror, that there was something quite patronizing about them.

'What are you building here, Judd?' she asked.

'To schematic ADAR 45A, as detailed in work roster.'

Suddenly Hannah remembered an earlier conversation she had been witness to, and things that had been said during their first tangle-box communication with Mars. Recalling this, the situation started to become clearer.

'I need to talk to Paul,' she declared. 'And to that lunatic Jasper Rhine.'

He remembered natural sleep, that moment of sliding from dream or nightmare to a semiconscious state wherein he could distinguish between the real and the unreal. He had reached it again both here, in his human body, and elsewhere in his backups and also in the computer systems of Argus. A fragment of his awareness recognized that consciousness for him was no longer the simple state experienced by any normal human being. He had too *much* mind at that moment for it all to surface to the real world, and simultaneously too little control over his disparate parts. And again, as his mental activity ramped up once more, and his mind coughed and spluttered like an engine with a broken block, he found his way towards that state experienced when he was first amalgamating with that AI copy of his mind called Janus.

Why?

Why exist at all? Continued existence was an artefact of evolution first instituted by replicators in the chemical soup of Earth's early oceans. It was a thing generated by chance, before minds had even existed on Earth. Everything else – every reason for existence that humans deluded themselves with – stemmed from this happenstance. All came down to replication, the avoidance of pain so as to evade damage that might interfere with the process; brute survival for no purpose other than survival itself.

He could readily die now. In a place where the human dead lay in mountains, and oceans of maggots squirmed, he could disconnect and divide. He could shut down the once-autonomous processes he now semi-consciously controlled. He could reach out from his backup and turn off the power that sustained his heart. He could do all this without pain, without feeling loss, and then sink into the nirvana of oblivion.

Why not just die?

Brute survival replied, 'Because of the wonders.'

A choice to live – a choice to die, and no reason for either.

'The wonder is the reason,' said a voice he now recognized as coming from within, yet from the shape of a mind not his own. 'Nothing worthwhile comes without effort, without sacrifice. If dying is so easy for you – and I think you're fooling yourself with that idea – then you must know it's not worthwhile.'

Circular logic.

'It's how we stay alive.'

The double fence of the Albanian enclave in the Dinaric

Alps stood over to his right, readerguns lying between its two layers, perched on squat and slightly corroded aluminium towers. He could walk over there, climb the fence, continue walking on past the guns. That was no guaranteed route to death, though, since the SAs here were considered just too valuable to be shot while trying to escape. Enforcers would come after him, track his implant by satellite and haul him back. Anyway, if he started heading over that way, his companion would soon grab him, stop him. She'd always known instinctively when he was about to do something that threatened his own survival.

When do you leave?

'Tomorrow.'

To build spaceships.

'Yes.'

To live, one must become all one can.

He gazed around at the enclosure, annoyed that visitors were prohibited from speaking to or even seeing any of the other . . . inmates. He would have liked Hannah to be here.

I'm getting out of here.

'You'll get yourself killed.'

Probably.

He felt an overpowering déjà vu and also an underlying nostalgia. He wasn't talking at that moment, he realized, but remembering something from the wreckage that interrogator Salem Smith had made of his mind. In that memory, he turned towards the one he had been speaking to, at last trying to identify her. But again that nameless woman he had seen communicating via the tangle box with Mars was back, and now gazing at him pensively.

He swung away, found himself again amidst the images of Earth's dead and pictures relayed from cams within Argus.

He gazed through the eyes of Judd and sensed impossible reaches of time, and also deep wisdom. Judd dipped his head in acknowledgement, being of the opinion that something had to be done, to complete and to make the machine work. Sliding away again, Saul touched this and that control, then nested in bones.

Mars

Driving out in a crawler towards Shankil's Butte, Var bitterly remembered the last time she travelled out here. Was there some irony in the knowledge that, just beside where this chunk of rock had been shoved up from the peneplain, lay the fault that Rhone and his assorted crew were currently widening? It was from this butte that Ricard or one of his men had fired the shots that killed Gisender, shots which to Var's mind had marked a point of no return. It had certainly represented such a point for her when she found Gisender's corpse, viewed the forbidden broadcast from Earth, then subsequently discovered that Ricard had sent a shepherd out to seize her.

A crump reverberated through the thin air, and a cloud of dust rose from the installation ahead. What looked like a number of large chemical tankers lay near the butte, but they were in fact atmosphere-sealed cabins. They had originally been used while Antares Base was being finished, and had recently been salvaged from their old site just outside Hex Four. Now they clustered about the foot of a derrick which supported heavy hydraulic motors driving cable drums, from which hung every last metre of heavy cable they had been able to find anywhere on the base. Beside this derrick also rested a small mountain of rubble hauled up from the blasting below.

Var drove through the thinning dust cloud, drew to a halt beside one of the cabins, sealed her suit and exited the crawler. The rouge of Mars began rising in a cloud about her feet, before tracking away in an arc behind her as she walked towards the excavation. Reaching the edge, she caught hold of one of the derrick's beams and peered down. The hole was nearly fifty metres across and cut raggedly down through dusty murk. However, she could just see a big skip down there, laden with rubble, and the work lights glaring from two stripped-down robotic diggers suspended by their own cables. It looked like a hellish place to work.

'Martinez is two hundred metres down,' came the comment relayed through her suit radio, which at that moment was set on line-of-sight com. She glanced around, to see Rhone rounding the nearest cabin and heading over. He pointed up at the derrick. 'We're almost at full extension now, but it'll be another hundred metres before we reach the big fault.'

'So, what now?' she asked, stepping back from the hole and turning to face him fully.

She wasn't entirely sure what Rhone was doing out here. Unlike her, he had no need to escape the hostile atmosphere inside the base; unlike her, he wasn't being viewed as a necessary evil. But, then, even that was better than being considered an *unnecessary* evil.

He came up to stand before her, resting his hands on his hips. 'Martinez reckons that cutting a ramp down towards the fault is the only answer. It will be heavy work but, so he says, without any extra cable it's the only way, and I'm afraid it's going to take a long time.'

'He's the nearest thing we have to an expert on this sort of thing, so we'll have to take his word for it.' Var suppressed her frustration. Delays were something she definitely didn't want to hear about, especially now. 'How long before we can start moving stuff down there?'

'A few months yet. Once we're through to the fault, we'll need to relocate the lifting rig further down, so as to lower a dozer. Once it's down there, we can use it to push the rubble up into a ramp, and to infill a road running along the bottom for about five hundred metres. After that, we reach the big ledge, which we'll need to level out a bit before we can start building.'

Perhaps Rhone had heard she was coming out here, so had come to play his new role as her close scientific adviser. Lately it had been difficult to avoid the man, and his reports and assessments.

'But if we had more cable,' said Var, 'none of this would be necessary?'

'Just infilling for the road,' said Rhone. 'If we didn't have to blast to make room for the ramp, and spend time building it, we'd gain a month or more.'

It was crazy. They had ways of making so many things on the base, but the kind of high-tensile cable needed for this purpose was, for the present, beyond them.

'It's suitable down there?' Var enquired absently, still thinking over the cable problem. 'I've only seen the seismic map.'

'Yes, it's suitable.' Rhone nodded. 'It's about three hundred metres wide and nearly a kilometre long.'

Another crump issued from underfoot and the ground shuddered. They quickly stepped back as a cloud of dust rose out of the hole.

'What about ice?' Var asked.

'Ten kilometres away,' said Rhone, frowning. 'Martinez

just wants to get on with this, but I wonder if we should ensure we can get to it – by taking some blasting gear and digging equipment through. We don't want to move the whole base down there only to find we haven't got access to water. That'd just mean slow death.'

'No,' said Var, 'this is where we are going. We don't have the time now to change our minds.'

Rhone turned and gazed at her. 'Bad news?'

'The *Scourge* is on its way,' she replied. 'Long-range imaging showed it blasting away from Earth orbit just two hours ago, but even if we hadn't seen that for ourselves, the jingoistic broadcasts on ETV would have been enough warning.'

'So we have maybe a year and a half?'

'Yes, that's all. We need to get this all done as quickly as we can.'

Considering how quickly things were proceeding here, even with the necessity of building a ramp underground, it still seemed that they had plenty of time. But Var knew better. Since their supplies of regolith bonding were limited, they would have to dismantle the original base, transport all the blocks over here and lower them down. The whole infrastructure would have to be transported: all the hexes piece by piece, Hydroponics, the Arboretum, the reactor. In fact she could think of nothing they could afford to leave behind. Their task was essentially like relocating an entire village down into a mineshaft.

'Do you want to go down for a look?' Rhone asked.

She did, in fact, but she said, 'No, I'd just slow Martinez down.' She turned away and headed towards her crawler.

'I'll tell him when he comes up with his next load,' said Rhone.

'You do that.' Var halted and turned round, a sudden thought occurring to her. Perhaps it was simply being here again, being reminded of Gisender and her ostensible mission to collect fibre optics from the old Trench Base radio station. 'We've got lots of equipment in Antares Base that came from the old Trench Base. How was it transported there?'

'By ATV, I think,' Rhone replied.

'That doesn't make sense,' said Var, feeling a sudden excitement. 'An ATV journey would have been thousands of kilometres. A more logical route would have been the direct one, which would mean going up the side of Coprates Chasma.'

'Cable,' said Rhone, catching on quickly. 'I'll need to check the base records. I can do that from here.' He stabbed a thumb towards one of the cabins. 'I should be able to find out for sure if there's anything still there.'

'Yes, you do that,' said Var.

'If there *is* cable there, I'll organize a mission at once. In fact I'll go myself, as I'm feeling a bit of a loose wheel lately. It's the practicality of people like Martinez we need most of all here right now.'

Var instantly did not like his eagerness to set off on such a mission. Was this something he had been aiming for?

'Maybe I'll go, too,' she said, just to test his reaction. 'It would be nice to get away from all the invisible daggers plunging into my back.'

He seemed to accept that comment at once. 'We'll need to take cutting equipment, and an ATV trailer with a motor and cable drum.'

'Check first,' said Var, 'then let me know.'

She turned away and continued towards her crawler, then climbed inside and just sat at the controls, thinking hard.

238

Maybe a little trip away from Antares Base would be a good thing in a number of respects. Maybe, by being at close quarters with the man, she could solve the puzzle that was Rhone of Mars Science, and find out for sure if he intended to stick an even more visible knife in her back.

Earth

From an interminably boring childhood to supervised school and then university Serene had never really had any friends. Family being something she wanted to forget, she had quickly forgotten. All she had were colleagues, who would receive the brief and snappy response of, 'I am interested only in now and in the future,' if they ever enquired about her past. As far as she was concerned, the immutable past had formed her as she was, and she was satisfied with that. She did not like to think too much about her formative years, but she was thinking about them now.

'A specialized search program picked it out of the, on average, seventeen million personal messages directed towards you every day, ma'am,' said Elkin, the new leader of her team of PAs.

Serene gazed steadily at the text message relayed to her palmtop, reading and rereading every word of it, a deep feeling of puzzlement growing within her. He was *alive*. She had never even considered the possibility. She sent his citizen code to the house mainframe then, forcing her face clear of expression, looked up at Elkin.

Her PA leader was a big-breasted, wide-hipped woman who dressed to try and hide her obvious womanhood. But even clad in a loose grey business trouser suit, with her black hair in a pageboy cut, she still oozed sexuality. Serene smiled to herself, at the forefront of her mind being the knowledge that Elkin quite enjoyed sessions with three men at a time, claiming, as she had recently explained to the three enforcers currently satisfying her needs, that she liked to be 'all filled up'. Serene regularly watched the security tapes, which were quite a bit better than much of the porn she had seen.

'Thank you, Elkin, that will be all.'

The woman gave her a brief nod and retreated.

Now alone, Serene called up the file located under the citizen code she had input, studied the current image of a squat muscular man who, after the treatments he could obtain as a valued SA, appeared to be in his forties. This man was actually eighty-six. She reflected on her brief thoughts about sex and, understanding where they had come from, felt a sudden annoying surge of unaccustomed guilt. She checked his history, starting from twenty-eight years ago at the point where she herself had diverged from it. Under tight political supervision, he'd spent a further nine years in Berlin, in the Brandenburg Tower, continuing his research on population genetics, related dynamics and psychology. He'd provided statistical analyses of great use to the Inspectorate: data that had resulted in large savings on resources. It was always useful to know precisely how hard you needed to wield the big stick, and precisely what degree of control might be necessary when dealing with vast populations.

At the end of those nine years, he had taken a partner, and produced twin daughters who, due to his past record, were immediately taken away from him. Next working in South America, his wife of four years, having been caught making illegal enquiries about his record, was sent off for adjustment.

She died shortly after being released into supervised accommodation. The surface report cited a domestic accident with some kitchen appliance. The underlying report noted that her kitchen cam had failed and gone into a maintenance backlog, while she had sliced open her wrists with the blade removed from a Safecarver and bled to death on the kitchen floor.

Five years ago he had been sent back to work in Europe, sometimes in the Brandenburg Tower again, more often as an adviser to the four main European delegates. It annoyed Serene that he had been so successful in his way. Her aim had been to get him sent for adjustment twenty-eight years ago, but he had been far too useful for that.

Serene input his call code, ensuring a console contact only, since she wanted to see his face. He must have been waiting because he answered within just a few seconds. He looked haggard, dark under the eyes and, when he saw her, he jerked back from the screen, his expression showing a commingled disgust and fear. She couldn't understand why he had sent her a message, then she noted him fingering his collar and realized why: he'd grown tired of waiting for the axe to fall.

'Hello, Papa,' she said, smiling calmly as she remembered her love for him despite his dictatorial ways. She remembered how, with her mother dead, she had tried to help him, tried at the age of twelve to relieve some of the pressure he was under. Serene knew all about sex, all about the needs of men, since her political officer had already shown her, and she wanted to take control. She wanted to supplant the various 'nannies' that visited, taking his attention away from her. But when she had tried, he had pushed her away, and that was the first time she saw that look on his face. The pain

241

of rejection sent a wave of heat through her even now. Yes, she understood his fear, and she understood how he would have felt that to respond to her was plain wrong. But they had been different: they had always been different.

'Serene,' he said, 'I see you've done very well for yourself.'

Serene had already found and cued up the code to his collar, and her finger now hovered over the send button. Then, as she gazed at his face, she withdrew her finger. She was now the dictator of Earth, with all Earth's resources at her disposal. A sudden twisted excitement arose in her, almost sexual. She could do anything she wanted. She was in total control.

'Yes, I have done very well, Papa,' she replied. 'I see that you haven't done so badly either. You were an adviser to the four top European delegates, I understand.'

'I did do well,' he said bitterly, 'despite being accused by my own daughter of beating and raping her. But I haven't been trying to reach you so we can discuss the different routes our careers have taken . . . daughter.' He spat out the last word, then reached up and touched his collar. 'I want to know about this. When, Serene? When are you going to send the code to this and finish off what you started?'

What an arrogant self-obsessed idiot he was. That he wore such a collar was just chance, just wherever he came in the list, which included over half a billion other SAs. But through his self-obsession, through his belief that this had to be personal, he had revealed himself to her. Now she knew he was alive and well.

'You are just one of many, Papa, but since you are my father, I will order that your collar be removed at once.' No way did she want one of those occasional collar malfunctions to take him out, for they still had unfinished business. She paused, momentarily puzzled, not entirely sure what that un-finished business was. 'I will also be sending an aero for you.'

'Why?' he said. 'Do you want me to be facing you when you kill me? Didn't you do enough when you reported me to your political officer for the very offence I refused to commit?'

Apparently not, since he had survived the experience.

'And how did you do it? How did you fake the evidence?' he asked.

The fact that, at twelve, she was no longer a virgin had been taken care of by her political officer a few months before. She was one of the many young girls that that particular guardian of Committee ideology had used as part of his personal harem. Faking the evidence against her father had been easy. She just waited until after a visit from one of the 'nannies' he employed, and then scraped it off his bedsheets.

'That is all in the past now,' she replied smoothly. 'Right now I am in need of advisers in precisely your discipline, and your name has come up on a shortlist. It is in fact quite a happy coincidence that you yourself also tried to get in contact with me.'

'Well, I guess with two-thirds of the original upper execu-tive being fried, you need to know where to concentrate the razorbirds and shepherds next.' He grimaced, looked to one side for a moment, then focused back on the screen. She remembered that he'd done a lot of work involving the deployment of shepherds, and also on techniques to increase the public fear of them. 'But I think you're lying to me,' he continued. 'You were always very good at it.'

'We'll talk further after you arrive, and, Papa,' she gazed at him like a parent humouring a worried child, 'please understand that the past remains the past. We, here and now, are making the future.'

'Yeah, right.'

Serene cut the connection, then took a wet wipe from the pack on her desk, to cleanse her hands, which suddenly felt slimy. She felt her lies had sounded close to plausibility, but he had only accepted them because he had no choice. The only real alternative for him now, if he had even a gram of understanding, would be to kill himself at once. He must surely realize that the only person on the planet ever to have caused her to feel shame would have to pay a heavy price indeed.

'Elkin!'

The woman was back through the door in a second. 'Ma'am?'

'Send a grab squad to pick him up at once,' said Serene. 'And tell them that if he dies, then they die shortly afterwards.'

'Ma'am.'

'I also want you to get Interrogator Nelson here, quick as you like.' Serene waved a dismissive hand, noting Elkin's brief look of fear at the mention of that particular interrogator. No one liked Nelson getting too close. He was someone Messina had personally recruited from an Inspectorate HQ in Bangladesh, and everyone knew what he could do. In Inspectorate circles he was known as Leonardo. This related to the artistry of his work, just as that work of his called to mind the anatomical sketches of Leonardo Da Vinci.

10

Crowd Control

The extreme civil unrest that followed the Golden Decade looked, for a while, as if it might bring everything crashing down, especially when elements of the military and police forces of the world began to side with the protestors. The use of pain amplifiers began to bring this under control, but with the loyalty of those using them sometimes being questionable, governments wanted something more reliable. The first shepherds were quickly designed and rapidly hurried off the production lines. This could all have ended in disaster for the governments concerned, for the machines could have been laughable failures, inefficient, prone to breaking down, which was the usual way that state-instigated projects ran. However, because of the urgency in deploying them, bureaucratic interference in their design was minimal, and the roboticists came up with something fit for purpose, rugged, fast . . . and terrifying. During the first ten years of their deployment, they killed off the rioting and seated themselves firmly in the public consciousness – so much so that, even though better robots are now available, shepherds are the tool of preference for the riot breakers.

Scourge

After hour upon hour under massive acceleration, Clay felt the terror just grow tired and slink away, out of his head.

Finally the chemical booster detached, and small steering jets fired up on it to put it on course far behind a long train of other boosters from the old Mars Travellers, which were even now falling into orbit around Jupiter, where, some centuries hence, they could be salvaged either for their metals or for reuse. The floor tilted as the fusion drive took up the load, applying a full gravity of acceleration. For some while yet, crew and passengers would not have to tolerate zero gravity, though to get from one end of the ship to the other they would have to climb ladders as if they were ascending and descending inside a two-kilometre-high tower.

'Now for you,' said Scotonis, 'just a long and boring wait.'

'And for you?' asked Clay, undoing his straps.

'Weapons drills, training, stress testing and diagnostics, and we have to continue fitting out the interior,' said the captain. 'The ship is full of materials and components yet to be installed, supplies yet to find their proper home. And it's also full of people who'll die if they don't quickly acquire the right education.'

Clay stood up. 'I'll head for my cabin now.' He felt the need to add at least something else, as he gazed at the captain, his pilot and gunnery officer. 'Congratulations on a successful launch – may our mission be equally successful.'

'I'm sure we'll try our best,' said Pilot Officer Trove, while fingering her strangulation collar.

Clay headed out through the safety airlock at the back of the bridge, noting that it was even more difficult to walk in gecko boots in full gravity. Outside the bridge it took him a moment to locate himself on the simple map he had memorized: the internal floor and airlock now lying in a different position from when he had entered. Ahead of the bridge was where the railguns, missile ports, armoury for ship's weapons and access to the single turret-mounted maser were located. The passenger compartments lay directly behind it. Beyond this area lay the holds and barracks, which sat over the massive engine and surrounding engine room. He found his way to a cageway extending downwards, connected his safety cable to a bar beside one of the ladders within, and began to descend.

Halfway down, he paused to watch four crewmen descend past him on two other ladders. They did not have their safety lines attached and went down very fast, almost in a controlled fall. Finally, he reached the entrance into the passenger compartments and strolled along, checking door numbers until finding his own. He pushed his hand against the lock, whereupon a laser above the door briefly scanned his pupil while some other emitter doubtless also checked his implant code. The door lock opened with a clonk, and a push sent it swinging inwards. He felt almost disappointed to find a conventional hinged door here, having been raised on a diet of trashy politically approved SF where every door was inevitably a sliding version.

His one-room apartment was spacious, though that amount of space would soon decrease once he folded down the bed, pulled the shower unit out from the wall or expanded the collapsed cupboards and desk to accept his belongings, which currently resided in a plastic crate resting in the middle of the floor. He headed straight over to the collapsed cupboards and pulled them out from the wall, opened one of them and found a number of highly compressed packages. Clay stripped off his spacesuit, securing each component of it in numbered compartments allocated in the cupboard, then tore open one of the compressed packages. As he shook it out, the ship suit expanded, its quilted layers busily sucking up air.

He pulled it on, then tugged on the slippers also provided in the package, before heading over to the desk.

The desk also folded out from the wall and, once out, revealed an inset keyboard which, with a touch, started up the computer, the screen on the wall above instantly flickering on. Again a laser scanned his eye and another emitter read his implant, then he was in. His security clearance aboard this ship was the highest – higher even than the captain's – and, barring some override from Earth, there were things he could do in this cabin that he had, over the last few months, been unable to achieve.

Within a minute he was into the security system, knew the location of everyone aboard the vessel, and could check them with cams, and in some areas, if he wished, fire up readerguns. These guns were slightly different from the earthbound ones, in that they fired low-impact ammunition so as not to damage the infrastructure of the ship. Another option was inducers, usually in cabins or corridors, but not anywhere critical. He was now very powerful aboard this ship, but killing or tortur-ing anyone was not his aim. Checking the system, he found both the cam and the inducer in his room, and shut them down. After that he lowered the bed from the wall, stood on it and, using a small electrical tool-set, undid the light fitting to reveal the cam and the inducer inside, and disconnected them.

Clay found himself sweating, for such simple actions had long been classified as a capital offence. Now he opened his crate of belongings and took out three items, placing them on the bed. The first was a metal egg which hinged open to reveal a small compartment inside: numerous gold electrical connec-tions lining it and ready lights coming on across the now exposed face. He put it to one side, then picked up the next item: a tool rather like a gun but with a wide flat barrel, inside which surgical steel gleamed. He placed this down on the bed, too, then rolled up his right sleeve before taking up the same tool again and passing it up and down his arm. The thing beeped at one point, like a metal detector, and he finally positioned it so its tone was continuous, before pressing it against his skin and activating it.

Immediately that point on his arm grew numb, since the tool was emitting an inducer signal somewhat like white noise, effectively shutting down his pain response directly under-neath it. It did not shut down other nerves, however, and he felt the cut of the blades extruding from the barrel, the four-pronged forceps closing and pulling, then the cold of wound glue and the brief pressure of a clamp. When he took the thing away from his arm, there was hardly any evidence of it having done anything but for a small smear of blood. He opened the side of the device, popped out his implant and then inserted it into the compartment in the ovoid – this being a diagnostic tester which would persuade the implant that it still resided inside a human body. Apparently, Delegate Angone of Region SE Africa had kept his implant in precisely such a tester, which was why Serene had to use a TEB nuke to remove him from existence.

Clay inserted the closed tester into the top pocket of his ship suit. Now the only way his implant could kill him was if someone discovered his second capital offence, in having removed it.

The next device he held in his palm and contemplated pensively. It was just a small cylinder, no larger than a marker pen, with a button on one end and a torch switch to the side. He reached up and touched his strangulation collar. The thing about these collars was that they had fibre diamond imbedded and were ostensibly impossible to remove without specialist equipment that was now on proscribed lists. Even using diamond shears was a very risky option. If you could manage to insert one blade up between neck and collar, you had to then cut through the collar instantly in one go, for, the moment just one imbedded filament was severed, the collar would activate at its fastest setting – so miss just one strand of the diamond, and your head was on the floor. All this, Clay thought, gave the misleading impression that the device could not be disabled.

The device began whining as soon as he clicked on the torch button, building up a massive charge. The weakness in these collars was both the battery and the microscopic motors it drove. Clay took hold of the motor, to locate it precisely, then placed the end of the charging device directly over it. He found himself sweating again, contemplating the calculated ten per cent failure rate of this method, and the five per cent chance of it actually activating the collar instead. Then, when the device reached full charge, he didn't give himself a chance for further thought and pressed the button. The device made a crack, blue arclight flaring under his chin and the collar warming up under the EM radiation pulse. For a moment it felt tighter but, as he lowered the small DEMP emitter, he realized that was just his imagination, caused by fear. And, really, that fear would never go away because, though he knew there was a ninety per cent chance that he had rendered the collar inactive, he would never know for sure unless Serene sent the signal to tighten it.

Clay put away his tools, considered finding some way of disposing of them but then decided the risk of them being found was minimal out here, and he might yet have use for them. He reconnected the cam but left the inducer detached

– just a fault no one had yet picked up. Next, feeling as if he was being watched, he unpacked and stowed the rest of his belongings, before collapsing and putting away the crate. As he did all this, he wished his previous actions had not been necessary, but knew they were. He had finally come to understood that loyal service led to his knowing too much, and that made it all the more likely that Galahad would eventually kill him. Those close to her were in nearly as much danger as those who might rebel against her.

Earth

Messina had ensured that his house – being the residence of Earth's dictator for a lifetime he had intended never to end – contained everything he might need, hence the underground suite of sound-insulated torture and interrogation cells lying just off the wine cellars, which could easily be reached via the private elevator in his office.

'I'm an old-fashioned sort of guy,' said Nelson. 'I know that an inducer can deliver the same sort of agony as any torture ever imagined and that now, with cerebral implants, it's possible to convince the victim that he really is being physically tortured, but that's not the same.' He shook his head in disappointment. 'There's no artistry in it.'

There was something wrong with Nelson. That he was a state-employed psychopath was a given, in fact there was no end to such people available, but he was also something beyond that. She knew from the reports on him that the wiring in his head was linked up in all sort of odd ways, that he possessed a form of synaesthesia so that smells had colour and his sense of touch was audible, that his pain and pleasure

251

circuitry was all tangled and he used an inducer on himself for personal gratification – but he was also thoroughly, unconventionally brilliant. His deep studies of how a body could be ruined – transformed, as he would put it – and his endless exploration of pain and horror had perversely contributed a great deal to the advancement of medical science. In fact his research, statistically, had saved more lives than it had taken. Of course, that had never been his aim. He had only ever wanted to keep his victims alive in their agony for as long as possible.

'So, what can you do?' asked Serene, as she studied the white-tiled walls, the surgical table, and next to it the complicated metal framework for full-body restraint, alongside the heart monitors and other equipment usually the preserve of delegates' private hospitals.

As Nelson began to explain the sheer extent of his craft, Serene quickly realized that, if she actually went through with this, she would be taking a step beyond her purported aims. Everything she had done thus far, no matter how grim, or how cruel, had been justified for the future of Earth. The extermination of billions had been an act that had to be carried out before the pressure on Earth's ecology passed beyond the point of no return. Her concealment of the fact that she herself had committed this act had been necessary because, without that concealment, the degree of hatred that would have been aroused against her would make it impossible for her to govern. Her wiping-out of the remainder of the Committee had been necessary, too – things needed to be done quickly, so it was foolish to waste time in debate about who should be in power, and foolish to waste resources on infighting. That she had ruthlessly seized power was in itself proof of her fitness to rule. Subsequent exterminations had been necessary too, for Earth's population was still far too high, and therefore targeted exterminations, where they would do the most good, were the best option. She felt perfectly justified in all that she had done, and every person she had killed had been eliminated out of necessity. What she intended now, however, was altogether unnecessary.

'I'm bringing him down now,' said the voice over her fone.

'Very good,' she replied, turning away from Nelson's monologue. 'I take it he is still unharmed?'

'Just a few bruises.'

Serene swung back to face Nelson, who was watching her with almost childlike curiosity, his head tilted to one side.

'Go get ready,' she said, and watched him head over to a nearby sink to wash his hands, then don his aseptic overalls and pull on surgical gloves. Then she turned to watch the lights ranged on the wall just above the elevator. She suddenly felt hot and cold flushes that were a combination of both shame and excitement. From her childhood she recognized this sensation as the thrill of deliberately doing something she knew to be wrong.

The elevator arrived and the doors slid open. Sack stepped out, lizard-skinned and the colour of graphite, in a cream business suit, like some CGI fantasy figure. His hand lay gently on the shoulder of Donald Galahad, her father, as he guided him into the room. By contrast, her father's clothing was filthy and torn, with piss stains on the front of his corduroy trousers, his head dipped and his hands bound behind his back. He looked up and his eyes widened when he saw her, but he could say nothing around the big plastic plug jammed into his mouth.

'Keroskin,' exclaimed Nelson delightedly. The man was gazing at Sack. This new hard skin had not been approved for general use yet, but was known about in medical circles. 'How does it feel?' Nelson asked.

Sack gazed at him doubtfully with ophidian eyes, then glanced questioningly at Serene.

'Answer the man,' she said.

'Feels like a big thick scab all over,' Sack replied.

'We must talk further,' said Nelson, his attention already focusing on the captive as he said, 'He needs to be stripped.'

Serene felt a surge in her groin, and nodded to Sack. 'Go ahead.'

Sack first snipped the plastic ties binding her father's wrists, and one of his hands immediately went to his mouth to grab the plug and lever it out.

'Serene!' he hissed, fear and rage in his voice, then he tried to fight Sack off, which was a complete waste of effort as soon as Sack touched him with a disabler and dropped him, writhing into unconsciousness, on the floor. Sack then clicked open a flick knife and made short work of the prisoner's soiled clothing. Serene stared at her father's naked body, noted that it had changed very little in twenty-eight years, remembered the hot shame and excitement when, like a loving daughter, she had climbed into his bed to cuddle him, also remembered him violently pushing her away when she reached down and began rubbing his penis. The look on his face had changed from shock to disgust when he had gazed at her then, fear taking hold a second later when he realized the vulnerable position he was in.

'Into the frame,' ordered Nelson.

Donald Galahad finally regained consciousness as Nelson was scrubbing him down with some antibiotic and antiviral solution.

'Why?' he said, his voice raw. 'You already destroyed me.'

Serene stepped forwards, folding her arms. 'You know why you are here?'

He nodded once, briefly. 'I rejected you. I rejected the advances of a perverted precocious brat, and for that you hate me and will never forgive me.'

'Quite right,' said Serene. She glanced at Nelson but he didn't seem to be listening to this exchange. Instead he walked over to a large wheeled cabinet and folded it open. Then she glanced at Sack, but could read no expression in that lizard face, before returning her attention to her father. 'You are now,' she continued, 'going to experience the most unbelievable agony, Father, and it is just going to go on and on.'

'Please,' he said, 'just kill me. Just kill me, yourself.' He bowed his head and tears dripped from his eyes. She felt an odd rush of embarrassment at seeing this. 'Please, my little Serene. Please . . .'

After that 'little Serene' – which reminded her that he had never said it to her again after that time she climbed into his bed – tuned him out and focused instead on Nelson, who was viewing the surgical gear packed inside the cabinet.

'You can get started,' she told him.

Nelson did not waste a second. First he hooked up a couple of drips, into tubes of which he now injected various prepared concoctions. Her father remained with his head bowed, weeping quietly. Nelson then went back to his cabinet and, like someone choosing chocolates from a box, made his selection.

Donald Galahad's scream was an endless agonized full-throated warbling that just went on and on. Serene could detect notes of offence, disbelief, injustice – in fact a whole array of underlying emotions. She wondered if she could become a connoisseur of such noises, listening to them like some Epicurean listening to a Mozart clarinet quartet. Then, as Nelson finally reached the top of his victim's stomach, the note changed, probably because the muscles had been sliced open now and her father couldn't put everything into his scream.

'The trick, of course,' said Nelson, glancing round at her, while holding up the bloody electric cautery knife, 'is to give them a sufficient quantity of my special cocktail so as to keep them alive, but not enough to dull the pain.'

The split now ran from her father's groin right up to his solar plexus, layers of yellowish fat and muscle everting like obscene lips. However, the knife he had used had been designed for bloodless surgery, hot cells all across its surface detecting and cauterizing blood vessels just moments after the edge had passed through them. There was therefore hardly any blood at all. Nelson next put the knife aside and picked up a small conventional scalpel, pushed open the fatty lips of the wound and reached inside, snipped neatly at this and that, and then all her father's intestines flooded out into the wide stainless steel bowl positioned at waist level in front of his abdomen. He screamed again; more in disbelief than in agony as he stared down at his own entrails. Then he made a small grunting sound and his head slumped down on his chest.

'Ah,' said Nelson, pulling up her father's head by the hair and fixing it back into the clamp behind. 'Overload.' He turned towards her again, smiling confidently. 'Don't worry, five or ten minutes from now he'll regain consciousness and suffer just as much agony. Our only problem will be in trying to stop him wrecking his vocal cords.'

'How long can you keep him in agony and still alive?' Serene asked.

'My record has been one year and six months,' he replied

proudly. 'There's not much point in going on longer than that – because there's not much left, you understand?'

'I understand,' said Serene. She turned to Sack, who had been watching the proceedings impassively. 'You stay here for the moment. You can tell Nelson all about your new skin.'

He looked at her in puzzlement, but obeyed as she turned and headed for the elevator. The truth was that she didn't want him or anyone else near her right then. She managed to hold on until the elevator doors drew closed, then she went down on her knees and threw up on the floor. Big body-racking sobs ensued, until she stopped them by banging her forehead against the metal wall until blood ran and dripped off her nose. Back up in her private rooms, she sealed the wound with glue and further tidied herself up. A brief instruction then summoned one of the house staff to clean the elevator floor.

Mars

Shankil's Butte lay in a haze of dust far behind them. In the low gravity, dust and other particulate matter lingered in the air for a long time. The problem wasn't as great as in zero gravity – an issue Var had often needed to deal with during construction of those Mars Travellers she worked on – but it still was a problem. Down inside his hole, Martinez solved this with extractor fans pumping the thin air into big bonded fibre bags with a sufficiently loose weave.

'Thank heavens for the Hoover,' he had said.

By the puzzled expressions of the rest attending that particular meeting, Var realized they had no idea what he was talking about.

'Haarsen is doing well,' said Rhone from beside her. He had run out of conversation after a few hours, gone for a sleep in the cargo compartment of the ATV, but was now back again. She still couldn't quite fathom him, certainly didn't trust him.

She glanced at him now. The weapons expert, Haarsen, had rendered chemicals from the Martian regolith to turn into a usable explosive. Once he'd got the process nailed, he had turned it over to Leo in Stores, and turned his attention to other projects. He had designed easy and practical processes for manufacturing weapons, and was now well on his way to building a DEMP emitter.

'Yes, he is,' she agreed, 'but I wonder if it's going to be enough.' She stabbed a thumb behind them. 'He wants to put the DEMP in a bunker on top of Shankil's Butte. If the *Scourge* comes here, it can railgun the DEMP emitter then drop a nuke down the hole Martinez is digging. Failing that, the two thousand troops aboard can be landed and come down after us.'

They now knew that the *Scourge* possessed shuttles capable of descending through Martian atmosphere. And of course, even if the *Scourge* didn't come after them this time, it might come in the future, or some other ship would be sent, produced in that sudden hive of industry growing in Earth orbit.

'What other options do we have?' asked Rhone, and for the first time she saw fear in his eyes. Maybe until now it had all been just an intellectual exercise for him.

Var gazed steadily ahead, while considering how close Shankil's Butte stood to their rabbit hole. Perhaps there were some further options . . .

'We'll go with what we have now,' she decided, 'but maybe we should consider laying some of the new explosive around the butte. A series of properly placed charges might be our last option. You're the geologist – you tell me.'

'What do you mean?' Rhone asked.

'I mean, would it be possible to drop a few million tonnes of stone into that hole to plug it up?'

'Yes, it's possible.' Rhone seemed a little nauseated at the prospect.

Var recalled how, upon seeing the shepherd that Ricard had sent striding after her across the Martian landscape, she had thought it looked like something out of H. G. Wells's *The War of the Worlds*. Future Martians, she felt, only stood a chance of remaining free and surviving the dictatorship of Earth if they took the route of another such Wellsian creation.

'A future branch of the human race,' she said idly.

It seemed that Lopomac, who had been in the cargo compartment behind, with two recruits from Martinez's men, had been reading her mind. 'We become morlocks,' he said, leaning through into the cockpit, and seemingly amused by the whole idea. 'Historically, it's not unusual for rebels or freedom fighters to go literally underground.'

'And that will be our future?' said Rhone. 'Always under the ground and skulking in shadows?'

'I'd rather skulk in shadows that spend any time in a nicely well-lit adjustment cell.'

Rhone seemed to have no answer to that, and Var wondered if his problem was actually accepting that there was no way back to Earth for them. If that was the case, then he would be completely the wrong person to be leader of Antares Base. He would merely get them all killed.

Var pointed ahead to a distant structure now becoming visible and changed the subject. 'So, how much cable are we talking about?'

Rhone seemed happier with this question. 'The cliff that the lift was positioned above is nearly a kilometre high, and the cradle ran up and down between two cables, so at a minimum there's two thousand metres of it.'

'More than enough,' opined Lopomac.

The distant object was now clearer: a kind of frame around some sort of bulky object, probably a motor or cable drum, though much of it was concealed behind the line of the horizon. Maybe just another half-hour would bring them there and since, throughout the hours of driving, she had gained no further insight into Rhone's motivations, she decided it was time to be less circumspect.

'Tell me, Rhone,' she finally said, 'if you were in charge, what would you do?'

Rhone stared at her but, as ever, she could read nothing in his expression, so she returned to concentrating on where she was driving.

'There are so many variables,' he said, then seemed at a complete loss. Maybe he had never really thought about this too deeply. She felt certain he wanted her position but now wondered if that was actually not based on some deep conviction that he could do better, but simply stemmed from the kind of ladder-climbing found in any organization. It frightened her to realize quite how incompetent and *vaguely* motivated an enemy could be.

'We know some things for certain,' he continued. 'Serene Galahad will never leave us alone. We must either be punished or made to submit to her.'

After that, he said nothing for a long minute, so Var prodded him. 'Those are facts evident to anyone. I asked you how you would react to them.'

'If we stay on the surface, we'll be taken,' he affirmed. 'That's certain.'

'And?' Var turned to study him again.

He gazed back at her, puzzled. 'If you're asking me what I think I would do, in your position, I think the best answer would be that I'd faff about and be frightened of making such a drastic decision as your one to take us underground, and would probably end up getting us all killed.' He paused reflectively. 'And, in an attempt to be liked, I probably wouldn't push people as hard.'

He sounded so utterly plausible; every time she encountered a response like this from him, she found herself questioning her own sanity. Perhaps her paranoia was more evident to others than she supposed, and it was that which was driving them away from her. Even so, she could not ignore it; she could not afford to put such paranoia aside. Her own life and the lives of everyone at Antares Base depended on her judgement.

She now concentrated on the structure ahead, which had risen higher and was much more visible. It looked like the elevator equipment that would be found at the pithead of an ancient coal mine. From this oblique angle, it wasn't possible to see it clearly, but it appeared to be a framework in the shape of a pushed-over triangle, supporting a big wheel at its tip, right over the drop into Coprates Chasma. In the base of the triangle was a big drum and motor set-up, along with a small windowed cabin. However, they weren't close enough yet to see if any cable was available.

'I understand your anxiety,' Rhone continued abruptly. 'There's an awful lot of pressure on you, and perhaps too much responsibility.'

Patronizing prick . . .

'Var chose to take it,' said Lopomac from behind, 'and we agreed she should take it.' He paused for a moment, then continued, 'Power should always come with responsibility, and they should be equivalent. You get big problems when those who want power then renege on the responsibility.'

Was that it? Was it just Rhone trying to scrabble higher but not wanting the responsibility of the top job? Var chewed that one over in her mind as passing over another ridge brought the lifting gear ahead into full view. Now, seeing cables hanging from the wheel, dispelled such speculation from her mind. They had a job to do.

Argus

Obeying Hannah's instructions, Paul had arrived in Jasper Rhine's laboratory ahead of her and stood waiting as she stepped through the door, with Brigitta and Pike just a few paces behind her. She looked around, noticing how much things had changed here. The laboratory had been extended on one side to incorporate larger machines for the production of rectifier Casimir batteries, which were now steadily replacing every other battery used in every handheld device aboard the station. An adapted construction robot worked there, too, tending to the machines, packing batteries to be dispatched to station stores and, as a sideline, making stacked arrays of these same batteries to be used in some of the larger devices in the station, even in robots like itself.

Rhine himself was seated on a revolving chair encircled by a ring of benches, though he was almost concealed by the laboratory machines and the computer hardware stacked on their surfaces. Currently he sat before a scanning-electron microscope, eyeing its screen when not casting nervous glances towards Paul. Hannah strode further into the room, flicked her gaze towards a couple of screens up against one wall cycling grotesque images evidently from Earth, then averted her eyes, placed her hands on her hips, and gazed up at Paul speculatively.

'ADAR 45A,' she said succinctly.

Paul waved one of his big long-fingered hands in a curiously graceful gesture towards Rhine. 'The rough schematic supplied by Jasper Rhine was approved by the Owner. After the completion of the enclosure, work then commenced upon it.'

Hannah felt suddenly confused. She had expected lies, guilt, something human but got none of those. 'Why wasn't I told?'

Rhine had now come out from his little hideaway. 'Told what?' he asked.

She swung towards him, now finding a more viable target for her anger. 'Why wasn't I told that the robots are building your damned vortex generator in the outer ring?'

'Are they?' said Rhine, looking delighted.

Hannah swung back to Paul. 'This is madness. We can't afford to waste resources on this fantasy while the fucking *Scourge* is heading directly our way. Every moment of wasted effort gets us that much closer to either dying or ending up in an adjustment cell.'

Paul just stood there for a long moment, making no discernibly human response. Then he finally said, 'I am puzzled. You were unaware of ADAR 45A?'

'Yes, I was unaware of ADAR 45A,' said Hannah. 'So you need to shut down work on that and concentrate on our defences.'

'I am sorry, Hannah Neumann, but there is conflict and I am therefore unable to comply,' Paul replied.

'What?' Hannah stared at this unknowable being standing before her. She still felt angry, but that was being eaten away quickly by a fear that had been with her since she had taken over from Le Roque: that she was not doing enough, that she was losing control. 'What do you mean? You and all the other robots aboard this station were instructed by the Owner to obey me and me alone.'

'Yes, but obedience to you is secondary to obedience to the Owner himself.'

'He's awake?' Hannah asked, feeling a sudden surge of hope.

'He is not yet awake.' Paul bowed his head for a second, as if in thought, then continued, 'Before the Owner became comatose, he had queued up orders of primary importance, such as full enclosure of the station, securing the power supply' – Paul gestured towards the machines now making Casimir batteries – 'and, once resources were available after enclosure, then the construction of the vortex generator. When the threat of the *Scourge* became evident, ADAR 45A was moved to the head of the queue.'

By whom? Hannah wondered, but knew the answer to that already. Saul might have released his hold on consciousness, but his unconsciousness wasn't of the human kind.

'Surely you can see that wasting resources on this could kill us?' she said.

'On the contrary,' Paul replied, 'if we do not construct this device, we are finished.'

'Can you elaborate on that,' said Hannah, even though the meaning was plain.

'The *Scourge* will first disable us, then launch an assault. With two thousand troops at their disposal, and doubtless spiderguns too, it is a certainty that we would lose. The only uncertainty is whether or not their victory would be a Cadmean one, because the station and all aboard could be destroyed in the conflict.'

There it was, stated out loud and in plain terms: everything the tactical models had been telling them, everything Le Roque had banged on about in those early meetings, and everything they had since tried to ignore. She had often wondered about Le Roque's rather easy acquiescence to her; how, once it was evident she controlled the robots aboard Argus, he hadn't tried anything else. There had been no assassination attempts, no further efforts to take her captive, no angry protests – just acid observations. She now understood why. Le Roque had sought power not because he loved it, but because he knew *someone* needed to take charge. The moment Hannah took command away from him, he stepped aside with alacrity, because nobody ever wants to be captain of a sinking ship.

Hannah turned to Brigitta and Pike, who stood goggle-eyed as they listened to this exchange. Meanwhile, Rhine had returned to his equipment and was now frantically working a console.

'None of this leaves the room,' she declared. 'At some point wider knowledge of the construction going on out there will get out, so we need a story to cover it.'

'Ah, I see,' said Brigitta, who was clearly sharper than the other two.

'What do we do?' asked Pike.

Hannah focused on him carefully, feeling less sure about how he would react. 'I – and a few others I trusted – knew about this all along. I allowed construction of the vortex ring to proceed in secret, because I did not want its purpose generally known. Messina's clones currently aboard have been in regular contact with Earth, and I did not want them to find out about it and inform Earth.' It was essential that the likes of Le Roque and Langstrom did not know how this development had blindsided her. They might lose any confidence they had left in her; so might feel the need to try and take control again.

She glanced next at Paul but the proctor was unreadable. She then strode over to where Jasper Rhine sat working. 'What are the chances now of this vortex generator working?'

He glanced up with a slight dreamy smile on his face, which did nothing to inspire her confidence. 'I never checked this. It's amazing.'

'Answer the question, Jasper.'

He waved a hand at the console screen. 'Another two months and main construction will be completed, after which we'll need to connect it up properly to the station system. It will, of course, work – but there's much we still need to do.'

'Like what?' Hannah asked.

'I checked with our long-range sensors, and I also checked the old asteroid survey maps,' continued Rhine. 'We need to further alter our course by half a degree and begin decelerating in about a month, so that we can moor to asteroid HJI457.'

'You what?' asked Brigitta, from behind Hannah's shoulder.

'That's where we'll get the ore,' he explained, looking at her happily. 'We should be able to swing one of the smelters right round to it, and haul the stuff straight across. It'll be a low-temperature process compared to the usual smelting, and we can condense it in pipes cooled by vacuum, then use vacuum distillation to purify it.'

'This still isn't very clear, Rhine.'

'Nearly eighty per cent cinnabar and vermilion, eight per cent pure product, and the rest is just rock.'

'What product?'

'Mercury, of course,' Rhine replied, as if that was patently obvious. 'You didn't think the vortex generator would work without it, did you?'

Her throat trying to close up on her, Hannah asked, 'And how much mercury do we need, Rhine?'

'Oh, don't worry. There's enough there. We'll have to process about three-quarters of the asteroid to achieve about ten thousand metric tonnes of the pure metal.'

Pike grunted as if someone had punched him in the stomach.

'Oh, is that all?' he said.

Hannah closed her eyes, fighting the urge to start crying, then gritted her teeth as a call came through on her fone from Le Roque.

'What is it?' she asked sharply.

'We're in trouble,' he replied.

'Tell me.'

'The smelting plants just folded up their mirrors and are retracting into the station rim.'

'I see,' she replied. 'I rather think we've been here before.'

'Certainly,' he continued, 'and, just like last time, there's a course correction in the system queue – and it wasn't there before.'

'Let me guess: a correction of half a degree.'

'Is there something you're not telling me, Dr Neumann?'

An hour later she was standing in Tech Central, as the smelting plants locked home in the rim.

'What the hell is going on?' asked Le Roque.

Hannah turned to gaze at two unused screens. Nightmarish images appeared there, but they seemed hazy now and, just for a second, she glimpsed the image of one of Argus's steering thrusters firing up, its flame spearing out into the darkness.

Scourge

Commander Liang's cabin had been small and claustrophobic, and Clay had not wanted to stay inside it for long, but as the small Chinese man took him on a guided tour of the rest of the barracks decks, that claustrophobic feeling only increased. Squeezing past a group of soldiers gathered in the pipe of the hexagonal access tube, who were playing Yahtzee with sticky dice that they threw against a wall, and recording their scores on PDAs, he peered into the space they had abandoned. The hexagonal cabin was occupied by nine zip-up hammocks, and equipment secured to every wall made the space even smaller.

'They get a turn in the corridor every six hours,' remarked Liang perfunctorily. 'Then every forty-eight hours they get an hour in the spin-gym.'

'I guess they need it,' Clay noted.

'Six around each section,' explained one of Liang's three staff officers, pointing out the six doors ringing the tube. Clay glanced at the man and couldn't figure out who he was. Liang had named them all earlier, but their difficult names had since slid out of Clay's mind. Anyway, they all looked like clones of

Liang. Perhaps they *were* clones – as it wasn't exactly unheard of.

Clay stepped over to an open door, peering down into the cabin below it, which was still occupied – the soldiers ensconced in their hammocks because there was nowhere else for them to go. He looked up at the door above, which was closed, then ahead along the tube to the next ring of six doors and the next group of nine men hovering outside one. These had stripped out of their VC suits and were sponging out the insides of the garments. The barracks decks resembled a honeycomb, with hexagonal cabins ringing hexagonal access tubes. The designers had obviously called on nature for the best way of packing living beings into the smallest possible space.

'So, fifty-four troops in each separate section and four hundred and eighty-six in total along each access tube,' Liang continued. 'We've got six tubes altogether here, around which two thousand troops are bunked.'

'That doesn't add up,' observed Clay.

'They're not all troop cabins,' pointed out one of the clone trio accompanying them.

Clay damned himself for having made such a stupid comment. None of these living cabins had toilets or showers, so those facilities must be located somewhere. The men also needed to eat, drink and, of course, somewhere hereabouts was that 'spin-gym'. He put his error down to how disorientating this place was, how claustrophobic. At least now he had begun to get used to the smell, which was a ripe mix of body odour, stale cooking and sewage.

'Yeah, I can understand that,' said Clay. 'It must be hard for them living down here.'

'Not as bad as you might think,' opined Liang. 'They have

individual VR entertainment, and they have their tactical updates to learn – that stuff that was coming directly from Argus.'

These were updates which, since the Messina clones had been isolated and trapped in a hydroponics unit, hadn't really supplied anything useful for some time now. He nodded thoughtfully, as if this was all of great interest to him, but in fact he was wondering why Liang and his staff officers bunked down here alongside the men. After all, cabins had been made available for them on the executive deck, where Clay had his own cabin. He could only surmise that Liang and his men were the utterly loyal soldier-fanatic type. He'd seen plenty like them – men who focused totally on their 'duty' and utterly failed to question their indoctrination.

'They are also allowed an amount of chemical recreation,' Liang added.

Clay knew about the various pills and potions the troops were allowed. No stimulants, however; only the kind of chemical recreation that left men and women zoned out for hours on end. Another recreation, sex, had been barred because it might lead to friction of another kind. There had been no complaints about this, since the method of prevention had been introduced into the water supply down here.

'What about weapons drills?' Clay asked.

'Only in VR, at present.'

'Yes,' Clay nodded, 'I take it most of the equipment is packed in the hold.'

'It's not that; it's because of the lack of space.'

'So what do we have, then, in the hold?' Clay asked, intent on keeping the conversation running as he pushed his way past the next group of troops, even though he was already thoroughly aware of the ship's manifest.

'There isn't much in the way of heavy stuff,' said Liang. 'We've got eighty vacuum-penetration locks, some spiderguns and a hundred and twenty heavy machine guns – ten mils. The rest is ammo, portable weapons, medical supplies and food.'

Just another two groups of soldiers to push their way past, and they would reach the end of this particular access tube. Then Clay wanted some excuse to get out of here fast. After spending so long in his cabin, in the crew areas of the ship, in the hold, and as much time as possible in Messina's unfinished quarters, he had finally felt it was his duty to come here and 'inspect the troops'. He decided now that this would be his first and last such inspection. He halted, a tingling of his skin behind his ear making him aware that someone was trying to fone him. He allowed the connection by reaching up and pressing his forefinger against the fone there.

'Political Officer Ruger,' said Captain Scotonis, 'you wished to be kept updated of any changes in Argus's status. It has fired up a steering thruster and changed course, but only by about half a degree.'

Clay halted, his finger still up against his fone. 'Any idea why?' He glanced at Liang and the other three staff officers, who were gazing at him with a strange blank indifference.

'Not as yet.'

'I'm coming up to the bridge now,' said Clay.

'No need for that,' said Scotonis. 'It's not as if we need to go rushing about.'

War is one per cent terror and ninety-nine per cent boredom. Clay was not sure where he had heard that, but it seemed to apply perfectly to this particular journey. He'd been terrified during the initial acceleration of the *Scourge* but, as the interminable journey dragged on he'd felt as if he was increasingly losing his mind. Anyway, Liang could not hear

Scotonis's side of the exchange, so this seemed a perfect excuse for Clay to get out of this horrible place.

'I'm on my way,' Clay replied, then with another press of his finger he shut down the communication. Returning his attention to Liang he said, 'We'll have to cut this short, I'm afraid. Something has come up.'

Liang acknowledged that with a serious nod, but was unable to hide a flash of impatience. The man probably considered Clay a waste of time and space that was better occupied by another fighting man or maybe a few more crates of bullets. Liang was certainly all about the job, since his only recreation seemed to be playing fast games of mah-jong against a computer program, and constantly winning.

Scotonis and Pilot Officer Trove, who had now grown a scrubby Mohican to divide her narrow black skull, occupied the main bridge floor. Trove was in her seat, a virtuality mask over her face, while Scotonis stood towards the edge of the same bridge floor, talking with one of the crew who occupied a cradle suspended before a mass of overcomplicated-looking controls. What had one of them said – yeah, designed by committee. Clay walked over to stand beside the captain.

'Tell me more about this course change,' he said.

Scotonis turned towards him, his face devoid of expression. 'There's not much to tell, really. They altered their vector by half a degree.'

'Does this course take them towards an asteroid designated as GH467?' Clay asked.

Scotonis looked genuinely puzzled for the first time since Clay had met him. 'GH467?' he echoed. 'Why would that be significant?'

'Galahad offered to let them go if they moor a space plane

to that asteroid, but one that contained the Gene Bank data and samples – and Alan Saul,' Clay explained.

'Really?' said Scotonis, again surprised.

Clay continued, 'She made the offer because, if they accepted it, there would be less chance of the Gene Bank stuff being destroyed, and they would then be delayed by an appreciable time and quite likely already at odds with each other.'

'Ah,' said Scotonis, 'so it wasn't an honest offer.'

'Our mission remains the same: get those samples, and capture or kill the rebels aboard Argus. Then, if the Mars Traveller has not been destroyed, we place a small crew aboard the station, to dispatch it back to Earth, while we swing back to Mars and deal with the rebels there.'

Scotonis gave a brief nod to this, then headed over to Trove, who had just taken her face out of the VR mask. 'You heard?'

'I heard,' she replied sourly. 'This course change does take them closer to GH467, but not directly towards it. Incidentally, that asteroid was maybe not the best choice, since it is now widely diverging from the original route they took towards Mars.' She shrugged. 'I suspect it was chosen by someone unacquainted with astrogation.'

That was an unconcealed criticism of Serene Galahad, and this sort of comment was becoming more common from Scotonis and his senior crew as they realized that Clay simply could not kill them without jeopardizing the entire mission. He decided then that he would have to do something about this before it went any further, for he must maintain his facade of loyalty to Galahad, but not now. Instead he would wait until Trove returned to her cabin.

'So there's no guarantee that they are heading there?' Clay asked, pretending he hadn't noticed her sniping.

Trove shrugged. 'They could be, but we won't know for certain unless they make a further course correction within the next month, then begin deceleration – which is about the window they need for something as unwieldy as Argus Station.'

Clay headed over to his chair and sat down. 'I need to speak to Messina's clones.' Now familiar with the controls on the console that he could swing across before him on a jointed arm, he quickly punched in his instructions and made the call.

After the signal delay Alex's face appeared in a frame on the multi-screen ahead of him. Of course it did: it wasn't as if the two clones there had much else to do. The face was thinner now, and haggard. Trapped in the hydroponics unit, they weren't short of water or air, but their supply of food was meagre, for they could only take a limited amount from the food growing in the tanks without the agribots detecting the loss and reporting it. The degree of self-discipline that had kept the two clones inside that unit for so long, nibbling at a few leaves and the odd potato, while steadily making reports on what little data they could glean, had told Clay just how intense was their conditioning, and just how far away they were from being genuine human beings.

'What is your status today?' Clay asked, and waited impatiently.

'Unchanged,' Alex eventually replied. 'The android is still too close for us to risk leaving this unit and, as I stated before, if we don't leave here within the next month we will be incapable of ever doing so.'

'Understood,' said Clay, quickly continuing now the pleasantries were out of the way. 'You're doing very well there, and your sacrifice will be recognized. However, I have something more for you to do, in addition to your previous instructions. I need to you to find out whether the Gene Bank samples and data are being moved, and if a space plane is currently being prepared for launch. Do as much as you can now towards that end, with the data access you have, and, should you manage to get out of there soon, that is the first thing I want you to check.'

'Understood,' said Alex, once the instruction was received. 'Is there anything else?'

He hadn't even asked why – another sign of his lack of human characteristics.

'That's all for now,' said Clay, noting out of the corner of his eye that Trove had just stood up and was heading for the exit. He shut down the communication, got out of his seat and gazed across at Scotonis. 'I'll be here for his next sched-uled report, but if Alex gets in contact before then, I must be informed at once.'

Clay turned and headed after Pilot Officer Trove. Doubt-less now was the time for her break, and she would head for her cabin, where, if she followed her usual routine, she would enjoy a meagre meal of rice and reconstituted vegetables before sleeping for five hours. Upon waking, she would drink some coffee while awaiting the arrival of a ship's engineer who had taken her fancy, whereupon they would have frenetic sex for most of the remaining hour allowed to her. She would then wash, dress and return here.

Clay had seen how others entertained themselves aboard this ship and knew that his own method was unique, because he was the only one with such free access to the cam system. Now he felt it was time for him to utilize his free access to other equipment, namely the pain-inducer in Trove's cabin.

275

11

Fones

A great deal of time has passed since the days of the ancient telephone necessitating wired connections and finger-dialling or press-button keypads. The modern fone – a distinct spelling that rose into prominence with the first Internet – is an adaptable piece of technology that has taken many years, perhaps too many years, to reach its present state. More than a hundred years ago, computer voice-recognition enabled the owner of such a device to call someone just by speaking their name, and over fifty years ago the introduction of rugged implant technology ushered in visual cortex interfaces and sensitized skin controls – usually positioned at the temple – to allow us to call up menus to our inner vision, and thereby make all our calls that way. In fact, terabyte processors and old Bluetooth technologies have since made the fone a simple mobile Internet connection. However, it has still taken two centuries to get to where we are today, and those who all those years ago predicted technological singularity would wonder why such a simple thing had taken so long.

Earth

Nelson allowed Serene's father twenty-two hours to stabilize between each two-hour session. In the first week, Donald Galahad gained a four-day respite – if it could really be called that – when Serene dispatched Nelson to attend to some other work that was conducted before a private audience as an object lesson. It was the first and last time she used him like that, for the response had not been good. Many of the staff of the factory whose manager had been the object of that lesson failed to turn up for work the next day, until enforcers went and rounded them all up. Better to kill quickly and cleanly and move on. She had also quickly developed a loathing for Nelson and his 'art'. The man was like some poisonous insect in which one might show some scientific interest, nothing more. She therefore left him alone in the cellar with her father and attended just one further torture session, affecting a clinical detachment from it all but experiencing the same reaction in the elevator afterwards.

Why can't I stop?

She had thought she would enjoy this, but hated it from the start. She half-expected to come to enjoy it eventually – this personal exercising of ultimate power – but it seemed petty now, a foolish whim, altogether too frivolous. She understood herself enough to know that she would never want to admit to having made a mistake, and surely stopping Nelson from his activities would be such an admission, but there was something more to it than that. The last time she had come down here was after one of the exterminations necessary to rebalance Earth's ecology; when the Scour had wiped out three million people in the Northeast India region and then the big dozers and macerating machines went in to level that particular area of sprawl.

Am I punishing myself? she wondered. Had she found it necessary to come down here to feel shame, feel the gorge rising in her throat, for some kind of penance?

'The physical work is complete now,' said Nelson, stepping

back. 'The level of agony he will experience henceforth will be governed by electrical stimulation of his nerves and by the drugs employed. He will also experience pain from the various infections that will inevitably ensue. How long he remains compos mentis is now dependent on the degree of pain delivered, and how long he will last physically depends on the extent of those infections.'

Serene felt her father had already lost all the compos from his mentis over the course of the last week.

So this then was Nelson's art.

The frame holding her father's body now sported numerous silvery extensions supporting polished dishes and glass containers. He seemed a freeze-frame of an exploding human being. Opened up like a gutted fish, his internal organs were arrayed all about him, all the plumbing and nerves of his body stretched, force-grown or otherwise extended in order to support them. In some areas Serene could see his blood running through glass tubes. Wires were interwoven, electrochemical amplifiers connected here and there, nerve interfaces running optics between each other. Serene watched his heart beating in a glass vessel half a metre out from his chest, his kidneys throbbing on dishes up either side of his drooling face, his intestine formed into a neat spiral just below the plastic-enclosed mass of his liver.

She gazed at this display in bewilderment. Traitors should pay with their lives, and if they possessed information, they should be tortured until they revealed every last scrap of it; then they should be disposed of. The rebels aboard Argus Station and on Mars should face lengthy punishment before the eyes of the world, and an especial place should be reserved in Hell for Alan Saul. But this was far too much punishment for a man who had merely rejected the sexual advances of his own child; this was far too much even for the man who had made the dictator of Earth feel shame both when she was a child and again now.

It was time for this to end.

She swung her attention across to Nelson, and studied him intently.

His expression was one of childlike wonder, and his hand was inside his lab coat, where a bloodstain was showing through. He was probably tugging at one of his numerous piercings and, after she left here, he would doubtless end up jacking off on the output from a disabler. For putting temptation in her way, Nelson should be made to suffer. For distracting her from her prime purpose, he should end up on one of his own frames. But that was pointless, because with his screwed-up wiring, such pain as this would be the ultimate in ecstasy for him.

'Sack,' she said, glancing round and gesturing her bodyguard forwards.

Sack stepped up beside her with alacrity, but she had caught him out because it had taken him a moment to wipe from his face an expression of disgust that even showed through his keroskin. 'Give me your sidearm.'

He reached under his jacket, removed a heavy automatic, spun it round in his lizard-skin hand and presented it to her butt first.

'This was my father's,' he said, which gave Serene a moment of pause. Was that somehow significant? She shook her head in irritation, took the weapon and stepped forward, as close to her father as she could get.

Donald Galahad's gaze seemed to focus on her for a

moment, then drifted away again. He was making a throaty whimpering and when his mouth opened briefly she saw that he had chewed his own tongue down to a stub.

'Father,' she said, and his gaze drifted back to her. 'Father, I am going to end this now.' No reaction; his attention slid away again and more drool dripped from his chin.

'But you can't,' said Nelson. 'He is perfect now.'

How did she get here? How did this happen?

She raised the automatic and snapped off one shot, the recoil nearly throwing the weapon out of her hand. However, her aim had been true and the bullet punched a hole straight through the glass vessel her father's heart resided in.

'No!' Nelson yelled, throwing himself at her.

Sack intervened quickly, catching hold of the man and slamming him face down on the floor, a knee planted in his back.

Blood arced from the hole in the glass vessel and spattered the floor immediately to Serene's right. She inspected the weapon she held, realized it was of some antique design, hence the recoil. Now settling into a Weaver stance she fired twice more into the heart, watched it stutter to a halt, then transferred her aim directly to her father. His head was waving from side to side and his lungs, hanging in a large cellophane bag to the right of his heart, were still sucking and blowing. Obviously all the extra equipment here, the extra venous shunts and feeds of artificial blood, were keeping Donald Galahad functioning beyond the lifespan of his own heart.

Serene fired twice more, the first shot hitting his cheekbone and taking off the side of his face, the second demolishing his nose and blowing his brains out of the back of his skull. She lowered the weapon, suddenly feeling utterly calm again, utterly centred.

'I understand now,' she said, stepping back. 'In my position it is possible for me to gratify every human urge, every single whim. I can indulge in any cruelty, play power games, mind games and never lose. This was necessary.' She turned and gazed down at Nelson. 'Kill him.' Sack responded immediately, reaching down and twisting the man's head right round with a sound like a tyre going over an apple, then stood up leaving Nelson shuddering on the ground, his head facing backwards.

Serene handed over the automatic. 'I've outgrown such games now.' She gestured back to her father's remains. 'But I needed to find out.'

'Ma'am?' Sack asked, puzzled.

'Let us say I needed to get this thing out of my system, so I could at last see what is really important.' She headed for the elevator, knowing that this time she wouldn't be throwing up inside it. 'Clear out this cellar,' she said, 'clear it out completely.' She paused for a second. 'I want it remodelled. I want sun pipes leading down here, and I want a garden. Yes, I want a garden . . . with a pool . . . with carp in it.'

She glanced back at her bodyguard even as she reached the elevator doors, again catching one of his usually hidden expressions. Only when she was in the elevator and ascending did she realize what it might signify. She had never seen Sack actually look frightened before, and she found that oddly appealing.

Argus

Alex and Alexandra carefully exited the hydroponics unit airlock and looked around. The robots were gone but, when

Alex propelled himself to a nearby girder and paused there, he could feel the vibrations of their distant activity in the station rim. According to Alexandra, the robots were over two kilometres away right now.

Alex then launched himself towards the new structure just twenty metres away from the hydroponics unit, snagging a cable as he arrived and bringing his feet down on a thick mass of resin-bonded wiring. Alexandra caught the same cable, and pulled herself down beside him. He quickly reeled out their combined safety and communications line, and they connected up.

'They sure that's a fast transport system?' she asked as soon as they could talk.

'Looks something like a tubeway network,' he said. 'Tactical reckons that, with the interior being vacuum, they should be able to squirt passenger or cargo modules around faster than in a scramjet.'

'Crazy,' said Alexandra.

'Exactly,' he said.

Whenever the robots weren't actually testing this machine, communications with the *Scourge* had continued, Alexandra grabbing everything she could from the station system and sending it that way. All the weird images and sounds had been analysed, all the intercepted communications run through specialized computer programs. Tactical had thereby come back with what seemed to be the correct answer: Alan Saul wasn't dead but very badly injured, his brain damaged by Two's shot to the head, but, such was the hardware in his skull and his computer links into the system and to the robots, that he was impossible to cut out. The entire station was now being run by someone who had lost a large chunk of his brain.

'Okay,' Alex continued, 'the space docks next – check your rifle.'

Alexandra set her Kalashtech assault rifle to vacuum function and ran a diagnostic on it. 'If we have to use these, then that's probably the end for us.'

Alex switched his rifle over too, also running a diagnostic. Both weapons had recently been in a warm, oxygenated and moist environment, which usually wasn't a problem but could become one once they were moved into vacuum. Gas pockets forming in some components could expand and cause damage, as could the abrupt temperature change, and trapped moisture might turn to ice. There were no problems with either rifle, but, with the remaining ceramic ammo divided between them, they only had two clips each, one full and the other containing about half its usual load of eighty bullets.

'If we get into trouble and get separated,' Alex declared, as he led the way along the surface of the weird new structure, 'you must head straight for the plane. You know exactly what we want, so, if you encounter a problem there, head straight back to the hydroponics unit.' He paused reflectively. 'And you remember what to do if you're cornered, with no chance of escape?'

'I give myself up,' she replied woodenly.

He glanced round at her and noted her frown. It had been hard enough for him to accept that this was the best option, for his own conditioning cried out at the very idea of surrender. Alexandra, in her inexperience and her youth, had great difficulty first accepting that she had been subject to conditioning at all, and utterly rebelled against the thought of giving herself up.

As they crossed from the new structure to a cageway

leading into near-space levels of the rim, retracing the route they had taken earlier to get to the hydroponics unit before the robots started tearing this particular area apart, he once again ran through what he had been telling her repeatedly for some time. It was something she seemed to forget every time she slept, but every time he reminded her it seemed to stick in her mind a little more.

'We have nothing that will be of tactical value to the rebels, because those communicating with us have ensured that,' he said. 'We have both been conditioned to fight to the death when facing capture, because the Chairman did not want any information we might possess falling into enemy hands.' That was not strictly true, though it was what Alex himself had believed for about the first ten years of his life. But he had come to realize, over the ensuing twenty years, that they were conditioned to fight to the death simply because they were a disposable commodity.

'If we die,' he continued, 'we can do nothing for the Chairman and therefore will have failed him. If we are captured, though, there is still a chance, when the *Scourge* attacks, for us to free ourselves and rescue him.'

'I understand,' she said, but still she doubted him.

From the cageway they headed on round, two levels below the outer skin of the rim, towards the space docks. Here the beam-work of walls marked out corridors and rooms, but only a few of the wall plates – ten centimetres of insulation sandwiched between layers of bubblemetal – had as yet been welded in place. Work here had ceased completely during the struggle between Saul and Smith, and never recommenced. Half a kilometre further on, they reached a completed wall with a wide bulkhead door inset. Alex pulled down the manual handle – the fact that he could even move it indicating that vacuum lay on the other side – and they stepped through into a section of the level that was almost complete but had yet to be pressurized.

'What's that?' Alexandra asked, pointing to an object drifting through vacuum ten metres along the corridor they had now entered.

Alex focused on the thing she indicated. It must have been shaken loose during that recent course change but had yet to be dragged to the floor by the nigh-indiscernible gravity of the central asteroid, or pinned against a wall by station spin. For a moment he just could not quite process what he was seeing, so strange did it look in this setting. Then he understood.

'It's a boot,' he said. 'I think we just found the mortuary.'

It was through the next doorway, a long room along the back wall of which the casualties of past battles aboard the station had been stacked in two heaps, like cordwood. Alex stepped inside and viewed the scene before him. He knew that originally the corpses here had all been clad in fatigues or vacuum combat suits. Now, all the corpses in one pile had been stripped while those in the second pile were awaiting the attention of whatever robot had been given this task. Gazing at the naked dead, Alex could discern which ones had died in VC suits that had remained sealed or had sealed themselves with breach glue: they were the ones that had not deflated as the water evaporated from their bodies – it was now frozen inside them. They were the ones that looked less like something dragged from a hole in Ancient Egypt's Valley of Kings.

'We should check those.' He pointed to the heap of corpses that were still clothed.

'Why?' Alexandra asked the question in a whisper, as if her voice might disturb those here, even though vacuum lay between them and the dead.

'Ammo,' Alex replied succinctly.

He was about to step forward when her hand clamped on his shoulder and she abruptly jerked him back towards the wall adjacent to the door. He turned suddenly, grabbing her wrist and twisting, thinking for a moment that she was attacking him. Then he saw it, released his hold and squeezed back against the wall beside her.

In vacuum, it came through the door with eerie silence for something so large. Alex recognized it at once as the same design of construction robot that Saul had originally hijacked during his assault against Smith. The thing looked like a giant steel ant, pairs of limbs terminating in flat gecko-pad feet extending from its two rear sections; its front section, arrayed with glassy sensors, was raised up with two limbs extending from it, both sporting numerous cutters and manipulators. In one of these it was carrying a roll of material, which, when it reached the corpses, it shook open to reveal as a large netting bag. Steadily it set to work, picking up a woman in a VC suit and swiftly divesting her of her garment. The suit went straight into the bag, the woman onto the other heap.

'Out of here,' muttered Alex, and soon they were moving away from there just as fast as they could.

'What is that thing doing?' Alexandra asked.

'Maybe they've decided those VC suits are going to be needed,' Alex replied, trying to be pragmatic but, in his heart, failing. 'Come on, let's speed it up now.'

It took them two hours to reach the exterior of Docking Pillar Two, climbing an access tube for maintenance robots leading out of the rim and up between some fuel silos. Alex found it difficult to shake off the sense of doom that had descended on him since they saw the corpses and, from Alexandra's monosyllabic replies to anything he said, he knew she felt the same. He gazed out at the stars, trying to develop a better mood from the sight of them, but all he could think was how very far from Earth they were.

Directly above them, Messina's space plane occupied one entire docking face. Each such face could take two of the normal space planes, but the *Imperator* was much larger. Simply inverting themselves, they walked up the pillar until they reached the plane's nose, circumvented this and then walked up along one side of it.

'Access would have been easier from inside,' said Alex, 'but the cams are still operating in there and, even if there's no human watching, recognition software is sure to be.'

'Yeah, sure,' Alexandra grunted.

He continued, 'My guess is that someone *is* watching and that there will be guards inside. Because I'm betting there are some on the station who have contemplated stealing a plane and escaping.'

'They won't know about the hibernation equipment here,' said Alexandra, gesturing to the plane beside them.

'Here.' Alex paused beside a large bulge on the hull, reached out and took hold of a recessed handle and began turning it. 'No,' he went on, 'no one is likely to know about that but, as you grow in experience, Alexandra, you learn not to underestimate the power of human stupidity.'

After turning the handle five times, he pulled out a ten-centimetre-deep plug of nanotube carbon to reveal a simple keypad. He input the required code and stepped back.

'I bet there are those who, given the chance,' he said, 'are prepared to steal a plane and fly off to meet the *Scourge*, expecting to be picked up and eventually taken home. Scotonis would simply ignore them and continue his pursuit of this station, so they would die aboard their escape craft.'

The bulge rose a little, then slid aside to reveal an airlock. Here another keypad required a code to open the outer door, whereupon they both squeezed inside the narrow space for the lock to pressurize, before stepping on into the space plane itself.

'The air's good,' said Alex, sliding his visor aside.

The *Imperator* was luxuriously appointed. They had stepped into the section containing the rows of acceleration chairs, but even these were considerably more comfortable than any found aboard a normal plane, for each was even provided with its own mini-bar, swing-over table, screen and entertainment console. The real luxury, however, was in the suite of rooms lying beyond. Alex glanced without interest at a cocktail bar, a fully appointed kitchen, the massage parlour and the zero-G bathroom with its high-tech appliances making it possible for Messina to enjoy a jacuzzi without drowning. Upon passing through the door into Technical and Tacks, both he and Alexandra had to stop and scrape off the layer of fluff that their gecko-boot soles had picked up from the thick carpet. Shortly afterwards Alexandra came to stand before a console and screen.

'This is more like it,' she said, sounding a lot happier as she unhitched her pack of equipment, which she had not wanted to leave behind, and shoved it down beside the chair. Unlike the gear inside her pack, this console possessed the full complement of military software, including penetration and sabotage programs. She sat, cracked her knuckles, booted up the console, and was soon into Argus's system. Alex moved away, and began searching the plane for food, water and ammunition. Soon he returned to her with sealed packs of soldier's rations.

'That all?' she asked.

'That's all. All the Chairman's stocks have been taken – all the luggage too.'

'Figures.' Like him, she ate with slow care, aware of what such rich food could do to them after so long without.

'I'm seeing no sign that they're moving the Gene Bank samples, and the data remains as widely distributed as it was before,' she told him.

'Make absolutely sure of that,' he replied, 'then check to see if there's any sign that they've been preparing a space plane.' He moved off, hoping to find something more than the small box of ration packs he had shoved inside his backpack. Checking the kitchen, he found that it had been totally stripped, too, not even spices remaining. When he finally entered the armoury, just behind the plane's cockpit, he didn't even feel any disappointment, for he had expected it to be as empty as he found it. He returned to stand behind Alexandra.

'Something else is going on,' she said. 'I don't know why, but they're preparing one of the smelting plants for refining a huge amount of mercury ore.' Schematics began coming up on the screen.

'Where would they get the ore?' he asked. Then he realized: 'An asteroid.'

'But why?' she asked, now frantically searching.

'What's that?' he asked, seeing a system of pipes being highlighted in red.

'They intend to pipe it in . . . but that's odd.' She checked back through schematics, tracing something, then abruptly sat back. 'It's that thing the robots are building – it runs below the smelting-plant dock and there's some sort of junction there. They're going to pipe the mercury inside it, and there are plans here to connect the ring up with the station's astrogation system. It makes no sense at all.'

All at once it made perfect sense to Alex. 'That's no tube transport system . . .'

Just then, as they gazed at the screen, the soft thump of an airlock door opening was all too audible. Alex looked back the way he had come, from the armoury, to where the main tube airlock entered the docking pillar. Something came through fast, hit the ceiling above the door and bounced down to thump heavily against the floor, where it drove its piton feet straight into the metal.

'Drop your weapons.'

The voice speaking through the new arrival was recognizable as Langstrom's. Alex knew they were done, but in that same instant he knew for certain that his partner would not obey his earlier instructions.

'No!' he managed, just as Alexandra skidded her chair backwards, snatching up her weapon and raising it. Her weapon thundered, firing a full clip of ceramic ammunition at this jury-rigged mobile readergun. Alex himself staggered back towards the door as the robot replied with a brief burring sound, bright light flashing from its turret. Blood and chunks of flesh sprayed out from the back of Alexandra's VC suit, and bonelessly she slammed into Alex, knocking him further back into the room behind.

Alex pushed himself away from her, glimpsed the robot now tilted over, the legs on one side of it blown away. With his rifle still strapped across his back, he threw himself aside as its weapon burred again. One shot clipped his oxygen pack and another caught his shin and spun him round, but he fell out of its line of sight. He dragged himself along by handfuls of soft carpet, propelling himself onwards.

Those who had sent this robot in probably did not know about the secret airlock. He finally reached it, dragged himself inside, slapped a repair patch over the bloody wreckage of his leg, then watched breach foam boil out round that, even as the airlock evacuated. Next he pulled himself out into vacuum, and somehow just kept going.

For fifty minutes everyone hung on as the steering thrusters flipped Argus over and stabilized it. Half an hour after this, the big Mars Traveller engine fired up, and Hannah had something more than just her sticky boots to secure her to the floor of Tech Central. It was a weird feeling, and it reminded her of the boost out from the Moon's orbit and the relief she had felt then, the knowledge that they were moving away from Earth and the Committee. However, despite that memory, she knew that now the same sensation was bringing the reach of the Committee – albeit a rather changed version – closer and closer. As they now decelerated towards the edge of the Asteroid Belt, the *Scourge* would be rapidly gaining on them. They would have, at best, a month moored to asteroid HJI457 before it was fully upon them. Le Roque and Langstrom were thoroughly aware of this, too, and she could see it in their faces.

'A space drive,' said Le Roque, gazing disbelievingly at the images relayed to his three big screens from the interior of the rim.

The course correction, which had occurred just after she discovered what the station robots were building in the outer rim, had started Le Roque asking questions. The correction looked as if it had been in the system queue ever since they left the Moon behind them, but Le Roque declared otherwise. When it became evident that Saul was not regaining consciousness, he had checked everything so as to ascertain their status, ensuring there were no surprises awaiting him, and he had seen no course correction in the queue then. It seemed that Saul was giving orders from his sleep, and slipping them in under anything else put in after he entered that state. This present deceleration was a case in point. Le Roque had also found out about the work that Leeran and Pike were doing in one of the station's smelting plants, and by then Hannah knew she could keep it from him no longer.

'We can't allow this to be generally known,' she explained. 'We might have taken out one of Messina's clones, but the other one might still be able to send information straight back to the *Scourge*.'

'The woman we shot had a pack of jury-rigged com equipment with her, which was probably what they were using,' said Langstrom. 'And the man was shot in the leg, so he is more likely to be struggling to survive rather than trying to find a way to communicate with the *Scourge*.'

'Nevertheless,' said Hannah. 'We have to keep this under wraps. This is our edge, and this is what will enable us to survive.'

'If it works,' said Langstrom gloomily, turning to eye the proctor Paul, who, after Hannah had ordered Tech Central cleared, was the only other being present.

'It can work, Commander Langstrom,' the proctor assured him. 'All that is in doubt is whether it can be made to work in time. The extent of the damage we will receive upon entering the Asteroid Belt can only be calculated within limited parameters that range right up to the complete destruction of this station.'

'Oh, happy day,' said Langstrom. 'So how did the Mars Traveller VI avoid damage when it went there for the Argus asteroid?'

'Because when it went to the Asteroid Belt there was no disruption zone – it actually caused it.'

'Right, fair enough,' Langstrom conceded.

'So what do we tell everyone?' Le Roque asked.

'We're slowing so as to reduce asteroid debris damage,' Hannah replied, noticing that he had now called up another picture on his array of screens. 'They need know no more than that.'

Le Roque stood staring at the new image, which was a view up the side of the Traveller VI engine and out into space. Trust him to spot that one right away.

'This thing,' he said, 'is going to be built right across the mouth of the Traveller engine enclosure. Once it's there, we won't be able to use the Traveller engine without destroying this . . . vortex generator.'

'That's true,' Hannah replied, 'but if the space drive works, we won't need anything else again, and if it doesn't work, it certainly won't actually stop us using the Traveller VI.'

He grunted in agreement and continued staring at the screen. She decided not to add that if Rhine's space drive was a failure, whether or not they could fire up the Traveller engine was irrelevant.

The deceleration lasted for a month, bringing their speed down to just above ten thousand kilometres per hour. Hannah expected more, but there was nothing. For three further months life aboard the station continued. Leeran and Pike laboured to convert a whole smelting plant over to the refining of mercury extracted from its ore, and the robots continued building the vortex generator. Then, towards the end of those three months, they finally arrived at the periphery of the Asteroid Belt.

The dust came first, seemingly without any effect until detectors picked up a slight elevation in the temperature on the station's skin. Already pre-programmed, the steering thrusters fired up again, turning the Mars Traveller engine away from their course so as to protect it, and tilting the station so that the brunt of any impacts would be taken against its base.

'He prepared for this,' Le Roque noted.

'How so?' Hannah asked, yet thought she knew.

'The lower enclosure is thicker: thin case-hardened plates on the outside, closed-cell rock foam laminated with bubble-metal lying under that. The combination should act as a shock absorber, and take out most of the sting of anything small. Also, it appears that most of the collision lasers are concentrated down there.'

'Which only demonstrates how you must trust in his judgement.' Hannah kept her expression blank as she said it. The enclosure had been all but finished before they made the course change away from Mars, and she now remembered Saul saying something about Mars just being one stop on the way. But on the way where?

Yet another month passed, and then the collision lasers began to draw power from super-capacitor storage, perpetually topped up by the station's fusion reactors. Hannah watched the fireworks on a screen in her laboratory, while in her surgery James was detaching all but the monitoring equipment, the fluid and nutrient feeds and muscle tone stimulators from Saul. The spaces in his skull had filled with new growth, but what now resided within that was open to debate. New bone had grown across the gaps in his skull, and was slowly thickening and hardening, while his remaining injuries were just gradually fading scars. Hannah wanted him out of the surgery now so that she wouldn't have to go through the decontamination routine every time she went in to check on him. Saul had been installed in a bed for five days in her laboratory itself, when Argus Station received its first proper mauling from the Asteroid Belt.

A piece of debris weighing ten grams, which spectral analysis nailed down as eighty per cent nickel iron, came in so fast that the lasers only managed to warm it over. It hit the lower enclosure, fragmenting and melting as it punched through the laminations, then entered the inner station as a fountain of white-hot vapour which left a shiny plating on a nearby I-beam. A second and a third hit followed shortly afterwards, one failing to penetrate, but the next one cutting into a pressurized section of the station rim, the hole automatically sealed by the layer of rapidly expanding sealant within the walls, and causing a brief fire that was quickly knocked out by a computer-controlled jet of carbon dioxide.

'Breach protocols now apply,' Le Roque announced a short while later, after which everyone constantly wore spacesuits or at least the more flimsy survival suits. He also moved as many personnel as possible into the quarters located below Tech Central, where the bulk of the asteroid lying below would protect them from further impacts.

Over the ensuing weeks these became a constant, and initial terror lost its grip on the station population until one of the steering thrusters briefly fired up. The station was now being steered, as far as possible, to avoid some of the larger asteroidal chunks passing by outside. Then the fear generated by that began to wane as the firing up of the thrusters also became routine.

There was too much to do, and there was also a perpetual war for station resources between those actively at work. Power was at a premium. Le Roque refused to let super-capacitor storage drop below half, just in case the collision lasers had to deal with anything worse than they had encountered thus far, and Hannah agreed with him. However, the retracted smelting plant that was not being converted for mercury refining continued to draw in power to heat its furnaces because it no longer had the input of the sun mirrors. Here the components for the rest of Rhine's vortex generator were being manufactured, along with the mercury-refining components for the other retracted smelter and the nearly complete selection of new station weapons. Which of these was most important? Hannah asked herself, then, again considering the models that rated their survival chances at zero without having a space drive, she put weapons construction on hold.

It was a fortuitous choice, she felt, especially when a one-and-a-half-kilo lump of rock and iron smashed into the station rim and turned a ten-metre section of the vortex generator there into slag. Brigitta was soon there to disabuse her of any complacency over her decision.

'Say we build that thing and it works,' said the more gregarious Saberhagen twin. 'What then?'

'We've then got a fighting chance against the *Scourge*,' Hannah replied. 'But, more importantly, we've got an even better chance of running away.'

They were once again in Tech Central, and again debating the meticulous allocation of resources. Brigitta raised a silencing hand and pointed at one of the three big screens, this one now showing a small swarm of rocks like fragments of black glass. Perfectly on time, they felt the slight drag as a steering thruster again fired up.

'And how quickly do you think we will be able to get out of the belt?' Brigitta asked.

'She has a point,' said Le Roque. 'That first deceleration wasn't to slow us down to intercept that lump of mercury ore;

it was intended so we could get through this intact.' He gestured at the rocks on the screen, which were now sliding over to one side.

'We need those weapons,' Brigitta affirmed.

Hannah turned to Paul, who, as well as the spidergun, had become a constant companion. 'What's your assessment?'

'I can only give you highly variable percentages, Hannah Neumann,' the proctor replied. 'Without the vortex generator, we are dead. Without Brigitta and Angela Saberhagen's weapons, the *Scourge* could disable us while we are still manoeuvring out of the Asteroid Belt. If the generator receives no further asteroidal damage, then it will be complete in time so – on that basis resources can be diverted to finishing the weapons. If, however, the generator is again damaged, resources that were used to finish the weapons will no longer be available, and thus the ring will not be completed in time.'

'Toss the dice,' said Langstrom.

Hannah did. 'No work on the weapons until the vortex generator is complete.'

'I just hope that decision doesn't kill us,' said Brigitta.

'So do I,' Hannah replied. 'So do I.'

Mars

The two kilometres of cable had made a distinct difference, and now down in the fissure cavern after the dust had cleared enough for her to see more than a few metres, Var found it rather strange to be gazing at Hex One, with its branching wings already in place, but now located underground.

'Hex Four is a bit of a problem,' said Martinez, standing beside her.

'Why?' she asked sharply.

'We have to move the plants out first, so we'll need to find a place for them.'

Var nodded towards the structures lying ahead. 'I take it you're already getting infrastructure in place?'

'Yes,' said Martinez slowly, as if telegraphing that she was just about to make some mistake. This kind of attitude had become really annoying – people not telling her things outright.

She forged ahead anyway. 'Get lighting and heating for them up in the remaining wings, then you can move down Four.'

'The reactor,' said Martinez.

Var suddenly felt stupid. She put that down to merely being distracted by the tension she had been undergoing so long here at Antares Base – the expectation that someone, at some point, was going to turn against her. She returned her attention to the moment.

'Power is going to be a problem, whichever way you cut it,' she said succinctly.

'Yeah.' Martinez nodded. 'As it stands, the reactor supplies the energy for our population and for Hydroponics and for the Arboretum. If we move the reactor first, we'd have enough power in super-cap storage to support them for three or four days, but it'll take longer than that to move just the contents of Hydroponics.'

'But you have a solution?' she guessed.

'We move the contents of Hydroponics and the Arboretum into the remaining wings above, take apart those two hexes and assemble them down here, move super-cap storage down here, prepare the reactor for shut-down and removal, then shift population and plants down here all at once beforehand.'

'Which means you have only three or four days to get the reactor located down here,' Var observed. 'That can be done?'

'It'll be tight,' he said, 'but there may be a way to speed things up.'

'Tell me about it,' said Var.

'We now have enough cable, but what we could do with in addition is another lifting motor, cable drum and other related equipment.'

'You're talking about the trench lift?' she said.

He nodded, seemed reluctant to continue, then forged on. 'You were out there yourself with Rhone, while getting hold of that cable. I can't get anything out of him about the condition of the equipment out there . . .'

Var considered that statement. After his initial burst of enthusiasm, Rhone had retreated into Mars Science and become increasingly unhelpful. Perhaps their frank conversations out there had brought home to him that the top job wasn't so great and he was no longer manoeuvring for it. She suppressed that thought: she'd been wasting altogether too much time in worrying about what other people thought or what their motivations might be.

'I see no reason why there should be a problem with it,' she replied. 'There's no record of any of it ever going wrong. There's no likelihood of any corrosion problems, and the motor and the bearings will all have been sealed.'

'So I'm authorized to collect those items?'

'I already delegated this task to you, Martinez,' she said. 'Why are you thinking now that you need my permission just to do your job?'

He hesitated, then said, 'It's never been entirely clear what my job is – and I don't want to step on anyone's toes.'

'I thought it was perfectly clear that your job' – Var was

trying to control a sudden flash of anger – 'is to get the base moved down here, dealing with whatever problems arise. I would say that relocating the trench lift here is completely covered by that remit.'

'Okay.' He nodded.

'So why are you behaving like you expect me to bite your head off?'

He gazed at her directly. 'Because that has become a habit of yours just lately.'

The anger within Var ramped up by an order of magnitude, and she felt herself on the edge of shrieking at the man. Then, all at once, it began to wane, as the last few months seemed to unfold in her mind as a series of episodes seen from someone else's point of view. Previously she had seen herself constantly having to deal with problems created by stupid people who neither trusted nor liked her, and now she realized that on every such occasion she had found someone else to bawl at. Self-fulfilling prophecies . . .

She took a couple of steadying breaths, swallowed drily. 'Yes,' she said reluctantly, 'perhaps it has become a habit.'

They both just stood there awkwardly, finding nothing else to say.

'Is there anything else I need to know about?' she asked eventually.

'That's about it,' conceded Martinez reluctantly.

'Then I need to get back to base – or rather what remains of Antares Base,' she replied. 'We're coming up for another tanglecom with Argus, and I have some questions to ask.'

'It's odd,' said Martinez, obviously glad to move on to something else. 'When they made that first course change, I thought they were running away.'

'Apparently not,' said Var. The Argus Station was now

slowing into the Asteroid Belt, and even Rhone, when he had put in a brief appearance at the latest meeting, could think of no plausible reason why it was doing so.

'But why . . . why are they slowing?' Martinez asked.

'Rhone suggested they might be making a fuel stop at one of the ice asteroids there, but that doesn't add up,' Var replied. 'Two coms back, Neumann said they've got more than enough water for the Traveller engine and the station reactors.'

'Maybe they've built weapons and need more?' suggested Martinez.

'Only if they've managed to build more reactors, which seems unlikely.' Var shook her head. 'I'm sure there's a good reason and that this "Owner" of theirs has some sensible plan in mind.' She turned and began heading away.

'This "Owner" we've seen only once,' Martinez called after her, 'and who hasn't talked to us since?'

'That would be the one,' she replied, a shiver running down her spine. There was something about that man, about that brief sight of him on tanglecom, that made any mention of him seem to reach down and press buttons deep in the core of her being. She wanted to meet him one day, and then she hoped to understand why he caused such odd reactions in her.

12

Cry Wolf

The warnings of the Malthusians and promoters of environmental catastrophe have been with us, in one form or another, since the dawn of human history. They grew shrill as the media arrived to transmit their hatred of humanity around the world, and as the hungry beast of endless news fed on their trifles. They jumped on every theory or scientific study that could promote the prophecies of doom and demanded worldwide control, more regulation and the subjugation of the individual to the good of all. And it was true that a growing human population was bad for the planet, and that we polluted the air and the seas, destroyed the diversity of life, but it was also true that, by heeding their earlier cries and as new cleaner technologies came into play, we were pillorying the polluters and rebuilding ecosystems. It took the Committee, feeding on the catastrophists' pleas for worldwide control, to kill off any sensible environmentalism. With its Soviet attitude to industry and its power base built on exploitation of the massive zero-asset population, it again raised the spectre of a dying world. A combination of leaden bureaucratic oversight and plain incompetence eventually returned us to the pollution of the twentieth century, but on a now massive scale; while the catastrophists were silenced by the very mechanisms of control they had eagerly espoused.

Earth

The transmission delay was irritating, and Serene very deliberately fought to quell that sense of annoyance. It was a human reaction to something impossible to control, and was merely giving in to the animal element in her psyche – indulging it. In an attempt to avoid such indulgence, she had even limited these personal face-to-face communications to once every month, for her harrying of Clay was not going to get the *Scourge* to its target any quicker. Besides if anything important had happened, it would turn up in his regular weekly report, which in this case it had.

'Since there has been no mention of them in your weekly report, I think by now we can safely assume that Messina's clones are either captured are dead,' Serene said. 'I also take it that there has been no further trouble from the troops, especially after Liang recently killed a troublemaker aboard. Was that entirely necessary? Remember, the per-unit cost of sending you all out there has been very high. I also take it that there has still been no communication from Argus. I understand that the station has made further course changes and is now decelerating into the Asteroid Belt. They are not, however, heading towards the asteroid I designated.'

Serene paused for a moment's thought, slightly distracted. When her garden was finished she really ought to have the communications gear moved down to it. It would be so much more relaxing down there. 'In your previous report, you suggested that maybe they are still acceding to my demands but have chosen another asteroid. This lack of communication leads me to suspect that is not the case, and I have to wonder if their course is being set by the random impulses from a man who took a bullet to the head. Okay, reply.'

Serene stopped there, then glanced aside at the notes on her palmtop. This lumping together of the parts of a conversation had its usefulness, but it did not enable her to read his responses so easily. It also gave people some time to formulate a response, rather than answer on the spur of the moment. She sat back, rattling her fingers against her desktop, then opened up a subscreen on her main screen to watch the ETV news. After a few minutes of that, she turned it off again, bored with news reports whose contents she already knew.

Finally, after long tedious minutes, Clay replied, 'Since I disciplined Pilot Officer Trove, there has been no further trouble with the crew. However, the troops were getting bored and this resulted in some fighting amongst them, and necessitated the disciplinary measures I detailed earlier. The one that Commander Liang had executed was no loss. According to the army medic, he was developing a mental condition that would have required treatments unavailable aboard this ship, and he could no longer be trusted with lethal weaponry.' He grimaced and glanced at something to one side – probably at his own notes. 'We regularly ask for a response from Argus, but there has been nothing. On their current course, it seems likely they have slowed down to prevent heavy damage to the station, which presents such a large profile to the belt, much larger than that of the *Scourge*. However, Trove informs me that had they not changed course or, if they had chosen another course, they would not have had to slow so much. It seems they are aiming directly for some destination in an area of the Belt where debris is heavily concentrated. Still, as you say, if they had been intending to accede to your demands, they would surely have told us so by now.' He paused again, before going on to disagree diplomatically with her last point, 'The station does not seem to be under the control of someone brain damaged, since subsequent minor alterations in its course have taken it around some of the worse concentrations of asteroidal debris. Okay, I'm done now.'

'Very well, it seems we're not going to get an answer to this any time soon, unless those aboard Argus reply to you,' said Serene. 'How long until you intercept the station, and is there anything else you'd like to tell me? Over to you again.'

Serene tried the news again, was quickly bored again, and began reading a selection of reports sent her way by her staff. She became deeply engrossed in a report on the discovery of the bones of a deer around a campfire in the Eastern European Region, and the subsequent hunt for the zero assets that had killed it. These people were outside the system, of course, for they did not possess ID implants. They had yet to be found.

'As things stand at the moment, that'll be fifty-two days,' Clay replied.

Serene jerked out of her reverie, surprised that the transmission delay time had already passed. Then she struggled to remember what she had last said to the man.

'If they slow further to intercept some particular target, then we'll get to them all the quicker,' he finished.

Ah yes . . . the time it would take for the *Scourge* to catch up with Argus.

Clay now looked briefly uncomfortable – even guilty, Serene thought. 'I have a query,' he said, 'from Scotonis. We understand there has been a resurgence of the Scour on Earth, across the Asian regions, and also a number of police actions. ETV news is a little unclear on that. Perhaps you can . . . tell me something?'

'Yes, there was another outbreak of the Scour, which caused over a hundred million deaths, whereupon subversive elements in the regional administration took the opportunity to seize control of a ballistic-missile launch site and threaten the European regions. I necessarily replied to this with TEB. The damage that caused and the subsequent infrastructure crashes caused many, many more deaths. Back to you.'

Serene returned to the deer report, then issued instructions. The perpetrators of this crime were to be taken alive and held until she decided what to do with them. Admittedly she no longer countenanced petty vengeance, but an example would have to be made, on ETV. Humans needed to understand their relative value in the ecosystem of Earth.

'How many in total?' Clay asked her.

Again the time had sped by, and Serene sat back, completely focusing on him. There was something she had wanted to say about that whole farrago on ETV, something she had wanted to shout from the rooftops but knew she couldn't. The Asian extermination had been necessary because, despite everything that had happened, despite the fact that Earth might still die from the wounds inflicted on it by having had to support a population of eighteen billion, and despite the population strictures she had imposed, the birth rate in those regions had suddenly shot up. Her enquiries into this painted an unhappy picture of incompetence, mainly due to the lack of a sufficiently well-trained and ruthless administration – the blame for which she could lay squarely at Alan Saul's feet – also an abrupt increase in food supplies, and misplaced hope for the future in a highly family-oriented culture. She had selected the most inefficient regions and released the Scour on them, then taken out their administration centres with tactical nukes. Even now the dozers and macerating machines were moving in.

But none of this was what she wanted to shout from the rooftops.

Eight point nine eight billion . . .

A watershed had been reached. Earth's population was finally down to a sustainable level and, though the diversity of fauna and flora was still limited, the planet was starting to bloom again.

'Two hundred and sixty million is the initial estimate, though with the infrastructure problems it's difficult to be sure.' He just gazed at her, not reacting because he had not yet heard her words, so she continued, 'Despite this tragic loss, one must take the long view and realize that the Scour, as terrible as it is, has quite possibly saved us from an extinction event. Earth's human population is now down below nine billion.' There, she'd said it at last.

Now she sat back to await his reply, no longer able to concentrate on the reports in front of her. It seemed to take so much longer for him to come back and, when she checked the time, she saw that it had actually taken six minutes over and above the signal delay.

'Surely the Scour, in itself, is an extinction event, ma'am?'

She didn't like the tone of his voice, and she didn't like that hint of something she was noticing in his expression. Did he know more than he was letting on? He had been close to her during those first days, after all . . . She suddenly felt very uncomfortable and considered sending on its way the signal that would close up that collar around his neck.

'But I understand what you mean, ma'am,' he continued.

'We can never again allow the population of Earth to rise as high as it was, and must ruthlessly enforce population strictures. It is just worrying that this disease keeps recurring as it does, because it could as easily kill someone we cannot afford to lose, like yourself. I simply hope our scientists will find some cure for it soon.'

'Very true,' she said. 'But meanwhile I must soldier on, as must you, Clay. As before: keep your reports coming and get in contact at once should there be anything further I need to know. That's all for now.' She shut down com.

His return to normal deference had been plausible and it seemed likely he knew nothing about the Scour's true source. He hadn't been that close, and she doubted that his erstwhile senior had let him in on the secret. Even so, Serene felt that his attitude added weight to her earlier decision to place him aboard the *Scourge* as a disposable asset – as someone high status she could kill as an object lesson to the rest of the crew, should that be required. She now switched to images taken from various aeros and hovering razorbirds, which she had just lately found very soothing.

The huge sprawls in the territory that had once been called Pakistan now lay before her. Even as she watched, a giant two-hundred-storey arcology gouted smoke from its base and collapsed as if it was being sucked into the ground, dust clouds spreading like pyroclastic flows through the surrounding streets. As it went down, birds launched from its roof, but these were birds of metal, graphene and numerous sharp edges. To the left of this, Serene spotted a group of shepherds striding through the sprawl like herons hunting frogs, eliminating any survivors of the Scour, for such survivors had to be subversives who had removed their ID implants. To the right of the collapse, ten robot bulldozers and five excavators, all on caterpillar treads of which each link was bigger than the average hydrovane car, were carving a lane through the lower-elevation sprawl beyond.

Behind them came the even larger bulks of two macerating machines, their giant, toothed front rollers clawing up the rubble so as to pass it inside themselves – big industrial magnets and computer-controlled sorters inside extracting metals and other useful materials, which were regularly spewed out again into the backs of awaiting all-terrain trucks.

The first machine tore up and macerated the surface rubble, spewing out behind it a massive cloud of fragments of carbocrete, concrete, brick and other building materials, doubtless slightly dampened by the numerous human corpses it had just rendered to sludge. At its rear end were deep plough attachments that were busy hooking up foundations, sewers and other underground infrastructure to a depth of ten metres, which the ensuing macerator then chewed up, too. By the time the second macerator passed, its ploughs probing deep into the ground, there were patches of soil now visible amidst the thick layers of ground-up rubble. And these were patches that Serene knew would, given time, turn green.

She had seen that steady spread of green already; seen Earth healing its wounds. She never tired of seeing it, and intended to see a lot, lot more.

Argus

His suit had been leaking, both from the oxygen pack and the gunshot in his leg – the repair patch and breach foam not having proved sufficient to seal the damage. Running out of air, he took great risks in getting himself back to the hydroponics unit – the drugs his VC suit automatically injected into his system conspiring to make him less cautious. Nevertheless, he made it back there without being caught and, because of those drugs, managed to strip off his suit without screaming in pain. Once he had done so, he soon realized he would not be putting it back on. It had used up all its breach foam, the patch he had used was the largest available and it now fell away, and though the leak from his oxygen pack was slow, it was still losing air faster than the recharging pump could replace it.

Where the bullet had struck his shin, splintered bone protruded from his leg. He knew that if he wasn't to die, he needed to work quickly, for now, with the breach foam peeled off the wound, it was bleeding heavily. He opened his medical kit and first used a spray of artificial skin with an integral coagulant, then he dragged himself around the hydroponics unit in search of materials for a splint – finally detaching the legs of a mantis-like agribot for that purpose. He cut the right boot from his discarded VC suit and put it back on, attached the splints to it, then hung a roll of duct tape from the top of one of them, above his knee, in readiness. After injecting himself with a powerful painkiller, he lodged his boot in a framework and, looping his arm around a nearby strut, he pulled.

Splintered bone retracted into his leg and, maintaining the tension, he used his free hand to wrap the duct tape round several times above his knee. He then laved on an antivibact salve, followed that with another layer of skin spray, then wound the rest of the tape round his leg, down to his ankle.

I should surrender, he thought, at last. Then he considered how that thought had not occurred to him until now. What would happen if he did surrender? It was possible that the rebels would hospitalize him first, and then lock him in the cell block. However, Alan Saul had said right from the start that there could be no freeloaders, no people on this station who did not contribute to the overall running of the place and to the survival of its residents. They might just kill him out of hand. Then a further thought occurred to him – one that had not occurred while he was lecturing Alexandra about the benefits of surrender. They might simply do to him what they had done to the delegates here, and to Messina. They might erase his mind, and how then would he rescue the Chairman? He wouldn't even be able to remember that service to Messina was the sum purpose of his life.

No surrender, he thought, feeling a deep regret for everything he had said earlier to his companion.

The painkillers lasted him only for five days, the medical kit having been made for short-term use to keep a soldier alive until he could be taken to a hospital. The pain then returned, along with fever and hallucinations. He ate sparingly from the ration packs or from the produce grown inside the unit, gazing enviously at a crop of root vegetables being packed into a transport cylinder by the agribots, and wondering if he could get away with stealing more. On the twentieth day, his long rambling conversation with Alexandra and Alex Two, who regularly returned to the unit in ghostly form to check his progress, was interrupted by sounds penetrating from outside. Abruptly recalled to lucidity, he awaited his moment of capture. He then saw the first of the waiting transport cylinders sliding into the conveyor airlock at the end of the unit, and realized that the hydroponics unit had just been properly reconnected to the rest of the station.

Further time passed, and he lost track of it. His moments of lucidity increased for a short time – though interspersed with long periods of black depression, during which he just wanted to die – but they then rapidly began to decrease. In one of those moments, he recognized a smell in the unit over and above the smell of bagged-up excrement. It was decay – the stench of his leg going bad. He managed to pull things together enough to take an overdose of the last of the antivi-bacts, and then the real world went away again. The soldier's rations ran out, and he began to forget how much food he was stealing from the unit and, in fear of discovery, starved himself. Later, in one of his better moments, he started using his VC suit palmtop to record his thefts from the unit, and began to eat more.

When not crippled by depression, he towed himself around the unit, constantly searching for some means of escape. During one of these searches he rediscovered an entire hydroponics trough assembly that he and Alexandra had found previously and decided would be of no use to them. He assembled it and, little by little, tapped nutrient fluid into it. He also took the risk of breaking open vacuum-sealed cylinders of seed stock – a theft that would not be reported to system until the next planting took place here – and began growing GM beans, mustard cress and peppers. These seemed to sprout with incremental slowness, but still grew faster than any unmodified plant. Their growth and the departure of the transport cylinders seemed the only marking of time until, in another moment, while salivating over a handful of mustard cress, he remembered where he was and that he was alone, and checked the time display in the visor of his VC suit. An entire month had passed. He sank into blackness, could see nothing beyond the walls enclosing him in the unit, and the darkness in his own mind.

Lucidity returned again with a deep feeling of horror when he realized there was movement underneath the tape around his leg. He carefully stripped it off, the stink unbearable and maggots spilling out. There were flies aboard the station, but he hadn't noticed them here in the unit laying their eggs on his leg. He understood enough about such matters to realize that, though part of the wound there had gone bad, these creatures, in combination with the overdose he had taken, had actually saved him. They were eating away the dead matter. He cut a piece of material from his VC suit and wrapped up his leg again, leaving the maggots in place, and continued his enforced hermitic lifestyle.

Later, as the maggots turned to chrysalises, he washed them in plant nutrient and then ate them. Later still he removed the splints from his leg and cleaned all the disgusting detritus away to reveal raw but healthy flesh. The last of his skin spray went onto that, while he yelled in pain, then he wrapped it in further strips torn from what remained of his VC suit.

Another month passed, then another. It vaguely occurred to Alex that those searching for him had probably assumed he was dead by now, but he no longer thought much about anything outside the parameters of his small world. Small victories were all he knew: forcing himself out of depression, eating the top shoots of his bean plants and then eating the first raw pods; managing to plant small cuttings snapped off tomato plants; using composted excrement in his own hydroponics trough and seeing healthier growth resulting; watching the scar tissue form over his leg wound. Then the station suddenly moved, and that returned to him the perception that something lay beyond his own microcosm.

'I have to get out of here,' he told Alexandra, thoroughly aware that she was dead, but comforted nevertheless by the hallucinatory power of his own mind.

'*Yes, you must,*' she replied, noncommittal.

Again he began prowling around the hydroponics unit. He picked up the remains of his VC suit, considered what he might use to repair it, then discarded it again. The movements of the station continued intermittently, and out of his fugue he realized that it must now have reached the Asteroid Belt and was manoeuvring itself around space debris. Understanding this raised him to a new level of consciousness and, when he again examined a transport cylinder and wondered what of the packed produce there he might steal, he finally saw his way out.

Saul gazed at an asteroid of a deep red, and saw there all the blood he had shed coagulated into one massive lump. No, it was actually red because it was mostly made of cinnabar, with an outer dusting of vermilion. Closer inspection also revealed silvery veins of pure frozen mercury.

I brought you here . . .

The station continued to decelerate, which was enough, and some pragmatic partition of his mind went, protesting, into abrupt abeyance. He dreamed now of wondrous technology, formed in a perfect ring, and strange tall beings striding through a realm of metal. He descended into a nightmare in which fire blasted through the corridors of the Political Office and rendered the survival suits of five individuals molten on their very bodies, then was sucked away again and drew them out, through a hole with red-hot lips, to a place where the fluid in their charred skins boiled and bubbled them into grotesque parodies of human beings. They did not even get a chance to scream, but the single female survivor – safely clad in a VC suit – screamed for them.

Saul fled that terrible place and dreamed of a man and woman stepping back from the ranked globular shapes of ceramic furnaces, both standing with their arms akimbo as they studied with satisfaction the plumbing now put in place. Robots retreated past them, folding away tools as they headed for an airlock, before departing one after another into the station enclosure. There they fell in a stream, on a tower of electromagnets and began to take apart a section punched through with a hole whose interior gleamed bright copper. No rest for them, no sleeping, no dreaming.

'Call it conscience,' said the watching woman.

Nightmares resumed, but Saul was aware that they were now old ones. He felt the lasers draining their linked super-capacitors, the wrench of steering thrusters, then the insufficient blast of the Mars Traveller engine. He looked on in guilty helplessness as, unprepared, people fell against the direction of acceleration, slammed into walls, ceilings or floors, hard angles, pipes, beams. A symphony of breaking bones and screams played in his head. It all seemed summed up by one figure in a spacesuit hurtling across the station enclosure, clipping a beam and spinning helplessly down towards the central asteroid before hitting it with a blast of vapour and his suit helmet tumbling away.

Steering thrusters wrenched again, then the scene lit up with bright light as the fifty-kilo rock which the lasers had been unable to deal with, and the station had been incapable of avoiding, punched through below, turning half its mass to white-hot gas, then a further half of the remainder into molten debris as, like a bullet through a drinks can, it speared on through an accommodation unit before slamming its way out through the upper enclosure. Eight people had occupied the accommodation unit. The rescuers found nothing but an oily residue of them on the walls.

'Breach protocols no longer apply, people,' someone announced finally, 'and let me make this perfectly clear, showers are available.'

In space all around, it seemed that the asteroid debris was slowing as that one giant red asteroid loomed closer. Like a growing steel mushroom, one of the smelting plants began to extrude itself from the station rim, the computer feedback from it again waking up that closed partition in Saul's mind.

He now looked for Hannah, as he always did.

'Quite simply,' said Hannah, gazing at the other woman peering out from the oval screen, 'we were not sure of your situation there, and whether there might be those on Mars who would merely pass the information back to Earth.'

'Tanglecom is secure,' replied the same woman who had haunted Saul's dreams. 'I am alone, and what you tell me will remain between us. I will tell absolutely no one else.' She paused, smiled weakly. 'In fact, your wanting to talk to me in private like this is fortuitous, because I needed some privacy so I could send you something that may be of use to you.'

Something seemed to flicker through Saul's mind, then he saw Hannah turning to look at some schematics appearing on a nearby secondary screen.

'What's this?' she asked.

'I've told lies here,' confessed the woman. 'When we took over this base, I claimed that Earth could get nothing to us for decades. And when Galahad revealed the *Alexander*, and then renamed it the *Scourge*, I pretended to have no previous knowledge of the craft, so obviously I want you to refrain from mentioning this in your further communications with us.'

'You still haven't told me what this stuff is,' Hannah remarked, fixedly gazing at the small screen.

'Detailed schematics of the *Scourge*, down to its last weld and rivet.'

'You're sure?'asked Hannah. 'How could you possibly be in possession of these?'

'I'm sure,' replied the other woman, 'because I built the damned thing.'

Hannah switched her attention back to the main screen. 'What?'

The other woman nodded slowly. 'I got transferred out here after my political officer came to the conclusion that I was no longer to be trusted with handling the orbital tools I was using, because I'd discovered that my husband had recently died not in an accident, but in an adjustment cell.'

'I see,' said Hannah. 'These plans should be . . . very useful.'

'Now, moving on,' said the other woman, almost as if embarrassed by her revelation, 'I'm also quite sure that your diversion into the Asteroid Belt, which you've been evasive about for some time, offers you no tactical advantage against the *Scourge*; rather the opposite, in fact. So, can you now tell me straight why you are really going there?'

'I'd decided to trust you anyway, and now you've confirmed that I can.' Hannah paused to key something into the console before her. 'I've just sent you a schematic of what we've built aboard this station. We changed course earlier so that we could swing into the Asteroid Belt and there stop at asteroid HJI457 – which is a twenty-second-century designation for those identified as from Holocene Jupiter impact. There we must acquire the materials to complete our project – specifically ten thousand tonnes of mercury.'

'*You've* decided?' said the woman, turning her head, presumably to peer at another screen. 'I would have thought that would be down to this "Owner" of yours.'

Hannah showed a flash or irritation at that. 'I don't really like that title, Var, and I myself am currently in charge of Argus Station.'

Var?

'You don't like it? So what do you prefer?' Var continued looking off to one side, and then added, 'And what the hell is that thing and why would you need that much mercury?'

Varalia.

'It's something Rhine designed,' said Hannah. 'It's based on a theorized engine called an Alcubierre warp drive.'

The other woman returned her gaze to Hannah, her expression shocked. She obviously understood straight away what Hannah was talking about. She was obviously very quick and very bright this . . . *Varalia Delex* . . . for she at once continued, 'Manoeuvring will be a problem within the Belt, but once you're clear your problems should be over.' She paused again to gaze at that other screen. 'That is, if this drive actually works.' She shook her head in irritation. 'You said you are currently in charge of the station – so what's this Owner of yours now doing?'

Hannah replied, 'The Owner, Alan Saul, is currently in a coma.'

Further shock suffused the other woman's expression.

'Alan,' she said, her voice catching.

His name was so familiar coming from her mouth; just her saying it seemed to reveal some underlying structure to his mind, and out of that the memories surfaced. He now saw her walking beside him in that enclave in the Dinaric Alps of old Albania as he talked about dying, talked about escape. He remembered another escape – when they were children – from the suffocating care of their parents, out into a zero-asset area, and that glimpse of another world before the enforcers came for them and dragged them back. By groping for other such memories, he began establishing connections between the disparate parts of his mind. Finding only fragments caused a deep frustration, and made him push harder.

A muggy day spent in the constant roar of a city arose in his mind. The triple-glazed window shut it out as his gaze slid to a large computer screen showing the exploded schematic of a fusion engine, which was assembling automatically, then shrinking down small and dropping into another schematic recognizable as that of a Mars Traveller. The woman sitting before the screen sat back, for a moment studied the wedding ring on her finger, smiled at it, then swung her chair round to face him.

'Of course I can do better,' she said.

You were going to build spaceships . . .

Varalia Delex, whose second name she had acquired by marriage to her husband Latham Delex. Varalia whose maiden name had been Saul.

'Hello, sister,' Saul's voice grated, and he opened his eyes.

Earth

The four giant ships had been supertankers in a previous incarnation, and were the last of their kind turned out at the Port of Dalian shipyards. That they had remained functional for so long after the wells ran dry was testament to the then-innovative materials and technologies used in their construction: graphene and metals foamed on Earth before that technology really got into its stride in more suitable zero-gravity environments, new ceramics, tough new forms of glass, nano-coatings, clean-burn fission reactors and computer-controlled robots that continued maintaining those vessels during all the later years they served as floating prison ships. Now the prisoners were all dead: the ZAs killed by the Scour and the remaining SAs dying either of starvation or diseases prevalent amidst tens of thousands of rotting corpses.

'I am impressed,' said Serene, as she piloted the big aero down towards the landing deck. 'I didn't expect them to be ready so soon.'

The manager of the new project was a marine biologist called Michael Palgrave, a thin severe-looking man with blond hair and a badly sunburned nose, who stood nervously behind her; Sack was in the seat behind him, arms folded and a bored expression on his lizard face.

'We had the robots here, and it was simple enough to get them to strip out the cell partitions inside the old oil tanks,' he replied. 'We then constructed the nursery pools on the old prison floors and utilized plumbing already in place to get things started. It took longer to automate the sea-seeding system, and we have had problems with the stock.'

'I understand,' said Serene, quite happy to let the man ramble on because she was pleased with what was happening here.

As she finally settled the aero down on the landing pad, she glanced towards land and noted the green smear extending out across ten kilometres of sea. This was why they had chosen this area for the releases. The Dubai swamps had soaked up over two hundred million Scour victims and thus become poisonously anaerobic. However, from them this algae bloom had spread out to sea, and just beyond it the sea plankton had undergone a resurgence. There was food here now: microscopic food but billions of tonnes of it. She silently thanked the erstwhile rulers of the small but wealthy country that had once lain inland.

After surviving international crashes of the financial system with copious oil money, the rulers of Dubai had continued their project of turning their country into a tourist destination in readiness for when the oil ran out. After building the Palm Tree and the World island groups on their coastline, they became more ambitious and transformed that coastline from end to end. However, to maintain all this required the constant work of massive dredgers and underwater silt pumps the size of mosques. This was all fine while the oil money flowed and as it began to wane, when the influx of wealthy tourists took up the slack.

Serene stepped out of the aero behind her close-protection team, Sack immediately behind her and Palgrave a step behind him. She waved the marine biologist forward to stand beside her as her various PAs and other staff also exited the aero. 'So where first?'

He pointed ahead to one of the new buildings erected on the hectares of deck. 'We call it the panoquaria. It's where we harvest eggs, milt and spores from the adult fauna and flora, and it also serves as the hatchery.'

'Lead on,' said Serene happily, flicking another glance back towards the coast, and considering the disasters that occurred there before she was born.

The first oil-quake, which dropped the Burj Al Arab hotel and its population of four hundred and eighty billionaires into the ocean and left the Burj Khalifa tower tilted at twenty degrees, was also the first nail in the lid of the coffin constructed by Middle Eastern fundamentalism. Other nails were soon to follow. No one knew who had fired the missile at Tel Aviv from Iraq, but the warhead the ancient SCUD carried could only have come from Iran's shiny new collection. Mossad was blamed for the detonation of a similar device in a Baghdad cellar, and was also held responsible for the air-burst biological weapon detonated over Mecca during the Hajj, but that was only after the month-long incubation period of the virus, when it started killing returning pilgrims, as well as their families and friends around them.

After her close-protection team had checked what lay ahead, then signalled an all-clear, Serene followed Palgrave into the new building and gazed round in wonder. Along a row of tanks a group of human workers clad in hazmat suits – which were actually not protection for them but for what they were handling – were netting fish from tanks and gently squeezing milt and eggs from them into containers strapped to their waists. To her right a long, low aquarium swarmed with shrimp, while in others she spied prawns, crabs and various other crustaceans.

As she gazed at these, Serene considered the final chapters in the disaster that occurred inland of here. Resources – it was always about resources. As it was finally recognized that the human race had passed over the Hubbert Peak – that Peak Oil had passed – and as new technologies were finally taken out of the laboratory and applied across the world, Middle Eastern fortunes began to wane as oil magnates tried to cash in by overpricing a failing resource. The result of this was that the fundamentalists hereabouts soon learned that religious tolerance began and ended at the petrol pump, and no one felt any inclination to build the new fusion reactors in lands which, in public perception, had constantly supplied the world with bearded lunatics with strap-on bombs or home-brewed biological weapons.

When the Golden Decade came to an end in an overpopulated world where food and fresh water were running out and financial systems imploding, barren desert countries were the first to suffer, no matter how fat the bank accounts of their rulers. Then, as the nascent Committee gleefully began applying confiscatory taxes, Middle Eastern fortunes plummeted further. Here in Dubai the money eventually ran out and the island project failed, the island groups dissolving into a saltwater swamp that swallowed all the millionaire condos and tower blocks. But it was a failure Palgrave was now making use of.

'The fiddler crab population here shot up just after the Scour,' explained Palgrave, breaking into her thoughts as he pointed at a tank containing some examples of that species, 'then it crashed with the spread of a very specific fungal infection. That's our problem, you see. Monocultures are susceptible to that sort of thing, so we need more variety.'

'I am aware of that,' Serene replied, frowning, a little of the sunshine going out of her day, 'which is why, as you must be aware, the *Scourge* has gone after Argus Station. Once we have recovered the Gene Bank data and samples, we can introduce more variety.'

'Though admittedly,' Palgrave hurriedly added, 'every day we're rediscovering species long thought to be extinct. All it takes is one or two surviving eggs or spores on the seabed . . .'

There had been some cheering news over the last few months. Some old varieties of bees had been discovered building colonies in defunct agricultural plants – bees thought to have been wiped out in the twenty-first century by mite infections. Serene often found herself now wondering if Earth's biosphere could recover without all that stuff from the Gene Bank. However, every time her hopes were raised, something else came along and dashed them. The Mediterranean octopus was one example. Amazingly it still existed, yet the proof of that was only washed up on the shore *after* big infrastructure crashes in the Peloponnese had led to a case-hardening plant dumping a few billion gallons of toxic waste into the sea.

From the panoquaria they headed down below decks to the nursery tanks, all swarming with fish fry, crustaceans, mollusc larvae and seaweed spores. This place gratifyingly smelt of life, of renewal, of new beginnings.

'It's begun,' said Palgrave, pointing out one tank as it began to drain, its tonnes of fish fry draining out through metre-diameter pipes to outlets all along the sides of this erstwhile supertanker. She followed him along two kilometres of aisles, never feeling any of the inclination to boredom she felt in scramjet or space-plane construction plants. At one point, noting their lack of enthusiasm, she dismissed her PAs back up to the deck, retaining only Sack and her close protection team. By the time, four hours later, she reached an elevator leading back up to the deck, many of the nursery tanks had emptied and were now refilling with filtered and purified seawater.

It had begun; the renewal of Earth had really begun.

As they came back up onto the deck, Palgrave put his fingers up to his fone, then stumbled. He suddenly looked even paler than before, as he turned to stare at her with terrified eyes.

'A problem?' she enquired, immediately recognizing his reaction.

He glanced to one side, towards the distant deck rail. 'There was always the possibility—'

She held up a hand to silence him. 'What is the problem?'

'I have to check something.' Palgrave started to back away.

'Bring him,' she said, turning and heading towards the rail.

Palgrave let out a yelp of surprise and she glanced back to see two of her team grab him and begin dragging him after her. Heat haze shimmered over the deck ahead and the sunlight seemed suddenly too bright. Sweat immediately plastered her blouse to her back and she began to feel extremely irritated. She groped in her top pocket for her sunglasses, put them on, then quickly took them off again to wipe off the smeary fingerprints with a tissue. It was so difficult ever to obtain answers that weren't utterly distorted by the self-interest of her employees. Putting her sunglasses back on as she reached the edge of the ship, she rested her hands on the hot graphene rail and gazed first in puzzlement, then in growing horror at the scene before her.

'The pumps,' Palgrave said miserably, 'they've stirred up something from the ocean bed.'

Hectares of ocean were now covered with a scum of dead and dying fish. Nurtured inside this ship, raised healthy and ready to begin their task of renewal, they'd been pumped straight out into poison. Serene reached up to raise her sunglasses, scrubbed away tears, then slipping the glasses back into place she turned her gaze on Palgrave.

Of course, the man hung dejectedly between the two enforcers, and fully expected to die. She also noted that every one of her protection team, and Sack too, expected her to give the order, and were only waiting to learn how she wanted Palgrave killed.

'Release him,' she said.

The two enforcers did so, and Palgrave subsided heavily on his knees.

'In your effort to please me,' she said, 'you did not take sufficient precautions. You did not adequately survey this release area.'

He looked up at her, still waiting for the axe to fall.

She continued, 'Do not make the same mistake again.' She then turned and began walking back along the hot deck to the aero landing platform, gesturing Sack and her team after her. Always, she decided, there came a time to put away childish things, and killing out of spite was one of them.

13

Rest in Peace

Towards the end of the twenty-first century, with land at a premium and with old traditions dying and religions crumbling, human burial became increasingly unfeasible. In some places that old method of human burial whereby a grave was effectively rented, and the bones were later transferred to an ossuary, did gain a brief foothold but it was soon swept away. Public safety and the recycling meme of preceding decades were used by governments to enforce change. Burial was taxed and legislated into extinction, and graveyards soon cleared for either agriculture or building purposes. Cremations of the singular kind were killed off in the same way – pollution taxes and health and safety 'issues' soon making them prohibitively expensive. Communal incinerations quickly became the norm, with the bereaved storing their dead until there were enough for a single burn inside some combined trash-incineration and power-generating plant. Later changes, first in the biotech and macerating technology, then in the laws governing what could go into community digesters which provided methane gas supplies and compost for agriculture enabled a return to individual disposal, since there were no constraints on when a corpse could go into a digester. People could even bring flowers, too – to cast down, after their loved one, into the hopper and the macerating drums.

Argus

As Alex stood over a transport cylinder he was making ready, he felt an overpowering reluctance to follow through with his plan, then turned and gazed at his personal hydroponics trough. He simply did not want to leave his plants alone; nor did he want to leave his little refuge. However, his programming proved stronger, and he returned to the task in hand.

The lock on the cylinder lid had been first. He had removed a plate from the interior, which covered the mechanism, and now, with a pair of pliers from a simple toolkit, he could open the cylinder from inside. This he would only be able to do once it reached its destination – which would be one of the cold stores scattered throughout the station. If he tried opening it while it was being air-blasted along its transport tube, he'd probably emerge out the other end in bits.

The problem he now faced was a computer, one that Alexandra could probably have solved in an instant. He needed the cylinder to inform the hydroponics unit that it was full and therefore ready to be sent on its way. Five hours of working with the computer in the cylinder and in the unit itself got him nowhere. Then he traced some wiring and found the solution so simple it made him laugh hysterically. The cylinder broadcast its readiness to be filled after it arrived and its lid was opened. It then broadcast its readiness to be transported away again simply when the lid was closed.

Alex now collected all the items he could think of that might be of use when he reached the cold store, starting with his rifle. He then ate everything his plants had recently produced, followed by a portion stolen from the unit itself, drank his fill of the water yet to be laced with plant nutrient, then lay down inside the cylinder. As he reached up to close the lid, some strange memory niggled at him and he paused in puzzlement to try and nail it down. After a moment it became clear.

'Like a coffin,' he said out loud.

The comparison carried no emotional baggage. Coffins were something he knew about through watching some of the few politically approved films he had been allowed, and so possessed no macabre associations. Putting dead people in boxes in order to bury them was a waste of resources the Earth had been unable to afford for nearly a century. And a funeral was these days a short goodbye next to the hopper of a community digester or waste incinerator.

He closed the lid.

Oddly, lights immediately came on inside, but lights of a deep purplish blue. He realized he was being bathed in ultraviolet, which was regularly used to wipe out free bacteria and viruses. The cylinder began to move, and he felt the clonk as it entered the transport tube. He was on his way; this was going to work!

Then a sulphurous vapour began to fill the cylinder and he realized that ultraviolet was not all they used to prevent the spread of diseases. Immediately he was gasping for breath and then clawing at the lid above him, even as he felt the cylinder accelerate down its tube. He realized that opening the cylinder now might kill him, but the gas most certainly would. But where were the pliers? He groped about, just as the cylinder abruptly decelerated. He held his breath, was relieved to feel another clonk just as he found the pliers down beside his chest. Then, even as he scrabbled at the locking mechanism, the lid suddenly opened.

His eyes were watering and he just could not stop coughing.

Something was opening and closing above him, and he reached up and shoved at it and, with a whine of hydraulics, a jointed arm withdrew its four-fingered claw – the computer controlling it obviously confused over what it had found. He grabbed the same claw and used it to heave himself out, and propel himself away. Then, as his vision cleared, he studied his surroundings.

The cylinder had arrived in a hexagonal aisle, surrounded on all sides by translucent boxes packed with produce. Immediately he started shivering but, as he gasped, he realized it was lucky he was still able to breathe. This store had been made for human access so had been kept oxygenated. It was also for preserving food, so it was very cold. He propelled himself along the aisle to the end, out into a metre-wide space between the entrances to six other aisles and the end wall. The store seemed to be arranged like the ammunition cylinder of a six-gun.

In the centre of the near wall sat an airlock, which he immediately went over to and opened, pulling himself inside. Ensuring that the inner door remained open by jamming the pliers into the hole where the hinge curved into the wall, he moved over to the outer door and rubbed at a veneer of ice that was frosting a single porthole. Eventually he obtained a view he could understand. Outside, a cageway extended for ten metres then curved to the right, and visible through the cageway to the left was that thing the robots had been building in the outer rim. He felt like crying. The only improvement in his situation here was access to more food and this additional view. Without a spacesuit, he could go no further than this, and he could not stay here either. The cold in the store behind him, though not sufficient to freeze the produce and thus ruin it, would still eventually kill him. He turned, retrieved his

330

pliers and headed back to see if he could get the cylinder to transport him back home.

The oval screen before Hannah went to a holding logo, which had once been a United Earth one but was now simply a picture of Argus Station taken from one of the smelting plants. But then, oddly, that changed to a still image of Var Delex.

'Now that's strange,' said Rhine.

Hannah glanced across at him questioningly. He was sitting before another screen via which he had been monitoring tanglecom, measuring quantum effects within the tangle box itself or, as he put it, 'checking the cat's poison'. Now his screen also showed an image of Var Delex's face. Hannah turned to look at other screens in the room and saw that they too showed the same image.

'One of your quantum effects?' Hannah suggested, then abruptly grabbed the arms of her chair as a deep thrumming noise rose into being and seemed to penetrate her to the bone. It continued for a while and was so intense she saw a pen vibrate across the tabletop nearby and fall to the floor. 'Shit, what is that?'

Hannah could think of very little that could have caused it, but feared something major: Arcoplex Two itself going out of balance, or the massive motors that turned it breaking down. She punched some commands into her console and disconnected the screen before her from the tangle box, immediately calling up the station log to see if anything had been reported either by the system or by the staff.

'PA system,' said Rhine, the image of Var Delex banished from his screen and other data appearing there. 'Maybe he's having another nightmare.'

If Saul was stirring uneasily in slumber, the stuff issuing

331

from his mind into the station system had changed radically. Surely this was something else? The station log appeared on her screen, slowly scrolling as new events were added, then suddenly it blurred as the number of those events suddenly rose, and, just at that moment, she got notifications of four calls queued up on her fone. One was from her laboratory, the other three from Brigitta, Langstrom and Le Roque. She answered the technical director's call first.

'What is it?' she asked.

'Isn't that the question I should be asking you?' he shot back.

'Le Roque, the station log just went crazy after an image of Var Delex appeared on our screens here, and then some . . . noise over the PA system. I'm not keeping anything from you, so speak to me.'

'Same screen image in Tech Central,' he replied grudgingly, 'and, as far as I can gather, all across the station. That noise was odd because it was largely infrasound, which can have some strange effects. But that's not all that's happened. Grab yourself exterior cam views of your arcoplex, as you might find them interesting.'

She banished the log file and called up image feeds, selected four, and her screen now quartered to provide them. Her first impression was of metallic movement, more than should be registered through these cams, for all that should be visible was the steady rotation of Arcoplex Two. It took her a moment to realize that she was seeing masses of robots on the move.

'What the hell?' she said.

'So you know nothing about this?' said Le Roque.

Hannah selected another more distant view of the arcoplex and saw how robots were swarming around it like ants around a chunk of salami. There were thousands of them, maybe their whole population here.

'They just finished off whatever job they were doing and headed straight for Arcoplex Two,' said Le Roque. 'The only ones not included were the fixed robots, some currently working out on the vortex generator, and the proctors.'

Hannah stood and headed over to the door. 'Let me start checking things out – I'll get back to you.' She opened the door and looked out, and realized that her spidergun was no longer with her. Was this something else that had entered the station queue? Some new order from Saul's unconscious mind?

'Brigitta,' she said quickly, responding to the next call, 'I've no idea what's going on. Have you?'

'I take it you saw the robots?' the Saberhagen twin asked.

'I've seen them.'

'Every station weapon that was capable just powered up too.'

What the hell was going on?

'I'll get back to you.' She responded to the next call: 'Langstrom?'

'Why the alert, Dr Neumann?' the soldier asked.

'I'm trying to find out what the hell is going on, Langstrom. What alert are you talking about?' Maybe the PA system was still issuing infrasound, because her skin suddenly felt cold, as if in response to some invisible wind sweeping through the station.

'We just got instructed to go to full security alert – all station police called on duty and permission given to employ deadly force. Yet the arms caches are locked down. I checked with Le Roque and it's nothing to do with him. It makes no sense.'

'It's not me, either. I'll see what I can find out.' She shut off that line and noted the one left was routed from her laboratory. She then remembered that it was closed off, and that neither James nor any other member of her staff was there. Suddenly she had an intimation of what it might be. She opened the channel in question.

'Recorded Alert One,' her own voice told her. 'Alpha rhythms detected and patient conscious.'

It was the message she had wanted to hear for months but, now it had arrived, she felt numb. She didn't know what to say to the others. She had to check first. She turned to gaze at Rhine, who took one look at her expression and asked, 'What's the problem, Dr Neumann?'

'No problem, none at all,' she said, noting the slight edge of hysteria in her voice. 'It's Saul – I think he's awake.'

'At last,' said Rhine, looking somewhat smug.

She turned away from him, stepped out into the corridor and began walking. *The sleeping god wakes*, she thought, not sure where those words had come from. It was all right for Rhine to feel vindicated, to feel that an ally had returned to the conscious world, but he did not know what Hannah knew: that the one now waking up might not even know Rhine, might not even know what it was to be a human being.

Saul gazed steadily upwards, but could see nothing but weird rainbow effects spreading out in watery ripples. The bullet had all but destroyed his visual cortex at the back of his skull, but he had lain here for months with brain matter growing to fill the spaces, which he at once checked, sliding into Hannah's laboratory computer to assess the extent of the healing. His visual cortex occupied a larger area at the back of his skull than before, and its structure was substantially changed, as

were all the other portions of his brain that had been damaged. His optic nerve was also thicker, and the neural density
to the rods and cones of his eyes had all but doubled.

Saul groped for connections, activating dormant synapses
and firing up the somnolent nerve tissue lying between them.
His vision hazed in and out like a TV channel search. He
thought that it might be better if he actually had something
other than just the ceiling to focus on, so decided to sit up.
Just for a moment he could not, then further previously
damaged neurons fired up, fed back into a mental partition
that defined every function of his physical body, and in an
instant he remembered how to control it all, utterly.

The physical effort required in the arcoplex's gravity was
the only downside. He could define and minutely control
every muscle in his body, route blood to them and have them
working in perfect concert, but they were partially wasted
since muscle-tone stimulation though useful, was hardly
adequate. For a while at least it might be a good idea to
confine himself to the zero-gravity areas of the station.

Now sitting upright, he concentrated on his vision – still
trying to tune in to that station. Shapes began to appear and
he tried to resolve them, understand them. One came clear: a
circle, rainbow ripples distorting it and bright light burning
a hole through one section of the circumference. He tuned
out that light and the circle became clear. He saw a rim of
concentrically ridged plastic with an object lying across looking like a long curved claw. Scattered about this ring were
white crusty items like sheets of crunched-up and compressed
bubble wrap. He could comprehend none of these objects as
he next focused on the glassy eye this ring enclosed.

Here were lines, reflected lights and a distorted image
down towards the bottom. Unable to make anything of that,

he instinctively cleaned it up with a program now running in his visual cortex but more commonly found in cam systems. The distortions ironed out, presenting him with a clear image of his own reflection. But what was he being reflected from? Another program – a search through his distributed mind – quickly rendered just one result, and he then had to recalculate scale. He was focusing right across the room at one lens of a binocular microscope, and the objects on the plastic rim about that lens were a human eyelash and a scattering of skin flakes. And next, when the lights came on like a sun going nova, he realized he had been seeing that lens in infra-red.

'You're awake!'

Now aware of his visual error, he focused on Hannah entire, mapped her features, noted extra lines on her face, a healing cut on her earlobe and some new grey hairs on her head. He was seeing her complete, and not using the visual shorthand the human brain usually employed to identify someone. She was also thinner, he noticed, looking tired and worried. He read fear in her expression too: fear of him, and of what she was going to find here, which kept her hovering just inside the door as if ready to flee.

'I am awake,' he agreed, his voice hoarse, the very words opening to his inspection further connections inside and outside his skull.

The words appeared as text in the visual centre of his brain, and via new connections, were open to be expressed in any language he chose. This was just through a simple connection to the station network, which had located a language library. However, while he had been unconscious, the partition of his mind containing his language centre had already analysed that library in depth and he could not only speak the words in any tongue now, but place on them any nuance he required. His mind, partitioned throughout this particular body's brain, and throughout the extra neural tissue residing in two metre-square boxes in this laboratory's clean-room, and then throughout the station system, seemed to have been very busy indeed.

'How are you feeling?' Hannah inevitably asked.

'I will answer the question you *wanted* to ask, rather than give you the conventional response,' he said flatly. 'I am sane, I am functional and have become more than I was before I was shot and, to be specific, I will take charge once again.'

She moved further into the laboratory, some of the tension slipping out of her as she briefly focused on some of the laboratory screen displays. Saul knew what she was seeing there: glimpses of a mind functioning smoothly, while efficiently running the nervous system of a human body, revealing no signs of epilepsy or the other crippling effects of brain damage, instead operating in smooth waveforms. These reassured her, and perhaps she was discounting everything else that she could not recognize because she wanted him to take charge again. She wanted the *responsibility* taken away from her.

'More than you were before?' she asked, moving over beside him and immediately busying herself with removing monitor pads from his chest and skull.

'I kept myself functional because of this Scour, because we needed to know what it was all about. I should not have done so. My body, brain and mind required time to heal. I ideally needed to shut down to allow that process to commence properly. However, our situation was too dangerous for me to release my hold completely. I first ensured that the robots would obey you, and you alone, then as I slid into unconsciousness I partitioned my mind, delegating my will and intentions to its various parts.'

'It seems that you achieved a lot in a very short time,' said Hannah, spraying antivibact on the skin behind his ear as she pulled out a hair-thin optical probe penetrating the inside of his skull. 'I thought you could hardly manage to look through one cam, at the time.'

'It was instinctive,' said Saul dismissively, then added, 'though instinct is a questionable description of what I did.'

'Like, for example,' said Hannah, 'instinctively calling just about every robot on this station to your present location.'

In an instant he was gazing through cams located outside the arcoplex, then into the minds of the massed robots and isolating what had brought them here. It was something that had spread virally from the two spiderguns now stationed outside the door to this laboratory. He could define it as computer code, but an easier description would be that it was their protective instincts kicking in. He shut it down, he reassured them, and sent them back to work, watched them hesitantly moving away as if unsure that he knew what he was doing.

'They are returning to work now,' he said.

'Well,' Hannah shrugged, 'that certainly shows that you are in charge but, anyway, we soon found out that you never really weren't.'

'Quite so,' Saul agreed, 'though my awareness of that fact wasn't wholly conscious.' He reached up to pull the teragate plug from the socket in his skull, and switched the data stream going through it over to his internal radio modem, then continued, 'I lapsed into unconsciousness without preparing any way to wake myself. Partitioning my mind was almost a survival effort, but it has had some beneficial results.'

'What did wake you?' Hannah asked.

'Let me get to that in its turn,' Saul said.

'Okay, you're the boss.' Hannah's expression was wry, almost sad.

'The parts of my mind were not completely separate, however,' he said. 'There were those for my senses, the other functions of my body and the functions of my mind, but access was required to them for one other partition. I needed to analyse our situation perpetually and make the best decisions about what to do to improve our chances of surviving. Hence the orders for Rhine's vortex generator to be built, and the subsequent course changes – these decisions were made inside that partition.'

'It's an interesting theory,' said Hannah sniffily, 'and I would guess that from your point of view the different parts of your mind would seem like partitions. In reality the human brain, and thus mind, is already a divided thing.'

He understood her reaction at once and knew that she was uttering such half-truths because he had infringed on her territory, her expertise. Even in her computer as she tried to map what was happening to him, she had labelled the partitions. Therefore it was so childish of her to react in this way. He paused in that train of thought, and realized that he had sounded bombastic, pompous and patronizing. He understood that if he clearly stated his thoughts to anyone now, he would always sound that way, while much of what they said to him would seem like the wittering of children.

Re-establish humanity . . .

'Yeah, I guess so, but it's much easier to use computer

analogies' – he smiled ruefully at her – 'especially after some-one started sticking computer processors in my head.'

'Never by choice,' she said crossly.

'Ah, choice,' he said, humanity re-established. 'Anyway, those bits of my mind that were damaged eventually healed.' He studied her carefully, deciding it would be best for her to see it for herself rather than have him lecture her. 'You said the bio-interface in my skull would grow according to demand, and that those bits of my mind governing my senses, the processing of certain kinds of information like mathemat-ics, spatial ability, even aesthetics if there is such a part, were internalized, they had no reference frame . . .'

He saw her expression, blank at first, then frown lines appearing on her forehead as she realized she had something to think about here, rather than just absorb.

'Without any reference frame, without connections to the other parts of your mind, the bio-interface wouldn't have known whether or not there was demand,' she said. 'It would have had two options. It could simply stop growing its neural net or have it keep on growing.'

'It kept growing.' He stabbed a finger towards the clean-room door. 'And there was room for it.'

'But that's . . . separate . . .'

He nodded once, waiting for her to catch up – and she did.

'Of course, it continued to grow physically in your skull but informationally in your . . . spares.'

'My vision is a prime example of what's happened inside this body,' he said. 'The net has grown into my optic nerve and done a lot in my visual cortex. I can see into infra-red now, and a little into ultraviolet – though I think that's the full physical extent available to me. I'm also no longer using the usual mental shorthand for anything I see.'

'You're processing everything, every detail?'

'Different shorthand – using up a few more pages.'

'Omniscience?' Hannah asked, opening a container down beside his bed and taking out a standard undersuit for space apparel.

'Hardly.'

Swinging his legs off the surgical table was not quite so difficult as sitting upright had been, but still he felt exhausted after the effort. He felt disconnected too, but it was the familiar inertia experienced after a long deep sleep. An urgency in him was growing and his focus kept drifting away from this laboratory, out towards the smelting plant and the cinnabar asteroid, to the vortex generator and to the eight proctors now ranged all the way round it like priests guarding some temple relic.

'*We felt you,*' said the proctor named Judd. '*Your orders?*'

'*Unchanged by full consciousness,*' Saul replied mentally. '*You have done well.*'

'*There are inefficiencies,*' said the proctor Paul, who was currently with another proctor called David in the Arboretum cylinder world.

'*If you had taken full charge,*' Saul informed the android, '*station personnel would have rebelled, creating greater inefficiencies.*'

'*I understand.*'

'*Yes, of course you do.*'

These beings were something Saul needed to focus on closely when the opportunity arose, but right now he needed to get moving, to show himself to the people of this station, to optimize their chances of survival. Because, still, the approaching *Scourge* felt like a hot nail driving towards his eye.

'I need to run some tests,' said Hannah, frowning.

'Only for your own reassurance,' he answered. 'I know my condition.'

'Okay, so let me ask you again,' she said. 'How do you feel?'

He allowed the sensation of pain for a second, then quickly shut that down. 'Like I was shot three times and then operated on. Like my head has been opened up and most of the contents scooped out, and like I've been flat on my back for several months.'

'Then precisely as you *should* feel.' Hannah passed him the undersuit, then stooped down again to the container to begin unpacking a VC suit. In merely storing that clothing here, she had obviously tried to remain optimistic. 'Do you need any help?'

Despite her keeping garments ready for him, her tone told him she didn't approve of him getting out of bed now without her checking him over. Perhaps she didn't understand just how irrelevant his body felt to him. It was a much more complicated device than the robots he had earlier controlled and was now reassuming control of, but to him it was still merely a telefactored biological machine.

Considering that, his mind wandered off into some half-fugue state. There, in a strange way, he felt grateful for the shooting for, even though the manner of its occurrence was catastrophic, Saul had been pushed to what seemed like the next stage of his personal evolution: immortal mind – distributed, copied, safe, and his physical body just one of many he now controlled. In that moment he saw a possible future. As his abilities and the technologies he controlled increased, eventually there would come a time when he could grow replacement versions of himself, place within them the minds he required for any particular task and reabsorb that mind into his whole self after it completed that task.

Then reality came back. All that was still for the future, and he had to survive the now.

'I can manage,' he replied – the answer intended for her and for something inside him.

Slowly and methodically he eased himself from the bed, pulled the undersuit on over his scarred and tender flesh, then donned the vacuum combat suit, meticulously tightening its concertinaed seams. As he did this, he was also aware that when the alert had been transmitted to Hannah's fone to bring her here, she had told Rhine what she was responding to. Rhine had quickly taken an almost childlike pleasure, which wasn't without malice, in telling Le Roque. The technical director froze like a rabbit in the headlights before informing Langstrom, who had looked equally as frightened before getting himself under control and informing his staff. Thereafter the news had spread by fone and computer throughout the station.

'How do I look?' he eventually asked.

'Like something hot from a Transylvanian tomb.'

'Thank you for your support.' He paused, now considering whether to answer her earlier question, and decided there would be no advantage in her not knowing.

'You asked what woke me,' he said.

'Yes – you haven't really explained that.'

'It was a connection to the outside world, the conscious world, a connection running so deep it could not be ignored,' he explained. 'Even in the state I was in, I was still watching this station and still listening. I heard your recent tanglecom exchange with Varalia Delex.'

'I don't see any deep connection,' said Hannah, puzzled.

'Perhaps you did not notice her reaction when you told her my name. Maybe it's understandable that you missed it. As for me, I hardly recognized her – since so few of the memories remain.'

'Memories of what?'

'Her name is Varalia Delex, but that's her married name – from her husband, Latham Delex. Her maiden name is Varalia Saul. Hannah, she's my sister.'

Hannah's expression registered shock, then all sorts of rapid calculation and reassessment. 'You knew she was out here?' she tentatively asked.

'I knew she was offworld but I had no idea where. Perhaps that knowledge was a subconscious driving force, but I can't even speculate on how much influence it has had on my actions and decisions since I found myself on the way into the Calais incinerator.'

'You knew,' Hannah asserted.

'I thought you only dealt with empirical fact, Hannah?'

'Yes,' she said, obviously still thinking hard.

'Let's get moving, shall we,' he suggested.

She gazed at him dubiously for a second, then reached up and touched her fone with her fingertips. 'Langstrom is waiting for you outside, and Le Roque awaits you in Tech Central.'

'Yes, I am aware of that.' Saul smiled.

'What are you going to do?' she asked.

'I am not going to kill anyone, Hannah.' He knew about Le Roque and Langstrom's attempt to take control of the station, and he understood why they had felt the need.

A dizzy spell hit him as he began to walk, and his vision doubled for a second as he established further control over his brain's visual centre. Elsewhere within that organ, he could feel other control firmly establishing itself: the unsteady beat of his heart stabilizing as he finally relinquished remote control of it; other functions consciously controlled sliding over to autonomous function; memories copying back from his 'spares' as structures connected up in this physical body's brain to contain them; the new neural network from the biochip firming up and windows flashing open and closed into the virtual world of the station. Opening the door and stepping out, he turned to his police commander, who was now accompanied only by the repro Manuel.

'Langstrom,' he said, noting the addition of lines of strain in the man's face, a few grey hairs and a slight indentation to his jawline that signified the man had lost a tooth and had yet to have it replaced.

'You're . . . okay?' Langstrom asked, gazing at him wide-eyed. 'I didn't quite believe . . .'

'I am functional.' Saul paused, remembering to appear human. 'I'm in surprisingly good shape considering what happened to me, but we have the advanced medical technology here and the expertise.' He reached over and clasped Hannah's shoulder. 'I'm alive, let's put it that way.' He smiled, then realized from Langstrom's expression that he hadn't managed that correctly. The repro, of course, hardly noticed. 'So, what news on this remaining Messina clone?'

Langstrom looked suddenly shamefaced. 'No sign of him since a robot winged him when we ambushed both him and his partner aboard Messina's space plane. I'm beginning to wonder if he just crawled away and died.'

'We'll find him,' Saul assured the man. 'Come.' He set off

along the corridor, meanwhile sending a mental summons to certain others whose presence he required.

The journey to Tech Central was fraught with dangers for him. The tightness of his VC suit helmet caused psycho-somatic pains he only managed to rid himself of by shutting down new nerve growth in his scalp. Outside the arcoplex, the zero-gravity falling sensations returned so strong he nearly lost control of his limbs, while also trying to again get the hang of using gecko boots. The weakness he felt from moving about after being so long bedridden could not be dispelled, and by the time he arrived in Tech Central he felt exhausted. How-ever, he maintained rigid control and did not allow these weaknesses to show as he stepped inside the main control room and studied the people here: *his* people.

Scourge

Activity in the *Scourge* had ramped up and every time Clay stepped out of his cabin there would be someone hurrying to some destination, with an expression worried and intense. Throughout the initial months of their journey, everybody had worked efficiently, just doing their jobs, being professional, but as time progressed such activity sank into a kind of robotic boredom. Then there was the fight in the troop section, and Liang's execution of one of those involved in it, but not its prime instigator. This had knocked any real trouble on the head, and discipline had further tightened up after Liang doubled up on combat theory and tests, for which the punishment for failure involved the use of a disabler, and he instituted weapons drills outside on the hull of the *Scourge*, which left the soldiers too tired to attack each other. Now that they were decelerating into the Asteroid Belt, however, they were all inside, constantly exercising in the ersatz gravity to rebuild muscle mass.

With the crew there had been no further problems since Clay's punishment of Pilot Officer Trove, and they remained completely correct around him, but distant. It was time for that to change, though Clay worried about what the extent of that change might be.

'You summoned me,' said Scotonis, after Clay had opened the door to his cabin. There was no audible resentment in his words, nor was it visible in his expression. But of course it was there, safely hidden.

Clay returned to his chair, beside his small computer desk, and gestured towards his bed. Scotonis entered, moving a little woodenly, and sat down on it. 'If you'll pardon me, Political Officer Ruger, I do still have many preparations to make.'

'Call me Clay.'

'Certainly, Political Officer Clay.'

Clay grimaced. 'Everything is thoroughly prepared and checked,' he said, gazing at the other man. 'Commander Liang is still keeping his troops constantly at the point of exhaustion, exercising them now we have gravity, then intends to take that load off them in about two weeks – two weeks before we intercept Argus Station. They will be in the very best condition for boarding the station, at least as far as training and physical fitness are concerned.'

'I am at a loss to understand what you require, Officer Clay,' said Scotonis blankly.

Clay held up a finger to still him. 'You are running your own crew ragged, but they are also willingly complying. Every system is being checked and rechecked, every error corrected

347

just moments after it occurs and every nut and bolt tightened because nothing must be left to chance, because we all know the penalties of failure.'

Unconsciously, Scotonis raised his fingers to touch his strangulation collar, then on realizing what he was doing, snapped his hand back down again. Clay had made his point, and now it was time for the gamble. Failure out here meant he would die, he was certain of that. If they failed to get what they wanted from Argus, yet survived that coming encounter, Galahad would send the signal to his own collar or perhaps to his ID implant and then, when it became evident that he had not died, she would order Scotonis or Liang to arrest him. His control of the inducers and readerguns aboard would give him some advantage over them, but what then? He couldn't fly this ship alone.

'If we fail out here,' he said, 'we all die.'

Scotonis warily nodded agreement.

'The least Galahad would do is kill both of us,' he continued, 'then perhaps kill some of your staff – but not all, because she'll want this ship back.'

'The least?' Scotonis enquired.

'I know her, Captain, and I've seen how she behaves. It's quite likely that in a fit of rage she would kill everyone aboard, regret that action afterwards because of the loss of this ship, falsify some story over ETV, then move on.'

'Our position is unenviable,' Scotonis suggested.

'So it is,' said Clay.

'But I see no way it can be changed.'

Clay tried to read the man, but failed. Time to start laying his cards on the table. He turned and punched a button on his keyboard to call up a video clip, and felt a lurch in his stomach at being returned to this familiar scene. The man and the woman were tied to office chairs, their clothing seared, their burns visible.

The woman was in better condition than the man, with only a raw burn on her neck extending down to show through her charcoaled lab coat at the shoulder. What could be seen of the man's head was completely raw, his face not visible because his chin was down on his chest. Behind them stood an enforcer; only his torso, legs and the disabler he clutched in one hand were visible.

Clay's voice then issued from the recording. 'The sooner you start talking to me, the sooner you get medical treatment.'

The woman grimaced. 'Yeah, but that will just be to keep us alive so we can be eventually interrogated into drooling wrecks.'

'It's evident that you've isolated the Scour and started to modify it,' said Clay. 'So, I'll want to know the names of those who diverted resources to fund this project, and I'll want to know what your first intended target was.'

The woman said nothing until the soldier aimed his disabler at the man and activated it. The burned man's head jerked up, exposing the ruin of his face, and he howled.

'All right! All right!' the woman yelled. 'You want to know the truth? All we've done is isolate the Scour as it is. We haven't modified it at all. That data you got was just a description of how it is – not anything we've done to it. And do you know where it comes from?'

'Please enlighten me,' said that Clay from the past, the one just about to be apprised of a horrible reality.

She nodded towards him, her gaze focusing towards what he had first thought to be the gun he held down at his side, but he soon learned otherwise. She was indicating his forearm.

She continued, 'The Scour is generated by a biochip – in

349

fact the body interface chip in your ID implant. Surely you should know that. You worked at the Aldeburgh Complex where it was developed, and from where it was distributed across Earth.'

'That's nonsense,' said that past Clay, though the present one remembered that he had believed her at once.

Galahad's explanation for why the plague had killed just about every ZA just didn't add up. The enforcer had believed at once, too, which was why – after he had told Clay about his part in ensuring the laboratory burned – Clay had shot him as well as the other two. The wiser Clay of the present paused the video clip.

'What?' Scotonis's Asiatic complexion had paled, and he seemed unable to summon up further words.

'I ran some tests of my own,' said Clay. 'It's all easy enough to see when you stick one of the biochips from a Scour victim under a nanoscope. Getting access to a nano-scope for that purpose wasn't so easy, however, since Galahad tightened control on their use and utterly clamped down on any Scour or ID-implant-related research.' Clay continued to gaze at the frozen image, his fingertips pressed together before his mouth, then he swung round to face Scotonis.

'It was Galahad's own solution to the population prob-lem,' he continued, 'and a rather quicker way of wiping out all the zero-asset citizens of Earth than sectoring followed by controlled extermination through starvation or orbital laser.'

Scotonis took a moment to find his tongue. 'But it didn't just kill the zero assets.'

'No,' Clay agreed, 'she had to cover up wiping out the delegates remaining from the old regime, so – and I'm guess-ing here – she also made a random selection of SAs too.'

'Random?' Scotonis echoed.

'Yes, but, as I understand it, your wife Thespina and your children were later victims of the Scour, who died some months after it first hit.' Clay paused for a moment, carefully assessing his next words. 'There are two possible reasons for their deaths. They were either located in an area that Galahad considered to be under a particularly heavy environmental load, so were what Galahad considered to be necessary deaths in order to save Earth's biosphere, or their deaths were deliberately intended to instil further impetus in you, giving you added motivation to complete your mission.'

Clay watched a whole mass of conflicting emotions flit across Scotonis's face, watched his eyes fill with tears, before they were angrily scrubbed away. It took some while longer before Scotonis could manage to talk again.

'We could remove our ID implants,' he said, 'and we could shut down all ID-implant reading and recognition aboard this ship, but that leaves us no better off.' He reached up and touched his collar.

'That is not entirely true,' Clay replied, opening a drawer in his desk and taking out the device he had used to fuse the motor of his own collar. 'We can be free of these collars too, but then, of course, we'd need to decide what next?'

Scotonis gave a slow nod, his expression grim but determined.

Earth

After the failure with the seed ships, depression settled around Serene like smog. It sucked out her energy and her interest, made everything around her seem dark and shadowed. As she returned to Italy, she had considered sending the order to have Palgrave drowned in one of his own aquariums, but then shelved that idea. Humans were wasteful and destructive creatures, but some of them were also the best able quickly to put right all the damage their kind had caused. Palgrave was a valuable resource. He had made a mistake that led to the failure of the first attempt at ocean seeding but, because of his knowledge, skill and organizational abilities, further attempts could yet be made.

As she sat in her office in Tuscany, listening to the sound of a diamond saw filtering up the lift shaft from below, where workers were turning Messina's torture chamber into a garden of her own design, she contemplated how right her decision had been. Her wall screen showed her a scene underwater. Submarine robots resembling giant iron lobsters were digging up barrels of toxic waste, dumped there from an inland silicon etching and plating plant that had been closed down eighty years earlier, and loading them into nets to be hauled to the surface, while other designs of robots were guiding enormous suction pipes to draw up contaminated sand into a recently recommissioned dredger. Palgrave opined that the entire area should be clean within a few months, since there would be no more seepage once the barrels were gone, and that the portion of the waste that had already killed the seed stock would itself break down in seawater within just a few weeks. Then the contents of the second seed ship could be released into the ocean. Serene hoped he was right because, even though Palgrave *was* a valuable resource, she could not allow a second failure to go unpunished.

Serene allowed herself a small smile, but didn't really feel it. The leaky barrels and contaminated sand would be dumped inland at the site of the etching and plating plant, now occupied by urban sprawl. It was some kind of repayment for any descendants of those who had worked in that plant, and who were doubtless still living in the area. She next turned her attention to other matters, reaching out to her controls to change the view, which immediately divided up into six frames. Each was recorded through the cam overlooking a cell in an Eastern European Region cell complex. Each cell contained a group of ZAs, their total number over fifty. None of them was identifiable, since none of them possessed an ID implant.

This was becoming something of an ongoing surprise, for just how large and widespread was the illegal population of Earth had only been revealed by the extermination of legal ZAs by the Scour. Really, all of these prisoners were guilty of a capital crime by dint of not possessing ID implants, but the criminality of one group – in cell B45 – was even more serious. Serene gazed at them, trying to summon up some interest in them all, then finally forced herself to open communication with the enforcer in charge. Another frame opened on the screen to show an eager-looking young woman in an enforcer's uniform.

'Branimir,' began Serene, 'I've read your report, but now I'd like to hear it from you in your own words.' It was merely a delaying tactic while she decided what to do. Really she just wanted to give an extermination order and then forget about it, but that was just due to her mood. She needed to step back and use her intellect, since the remaining population of Earth needed to learn a lesson from this.

'Ma'am,' said Branimir respectfully, 'after the bones of the only roe deer recently seen were discovered, you ordered that those who killed it be apprehended and for us then to await your decision on their punishment. It seemed unlikely to us that any of the remaining SA population was guilty of killing the deer and eating it, since the site where the bones were found was obviously an indigents' encampment. We also knew that de-implanted humans were present in the area. Using the encampment as a centre point, we set up a readergun perimeter extended twenty kilometres out. We then moved every implanted human out of the area—'

'How can you be sure that only indigents were involved,' Serene interrupted. 'Certainly that was an indigents' encampment, but I don't see them as being above selling fresh venison' – Serene felt slightly disgusted by the thought – 'to SA residents.'

'We ran stomach contents tests on them all, as they were moved out, ma'am.'

Serene nodded in acknowledgement of that. The report had been a little vague on that point, but this explanation accounted for the huge forensic investigation bill involved. Testing the stomach contents of nearly three million people was no small operation.

'Continue,' she said.

'Once the resident population had been relocated, we worked our way in, using human searchers and spiderguns, with razorbirds doing a thermal sweep, and in that way seized everyone else remaining within the area. Nine of the fifty-three we found registered positive to having ingested deer meat. We now hold them all at your pleasure.'

'That wasn't all you found,' said Serene, 'from the stomach contents analyses?'

'No, ma'am.' The woman looked slightly uncomfortable. 'Over eight thousand SAs, and all the de-implanted, registered positive for consuming human flesh.'

This hadn't surprised Serene, since cannibalism, as a response to famine, had been underway for a long time. What had surprised her was the extent and degree of organization evident in the long-pig black market. This extent had only been revealed as she began closing down the Safe Departure clinics, thus revealing just how many bodies hadn't made it to the community digesters. Big freezer warehouses had also been found, full of gutted corpses hanging on hooks, and processing plants where the meat was homogenized and turned into something that looked sufficiently acceptable. It had struck her as imminently sensible, so she had told the Inspectorate investigators involved to drop their investigation.

'I need to consider this,' she told Branimir. 'I'll get back to you shortly.' She then cut the connection.

So, what to do? Obviously every one of the fifty-three faced a death penalty, but the nine needed a special punishment. This wasn't about petty vengeance or childish spite but, as she had decided earlier, about delivering a harsh and memorable lesson to the rest of the population of Earth. She sat back and thought about the considerable range of options available to her. It would have to be something highly visible, broadcast on ETV, and fairly long-running. Unfortunately she had dispensed with the skills of Nelson, but there were others available with a similar proficiency.

She began scanning history files in search of ideas, and discovered that the region where the bones had been found had once been the country called Romania. With something tickling at her memory she searched further and soon found inspiration. It was a method that should work and, with modern techniques and medical technology, it could be extended for a long time – long enough to make it worthwhile instituting a real-time subchannel on ETV. Vlad Tepes himself had shown her the way to deal with these criminals.

14

And Down on the Farm

Out in the million-hectare fields of mass agriculture, leviathan multi-combines cruised about like mobile islands. These simultaneously harvested a crop, pre-processed it, compress-baled waste organics either for digesters or biofuel plants, and ploughed, fertilized, tilled and planted the cleared fields in a stroke. With little supervision, they then took their harvests to processing and distribution plants, from where the crop went by robot truck to be unloaded by robots in hypermarkets. The main human component in this circuit was consumption, and little else. However, humans did still work in other parts of the agricultural industry where a more delicate touch was required: fruit picking, the pruning of orchards and grapevines; anywhere the heavy and bumbling appendages of machines might cause damage. The development of multipurpose robots, eventually refined into the agribots, changed all that. The moment the hardware caught up with computer software, and the first grape picker displaced a hundred workers in the New World, was the beginning of the end of human participation in agriculture. The closest most people now get to the growing of the crops that feed them is as part of the fertilizer produced by community digesters.

Mars

As she pulled away from the remains of Antares Base, the work lights had picked out an ATV labouring away ahead of its train of linked trailers, each stacked with bonded regolith blocks from Hex Four. Over to the right of the hex, robots and a number of workers in EA suits had been further disassembling the roof panels, ready to be loaded when the ATV returned with its trailers empty. The move was going well back there, and everyone knew what they were doing, which seemed more than could be said for the team uninstalling the old lifting gear from the edge of the Coprates Chasma.

It had seemed to be a good idea to send Rhone out here to oversee the work, since he was a former chief of staff who no longer had a department to run – preparations currently being made to dismantle it for transport – but nevertheless he was fudging the new job. Martinez, apparently, could get no sense out of him and no reasonable explanation for the delays. Lopomac's earlier visit out here had not speeded things up either.

Things had been starting to look up as she had realized that the general mood of the base was more pessimistic than hostile and that it was not due to her. She pushed herself harder, becoming more diplomatic and more optimistic. She congratulated and cajoled, made frequent reference to what was happening with Argus, and noting what it might be possible to achieve. And, slowly at first, the general mood had changed to one of cautious optimism. However, as she now peered ahead through the Martian dawn, she felt a return of the anger she had managed to control since her brief exchange with Martinez.

The sun was casting a weak light across the Martian landscape as Var drove her ATV the last few kilometres towards the chasma, and now she could see that the lifting framework had still not been disassembled.

'What did he say: "all the bolts rusted solid and needing to be cut"?'

'That's what he said,' Lopomac replied from beside her. 'He did seem to have a case, but it wasn't corrosion – they'd used some sort of bonding in the joints.'

'Even so, he's had cutting equipment there for five days now.'

'Quite,' agreed Lopomac.

It wasn't entirely necessary for her to drive all the way out here to discover why there had been so many delays. Really, she could have ordered Rhone and his crew back, then sent someone else out here instead. However, she needed a bit of time away from the base to think some things over.

And there was a lot to think about.

My brother is the Owner. . .

She had been stunned by the discovery, but the more she thought about it, the more it made sense. She could think of no other single person more likely to manage what he had clearly achieved. If, in the past, someone had asked her to identify one person who could make a difference to the situation on Earth, after she had dismissed the likelihood of someone like Chairman Messina making any changes, Alan would have come to the forefront of her mind. But even Messina, who thought he could have made great alterations to how things worked on Earth, could never have managed the things Alan had done; like getting himself aboard the Argus Space Station, stealing it, then destroying Committee infrastructure on Earth . . . And now, with the station under his control, a space drive . . .

It was, she felt, a terrible shame that one of the greatest steps forward in human history was being made at a time when humanity itself was in such a dismal position. What Alan was doing aboard Argus Station should really be marking the beginning of some golden age, as wonderful horizons opened up for humanity. It should not be something born out of necessity just for some people to escape the grasp of nightmare totalitarianism. But then, it was ever thus. Hadn't some of the biggest advances of the past been the result of the horrible necessities of war? Hadn't nuclear power generation arisen from the ashes of Hiroshima and Nagasaki?

But still.

Var understood herself enough to know that her recent disconnect from the exigencies here, and her present focus on what Hannah Neumann had told her, was a purely selfish thing. In her childhood she had been obsessed with the idea of space travel; as she grew up, that obsession had never waned, and eventually she'd arrived at precisely where she wanted to be. Admittedly her parents had helped her up the first steps of that ladder, but it was her own ability that had taken her all the way to the top, to become the chief overseer of the Mars Traveller project, and of the *Alexander* – now named the *Scourge*. And now her brother was about to test out what seemed likely to be one of the biggest advances in the technology of space travel that the human race had ever experienced.

She wanted to be there for it.

'Here we go,' she said, as she drew the ATV to a halt.

Securing their EA suits, she and Lopomac climbed out of

the vehicle and looked around. Two other ATVs, both with trailers, were pulled up nearby. A power supply of stacked super-capacitors rested next to the lifting gear, in the framework of which a few people worked. The buzz of a diamond saw could be heard, just a weak mosquito whine out here, and some lengths of the framework had already been stacked on one trailer. It wasn't enough, though – they should have been a lot further ahead than this. Then her gaze came to rest on one of the ATVs, and she saw something that immediately made her suspicious. The vehicle was one of those possessing a standard-fitting satellite dish, but why was it unfolded and pointing upwards? She began walking towards it.

Rhone shortly stepped out of the ATV concerned and walked over to them. Two others who had exited the same vehicle before him were already carrying heavy tool bags towards the lifting gear. A routine tea break maybe?

'I suppose you've come here to tell me off,' said Rhone.

'Not really,' Var replied, 'but I would like some explanation of why it's taking so damned long.'

He gestured towards where the work was in progress, then led the way over. Soon they stood beside the towering framework. Over to their left lay the drop into the chasma itself, and beyond it a superb view of the gorgeously unreal landscape. Rhone pointed out one of the joints in the framework.

'I told Lopomac here about the joints,' he explained. 'I earlier made the mistake of assuming it was some form of electrolytic corrosion, but he then helpfully pointed out that it looked like epoxy bonding. He was correct.'

'Seemed fairly obvious,' said Lopomac.

'So,' said Var, 'the fixings are bonded. We cut through them, and just weld the framework after we get it back to Martinez.'

Rhone nodded and dipped his head down to peer more closely at the joint, as if further considering her words. At that moment a dull clattering issued from where the workers were located inside the framework. Over radio came an odd crunching sound.

Rhone now stood upright. 'I knew you would come out here eventually,' he said.

It took her half a second to realize what had happened. She whirled round to see Lopomac falling, his visor smashed and spattered with blood, vapour issuing from an exit hole that had removed the back of his skull. As she turned back, Rhone had moved out of her reach, and the two who had left the ATV before him were stepping forward. Both of them carried Kalashtech assault rifles that were aimed at her. Var backed up, expecting a bullet at any moment.

'Traitor,' she spat.

'No,' Rhone replied, 'just someone who wants to survive. Your arrogance will kill us all. We stand no chance against Earth.'

'So you've been talking to them,' she said. 'You've been talking to the *Scourge*?' She glanced around but could see no way out. They were going to kill her here and now, and that would be the end of it. 'They'll just stick you on trial, then in an adjustment cell. Your torture and death will probably appear on ETV primetime.'

'On the contrary,' said Rhone, 'I've been talking to Serene Galahad directly and she has made guarantees.'

'And you believe her?'

'I believe her guarantees more than I believe that we can survive here unaided. I believe her guarantees more than I believe your fantasies, Varalia Delex.'

Var realized she had backed up right to the edge of the

361

chasma. She was doing their work for them. When they shot her, she would topple into it and they wouldn't have the messy task of throwing her over the edge. Doubtless Rhone would then return to the base with some story about a nasty accident occurring out here. They weren't that uncommon.

'I suppose you killed Delaware just to undermine me,' she said desperately, turning now to glance down at the long drop behind her. She noticed then how there were rails bolted against the surface down which the lift-cradle had run, because the drop wasn't sheer.

'No, that wasn't the main intention,' Rhone replied. 'I killed him merely to shut him up. I wish the distrust in you that his death engendered had been enough, but it wasn't. Those fools back there still carried on believing in you.'

How badly she had misjudged the base personnel in that, and how right she had been about Rhone. She should have been altogether more ruthless.

'And so you're going to kill me,' she said, trying to extend the verbal exchange further as she desperately searched for a way out. 'Do you really think anyone will believe whatever story you're likely to concoct?'

'I've no intention of lying to them,' Rhone replied. 'Once they know that Galahad will let them live, and that she only wanted the true rebels here dealt with, they'll just do what they're so used to doing, which means whatever they're told.'

'You won't get away with this,' she said, feeling like a cliché from a million fictional dramas.

Rhone reached out a hand and one of his two men handed over his rifle.

'I'm just playing the odds,' he said, raising the weapon.

Var turned round and stepped off the edge. It was likely she would not survive this fall, but it was even less likely that she could survive the ceramic bullets about to punch through her suit. She, too, knew how to play the odds.

Argus

Hannah glanced at Saul as she walked along at his side. So, his sister was still alive, and was actually the technical director of Antares Base. Hannah felt uneasy about that news, felt it was some kind of game changer, but she could not logically nail down why. He had said the fact that Var *Saul* was offworld might have been an unconscious driver of his actions, but how could something like that be quantified? She wanted to ask him about that further, try to see her way clear, but in the end what use was such knowledge to her? He was in charge of Argus Station. He was the de facto dictator here and his decisions were final.

She followed him into Tech Central and gazed at the new equipment recently installed: the big console with three seats before it, and screens extending above. A couple of technicians had taken a large portion of the floor up and were busy installing optic cables and junctions. From here the adapted EM radiation field could be controlled, as could the vortex-generator ring itself, and the place now looked more like the bridge of the massive spaceship that Argus Station had become.

The murmur of conversation ceased once all present saw who had entered.

'Welcome back,' said Le Roque, somewhat pensively.

'Glad to be here,' replied Saul, his voice remote and carrying no hint of being annoyed or even happy, no hint of human emotion at all. 'Everything is proceeding to schedule?'

His gaze strayed to the three main screens up on the wall. Hannah noted that they showed various views of the nearby asteroid. One was from the dock for the smelting plant that had recently been extended, which showed the plant now merely tens of metres from a surface that glared red under powerful work lights. Another was taken from the smelting plant itself, showing the big anchor cables that had been extended across, along with all the umbilicals connected to an excavator robot down on the surface. And the third, from the robot, showed its big rotary digging blade already gnawing into the cinnabar and feeding it into the machine's maw.

Le Roque watched Saul for a moment, then swung his attention round to Leeran and Pike. It was Pike who responded.

'We've already filled up our first furnace,' he paused and shrugged, 'though the word furnace implies temperatures that we're not using. Better to call them ovens. We're cooking up the first batch, and already mercury vapour is going into the condensers for primary condensation. Secondary condensation – purification – should begin within six hours, and about eight hours after that we should be ready to start pumping pure product directly into the vortex generator. But, of course, we won't be able to do that until they've completed the ring – and put the section in over the Traveller engine.'

'Good,' said Saul, 'then I won't delay you here. I want you back out at the smelter plant, making sure nothing goes wrong.'

Pike gave a brief nod. 'Good to have you back. Things have been edgy.'

'Yes,' Leeran agreed, 'it's good to have you back.'

Hannah watched them both obediently depart.

'Brigitta and Angela,' Saul now addressed the two grinning

Saberhagens, 'you have the time now to commission all the station weapons you've built.' He glanced round at Hannah. 'At this juncture it is pointless building replacement sections for the vortex ring. If it is hit once it's up and running, it will tear apart the outer ring of the station.'

The two twins sobered instantly and Hannah immediately began to review recent history. She'd given the orders for spare sections to be made. If she'd checked the running specs of the vortex generator she'd have known that they were redundant. But she couldn't think of everything, because she wasn't omniscient.

'Now would be good,' Saul added.

The twins left, and in a like manner he disposed of all those others who had gathered here: giving orders to secure the various hydroponics units, to ensure the cylinder brakes were working in readiness to stop the spin of the cylinder worlds and lock them down, and numerous other orders besides. But Hannah knew that he could have issued all these orders just as easily through the system; and could probably have carried out the tasks himself without further human intervention. He was here just to show himself, to demonstrate that Argus now had a firm hand on its helm.

Finally, the only personnel remaining were Le Roque, the working technicians and a few of his staff like Chang, along with Langstrom and herself. She felt a sudden familiar tightening in her torso and in the back of her throat. Though she recognized the first signs of a panic attack, they came to her almost like a balm. Her liar panic attacks only ambushed her when there was nothing actually to panic about. He was back in charge, and she could now return to her laboratory.

'Langstrom,' he said, turning to the police chief, 'I have just started running diagnostic checks on Chairman Messina's

space plane, the *Imperator*, and fuelling has also commenced.
I want you to choose the required crew to fly it, and a six-man
team of the best EVA workers you have and get them aboard
the plane, ready for a flight in twelve hours.'

'Yes, sir,' Langstrom replied. 'Might I enquire why?'

'The *Imperator* is armed, and it even has five tactical
atomics aboard. I intend to make things a little difficult for
the *Scourge*,' Saul replied. 'Get on to that now.'

Langstrom obviously wanted to ask more but, grateful to
still be alive, he quickly headed off, taking the repro Manuel
with him.

'Now you, Le Roque,' Saul said, and the man immediately
looked as if he expected the hammer to fall, 'you've been
receiving requests from the *Scourge* to open communication.'

'We've said nothing to them,' said Le Roque hurriedly.

'Well, now it is time to talk,' Saul replied.

'Why?' asked Hannah. 'They want us all dead or captured,
and this station back under their control.'

'You will see shortly,' Saul replied, as Le Roque turned to
the console below the three big screens and punched in a
command.

The screen just flickered for a moment, and then a tough
Asiatic face appeared. It was the man Hannah recognized
from the *Scourge* broadcasts as Captain Scotonis.

'So you have seen fit to reply at last,' said the captain,
then his eyes widened fractionally as he took in whatever was
visible to him on his screen. 'Who are you?'

'I am Alan Saul.' He stepped closer to the screens, and
Hannah guessed that he had routed an image of himself,
rather than the image the screens, with their integral cams,
would be currently picking up of Le Roque.

'So rumours of your demise have been exaggerated,' said Scotonis.

'Not entirely,' Saul replied, 'but then death has become a rather movable feast with me. Do you yourself have complete authority aboard the *Scourge*, Captain Scotonis.'

The captain looked momentarily baffled, then said, 'I'm handing you over to Political Officer Clay Ruger right now.'

The next image to come up on the screen was another that Hannah recognized from previous attempts at communication with them from the *Scourge*. The man was also recognizable in another sense, for he was a type. Handsome but cold, there was a kind of blankness there, indicating the archetypal murderous Committee bureaucrat. However, upon seeing Saul, he did show a modicum of shock, albeit quickly concealed.

'Alan Saul,' he said. 'You have a great deal to answer for.'

'Substantially less, perhaps, than your new leader Serene Galahad, since I did not send the signal to release the Scour from eight billion implant biochips.' Saul paused for a second. 'But I sense that this is old news to you.'

Ruger appeared momentarily fazed, but then continued smoothly, 'That's complete nonsense. Everyone on Earth knows how you inflicted the Scour on them.'

'Whatever.' Saul waved a dismissive hand. 'I haven't contacted you to waste time in such recriminations. And certainly I can't apprise the people of Earth of the truth, since it seems that Galahad now has her own comlife guarding Govnet.'

Again Ruger took a moment to recover. 'Then why have you called?'

'To make you an offer,' Saul replied. 'Twenty minutes ago I began making a copy of all the Gene Bank data we have stored aboard Argus, so I can begin transmitting it to you at once.'

Again Ruger's response was slow, but now Hannah realized that this was due in part to transmission delay, which seemed to emphasize his hesitancy. She studied Saul's face. What was he doing?

'And what would you want in return for that?'

'Despite my demonization on ETV, I am not actually a nihilist. I would like to see that data used on Earth to try and restore its biosphere, and it is little enough trouble for me to send you a recording of it.'

'What about the physical samples?'

'Unfortunately, making copies of them would take months, if not years, since it would involve some lengthy biotech processes. I could, however, set such processes in motion should you be prepared to stand off and wait.'

'I would have to put this to Chairman Galahad.'

'I understand.' Saul nodded. 'I have now begun transmitting the data to you, and I do have one small thing to ask in return.'

'And that is?'

'Tell me, what is that object fixed around your neck?'

Ruger really did look put out this time. He unconsciously reached up to touch the metal ring, and seemed to be searching for the right words.

'It ensures obedience,' he said.

'Strangulation,' Saul replied. 'Explosive collars are too messy, and inducer- and drug-administering versions are too complicated to manufacture in large numbers.'

Ruger just gave a tight nod.

'Get back to me when you've received a reply from your chairman,' Saul finished.

The screen flicked back to show the mining robot still hard at work.

'What was the point of that?' asked Le Roque. 'You're throwing away one of our biggest bargaining chips.'

Saul turned to him, and Le Roque abruptly took a pace back.

'I agree with him,' Hannah interjected, not so much because she did agree but in the hope of forestalling any nasty reaction from Saul.

Saul watched her as she moved round to stand beside Le Roque, his face expressionless until he remembered to appear human, and he smiled ruefully.

'It was, in effect, about a number of things,' he replied. 'I actually do want a copy of that data back on Earth, in fact as many copies as possible, because I am *not* a nihilist and the death of Earth's biosphere concerns me as much as it concerns those still living there. However,' he held up one finger, 'consider just how much data that copy will contain. It would consist of the DNA maps for maybe twenty per cent of Earth's species, which incidentally includes most of the macro fauna and flora of the planet. It comprises literally terabytes of data – more than could possibly be checked through by the *Scourge*'s computer security.'

'You're making a link, then,' said Hannah. 'You're going to take control of their ship.'

'I hope so,' he said, 'though it is quite possible they will route the data straight into completely isolated storage. My hope is that, instead, they will then begin transmitting it back to Earth, where it is more likely that someone will be careless in their handling of it.'

'What's the benefit to us?'

'There is a small chance that it won't go into isolated

storage, and right now we need to grab every chance we can get. It's also the case that, if it is routed back to Earth, it could come in useful in the future . . . if there is a future for us at all.'

'You said something about comlife back there,' said Hannah.

'While I slept, I felt it,' he supplied, 'but just before we came in here I tried to obtain data from Govnet. This Galahad has set her own guards on the computer networks of Earth, seven of them. They do not have my grip on the data world, however, so I suspect the bioware used was an earlier version of yours, but with transmission delays they are enough to keep me out. However, if what I am currently weaving into the Gene Bank data is released there, I will gain a foothold.'

'A foothold in the future doesn't help us now,' said Le Roque.

Saul shook his head briefly, as if in irritation. 'Again you fail to grasp the danger we are in. I had to send it simply because of the small chance of it being effective on the *Scourge*. But, of course,' he continued, 'I am not betting our lives on that possibility.' He turned towards the door. 'We need that drive, we need those weapons, and we need to do all we can to give us the time for them to be completed.' He paused at the door, and Hannah hurried to catch up with him. Before stepping out, he added, 'And one way of giving us some time is to lay a minefield.'

Earth

It had taken some weeks to prepare the place, because Serene had wanted it open and with no buildings in sight. She had ordered that the entire area previously evacuated during the search for the deer killers should remain unoccupied – its three million previous residents being reassigned to accommodation emptied by the Scour. Next the big dozers and ploughs were flown in, first clearing a mountain in the misnamed Transylvanian Plateau of its infection of apartment blocks and then heading outwards, tearing up further buildings and dumping their rubble in various valleys, canyons and gorges. Serene estimated that by the time the machines had finished there the place could truly be called a plateau.

The polished aluminium spikes specially commissioned for this site were erected on hinged brackets attached to a concrete dais – the medical monitoring equipment inside them constantly checked until the arrival of those who would require monitoring. The nine had been well fed, all their medical needs had been attended too, and they were probably the healthiest they had ever been throughout their miserable lives. As the doctors attached further monitoring devices, injected them and attached fluid and plasma feeds, they remained subdued and compliant. But when they finally saw the nine spikes tilted over on their hinges, ready to receive them, their reaction was not unexpected.

With a hard-faced expression, Serene watched the whole process through to its completion, watched the spikes raised with the nine writhing and screaming in inescapable agony, silhouetted horrifically against a dull iron sky. It soon began to snow, big flat flakes of it tumbling down. She cut the sound of screaming when, after the ETV compère of the show had finished his narrative, her own lecture began.

I did not enjoy that, she told herself, *but it was necessary.*

She flicked to other cam images and now watched the dozers at work some kilometres from the scene, pushing over buildings and exposing long-hidden earth. Here was something really necessary that she enjoyed so much more. Elsewhere on Earth the scene was being repeated now that surviving populations were being moved to population centres. Whole swathes of sprawl were being cleared. New rock-grinding machines were turning concrete and carbocrete to sand and the contents of now-redundant digesters were being spread. Satellite pictures showed a steadily climbing percentage of greenery all across the five continents, and further massive algae blooms had appeared in the oceans.

She had done so much but was aware that her achievements were fragile. With the new resources that had become available after the Scour – the plentiful food and energy – Earth's population was again rising. Even after the hard lessons of the last century, it seemed that people refused to learn. This was why Serene now returned her attention to the work she had paused while watching the execution of sentence on the nine.

The Safe Departure clinics needed to be reopened, for clearly she had been premature in her closure of them. However, new rules needed to be enforced. In the past, safe departure had been a voluntary exercise, though there had been a great deal of social and state pressure on those whose working life had ended to take that route. It must now be made compulsory. She would not be so foolish as to set some arbitrary limit as, generally, with modern medical technology, the working life of a citizen could be extended into a second century. It would all have to be based on a finer status system than the old ZA/SA system. This would grade how useful a person was to the state, and in that respect it would encourage people to try to become as *useful* as possible. The nonproductive could no longer be tolerated. She would set up a focus group to look into the details.

Then there was the birth rate. During the last twenty years the Committee had brought in the one-child-per-couple rule in an attempt to reduce the population, but many had flouted it, especially those who worked for the state. This could no longer be tolerated. Previously, those who had more than one child were demoted to ZA status, sterilized and had their children taken into care. But this was not sufficiently harsh to overcome the human breeding instinct. The one-child rule would remain in force until the human population sank below her ideal target of five billion. Compulsory sterilization would be introduced for parents who already had one child. Anyone who found a way round this, no matter their status, would face summary execution, with no exception. Also any extra children they had produced would be disposed of, too.

Was this enough?

Serene sat back with her hands folded behind her head and gazed at the screen. She felt a tightness in her stomach, a frustration and impatience. Surely there were more measures she could take? Surely there must be some way to bring the population quickly down to a properly sustainable level? She could use the Scour again, of course, but recently she had learned that its reoccurrence tended to undermine her authority; tended to leave populations with the impression that she wasn't quite in control. Then, again, did anyone have to know?

Madagascar.

For a moment she wasn't quite sure why the name of that island popped into her head, but then remembered a report she had seen, a few weeks back, of lemurs being spotted there.

Now she immediately began to think about bones scattered around a campfire . . .

Nature reserves . . .

Yes. Serene began her research, soon finding that, apart from fish farms and palm-oil plantations, the island produced very little that was of value. Since the Scour the population had dropped to thirty million and some jungle was re-establishing itself in sprawl clearances. How difficult would it be to shut this entire island nation out of worldwide communication? The answer was quite simple: the same safety protocols that shut down Govnet during Alan Saul's attack on Earth were still in place, and they could be applied regionally. Any communications outside of Govnet could be safely ignored, since there were no longer any free media organizations to pick them up.

Even as she considered how this could be done, Serene set the process in motion. She also began issuing orders to all shipping and all air transport in the area, diverting away any of those that were heading towards the island.

What else?

Expert programs were available to her and she used them. She closed out the island, isolated it, made it remote from the world. Of course, administration staff on the island would have access to their own means of transport, but it was a small matter to relay the coordinates of each of the one hundred and three airports, rotobus ports and private airfields to East Africa Region Tactical Excision, to specify chemical explosive warheads rather than atomic ones, and a smaller matter still to palm in her approval and allow her retina to be read.

It was happening. It was happening now.

She felt like a god.

Light touches on a few more controls selected a list of all

the ID implant numbers on that island, whereupon she added the code to initiate the Scour. Her finger hovered over send, then stabbed down.

Done.

Serene realized she was sweating and full of mad excitement. She tried to call up cam images from the island, but found that wasn't possible while Govnet was shut down. She felt foolish, searched for other images and got them by satellite. No missile hits yet, but they were certainly on their way. But satellite images meant that others would be able to see what was happening there. Was there some way she could shut that down?

Ridiculous. I am not a naughty schoolgirl.

What did it matter who found out what? She was the absolute ruler of Earth and there was no one who was out of her reach . . . no one on Earth. She was what dictators of the past could only dream about being.

The excitement began to wane, like the effects of a drug, leaving her empty and drained. In about a century from now, when all was done, when the buildings were all down and their ruins ground to sand and the corpses rotted away, she would have created Earth's first nature reserve. It just needed more wildlife to occupy it and so, inevitably, Serene's thoughts turned outwards. Soon enough the *Scourge* would reach Argus Station, and she would see the results of that venture. Meanwhile? She returned to watching the nine criminals writhing and groaning on their polished aluminium spikes. She didn't really enjoy the show, but felt it her duty to witness it.

Scourge

The interruption from Alan Saul had made no difference. Scotonis still wanted to go ahead with the removal of his collar, and now they were back in Clay's cabin.

'There's a ten per cent chance of failure and a five per cent chance of the collar activating,' warned Clay.

'Just do it,' Scotonis replied.

Clay pressed the EM radiation pulse device against the captain's collar motor and fired it off. A crackling sound ensued, along with a brief flash, and Scotonis yelled and threw him back, pulling the smoking collar motor away from his neck. He hit the wall and slid down it, his body shuddering. After a moment the shuddering stopped, and Scotonis let out a sharp breath.

'Battery,' he said. 'It discharged into my neck.'

'That didn't happen with mine,' Clay said, suddenly feeling very worried. Maybe this was what *should* happen when a collar was properly and permanently disabled, therefore maybe his own hadn't been? He set the EM radiation device to charging again, but the red LED was blinking, indicating that its battery didn't hold enough energy to charge up the capacitor. No problem, he walked round to a multipurpose induction charger sitting on a shelf by his bed, and inserted it. When he turned round from doing that, Scotonis was on his feet again.

'So who next?' Clay asked.

'Cookson and Trove,' Scotonis replied, watching him carefully.

'I hope Trove will not continue to resent me,' said Clay. 'I felt I had to behave perfectly in keeping with my role until now.'

'So what's changed now?'

'The communications delay,' Clay replied. 'Galahad has almost a sixth sense for liars, but she's becoming impatient with the com delay so she's talking to me less, and with that delay she's finding it more difficult to read me.'

Scotonis acknowledged that explanation with a brief nod, then asked, 'What about the ID implants?'

Clay opened the desk drawer and took out the device he had used to remove his own implant. 'I'm told these were made to turn a profit, so aren't made to last and can take out only about ten implants before they fail. I think the next person on your list should be your crew medic, Dr Myers.' He handed the device over.

Scotonis took the thing warily, glanced at his own forearm, then returned his gaze to Clay. 'Then what?'

'We could have done nothing – kept our collars and our implants and hoped for success. But you agreed that it wasn't worth risking.'

'No,' Scotonis shook his head, 'I wanted to be free of Galahad – simple as that.'

Clay paused for a moment, tried to order his thoughts. 'We're not transmitting the Gene Bank data back to Earth,' he said. 'And we will attack Argus to grab the physical samples, prisoners if we can, and the station. These will be our bargaining chips. Maybe we can then—'

'You haven't thought this out at all,' said the Captain. 'You only looked as far as ensuring your own survival.'

Clay tried to keep his expression calm, but in truth Scotonis was absolutely right. Clay had removed the immediate threats to his own life – the collar and his implant – then moved on to the next threat, which was Galahad discovering that he had done so; then to the further danger to himself, which was that he could not survive out here alone.

'This is not an easy situation,' he said.

'It doesn't matter what bargains we strike with Galahad,' said Scotonis. 'If we fail and she finds out we've disabled our collars and removed our implants, she'll still kill us once we set foot on Earth. So, unless you've already planned to spend the rest of your existence aboard this spaceship, we need another option.'

'You have a suggestion?'

'I do,' he said. 'We carry on through with our mission, and what we then do depends on whether or not we succeed. We have the capability aboard this ship to rig up some way of storing ID implants so they don't deactivate. We should even be able to find a way of removing those biochips from them. If we succeed in taking Argus Station, we'll head on to our next objective: Mars. As we head back to Earth, we can put our implants back.'

'And if we don't succeed?'

'Galahad will quickly learn what we've done, so we still head back to Earth. Almost certainly she'll be in the process of upgrading orbital defences right now – they'd started on them before we left – so we buy ourselves safe passage into orbit with the Gene Bank data we already have aboard. Once we get there, we make Earth safe for us.'

'How?'

Scotonis shrugged. 'You know what armaments we have aboard. It'll just be a case of locating her. Even if she goes to ground in one of the deep Committee bunkers, a number of nuclear strikes should cut her off from the rest of Earth and seal her inside it.'

'I see,' said Clay. And he did. He saw that, by telling Scotonis the truth about what had happened on Earth, he had set events in motion he could no longer control. He saw that, even if they did succeed out here and take Argus Station, retrieve the Gene Bank samples and capture the rebels, Scotonis still aimed to carry through his proposal in the event of failure. No matter what the outcome, Scotonis intended to kill Chairman Serene Galahad.

Searching his conscience, Clay could see no reason why this might present a problem for himself.

Argus

The proctor awaited Saul in the docking pillar, some distance away from the cylinder airlock leading into the *Imperator*. As he stepped out on the walkway beside the dock railway, Saul probed this proctor in the virtual world, but found some barrier in his way. It wasn't something that could bar him – he could break through it in an instant, for it was more like a curtain put up for privacy, which relied on the good manners of anyone approaching it. Saul decided then to respect it, focusing his attention elsewhere.

The robots had finished cutting away and grinding down the welds on the docking clamps holding the *Imperator* in place, and began obediently trooping away to rejoin the bulk of the station robots which were now hard at work on completing the station weapons. Other robots were also routing optic controls from those same weapons to Tech Central, while yet others were completing the alterations to the station's EM radiation shield projector.

At the moment this last task entailed adding separate linkages to each section all around the station rim, and further controls in the transformer room so the shield would possess more states than just 'on' and 'off'. When they had finished, the shield strength would be variable as a whole and also in sections; its frequency could then be changed, as could its shape – all to interact with the 'tensioning' of space-time caused by the vortex ring, and further interact with eddy currents within it. It should be possible then to set the course of the station, though some calibration would be required.

Now focusing through cams set inside the *Imperator*, Saul saw that the crew consisted of the six EVA workers he had requested and also the pilot – which role Langstrom had assumed. At present they were going through some unnecessary system checks or stowing away the gear Saul had instructed them to bring along. After ensuring that everything inside the craft was as he wanted, he propelled himself down towards where the proctor still stood on that docking face. He landed perfectly in front of it, but he still felt annoyed at the weakness of his muscles.

The proctor Paul was clad in a survival suit, with extra material added to encompass the humanoid's huge frame. Saul focused on its face, behind the mask, studying it intently with his new depth of vision, enough even to pick out the excretory pores and optics in its skin. But still there was nothing human there for him to read.

'So why the suit?' Saul asked, addressing the humanoid directly by radio.

'It offers me protection against hard vacuum, of course,' Paul replied.

'Which you don't need.'

'It is more comfortable, and on my body's stocks of oxygen I would not be able to survive in vacuum for longer than a few days.'

'And by wearing it you demonstrate a vulnerability you do not actually have, and thus appear less threatening to the humans aboard this station.'

'Very true.'

'So what is there for us to discuss?' Saul asked.

'We are agreed,' said Paul. 'You allowed us to emerge into existence but we feel this is no more than the debt any human owes to its parents, which means none at all, because in either case there was no altruism involved. However, our position aboard this station is essentially the same as that of the humans here: we serve you in order to survive. But, in the end, we feel more *comfortable* in supposing that we have a debt to pay.'

'There are ten of you,' said Saul. 'If you so wished, you could kill me, take control of this station and do precisely what you wish with it.'

'This is true.'

'Why not, then?'

'Such an act would be immoral. Also the future bears down on us with the weight of its ages. You are a being in transition, hardly out of your chrysalis, and you are a key opening probabilities and possibilities that extend into the future. We will serve you.'

'Cannot every being open the same? Cannot you and your fellows do so?'

'It is not the same – as Judd has seen.'

'So the vortex generator will work.'

'Yes.'

'And Judd, working close to it, is already peering through the wounds in causality.'

'Yes.'

'But there is no such thing as destiny or fate?'

'Only probability.'

'How long?' Saul asked.

'We will serve you either until you die, which could be at any moment from now on, or in ten thousand years.'

Even in his enhanced state, and understanding so much beyond this quite opaque exchange of words, Saul felt appalled.

'One of the penalties of power,' he remarked, turning away.

Paul's next words ghosted after him: 'But only if you have a conscience.'

Alex devoured the tomato, relishing every bite, carefully ensuring that not one drop of its juice escaped him. Next he began eating a handful of beans. He would have liked to see them grow bigger but had been unable to resist the temptation, having already picked them before it even occurred to him to leave them till later. It was worrying how slow his thought processes seemed to have become. It was a fact that sometimes three or four days passed without him remembering much about them. And when he did surface out of his fugue to consider his position, to remember that Messina lay beyond his reach, and that in any case affecting events unfolding beyond this hydroponics unit was impossible for him, the sudden guilt he felt made him once again close down his own thinking.

Perhaps he should take another trip to the food store. His trips there had been stalled by it being moved out of the path of that thing the robots were building in the outer rim, and automatic transport to and from it had only just been reconnected. However, someone must have gone in there between his last two trips because containers of sweetcorn had gone missing. Maybe if he spent more time there he would have a better chance of intercepting someone, and thus obtaining a spacesuit. The big problem was that his visits there were necessarily limited by the cold.

He turned his thoughts again to that object under construction in the outer rim. After Alexandra's discovery that it was linked in to the station's astrogation system he understood that it must constitute some way of moving the entire station, but how? Maybe it produced some kind of gyroscopic effect that would enable the station to dodge missiles. That was the only answer he could come up with. They should have sabotaged it while they had the chance.

Alex chewed and swallowed the last bean, but the meagre meal had done nothing to assuage his hunger. Maybe, since the store wasn't connected up to the automatic distribution system, it hadn't been connected to the station manifest and therefore no one would notice if he pilfered larger quantities—

Something clonked against the outside of the hydroponics unit, Alex jerked his head up and, in frustration, scanned his surroundings. He had heard sounds like this before but nothing had ever come of them. He assumed they were caused by robots moving past and maybe using the unit to bounce off and change their course through the interior of the station. However, this time another sound ensued that he did not recognize, until after it there came a hissing of air. The airlock was filling. Someone was coming in!

Numb and confused, he gazed at the detritus surrounding

him. He had no time to clear up his mess, to conceal that he had been living here. He had no time to empty his own hydroponics trough and pack it away again. Abruptly he realized he must act, he must move. He propelled himself towards the airlock, halting his approach carefully with a foot set against the wall, then pulled himself up among the frameworks extending across the ceiling, and waited.

The inner airlock door opened and someone came through, walking on gecko boots. This figure halted just a metre inside, then reached up to disconnect and take off the helmet of its spacesuit. Alex stared in pure curiosity, long starved of something new to see, and feeling a sudden surge almost of love for this individual – this middle-aged woman, from what Alex could see. Then he threw himself down on top of her, looped his left arm around her neck and locked his right behind it, applying the sleeper lock as she fought to free his hold. They both bounced up against the ceiling framework, then tumbled along through the hydroponics unit.

When she was finally still, Alex quickly set about removing her spacesuit. It wasn't a VC model but at least it also wasn't one of the older more bulky suits still much used aboard the station. He removed her undersuit, too, leaving her naked, donned that, then put on the spacesuit itself. He then considered tying her up, but eyeing her flaccid muscles and recalling how ineffectual she had been when he attacked her, he didn't think there was any need. Instead he settled down to wait until she regained consciousness.

Eventually she shifted position, shuddered then threw up, most of the vomit spattering onto the floor but little globules of it sent tumbling through the air. She raised her head, saw him, then tried to scuttle away from him. But she only managed to propel herself upwards from the floor, and ended up merely drifting, making odd panicked grunting sounds as she tried to grab hold of something. Alex stepped forward and grabbed her, shoving her down beside one of the troughs, to which she clung, cringing, a jet of urine squirting out of her and splashing against the floor.

'Don't hit me,' she babbled. 'They told me to come here. It's not my fault.'

There was an odd tone to her voice: here was a fully grown adult, yet speaking like a child caught misbehaving.

'Why do you always have to hit me?' she whined.

Alex stepped back, out of range of the spreading cloud of golden globules, and just stared at her, some memory niggling at the back of his mind. Then, causing a lurch in his chest, the memory became clear.

'What are you doing here, Delegate Vasiliev?'

She stared at him blankly for a moment.

'Why do you keep calling me that?' she complained. 'I'm just here to put on the trough covers and the plant nets.'

It suddenly became clear that she thought he was one of the station personnel. And that 'you' she kept mentioning referred to those on the station who hadn't accepted that little remained of the Committee delegate this woman had once been. But what should he do with her now?

Alex considered killing her. He could clear up the signs of his occupation of the hydroponics unit, then take her body out through the airlock and conceal it somewhere. This would at least delay any searchers from realizing what had really happened. However, the time he would need to expend in doing that would be better spent on him getting away from here and finding somewhere else to conceal himself. He decided to let her live.

'What's your name?' he asked.

'Janet,' she replied.

'I'm sorry to have taken your suit, Janet, but someone will be returning here soon with another one for you. Meanwhile you must continue with your assigned task. Do you understand?'

She nodded sulkily. Alex quickly put on the suit's helmet to cut out the smell of her vomit and piss, then headed for the airlock.

15

The City Sleeps

In the twenty-first century, the concept of the individual 'city' was only just clinging on, as suburbs, industrial complexes and new towns kept spreading and beginning to link up. Already places that were once thus designated had begun dropping the word 'city' from their names. As the century progressed, these urban conglomerations absorbed smaller towns and villages, until those living in these areas began to lose any concept of local community. In fact, the ideas of towns and villages were becoming tribal – merely subsets of what was engulfing them. As the Committee – and the nation conglomerates that formed its parts – took a tighter grip on power, it began eliminating old borders and dividing countries up into more easily governed 'regions', then arbitrarily dividing those regions up into sectors and areas with numerical designations that nevertheless failed to erase the old names from public consciousness. Such regions were soon appended with the name 'sprawl'. In high administration this fact was much debated, but in the end simply accepted. It didn't matter any more: the nation states and national identities were dying, which was the main aim, so a few archaic names surviving gave no cause for concern.

Argus

The *Imperator* detached from the docking pillar with a resounding crash. Then with a blast of compressed air through the nozzles of its steering jets, it began falling away from Argus Station. Langstrom manipulated the joystick, began fuelling those steering jets, igniting thruster flames in order to turn and cant the plane just so, while bringing the station up in the main screen.

Saul was amazed to find he still possessed some capacity for awe. The massive disc-shaped station seemed like some odd creature of the abyss that had extended a feeding tube into a random chunk of marine debris. But it was neither shape nor analogy that impressed him, rather a combination of the sheer scale of what he was seeing and the knowledge of their position and intent. Here they were, three hundred million kilometres from Earth, engaged in mining an asteroid, while getting ready to start up an engine that was a wet dream of science-fiction writers of the past.

'So where to?' asked Langstrom.

From where he was standing by the rear door of the cockpit, Saul glanced back at the six EVA workers, who were now ensconced in the forward travel compartment where Messina himself and anyone with him would have strapped themselves in during either launch or docking. They were gazing at the big screen on the cockpit bulkhead, which displayed the same view as from the cockpit itself. None of them was strapped in, for out here they would be experiencing no unexpected decelerations or course changes. In fact, barring the possibility of the plane crashing into something, neither was possible.

'The coordinates of the first target are on your screen,' he replied.

Langstrom swung the nose of the plane away from Argus, steadied it on blackness punctuated by the cold glare of stars, then fired up the main engine. Saul just leaned back against the wall for the duration of the burn. While this was occurring, he could feel his links to the station stretching, delays increasing in ways only noticeable to a computer, or maybe to a being with a mind that was half computer. And now, with this minuscule transmission delay giving him an ersatz breathing space, he began thinking about certain things he had effectively put on hold.

My sister is alive.

It was only as he arrived on Argus Station that he started to realize that, though his motives had seemed quite plain – namely freedom from and vengeance upon the Committee – they were not. Something else in his subconscious had also been driving him, something left over from the person he had been before Smith had destroyed his mind. That earlier self wanted to find his sister, and it was now a moot point as to whether that was the main driver of his actions or just an incidental goal. But, now he had effectively found her, what next?

Using Var's face, and a program related to facial recognition, he ran a search through his extended mind. Immediately data began to accumulate, and he needed to delete everything concerning recent communications from Mars. What remained was both fascinating and frustrating. Fragments of memory surfaced: escaping their tutors as children and entering a zero-asset area, but no memory of what had occurred before or afterwards, and no memory of what their parents had looked like; talking about death in the Dinaric scientific community, again a dislocated memory, nothing before or after; remembering her determination to build spaceships, the conversation conducted somewhere he just did not recognize; then something new with a brief vision of him gazing over the rim of a glass at her, her arm wrapped round a man. Just using logic, Saul could place these memories in time, but they were like fragments from a film and possessed no emotional content. Really, he didn't know her any more – hadn't even been able to recognize her face – so what was he supposed to do about her?

'It's an asteroid,' Langstrom commented.

Saul focused on him as the space plane's acceleration began to wane.

'No, it isn't,' he replied. Langstrom peered round at him in puzzlement, so he continued, 'Like a lot of objects out here, it was identified as an asteroid hundreds of years ago, and that designation was never changed despite contrary evidence, and is still retained in astrogation systems. When we get closer, you'll see what I mean.'

Saul turned and ducked into the passenger area, the six EVA workers watching him with cautious curiosity. He crooked a finger at them. 'I need two of you with me now.' He had expected reluctance from them, but was surprised when all of them began to rise. 'Bring your helmets and the tool chest.' He gestured to the heavy box that he had ordered to be brought aboard.

Leading the way out of the section occupied by acceleration chairs, then through Messina's luxurious private apartment, he glanced back to notice two of the EVA workers had fallen in behind him, one of them towing the tool chest, while the other four were hesitantly tagging along beyond them. He had no problem with that, just so long as they didn't get in each other's way. Finally he entered the plane's cargo hold, which was cold and empty, and turned to the six as they finally all trooped in behind. He pointed down to the floor at a panel measuring two metres by one metre, which was secured by a series of heavy bolts set only ten centimetres apart around its rim.

'General arming or disarming of this plane was carried out from outside, and usually when it was grounded,' he explained. 'We could go outside now and use the same route, but there's an easier way. The missile cache is right underneath here and it contains four thirty-kiloton warheads. I want them taken out and laid on the floor, then secured with magnetic clamps so that I can work on them.'

A heavy shaven-headed individual with the singular name Ghort, whom Saul had already recognized as being one of Messina's former bodyguards and who surprisingly had not joined Langstrom's police force but opted for a job in maintenance, gazed down at the floor contemplatively before saying, 'If they were loaded from the outside, then the compartment they're in might not be pressurized.'

Saul simply pointed at the space helmet Ghort was holding.

'Ah, I see.' Ghort turned to the four that had trailed along behind and gestured for them to move back, himself walking over to the hold door they had all come through.

'As you see,' said Saul, 'you can seal this entire hold while you work. You have two hours now before we start decelerating, so I'm hoping you can have them out and secured in just an hour – which should give me time to prepare them. I'll leave you to it, then.' He headed for the door.

'If I might ask,' said Ghort, a slight edge to his voice that intimated at hidden resentments, 'what do you intend to do with them?'

'As our first target becomes visible, I'll explain,' Saul replied. 'It'll become clearer then.'

As he left them, the four who had followed remained behind, donning the helmets they had brought. Ghort opened the tool chest and he and one other stooped over it to take out powered socket drivers.

'You're going to use the tactical nukes?' said Langstrom when Saul returned to the cockpit. 'They'll certainly make a nice display, but they've got a lot of space to cover.'

Saul reached over and patted his shoulder. 'Patience, and you'll see.'

Langstrom looked round at him in surprise, but didn't have anything to add. Saul returned to the passenger compartment, sat down in an acceleration chair and strapped himself in. He then simultaneously watched feeds from the hold where Ghort and the others were working, from the mining of the cinnabar asteroid and from anything else his attention was drawn to in Argus Station. Even while observing these, he continued working on the esoteric maths and theoretical stats of the station's space drive, both modelling how it should work and figuring out what adjustments would need to be made to the magnetic field in order to make it perform just so. As Ghort and crew were fixing the last missile to the deck, securing the floor plate again and repressurizing the hold, a new feed from Argus drew his attention.

The naked woman that had once been Delegate Vasiliev was donning a fresh spacesuit brought for her, and now telling her story. Saul felt a sudden surge of annoyance. The hydroponics unit had stayed out of his mental compass because it was moved, and while he had still been unconscious. This was

392

why the Messina clone had managed to stay hidden. Additionally irritating to know that, with everything that was currently going on aboard the station, the clone might yet continue to evade capture. Saul stood up and headed back to the hold where, watched by the EVA workers, he removed the warheads from each missile and attached coded transponders. He could now detonate them with just a thought.

Deceleration ensued, and at length their first target came into sight, observed by everyone aboard, all now crammed into the cockpit.

'An asteroid,' declared Langstrom, obviously puzzled.

'Give it a few more minutes and resolution will improve,' Saul advised him.

His own vision had resolved the grey blob on the screen and programs in his mind cleaned it up, but it would be a short while before any human eyes could detect what it really was. After a minute it became evident that this was no single lump of asteroidal rock, but a huge conglomeration of boulders.

'It's a rubble pile,' observed Ghort.

'Precisely,' said Saul, 'rocks and dust accumulating – one might say coagulating – over billions of years and all held together by minimal gravity. It is not particularly stable despite its great age.'

'And this helps us how?' asked one of Ghort's companions.

'Consider what a sixty-kiloton detonation on one side of this will do.'

'Make a hell of a mess,' someone joked.

'I get it,' said Langstrom. 'And, funnily enough, it looks perfectly in keeping.'

'Yes,' said Saul. 'Just like an ancient fragmentation grenade.'

Mars

Shots cracked over her head, so close. *Approximately one-third the gravity of Earth, air resistance . . . not very much, acceleration three point seven metres per second.* In the time it would take them to reach the chasma's edge, maybe five seconds, she would be forty-five metres below them and accelerating. These thoughts flashed through her mind just before she hit the angled-out cliff face and tumbled. Rhone wouldn't even bother to shoot at her now. With a straight fall of one kilometre, she would be travelling at a hundred and fifty kilometres an hour by the time she hit the bottom. That would undoubtedly kill her. She had to slow herself down.

And if she survived?

Nothing . . . she would die when her air ran out. But still that brute instinct for survival took over.

Var grabbed for holds and felt them being torn out of her hands, wrenching her arms. Each time she hit the cliff she scrabbled desperately for some way to slow her descent, using palms, boot soles, anything. The material of her suit could take it, and anyway, so what if it couldn't? *Play the odds.* At one point she noticed a row of ridges below, to her right, and on her next contact with the cliff propelled herself in that direction. They came up very fast and the first one slowed her abruptly, before shattering underneath her. No pain, though she knew for certain that she'd cracked something. Big adrenalin rush. Further ridges jolted against her and, for an insane giggly moment she thought, *speed bumps*, then was falling alongside a straight drop.

An angled surface came up at her hard and she turned her shoulder to take the impact, hoping to roll with it. Dust exploded around her and she went tumbling through it, blind. Next she was in free fall again, glimpsing the cradle rails far over to her left. They'd run the lift straight up the steepest section of cliff, but she was well away from that now. Debris fell all about her and then she was in against the sloping cliff face, trying to slow herself with palms and soles, rocks falling with her seeming to touch her gently then bounce away.

Then at all once she was tumbling in a great cloud of dust and rubble, instinctively grabbing and trying to slow herself, expecting some bone-crunching impact at any moment. It seemed to go on forever but could only have lasted a few seconds. Twenty-three seconds she calculated for a straight drop, but overall this had to have been longer. She tumbled out of the dust cloud on a forty-degree slope, loose rocks racing her down, shale dragging at her limbs . . . then she was sliding, coming to a stop.

Var lay there panting as the dust cloud caught up with her like a shroud, then she quickly ducked her head and covered it with her arms. Having survived that fall she did not need some boulder to come slamming into her helmet. An age seemed to pass.

'Well, I wonder if you survived that,' said Rhone from above.

He had to be peering over the edge now, or line-of-sight suit radio wouldn't have worked.

Var considered replying, then thought better of it. Bullets could travel the same distance she had travelled, but so much faster.

'It doesn't really matter if you did survive,' he continued thoughtfully. 'Even if you could manage to climb back up here, you'd have a long walk back to base – somewhat longer than your air supply.'

The dust rushed on past, the thin air around her clearing. 'Yes,' said Rhone, 'dump him over.'

Something glinted as it tumbled down the slanted cliff face. They'd just thrown Lopomac over the edge. She watched him disappear in the dust and debris created by his impacts against the cliff face, then a big explosion of dust as he hit the bottom. The anger surging inside her was strong and bitter, but frustrated. She had survived the fall but the likelihood of her surviving afterwards and getting some payback was remote. Climbing the cliff to the top would take her at least an hour and, if she wasn't shot while climbing, by the time she arrived there Rhone and his crew would be gone.

Optimize my chances, she thought.

Heaving herself upright she felt her ribs protesting. Inevitably she had cracked a few of them but they didn't hurt enough to signal that they were completely broken. She tentatively started making her way across the slope, causing little landslides with every step, expecting pain from some further quarter, but there was none. Was that lucky? It meant that if there was some way for her to survive, she had a better chance of discovering it. However, it also meant that, if she was doomed, she was doomed to die of suffocation.

She picked up her pace across the slope towards the settling dust cloud where Lopomac had fallen, finally finding him buried up to his waist in rubble and powdery sand, his busted-open helmet still issuing vapour as the Martian atmosphere freeze-dried him. She dragged him out of the debris and then took everything from his suit that might be of value to her. First his oxygen bottle, fitted over hers to give her a further eighteen hours of air, then all his suit spares and patches, super-caps for his suit's power supply, his water bottle, a small ration-paste pack and a geologist's rock hammer. Then she stepped back and gazed down at him. She wouldn't waste time burying him – and knew he would have understood.

Now what?

Even with the extra air, she would not be able to walk the distance back to Antares Base. She only had one real option, therefore. There was more than enough air to get her to the remains of the old trench base which, as she recollected, had often been used as a supply station, so there was a chance she might find more air stored there. After that there was another option. Opening not far from the old trench base, an underground fault stretched into the cave in which Antares Base was being relocated. If she could find some more oxygen, maybe she could use that as her route back, which would get her close without being seen. Then, given the chance, she would need to be as ruthless as she had been with Ricard.

Var turned and headed downslope in big gouging strides that brought a lot of the slope down with her, determinedly refusing to think too deeply about any doubts, because to do so might result in her just sitting down on a rock and waiting to die. Within a very short time she reached the bottom, but pressing on to get herself ahead of the landfall that had accompanied her down. She then headed along the base of the chasma, and soon began to notice human footprints here and there. Next, some paths made by one-time residents of the trench base became distinguishable, until she passed an area scattered with cairns composed of rounded black stones, and realized she had stumbled upon the trench-base grave-yard. Had she not known precisely where she was she might have assumed from her surroundings that she was walking through a mountain gorge, rather than a canyon. As she progressed, the rising sun slowly ate away the shadows from the cliff faces and slopes, revealing colourful layers of sedimentary rock and rare layers of obsidian jutting out like black bracket fungi. She would enjoy a few hours of the sunlight, which would save her some power – maybe an irrelevance since her air supply would run out before her power supply, and she would suffocate before she froze.

Further signs of previous human habitation began to appear, including the stripped-out hulk of an ATV resting on its side. This was one she already knew about, since a report existed in the Antares Base system suggesting that it should be retrieved for its reusable metals. This meant she was only a few kilometres away from the old base; in fact, several of the boulders from the landslip that had destroyed most of it were now visible. Impatient now, she picked up her pace and, trailing a cloud of dust, soon arrived by a wall built of regolith blocks. After a moment spent surveying her surroundings, she got herself oriented and headed for the one building that was still standing – a long structure with a roof fashioned out of curved bonded-regolith slabs. The edifice looked like an ancient Anderson shelter, and it was here that the personnel from Antares Base usually kept a cache of supplies.

The airlock and windows had not been removed from this structure, and a solar panel on the roof topped up a supercap inside, which in turn provided enough power to provide light. However, there wasn't enough power available to run the airlock's hydraulic motors, so Var had to struggle to open it manually. Within a moment she stepped inside, the low-power LED lights flickering to life in the ceiling, and looked around.

Against one wall stood an old-style computer, cables leading from it snaking up the wall to penetrate the roof. Var felt a sudden surge of excitement as, only then, the realization dawned on her that the solar panel was not all that was installed on the roof. There was a satellite dish up there, too. She headed straight over and pulled out the single desk chair, and sat down. The keyboard, of an antique push-button type, had a brush lying on top of it, the need for which she understood the moment she picked it up. The keyboard was thick with dust, likewise the single-pane perspex screen standing behind it. She brushed them off meticulously, then finally hit the power button. The single-pane screen went from translucence to blank white . . . then a menu appeared. If she was right, here was a satellite uplink – and therefore a way she could communicate with Antares Base. She should be able to get hold of Carol, or else Martinez, maybe get something in motion even before Rhone got back there.

Words appeared on the screen: NICE TRY, VAR.

She gazed at them with a feeling of hopelessness overcoming her. Rhone must have taken precautions, and now he knew she was alive.

AMAZING THAT YOU SURVIVED THE FALL.

Did he want to chat now? She sat back and just stared at the screen. He continued:

WITH THE OXYGEN YOU TOOK FROM LOPO-MAC, I'D GIVE YOU MAYBE FORTY HOURS. THERE'RE NO OTHER SUPPLIES OF OXYGEN DOWN THERE. SORRY, VAR, BUT I CAN'T LET YOU KILL US ALL. I'M SHUTTING DOWN THE SATELLITE RECEIVER NOW.

She stared at the words, desperately thinking of some reply that might change his verdict.

WAIT, she typed. DO YOU REALLY THINK SOMEONE WHO HAS KILLED BILLIONS ON EARTH IS

GOING TO LET YOU LIVE? She hit 'send' and waited. A loading bar appeared briefly, then blinked out.

UPLINK DISCONNECTED were the next words to appear.

Var just sat staring, angry and frustrated. She just wanted to get Rhone within her grasp, but now knew that would never happen. She was dead, there was no doubt about it. She would do everything she could to survive, but just forty hours of oxygen was nowhere near enough to get her back to Antares Base on foot.

However, while still gazing blankly at the screen, she realized that there was at least one blow she could strike against Rhone. She reached out and flicked the screen back to the main menu, from there entered the uplink menu, and after a moment found 'dish positioning'. After studying that for a moment, she keyed through to an astrogation program and ran a coordinates search, found what she was looking for and input some coordinates. The dish on the roof repositioned; the power drain involved was enough to knock out a few of the interior lights.

After two hours fifty-three minutes of further rotation of Mars, the dish would be in the right position. If she connected up the super-caps she had taken from Lopomac's corpse, she should then be able to keep it on target for the ensuing six hours. An icon down in the bottom right-hand corner of the screen indicated that it possessed an integral cam. All she needed to do now was decide how she would inform the people on Argus of the betrayal here.

Argus

At the base of the smelting-plant dock, the giant ore carrier looked like the framework of an ancient zeppelin standing on its end, attached by one of the cables leading out to the smelting plant itself. However, a small compartment occupied the lower end, and it could be reached by an extendible airlock tube. This was how those working out at the smelter – any who weren't robots – travelled back and forth between it and the station.

Hannah gazed up towards the plant itself, silhouetted against the lit-up asteroid. A half-metre-wide ribbed pipe carrying the mercury flow extended down from this, well outside the path of the ore carrier. All along its length were reaction motors, computer controlled to keep it in position against any station or asteroid drift. Presently the flow rate measured at under ten tonnes an hour – and that wasn't enough.

Hannah turned away from the porthole and continued along the corridors which, having to skirt an evacuated area of the outer rim, would eventually get her to that same airlock tube. She had tried to contact both Leeran and Pike but received no response. An attempt to question Le Roque on her concerns had elicited just a shrug and, 'He knows what he's doing.' Now she felt she had to get some answers, and just retreating to her laboratory wasn't an answer.

Eventually she reached the airlock tube and boarded the ore carrier. It jerked into motion once the airlock tube detached, and rose up towards the smelting plant. A hard vibration within the carrier as it rose impelled Hannah to grab hold of one of the handles on the wall to steady herself. She didn't know if such a vibration was usual, never having travelled this route before. Twenty minutes later, she left the carrier compartment and ascended a tubeway taking her up to the control block. Even here that vibration persisted, and Hannah assumed it must be down to the processes they were currently employing.

She found Pike and Leeran inside. The former stood facing the inward windows that overlooked the interior of the plant, while the latter was working at a bank of screens that displayed various views of the asteroid.

'Yes, I know,' said Pike, without turning. 'I just read your messages. At our present rate, the *Scourge* will be here before we've finished.' Now he turned. 'But that will change.'

'How?' asked Hannah, as she removed her helmet, feeling slightly uncomfortable in asking. She wasn't in charge of Argus Station any more but, while browsing the station stats, she had found herself unable to ignore that the refining rate simply wasn't fast enough, and that intended alterations to the process still wouldn't speed it up sufficiently. It seemed that when you started taking responsibility for something, it was difficult to give it up.

'The ovens aren't anywhere near up to capacity yet,' Pike replied, 'but we'll soon sort that out.'

'As I understand it,' said Hannah, 'you're about to send over another mining robot – the one that's being transported up from underneath Tech Central right now.'

'That's true,' replied Pike, almost dismissively.

'So that will effectively double the rate,' Hannah suggested, again making the mental calculations she had made already, just to confirm. 'That's still not enough, as we'll only have three-quarters of the mercury we need before the *Scourge* arrives.'

'Yes, but those are the only *mining* robots it's feasible to use,' said Pike.

Hannah just stared at him, appalled. How was it possible that she was here having to ask these questions? Why hadn't Saul seen this and done something about it, rather than go gallivanting off into the Belt, as he had?

'Is that all you can say?' she asked.

'He is merely stating the facts, Hannah.' Saul's voice issued from the PA speakers near to hand. 'We could move one of the big mining robots out, but that would probably take us a week to achieve.'

'Where are you?' Hannah asked.

'Just coming in to dock.'

'So, tell me, how the hell are we going to get enough ore mined quickly enough?'

Saul simply said, 'Show her, Pike.'

Pike gestured Hannah over and pointed into the plant's interior. Extending along one wall below, an ore tube was feeding the distributor into a row of oblate furnaces. The distributor itself was a large rectangular container that divided up the ore and impelled it, by Archimedean screw, down into each furnace. The furnaces meanwhile had been disconnected from the usual processes they served in this area of the plant: the ceramic pipes and metal-foaming tanks, the carousels of moulds; the wire, bar stock and sheet-making machines. Instead, new pipes had been connected to the furnaces, leading to rotary pumps then to cylindrical purification columns. From these, further pipes entered a single large pump from which extended the half-metre-wide pipe she had seen outside.

'There,' said Pike, pointing upwards.

'What am I looking at?'

'The installation hatch is opening,' he replied. 'The interior is normally pressurized, so we had to make some adjustments to open it up to vacuum. Now it's ready.' He glanced at her. 'Do you feel them?'

'Feel what?' Hannah asked, irritated.

'The vibration.'

'I thought that—'

Hannah now saw the big hatch opening, where Pike had pointed. It was just wide enough now for the first construction robot to come through, hauling a huge compressed-fibre sack. It attached this to the neck of a port in the upper surface of the distributor and, like a spider handling a silk-shrouded corpse in its web, squeezed the contents down into the distributor. By the time it detached the sack, another construction robot was attaching its own sack to yet another port, and had begun emptying it.

'They started arriving just after you began heading up here,' said Pike, gesturing back towards Leeran. 'I thought you knew.'

Hannah turned to look at the other woman, who now sat back with her fingers interlaced behind her head and a smile on her face. The screen she was looking at displayed a view of the entire asteroid, now resembling a fallen apple covered with steel ants. Hannah at once understood that these vibrations were nothing to do with the usual processes conducted within the plant, but signified the arrival of Saul's robot army – now diverted to the task of mining.

'So everything is under control,' she said.

Pike shrugged, and it was Saul who replied. 'If the two little surprises I've left out there sufficiently slow down the *Scourge*, and if the drive works as predicted and doesn't fry us with Hawking radiation, then our chances have significantly improved.'

A super-mind he might possess, Hannah decided, but he still needed to learn a little diplomacy.

Earth

The garden was now finished: water tinkled down an obsidian waterfall into a long pool two metres wide, which extended from one side of the erstwhile torture chamber to the other. An arched bridge crossed the centre of this pool, taking Serene from what she had called the jungle garden into her own little hideaway. Here, a Japanese pagoda shaded her from the output of the sun pipes above. Underneath it, she sat in a comfortable lounger, which could be turned by means of a ball control lodged in one arm to face any of the four big free-standing screens positioned amid the surrounding undergrowth.

All morning she had worked with her fold-across console and a small screen, checking reports, approving actions, sending queries, keeping her finger – as best she could – on the pulse of a busily functioning world. However, it was gratifying that her underlings were now handling most of the detail, and much less was getting flagged for her personal attention than before. It was possible for her to go for hours at a time now without having to respond to some query, and she utilized that extra time well, studying her world, flicking from one scene to another on her screens, trawling up data that was of special interest to her, life-affirming data. Sometimes she even managed to grab herself some hours of natural sleep.

The screen she was presently studying showed various views and data displays from the Mars Traveller construction station. Every now and again an image or a report would appear on one of the subdivided screen sections, a colour-coded marker up in one corner signifying its degree of importance. Generally all of these were low on the spectrum, and quite often blinked out again as soon as one of her staff began dealing with them. They would only be passed on to her if some major decision was required that directly affected the goals she had laid out. The commissioning of the station was going well. Already most of the fusion reactors were up and running, and fresh spaceship components were being manufactured. Admittedly there had been, thus far, nine hundred and sixty deaths in the process, but not one of those who had died was irreplaceable.

The adjoining subscreen showed views of the Asian clearance, and they were quite astounding. After a recent monsoon, the soil exposed between the mountains of unburied rubble had sprouted plants in an almost desperate profusion. It was as if the spores and seeds that had been trapped under the stony layers of the now-obliterated sprawls had at last seen their chance, and thrown all their effort into new growth. It was as if Serene had at last allowed Gaia to breathe. But, again, the teams of biologists she had sent out there reported back much the same as did other teams elsewhere: a lack of diversity, acres of plant life consisting mainly of human food crops, very few pollinating insects, a dearth of rotifers and the kind of subterranean life necessary to return the soil to its optimum condition.

The same was true of the Madagascan clearance, even though it was still some way behind the Asian one; but the story in the surrounding seas was a better one. Serene had ordered demolition teams in to destroy the walls of the thousands of square kilometres of west-coast fish farms. Changes in tidal patterns and a subsequent algae bloom had led to a small resurgence of sea life between Madagascar and the coast of Africa. Palgrave's opinion on this wasn't all that enthusiastic, since that sea life generally consisted of genetic-ally modified sea foods that were not sufficiently diverse to avoid being swiftly destroyed by some viral infection.

They still desperately needed the Gene Bank data and samples, which, since recent events on Mars, was now the *Scourge*'s only mission.

This last thought focused her attention on the next screen. Four screen sections there showed frozen images of four people. These represented reports from Clay Ruger, Captain Scotonis, Commander Liang and – ever since Serene's private message to the woman – from Pilot Officer Trove. She had hoped that by demanding weekly reports from Trove, whom Clay had punished with her own cabin inducer, she would get a truer picture of the situation aboard the *Scourge*. Trove would surely report any misbehaviour on Ruger's part. How-ever, all the latest reports had been perfectly in order and everything seemed to be proceeding according to plan. All four reports had been quite similar in nature, which seemed somewhat suspicious, but Serene put that down to her own 'leadership paranoia'.

Yet another screen section showed the current Hubble image of Argus Station, which, just like any broadcast coming from out there, was always going to be nearly half an hour old. Her experts had told Serene that the asteroid it was moored to consisted almost entirely of mercury ore, but few of them seemed to be able to come up with a plausible reason why it was being mined. But maybe this related to some startling news she had received from Rhone on Mars, who had apparently found something in Var Delex's files which in turn related to an earlier report from a professor working in the South African Region nanotech development division. The professor's verbal report she kept readily available to her on this same screen, and she now set it running again.

The grey-haired black man resembled a screen actor of the twenty-first century. Serene couldn't remember the actor's name, but did remember that he had played the role of an American president, when that nation still existed, in a film she had watched during her history lessons. There had been something reassuringly mature about him, and the same applied to this Professor Calder.

'It is probably not generally known, because it was one of Messina's private projects, that Professor Jasper Rhine was aboard Argus Station when it was stolen,' Calder had said.

'And what precisely is this Professor Rhine's field of study?' Serene had asked.

'His speciality is zero-point energy or, more specifically, realspace interaction with the zero-point field . . . that's about as close as I can get, because then it all gets pretty complicated.'

'I know what zero-point energy is,' Serene responded. 'You forget that my own speciality was nanotech.'

'Yes, quite so,' he had responded. 'When he was down here with us, Rhine was working on Casimir batteries and quantum-entangled materials that might lead to instantaneous communication. He did actually construct his tangle boxes, as he called them. One was transported to Mars and the other remained here on Earth. When they didn't work, Messina had him moved to Argus Station to conduct research into . . . erm, the more esoteric areas involving the implications of zero-point energy.'

'I think I can guess what that was, knowing Messina's obsession with immortality,' Serene had replied. 'But how does all this relate to that device reportedly now being built in the rim of Argus Station?'

'Rhine was a serious researcher and development engineer, ma'am,' had been Calder's reply. 'He actually did develop functioning Casimir batteries, though unfortunately our political masters here did not see fit to pass that knowledge on.' Calder paused, looking a bit uncomfortable. 'He might well have conducted the research required of him by Messina, but he would not have given up on his personal dream.'

'And that is?'

'An FTL drive.' Calder nodded to himself. 'Judging by all the information that was sent to me by your tactical team, that might well be what you are now seeing in Argus Station.'

She had thanked Calder for his input and cut him off, then considered sending someone to arrest him for wasting her time. However, she had decided against that, and hung on to this recording. Now she moved a cursor down to the bottom of the frozen screen section and hit the link to reopen communication with the same man.

After a five-minute delay, during which the screen segment just showed a wall mostly covered with a huge nanotech-development cladogram, Calder arrived and sat down, obviously out of breath.

'Ma'am,' he said, 'how can I help you?'

'It's regarding our previous conversation,' said Serene. 'You expressed the opinion that the structure being built within the rim of Argus Station might be something related to

Jasper Rhine's research.' She found it difficult to herself say what Calder said next.

'An FTL drive, yes.'

'You are still of that opinion?'

Calder looked abruptly worried. 'I'm merely putting that forward as a possibility. I expressed no opinion on whether it might be a working proposition.'

'Alan Saul,' said Serene, 'is what we are now calling here on Earth a "comlifer", that is a human mind melded with computer systems. In his case, it gave him the ability to take over Argus and thereafter trash a large portion of the Committee infrastructure on Earth. One would then suppose that someone possessing such abilities would not be fooled by any pseudoscience.'

'Yes, ma'am.' Calder hesitated.

'Do go on,' said Serene. 'You will not be punished for voicing a reasoned scientific opinion.'

'Very well. I was given data to assess, but I was also told that Alan Saul had been seriously injured and might even be dead. A further implication was that this project might be the result of his injured mind still holding sway over Argus. Perhaps, in such a condition, he could have been persuaded by pseudoscience.'

Serene just stared at him for a long moment. 'What is your opinion of Rhine?'

Calder ducked his head as if trying to physically evade the question, but then he grimaced and replied, 'He is undoubtedly a genius, unstable, but still a genius. Even putting aside his zero-point research he has made some huge advances in nanotechnology.'

'What is your opinion of this theorized space drive of his?'

'The theory itself is old,' said Calder, 'first propounded by the physicist Miguel Alcubierre in the twentieth century. His drive required all sorts of things that just weren't considered possible back then, like exotic matter, so was shot down as unviable because of the huge energy requirement calculated, and the probability that anyone using it would be fried by Hawking radiation.'

'But what's Rhine's take on it?'

'Brilliant as ever. You don't need exotic matter if you can use normal matter to create the same effects. You don't need vast amounts of energy if you're persuading the universe itself to comply rather than trying to force it. The Hawking radiation thing might still be a problem, but only at or above the speed of light, but even then the theory has its holes.'

'So you think it's possible?'

Calder's hunted look had become more pronounced. 'I'm not sufficiently qualified to judge, but I'm certainly not sufficiently qualified to dismiss anything undertaken by Rhine.'

'Thank you for your honesty,' said Serene. 'You will be receiving a ten billion Euro supplement to your funding, which you will then use to conduct research into this . . . Rhine drive. I am presuming Rhine's data and research notes are still available here?'

'Every . . . all . . . everything before Messina moved him,' Calder replied, stunned.

'Then I will leave you to get to work, since you have much to do.'

Serene cut the connection and sat back. Vast possibilities were now opening up. If this space drive really was a possibility, then it was even more essential that Argus Station be seized. Jasper Rhine needed to be moved onto the list of those who must be captured alive, and, though minor damage of what had already been built in Argus's rim might be required to prevent the entire station escaping, its destruction could not be countenanced. Serene at once began recording a message intended for Clay Ruger and Captain Scotonis.

Argus

Much had been torn out and altered to accommodate the new structure in the outer rim. Gazing at it again, Alex now saw what he should have noticed before, which the advisers back on Earth should have seen too. How could this thing possibly be some sort of fast transport system for running personnel and materials around the rim? Before it was closed off, he recollected that the internal pipe had been only half a metre across, which could just about accommodate a man if he was prepared to squash himself into something like one of those hydroponics transport cylinders. Also, the great bulk of electromagnets wrapping round the pipe – expanding the machine to three metres across – seemed far in excess of what would be required for such a purpose, just as the heavy beam-work supporting the thing seemed far more than might be required to keep it stable. This was definitely designed for something else.

Alex crossed the area it occupied, gazing right along its length to where it curved out of sight in the distance. He then followed familiar routes to his destination, and when he arrived he was thankful that things had not changed drastically there. The mortuary was still in place and, after watching it for a while, he ascertained that the robot that had been working here earlier seemed to be absent now. Alex eventually ducked inside to inspect the mortuary's contents.

The corpse piles were smaller – many more of them now

probably having passed through the station's digesters – and thankfully the robot had not completed its assigned task, no doubt having been reassigned to something more relevant to the very survival of the station. Two piles of corpses still occupied the room, those in one pile yet to be stripped of their spacesuits. Alex headed over and began turning some of them over, finding sometimes he had to apply his boot to separate those that were frozen together. He meticulously checked five of them until he found one whose VC suit seemed undamaged, then ran a diagnostic through the suit's wrist panel. The suit was clearly fine, so he stripped it off, rolled up its bulk as best he could, strapped it to his back and set off. Now he had a spare and with luck wouldn't again end up trapped like he had been in the hydroponics unit.

Next he needed to communicate with the *Scourge*. Plenty of options to that end lay further in towards the centre of the station, but unfortunately the closer he got to the centre the more likely he was to be captured. He headed out, trying to remember the schematics he and Alexandra had used, forever on the lookout for some viable alternative. Eventually he climbed out onto the rim itself and gazed around, astounded by the view.

What the hell were they up to? Only now, out here on the rim, did Alex realize that Argus Station was no longer speeding through vacuum. Yes, while he had been in the hydroponics unit he had felt the changes in acceleration, but his mind hadn't been functioning at its best, and the effects he felt could just as easily have been the result of ordinary course changes, since at any one time he hadn't known the position of the hydroponics unit relative to the station's direction of travel.

Gazing at the red asteroid far over to his right and partially obscured by the station itself, Alex finally gained some sense of scale and began to understand fully what he was seeing. A smelting plant had been extended all the way to the surface and the activity he could see – the movement of glittering metal under the work lights and the steady flow of objects between the plant and the surface – was simply robots on the move. This might account for the absence of the corpse-stripping robot, and why he had spotted no others inside the rim. Maybe heading towards the centre of the station would not be as dangerous for him as he had feared, but there was something else he needed to check out first.

He turned and crossed a few hundred metres of rim to bring himself into the shadow of a steering thruster, and stepped up onto its massive turntable. The device was so crusted with soot that it took him some minutes of scraping to find an access panel. Undoing the bolts that secured the panel was slightly beyond any of the manual tools he had in his small toolkit, but he did have a small diamond wheel cutter that ran off his suit's power supply, so he merely sliced the heads off the bolts. The panel popped out easily – two layers of bubblemetal sheet sandwiching ten centimetres of insulation – and he placed it down on the deck, holding it in place with his foot. Revealed inside was the control circuitry and, as he had hoped, a secondary transponder should the optic wiring to this steering thruster fail. He unravelled his suit's optic connector cable and inserted its plug into the first of the transponder's four ports.

After a second, a display opened in his suit's visor and, using his wrist panel, he began sorting through the options now available to him. Changing the set-up was a lengthy task, but one he was trained for. He reset the output frequency, input a channel code, but then the suit display informed him of a hardware failure. Biting down on his frustration, he checked through the whole process again, then, feeling like an idiot, stretched a finger out to the transponder board and flipped over a small breaker to power it up manually.

HARDWARE INSTALLED, the display informed him.

Now his suit radio was connected to the more powerful transmitter located in this thruster, so its range now stretched somewhat beyond just a few kilometres.

'Hello, *Scourge*, are you receiving?' he asked, then kept repeating the same words every ten seconds over the next five minutes.

Eventually a reply arrived. 'This is the *Scourge*. Com Officer Linden speaking. Who is this?'

'I would have thought,' said Alex, 'since I am using this particular coded channel, that who *this is* should be obvious.'

'If you are who I hope you are,' said another whom Alex recognized as Clay Ruger, 'you will be able to tell me where Alexandra obtained her Argus system modem.'

'Rim storage 498A – a storeroom listed on the station manifest, but which hadn't been used for at least two years and from which, according to Tactical, it was highly unlikely anyone would notice the loss.'

'Welcome back, Alex. Long time no hear,' said Ruger. 'Where have you been?'

'Hiding in that hydroponics unit Tactical directed us to,' Alex explained. 'My suit was damaged so I wasn't able to leave the unit.'

'And Alexandra?'

'Dead.' It surprised him how much it hurt to say that.

'That is unfortunate,' said Ruger, his tone hardly sympathetic. 'What is your situation now?'

'I have no resources but for the standard-format spacesuit

I'm wearing and one VC suit I managed to steal. Right now I'm standing on the station rim, boosting my suit signal through a thruster's secondary control transponder, and the longer I stay here the more chance there is that I'll be spotted.'

'Wait one moment. Let me check something.'

'I can't keep waiting out here.'

'Patience, Alex.'

Alex waited, glancing around frequently to check. Long slow minutes dragged by until Ruger replied.

'The transponder you are using is a plug-in board with the digits ELEC105 on its disc-chip?'

'It is,' Alex replied.

'It's not just a transponder.'

'No, really?' said Alex sarcastically. Of course it wasn't. A transponder occupying a four-centimetre-square board was only something you would find in a museum. The transponder itself was probably too small to even see.

'The board the transponder is sited on also serves as a navigational computer and diagnostics platform,' said Ruger calmly. 'In the event of hard-wiring failures, it responds to signals from the other thrusters and fires itself up in consonance. It contains judgement software too, transponder linked to station sensors – therefore a very complicated piece of kit. However, it has its own rechargeable power supply and can be unplugged.'

'So I can get myself out of here now?'

'Wait and listen,' Ruger snapped. 'If you pull that now, you won't be able to communicate with us. On the back of it are four terminals marked AER 1 to 4. You must use just AER 4 to connect to a monopole antenna. I am told that, with our distance from you now, all you will need is a couple of metres of metal.'

'Is that all?' Alex asked.

'How are you for air?'

'Three hours left in this suit and about an hour and a quarter in the VC suit.'

'That should be enough for now,' Ruger replied. 'Hide yourself while I get our tactical officer here to assess your situation. I will speak to you again in precisely two hours, Ruger out.'

Alex quickly detached the transponder board and, like a night creature fleeing from the glare, returned inside the shadows of the station rim.

16

Rock Fall

Mars looked ancient, unchanging and eternal. It had remained the same for billions of years, so how could humans possibly hope to make any impression on such immensity? What wasn't taken into account was that for billions of years the strongest force on the surface of Mars had been the blowing of winds that, in the thin atmosphere, would struggle to turn a terran wind turbine, but which had nevertheless sandblasted the planet's valleys over eternities of time. Putting a human colony, with all its disruption and its machines, in Valles Marineris was like allowing a family of mice to take up residence in a house of cards. Boulders which would have fallen from the cliffs only after a thousand years more of attrition by the dust storms, now came loose very quickly and fell. The warnings were there, but the colonists ignored them and instead decided rock climbing might be a good recreation. The result would perhaps have been less unfortunate if they had not decided to scale the cliffs and slopes directly overlooking their base.

Mars

After finishing the recording in the computer, Var cued it up ready to send on repeat, then she stood up. She had to keep moving, had to keep searching for some way to change her seemingly inevitable death sentence. Inserting Lopomac's

418

super-caps into the power box of the building brought all the light back on, and enabled Var to search through the containers scattered around inside. Rhone was right: there was no oxygen here, but she did find a ten-litre barrel of water that was frozen solid. She gazed at it for a long while, considering what would be required to crack the water to source its breathable oxygen, but the sums just did not add up. She would first have to thaw the water, then it would be necessary to find some kind of electrolyte to mix into it. Next she would have to rig up some method of getting the resulting oxygen into her suit, maybe using the bottle-recharging pumps to compress and store it. All that would take too much power, so it wasn't an option.

Within the building she also found some tools, a couple of radiant heaters that would have drained the super-caps within an hour, and some packets of dried soup. All of these were useless to her.

Outside. . .

She mustn't simply accept Rhone's word about the lack of oxygen here, because if there was any here he clearly wouldn't have told her. She stepped out through the airlock into Martian twilight, now that the sun had gone down behind the mountains, then paused. Perhaps it would be better to wait until morning. She would still have enough air, and the light would be better. To do a proper search of her surroundings now would require her using her suit lights, which would again use up her remaining power supply. She decided therefore to search as best she could without the benefit of lights. Even though such activity would burn up her air supply quicker, she could not contemplate just sitting inside doing nothing.

First she checked behind the nearby regolith-block walls,

looking for crates, containers – anything. So desperately did she want to find some way to survive, she could almost visualize some tarpaulin-shrouded supply dump just waiting for discovery around the next corner, or down in the shadow of that boulder over there . . .

After one hour of searching, the light growing increasingly dim, she noticed something that didn't seem to make sense. One building was just a great mass of tumbled rubble, but why it had collapsed did not seem evident, for there were no boulders anywhere nearby. Perhaps one had struck it in passing and bounced on? And there at the foot of a five-metre slope of rubble, lying flat against the rusty Martian dust, protruded a human hand.

Var began walking over, assuming this must be some formation in the dust that just looked like a hand. She squatted down and stared at it and, close up, it still looked like a hand. Then noticing an exposed blue logo along the forefinger, she realized what she was seeing was an EA suit glove. She felt a sudden hysterical relief and reached down to pick the thing up, but the euphoria dissipated when she could only lift it a little way, and realized it wasn't empty, but attached to an arm extending out from underneath the rubble pile.

She sat back on her heels. Surely all the dead from the Valles Marineris disaster had been found and buried? That was certainly her understanding but, then again, how much time would the survivors have spent searching for corpses? Most likely they looked just for as long as they expected anyone thus buried to survive, even clad in some sort of protective garment. After that they must have had quite enough to concern them in merely eking out their supplies until the arrival of the next Mars Traveller. Thereafter, when their efforts were devoted to building Antares Base, how many more searches would have been likely out here? She had no doubt that officials like Ricard would have considered any such search a waste of valuable Committee resources.

Var unhooked Lopomac's pick from her belt and scraped away the regolith from immediately about the hand and arm. She then stepped over to the rubble pile and heaved up the large block from underneath which the arm extended, and tipped it aside. She was aware that in Earth gravity she would never have been able to lift it, but also knew that if her muscular development had been similar to that of someone on Earth, she could have even more easily tossed the block to one side. Further rubble tumbled down, but that did not deter her. She kept at it because if this individual clad in the EA suit had been killed by the collapse of the nearby building, then there was a chance of finding an oxygen bottle here with something still inside it.

After a few minutes, during which she exposed yet more of the arm and brought down more of the rubble slope, Var turned on her suit light. She worked methodically, trying not to get herself in a sweat and trying to keep her breathing even. Two hours later, she had exposed the helmet and upper torso, almost completely buried in the ground, with the other arm obviously folded underneath. The style of EA suit was the same as her own in that it would have the oxygen pack strapped across the belly, so it was now underneath the corpse. She would need one of those heavy picks inside the building to unearth it, and it was time to return inside anyway in order to send the recording she had made.

As Var headed back, it occurred to her that there might be other corpses under the rubble, and so further oxygen bottles, too. She allowed herself to hope.

Argus

The robots were flowing back down the cables that extended to the smelting plant, even as the flow through the pumps within the plant ceased. Pike had insisted on running the furnaces for another hour, to build up a stock of a further fifty tonnes of liquid mercury. Maybe it would be required if there was damage or leakage. Saul allowed that overrun, since it did not slow down the vortex generator start-up test, and the mercury might be useful later, should they survive. However, if there was any damage to the ring while they were using it, and therefore leakage, the chances of making repairs were remote. Saul guessed that it hadn't occurred to Pike what would happen if damage occurred to a tubular ring around which mercury was being propelled at relativistic speeds.

The lights dimmed, and stayed dim. Saul headed over to the three recently installed acceleration chairs in Tech Central and peered at the displays positioned before them. Rhine occupied one of these chairs, overseeing the start-up test. One of the other chairs was for weapons control and presently unoccupied, while Chang sat in the third chair. He was effectively their pilot and was currently laying in a selection of courses they could take. His was an onerous task, since what course they took was dependent on how well the station could be set on a course, which wasn't yet known. Saul simultaneously inspected their efforts from within the station system, and retained the option to take control at any time.

'Pike is annoyed,' called Le Roque from his main console.

'Why's that?' asked Saul, already knowing the answer.

'The energy drain has cut out the smelting-plant cable motors,' Le Roque replied. 'It's not winding in any more.'

'Jasper?' Saul enquired.

'Can't it wait?' Rhine asked, exasperated.

'Yes and no,' said Saul, closely inspecting the thin white scars that covered the man's face. 'Incidentally, your test results should be coming in by now.'

'Yes,' Rhine agreed. 'But, once I've checked them, we should go straight into actual start-up.'

'But whichever way you cut it,' said Saul, 'you'll still have to divert power to bring in the smelting plant, since we can't go anywhere with it still dangling out there.'

'Yes, all right,' Rhine said grudgingly, stabbing at his controls.

The lights grew brighter for a moment, then dimmed again. Almost like a grumble in his gut, Saul felt the big cable-drum motor being set in motion again, once again winding in the smelting plant. In the virtual world, he also studied the results of the start-up test. Every single electromagnet, inductor and electro-stat plate on the vortex generator was functioning within desired parameters; all the alterations to the EM radiation transformers and emitters were also up to spec. Moreover, Rhine was correct to say that they should go straight into start-up. Even with the immense drain from station super-capacitor storage, the huge load on every single fusion reactor and the necessity of cutting life-support and all other activities down to a minimum, it would take many hours to run the generator up to speed. It would be tight, but only because Saul had needed to ensure that all the work was completed to the highest standard possible within the time available.

Saul turned now to watch as Hannah, the Saberhagen

twins and Langstrom arrived in Tech Central, perfectly on time. He stepped away from Rhine and moved over to stand behind Le Roque. The man glanced back at him expressionlessly.

'Everything is good?' Saul enquired, nodding towards the images on the three big screens. Two of them showed exterior images of the Arboretum and Arcoplex One cylinders respectively, while the third showed the smelting plant being towed in from the cinnabar asteroid.

'Do I really need to tell you?' Le Roque asked, turning back to his controls.

'Yes,' said Saul, 'I understand that my supposed omniscience is a slight bar to civil exchange.'

'It is,' said Le Roque, 'but only in conjunction with paranoia inspired by a lifetime spent under the Committee.'

'Except,' said Hannah, at Saul's shoulder, 'under the Committee you would have faced an interview with your political officer concerning your "unhelpful attitude" and, if your responses weren't satisfactory, perhaps a little adjustment would be prescribed.'

Le Roque glanced at her briefly, then concentrated fully on Saul. 'Everything is secure inside the cylinder worlds, and I've cut power to all the motors and have let them lose their spin at their own rate. It should take two days before they're near to stationary, then I'll apply the cylinder brakes. The smelting plant should dock and lock down in just five minutes or so, but then Leeran and Pike will have to secure everything inside it.'

Saul looked round at his newly arrived audience. They had come here because of what Rhine was doing, and because now was precisely the right moment to set certain events in motion. 'Time for a change of view,' he declared.

Saul mentally adjusted and focused the station's main visible light telescope array, selecting three portions of the asteroid belt and routing the images through to Le Roque's screens. The middle screen just showed blackness, while the two other ones showed conglomerations of rocks and dust only visible at extreme distance.

'And these are?' asked Le Roque.

Saul fought the inclination to tell him that he already knew. That was a game they had already played.

'The middle view is effectively what you would see if you stood out on the rim, looking towards the *Scourge*'s approach route,' he explained. 'The two rubble piles are those I visited with Langstrom.'

'There's no way they would not have seen us,' interjected Langstrom.

'True,' Saul agreed, 'and they might even have worked out what we were doing. However, they will know that, over such distances, a booby trap is nigh impossible, and so they will save any course corrections they need to make until the last moment.'

'What sort of distances?' asked Brigitta.

'Those two rubble piles are one point two million kilometres apart, and nearly the same distance away from us. The *Scourge* is just half a million kilometres beyond them.'

'What's your window?' Brigitta now asked.

'With the likely spread,' said Saul, 'twenty hours, but right now is the best time.'

He sent a coded command to one of the radio transmitters on the rim, and just a few seconds later all three screens blanked for a moment then came back on. The middle screen showed two glaring eyes of red and orange, steadily expanding. On the other two screens the two explosions were expanding oblate discs of fire beginning to extrude spindles of flame above and below. Just visible, within the sides of each disc, were arc-shaped clouds of shattered and molten rock.

'By the time the shrapnel from each explosion intersects with the *Scourge*'s course, it will be spread across nearly a million square kilometres,' said Saul. 'That ship of theirs will have to change course, and soon, or else it will end up amidst chunks of rock travelling fast enough to punch holes right through it.'

'And *will* it change course?' Hannah asked.

Saul glanced at her. 'Maybe not, since the crew might be more frightened of Galahad than the possibility of their ship being hit.'

Scourge

A sound like the rending of metal impinged on his hearing, but it was brief, echoing and distant, and Clay found himself once again in Serene Galahad's aero as it plummeted towards the ground. Then the side of his face smacking against his bedside shelf brought him rudely back to consciousness. He swore, realizing his cabin seemed to have tilted up on one side, and was glad that he'd taken the precaution of climbing into his anchored sleeping bag. He pushed himself away from the shelf, as a further sound like wind howling down a pipe told him one of the side-burn fusion engines had fired up. As his cabin seemed to right itself, he quickly contacted Scotonis.

'What the hell is happening?' he demanded.

'We're changing course,' replied Scotonis. 'We'll be making another correction in fifty minutes.'

'Changing course? You don't say.'

'I'm sure I just did,' was Scotonis's laconic rejoinder, and then he shut down the call.

Clay swore again as he struggled out of his sleeping bag and into his ship suit. It was frustrating that, now he and Scotonis were effectively conspiring against Galahad, the captain felt free to voice opinions he would otherwise have kept quiet. It would have been nice to be able to reinstate, in all crew cabins, the inducers he had taken offline, but such an act would probably get him killed. Scotonis, Trove, Cookson, and the others among the crew whom they had selected to have implants removed and collars shut down, neither trusted nor liked him.

Once out into the corridor, he quickly began to make his way towards the bridge but, after fifty metres or so, he came up against a closed bulkhead door. He slammed his fist against it. They were cutting him out, they were either going to betray him to Galahad or just . . .

Then he spotted a red light flashing on the panel beside the door, and belatedly remembered what that meant. The section of the ship beyond the door had depressurized. Now he remembered the sound he had heard in half-sleep. He again called Scotonis.

'Have we been hit?' he asked.

'Twice,' said the Captain.

'I can't get to the bridge,' said Clay, only after he said it realizing how self-concerned that sounded, and quickly added, 'Was anyone hurt?'

'The first glanced off the hull but the second penetrated,' said Scotonis. 'And, yes, people were hurt. In fact, you'll be able to see for yourself shortly. The hole was sealed by automatics and the damaged area is repressurizing right now.'

Clay wanted most of all to turn round and head back to

his cabin, but forced himself to stay. He leaned against the wall, staring at the panel as the light changed from red to orange, then to yellow and gradually to green. The door emitted a thump as it came off its seals, then, on its top pivot, it swung up inside the wall. Two corpses fell through at Clay's feet, while another one behind them still seemed to be trying to hold on to the floor.

Clay stared at them in horror. It wasn't as if he hadn't seen corpses before; he doubted there was anyone on Earth who hadn't, even before Alan Saul's attack and before the Scour. How could he have been a close adviser to Galahad and not see them? In fact, how could he have not seen every stage in the transition from living human being to the bulgy-eyed sacks of flesh lying at his feet? His horror stemmed from the sure knowledge that if he had woken just a few minutes earlier, it might have been him caught in this corridor trying to breathe vacuum. It would have been him lying there with his tongue protruding, broken capillaries in his eyes and face, and vacuum-dried blood in his ears.

He stepped over them and moved on, the air smoky all about him, only realizing after he was ten metres beyond them that all three casualties were crew, and that two of them were ones who had joined his and Scotonis's conspiracy. Moving further along, he found another crewmember simply standing with her back against the wall. This woman had managed to pull on a survival suit and just stared at him without com-prehension.

Beyond her the corridor was a mess. A hole a metre across had been punched through the wall; whatever made it had come down at an angle, so as to take away most of the floor. Jagged twists of hot metal splayed out from around the edges of the initial hole, insulation hanging like moss below it, and the whole area was now iced with fire-retardant foam. Clay walked up between both the holes and peered into them in turn. The one in the wall was only a few centimetres deep, having been otherwise filled with breach sealant, but the one in the floor went down at an angle for at least twenty metres before terminating at more breach sealant. It seemed likely that whatever had hit the ship had cut right through it.

Hearing a sound behind him, he turned quickly, almost feeling panic. When he saw a maintenance team arriving, hauling sheet metal and a welding unit, he turned away and quickly picked up his pace, only relaxing a little when the bridge airlock closed behind him.

'How bad?' he asked, as he strapped himself into his acceleration chair.

'Bad enough,' said Scotonis. 'It was a mistake to try and head through it.'

Clay gazed at the captain for a moment. There seemed something odd about him, something different, but for a moment he couldn't quite figure out what. Then, with a sinking sensation in his gut, he saw that Scotonis had removed his strangulation collar – which seemed like a statement of future intent. Clay shook his head, trying to dismiss what that implied. Best to focus on the immediate problems.

They'd watched Messina's space plane head out and moor to two asteroids in turn. Resolution had been good enough for them to see the warheads that the EVA team had secured to each one. Trove had given the opinion that to divert around the debris clouds the explosions would certainly generate would add at least two days to their journey, and the decision to do that had been deferred until a tactical assessment could be made. Unfortunately they had all been due to send their latest reports to Galahad, and there was no way any of them could get away with neglecting to mention this development.

'She's not going to like this,' said Clay. 'By how much is this going to delay our arrival now?' He glanced at Trove.

'Maybe a day,' she replied.

Galahad had replied very quickly. An Earth-based tactical assessment put their chances of getting hit by something at above fifty per cent, but their chances of being completely destroyed at below twenty per cent. They must not change course; they must take the quickest and most direct route to Argus Station. She had then gone on to explain why.

'And even in that short time,' said Clay, 'Galahad reckons they might manage to start up this inertia-less drive and escape.'

The other three exchanged sceptical glances.

'You don't believe her?' Clay asked.

'Do you?' spat Scotonis. 'Which is it? Some admittedly technically adept rebels have genuinely managed to build a fantasy space drive, or a psychotic dictator, showing increasing signs of losing her grip on reality, has finally tipped over the edge?'

'It's the latter, for sure,' said Trove, before Clay could speak. 'You just can't fuck with causality like that. Yeah, there've been lots of interesting theories, but they are all over-complications aimed at a desired result. You don't do science like that. You don't twist your maths because it's not giving you the answer you want. I know, because I've seen what happens.'

She sounded quite bitter on the subject, Clay thought.

'*How* do you know?' he asked

'I originally trained as a physicist and astrophysicist, but I ended up here,' she said. 'I pushed for it because by then I'd given up in the so-called academic world. The only advances we've made on Earth over the last half-century have been more through luck than judgement. Nothing is discovered when your political officer is telling you what your results must be.'

'That's nonsense,' said Clay. 'What about . . . what about Alan Saul and what he has become?'

'Yeah, some meagre advances on the technology we already had a hundred years ago,' she snapped. 'Our technology and our scientific knowledge once had some momentum it took the Committee decades to kill.'

Clay turned back to Scotonis. 'This is all beside the point,' he said. 'Galahad will be contacting us again soon. She may even be sending a signal to a few selected implants or collars right now. You have directly disobeyed her.'

Scotonis shrugged. 'She can't kill us any longer, but another lump of rock like that last one could, and we were only into the very edge of the cloud.'

Clay felt no inclination to argue with that, but the captain's attitude seemed to confirm that the man had no intention of ever putting his implant back in. And that he fully intended to return to Earth and bomb Galahad herself from orbit. Here then was Clay's penalty for telling the truth: his life was now in the hands of an angry and vengeful man.

However, the previous message from Galahad seemed also to confirm that Clay had made the right move. Seizing the Gene Bank data and samples seemed a difficult enough task as it was, but the plan for disabling and then assaulting the station *without* wrecking this mythical space drive and *without* killing this Professor Jasper Rhine made it nigh impossible. Galahad might as well have demanded that they capture the

431

station without knocking any leaves off the trees in the Arboretum cylinder.

'Perhaps we should just forget about attacking Argus at all,' he suddenly suggested.

'No,' said Scotonis, 'we complete our mission. We assault the station.'

Clay studied the man carefully but couldn't read him. Certainly there was something Scotonis wasn't telling him, didn't sufficiently trust him to reveal. Clay now firmly believed that Scotonis's main aim was to return to Earth and attack Galahad, so why would he bother with this risky assault on the station?

Argus

The tone, that perpetual sound of the station that the mind tuned out after being here for any length of time, had somehow changed. Hannah remembered experiencing an earthquake when she had been working at the enclave in the Dinaric Alps, and this sound reminded her of that event. In the case of the earthquake it was like thunder, but underscored by a feeling of huge movement that seemed to penetrate to her bones. This new sound reminded her of an old jet turbine steadily winding up to speed, but deeper in pitch, with hints of vast heavy movement and the unavoidable sensation that she was sitting right inside the turbine itself. Or perhaps she was just being overly melodramatic, for if she hadn't known where the sound was coming from, she probably wouldn't have put that interpretation on it.

She stretched out her hand and shut down her screens.

The samples she had taken from herself, from Rhine, Le Roque and the Saberhagens were all growing well. Given another twenty days, they could be inserted in aerogel matrices and force-grown to occupy them completely. However, for them to work as backups, those people would need hardware inside their skulls so that they could make a connection. And for them and any others on this station to have their crack at immortality, they first had to survive the next few days. The *Scourge* was now just two days away from them; meanwhile Rhine's vortex generator had built up most of its required momentum. Shortly it would be time for Chang, their pilot, to take his foot off the clutch.

Standing up, Hannah had to catch hold of the back of her chair to stop herself sailing up towards the ceiling. Despite Arcoplex Two now being all but stationary, and with zero gravity inside it, she had forgotten that fact. Carefully ensuring her gecko boots were properly engaging, she headed for the door and then for the exit from the arcoplex. The top of Tech Central still protruded from the station enclosure, and the view from there would be the best. Hannah had decided she wanted to see what a space-time bubble looked like.

In the arcoplex corridors she noted how others were on the move too, some of them clearly worried and hurrying back to their apartments, all clad in spacesuits or plain survival suits. Others were securing loose equipment, battening down the hatches. As she reached the airlock elevator, there was a resounding boom and she realized that the arcoplex brake had finally been applied.

Outside the arcoplex, similar activity was visible but with fewer signs of anxiety. Robots were still at work tying down unsecured equipment or finishing welding jobs, while others were forming themselves into interlocked masses at beam junctions or up against various enclosed units located within the station structure.

On entering the upper control room of Tech Central, she saw that most of the usual crowd was here, all secured in acceleration chairs in front of various consoles. She headed over to Saul, who stood by a line of unoccupied consoles, with his arms folded as he gazed out the windows at the view across the newly fashioned outer skin of the station towards the space-plane docks.

'I see that everything is being secured,' she said, 'just as it is before the Traveller engine is ignited.'

He flicked a glance at her. 'Yes, it is.'

'This Rhine drive,' she said, slightly uncomfortable with this new expression, 'is an inertia-less drive, so we should feel no effects of acceleration or deceleration at all.'

'The gap between what should happen and what will happen is somewhat variable when you're fucking with causality,' he replied. 'Not taking any precautions would be arrogant.'

Hannah managed to stop herself snorting at that, and instead asked, 'How long until it fires up?'

He stabbed a thumb back towards the consoles at which Rhine, Brigitta and Chang were sitting. 'Rhine is doing the calculations now. I estimate he'll start running the eddy currents in about two minutes, then charge the EM field shortly after that.'

'You estimate?'

'Yes, I estimate.' Saul allowed himself a grimace. 'Even now the vortex generator is running outside calculated parameters, so he's having to recalculate perpetually.'

Hannah focused on the view, blinked and rubbed at her eyes, then realized there was no problem with her vision. The rim of the station did seem to be higher than a few minutes ago, and the enclosure skin, which only a moment earlier had seemed to slope down from them, now seemed to curve upwards. Also, out at the rim itself, something like a heat haze was shimmering in vacuum.

'Weird visual effect,' she said, hoping for some explanation.

'Yes,' was Saul's curt rejoinder.

Hannah folded her arms, too, feeling cold and thoroughly vulnerable. Secure inside Arcoplex Two, it had been easy to forget that she was just a fragile creature kept safe from the indifference of a lethal universe by only a few layers of metal. Now, looking out into the night as they played around with fundamental physics, she couldn't help but feel they might make the universe just a little less indifferent to them, which did not strike her as a great idea.

'Introducing the eddy currents now,' Rhine announced.

The general muttering throughout the control room abruptly stilled, then Le Roque began making announcements over the station's PA system, ordering all tasks to cease and for everyone to get secured. Even as he spoke, the background noise began ramping up. It seemed almost as if someone had just opened the air inputs on a scramjet ready to take over from the turbine. She glanced round, then jumped as Saul reached out and touched her arm. He gestured to the two empty acceleration chairs next to the nearby consoles. Hannah quickly sat down in one and strapped herself in, while Saul did the same beside her.

'What happens now?' she asked.

'We encyst in the universe, and we move,' he replied, interlacing his fingers over his stomach as if he was feeling perfectly relaxed about all this.

Hannah switched her gaze again to the view. That odd visual effect was now gone, but another quite unpleasant effect was impinging upon her. Everything she could see out there – in fact, everything she could see in here too – seemed stretched taut and tensioned to an unbearable level, as if at any moment it might snap and just curl up into nothingness. Someone screamed, a short panicking sound, and Hannah looked round to see the woman Leeran covering her face with her hands.

'Bringing up EM radiation,' Rhine announced excitedly.

Now even the stars changed, abruptly dimming and changing colour, speckling vacuum like amethysts, then slowly shifting to a deep indigo, then blue, then to an odd mouldy green. As that green tinge began to lighten, Hannah realized they were running through the entire visible spectrum. When their colour became a gleaming topaz, the underlying sound changed, smoothing out, and Hannah's ears began to hurt. Next the stars turned to rubies, gleamed intensely bright – and winked out. Now utterly impenetrable blackness lay outside.

'We're in,' said Rhine, his tone hushed but the words carrying despite the constant din.

Next came a shuddering crash that shook the chair Hannah was sitting in. She glanced enquiringly at Saul, who shrugged and observed, 'Slight fluctuation there. We just lost about four metres of the space docks.'

Slight fluctuation?

'Chang,' he continued, 'move us now.'

'Will do,' Chang replied. 'One million kilometres, as discussed. I need those updates, Jasper.'

'I'm feeding them through now,' Rhine replied. 'You should have a full update in twenty seconds.'

Saul turned to Hannah, then with a tilt of his head he indicated the blackness outside the station. 'Just beyond that there are massive tidal forces,' he said. 'In essence, with this drive, we really won't need the weapons the Saberhagens built.'

'We could just ram the *Scourge*,' suggested Hannah.

'Yes.' He nodded and gave her a cold smile. 'That would knock out the space-time bubble, but there wouldn't be anything left of that ship to bother us.'

'So why didn't you do that?'

'Perhaps I'm getting soft.'

'I'm updated now,' said Chang. 'Commencing field shift.'

Was it fear that made her feel so hot now, Hannah wondered, then realized that it *had* grown very warm inside the control centre. Next an arc-bright light opened around the rim of the station, and an effect much like the Northern Lights wiped out the blackness. Another crash ensued, her safety straps bit into her, and surrounding space filled with fire, shattered rock and laceworks of glowing magma.

Scourge

One of the side-burn fusion engines gave its hollow roar and something tried to shove Clay into the corridor wall. He paused there, gasping as he waited for it to end. What the hell was Scotonis doing?

The burn finished and Clay checked his watch. The time was 10.15 a.m. ship time, since they had retained earth time aboard. He wiped the sweat off his forehead and wished now that he had done the same as Scotonis and removed his collar completely. Then he would have felt absolutely sure. As he set off again and passed through the damaged stretch of corridor, he further considered Galahad's recent transmission to him. She'd been sitting in a garden somewhere, and had seemed calm and balanced. Her words, however, had reached right into his gut and twisted.

'Obviously it was Captain Scotonis's decision to change course,' she had remarked, 'so to a limited extent I understand your lack of intervention. You probably told yourself that, being no expert in the dangers of space travel, you should defer to him. You should not have reacted thus. I gave you risk percentages that you should have perfectly understood, but which you ignored. That the ship might have been struck by asteroid debris did not change those percentages, Clay Ruger, and now you must be punished for your inaction. This will be a sharp reminder for Scotonis. Enjoy the time you have left, Clay Ruger. You will die at precisely 10.30 a.m. ship time.' She paused, turned to gaze at something else for a moment, then turned back. 'And it will be slow, Clay, because that is the best I can do to adequately punish your betrayal of me and of Mother Earth.'

It was almost as if she had put him aboard in the first place just so, at some future time, she could deliver an 'object lesson'. Punishing someone lower in the hierarchy wouldn't appear shocking enough, while punishing someone high up in the crew would hinder the mission's chances of success. The words 'sacrificial goat' sprang to mind.

As Clay entered the bridge, Scotonis, Trove and Cookson turned to gaze at him. He saw that all three of them had now completely removed their collars. He hesitated: maybe he should just turn round and head as fast as he could to the engineering shop and employ the diamond shear there. No, the reality was that if his collar wasn't disabled, then trying to slice it off would be fatal. If it was disabled, then he had no problem and could remove it later. He entered, aware of them still watching him as he sat down and strapped himself in. He noticed that Scotonis now wore a sidearm. Maybe this would be Clay's last resort if his collar was still functioning?

'I take it Galahad told you her response to our course change?' he asked.

'She did,' said Scotonis. 'Obviously she considered a political officer less essential to the success of our mission out here than me or any of my crew.'

'Obviously,' said Clay bitterly. 'Did she happen to notice that you weren't wearing a collar?'

'I put it back on whenever I record a report for her,' said Scotonis.

Clay acknowledged that with a dip of his head, then, finally looking up from his straps, asked, 'Why another course change?'

'The situation is no longer the same,' Scotonis replied, gesturing towards the panoramic screen before them. 'This is a high-resolution recording of what happened just ten minutes ago.'

Clay focused on the multi-screen. The frozen image of Argus Station lay clearly visible in a single frame, with the red blur of what he assumed must be the asteroid they were mining lying just behind it.

'Okay,' he said, and Scotonis set the recording running.

The Argus station just continued hanging in space, the image unremarkable for a few seconds, then things beginning to change. Any light from behind it faded away, until it lay in a circle of blackness. It distorted, as if that circle outlined the position of a concave lens, then it was gone, completely enclosed in a large silvery bubble. It was a flattened sphere dimpled at the pole, on the side they could see, rather like a doughnut whose central hole had just about closed up, while right on the edge of that bubble some sort of explosion ensued, then the image froze again.

'That blast came from part of the space docks,' Scotonis noted, 'sheared off then torn apart by tidal forces.'

'What?' Clay had no idea what he was talking about.

'The next bit,' Scotonis continued, 'we put together from the cams we're using to detect debris, because the cam originally focused on it soon lost sight of it.'

The image was set in motion again: the stars behind the bubble blurred as it slid off frame. Another frame recaptured it to one side of the first, the object bobbing up and down and then jerking from view again, until another cam feed picked it up in yet another frame on the multi-screen. Clay was left in no doubt, as the frames proliferated across in front of him, that he was seeing footage of something travelling very fast indeed. Then the bubble slammed to a halt and a bright flash obliterated the view for a second. The image next slid back from pixelated chaos to show the Argus Station at the centre of an expanding globe of glowing matter and rocky debris.

'It struck an asteroid half a kilometre across,' explained Scotonis. 'The asteroid was destroyed, but the station itself appears completely undamaged.'

Clay just kept on staring at the image and, as he finally managed to absorb what this meant, he could not resist turning to Trove. 'Seems you *can* fuck with causality.'

She just glared at him.

'This changes things,' he continued. 'How far did they move?'

'Six hundred thousand kilometres in about eight seconds,' Scotonis replied. 'They were travelling at nearly a quarter of the speed of light.' A short silence ensued as they all took that in, then Scotonis continued, 'It doesn't make much difference to our arrival time since they seemed to be trying to take the clearest route out of the belt, which ran transversely to our own approach.'

'But, still, what is the point in us going after them?' Clay asked.

'I'm still amazed at your stupidity,' Trove interjected. 'We have to go after them because if we don't, we're dead.'

'Why? I just don't see your reasoning.'

'What is your opinion of Commander Liang and his staff?' asked Scotonis.

'He's a useful idiot,' replied Clay, 'your archetypal fanatic . . . oh.'

'Oh, indeed,' said Scotonis. 'He and his staff command two thousand troops, most wearing vacuum gear and all heavily armed. If we mutiny now, all the readerguns aboard would not be enough to stop him taking over this ship.' Scotonis grimaced. 'Galahad was careful to ensure that it would be difficult for any of us to tip the balance of power aboard. That's either because she's very clever or very paranoid.'

'I'd plump for the latter,' said Clay. 'So why didn't you tell me this before?'

'Because you are an untrustworthy little worm,' said Trove, before Scotonis could reply.

'And you trust me now?' Clay asked.

'We don't have to,' said Trove. 'You're dead, remember?'

Decidedly uncomfortable with the implications of that, Clay focused his attention back on Scotonis. 'So you intend to get Liang and his men out of the ship first?'

'Damned right,' the captain replied.

'But still you need to get to the Argus Station to do that.'

'Yes, and if that drive remains undamaged and they start it up again . . .'

Clay could see no way round that. After all this time, they were still days away from Argus Station.

'We'll have to talk to our friend Alex,' said Gunnery Officer Cookson. 'He's the only resource we can use.'

Clay nodded. 'If he can sabotage something—'

'Then, of course, we have another problem,' interrupted Scotonis, now drawing his sidearm and pointing it at Clay.

'Problem?' said Clay.

'Well,' said the captain, raising his left arm and peering at his watch, 'you were supposed to be dead as of two minutes ago.'

Clay didn't hear the crack of the gunshot, just felt the sledgehammer impact on his chest. Then he felt nothing at all.

17

Air Supply

For EVA work one of the largest problems to overcome in vacuum has been air supply. During the return to space in the Golden Decade, highly pressurized oxygen was used in combination with recycled nitrogen and carbon-dioxide scrubbers. However, even these oxygen supplies remained bulky if someone needed to work in vacuum for any length of time. They could also be highly dangerous if holed by any of the vast collection of micro-meteorites that had built up in Earth's orbit since the days of Sputnik. *The invention of the red-oxygen catalytic bottle solved this problem at a stroke. Red oxygen, otherwise O_8, is solid oxygen that has undergone a phase change which previously could only be achieved under massive pressure. The specialized nanotube carbon-vanadium catalytic grid in the new bottles enables oxygen to undergo this phase change at low pressures, and then remain stable – only sublimating upon a current being introduced across the grid. This resulted in oxygen bottles that could supply up to forty hours of air.*

Mars

The satellite dish was now centred on, and tracking, the portion of the Asteroid Belt in which Argus Station was located – or rather where she had last known it to be located. There should be no problem with the station receiving the transmission, since the beam would be a million kilometres across by the time it struck the belt. Var sat waiting, awake and motionless, hoping for just some sort of reply. However, the time necessary for the signal to reach Argus and for one to be returned passed with no result.

She continued monitoring, intending to stay awake throughout the six-hour window available to her, but weariness began catching up with her. Three hours into the transmission, she found herself frequently jerking out of a doze. Five hours in, she came out of an hour-long sleep to gaze blurry-eyed at her screen, to see that she had finally received a reply. Var woke up completely, but only to disappointment. Her signal had been received and recorded, but only by the computer system of Argus. Doubtless it would then go through some sort of robotic winnowing process, so whether it finally reached human ears was debatable.

Once the window closed, she decided to wait until daylight before further excavating the ruins outside to get to that corpse. She lay down on the floor, folded her arms and drifted into sleep so quickly that it felt like death.

Consciousness returned abruptly and Var sat upright, sure she had only slept for a moment, until she saw dawn light filtering through the building's windows. She suddenly felt optimistic: perhaps Rhone had failed and now Martinez or Carol were coming for her; maybe she would find enough supplies of oxygen in the rubble pile to get her safely back to Antares Base?

She stood up, took a drink from the spigot in her helmet but felt no urge to make that same spigot supply her with any food paste. She felt grubby and urgently wanted to get out of her suit – she had already used the suit's toilet facilities, but the seal on them was never great. Trying to ignore her discomfort, she selected a large pick from the abandoned tools, headed for the airlock, then outside into the Martian morning.

A light carbon-dioxide and water-ice fog hung in a metre-thick stratum at just about chest height, so, as she stepped outside, it seemed she was forging her way through a white sea. The fog was even then visibly lifting, and by the time she reached the fallen building it had risen up as far as her helmet. She set to work at once, digging out to a good depth around the corpse, in readiness to try lifting it. However, before she could do that, her head-up display warned her that her oxygen bottle was nearly depleted. Reality hit home hard and her earlier optimism evaporated like the rising fog layer all around her. Perhaps, she considered, it was just that kind of optimism that Rhone distrusted in her.

She kept working around the corpse, loosening the regolith, occasionally slipping the pick underneath the body to try and lever it up. She ignored the regular warnings until she was panting, eking every last molecule of her oxygen supply, then she switched over to Lopomac's bottle and checked its reading. Unless she found something else here, she had just eighteen hours of life left. Var began levering at the corpse again, not so tentative now because what did it matter if she damaged it?

With a crackling sound that turned tinny in the thin air, and a big puff of vapour, the corpse lifted from the waist. She realized she must have snapped the desiccated flesh and spine inside the suit for it to be able to fold up that way. She must also have fractured a decayed suit seal to let out that puff of vapour, which was encouraging, since it meant the suit had remained pressurized. She dropped the pick and took hold of the corpse in both hands, forcing it up and back until it was resting against the rubble slope, unnaturally bent at the waist.

Caked in compacted regolith, the flat oxygen bottle was now visible to her.

Var dropped the pick and knelt down before the bottle. She half-expected to need further tools, but the bayonet hose fittings popped out easily releasing a little puff of vapour. She then pulled the bottle from its velcro backing and rested it in her lap. Next she disconnected her hoses from the bottle she had taken from Lopomac and plugged them into the new acquisition. She gave it a moment, then using her wrist panel summoned the head-up display and checked numbers. She had just acquired another ten hours of air.

This now meant she would run out of suit power before she lacked air. The power in the building, from the solar panel, would help her in some way, but suit heating tended to eat up watts, despite the insulation. Var returned her attention to the corpse, but realized she would have to unearth more of it to get to the utility belt where any super-caps might be found.

She stood up and started digging again.

Earth

Serene glared at the images on her screen. When she had told Ruger and Scotonis that they must hurry to Argus Station because it seemed some sort of inertia-less drive was being developed there, she had felt like a fraud. She felt like a fraud now, and long moments of introspection occurring while she watched this video clip, again and again, had presented her with an uncomfortable result. She had found a reason to influence events far away from her, and she *had* influenced them, because she could – because she simply enjoyed exercising power. Those were her prime reasons for telling them that they must not change course. The possibility that this Jasper Rhine could develop an inertia-less drive aboard Argus had been remote, theoretical, producing a reason to throw her weight around but no reason for alarm.

But now she *was* alarmed. This was a game changer.

She abruptly changed the view and gazed at a massive modern factory complex shimmering in South African heat haze. Over to one side, a shanty town had been bulldozed aside, its debris forming a small mountain range, and in the cleared area new buildings were going up fast. Amidst them was something that looked like a sports stadium, but only if those sports involved games with particle accelerators, fusion reactors and giant silos filled with liquid mercury. Professor Calder had already taken a huge bite out of his budget.

Serene's gaze now strayed to a flashing icon at the bottom of her screen. Calder had received her latest message and was ready to speak to her. She instinctively wanted to keep him waiting, but felt the situation was too critical to waste time on playing minor power games.

'Professor?' she said, responding at once.

'Ma'am,' he replied with a respectful dip of his head.

'You've been analysing the video and data feeds from the *Scourge*,' she said. 'You've seen that there is indeed an inertia-less drive aboard Argus. How far along are you?'

'My initial tests look promising,' he replied, 'but building such a drive will have to be conducted offworld. In a way they were lucky, because they had the structure in which to build a wide enough vortex ring, and they already had the required EM field-generating capability.'

'How long?'

'We could begin building some elements of the drive at

once,' he replied. 'How long thereafter it would take to get ourselves a working drive just depends upon how much in the way of resources you are prepared to dedicate to this.'

Serene gazed at him steadily for a moment, but he showed no signs of getting nervous about that scrutiny, so she continued, 'If the Argus Station escapes, and retains its ability to travel as fast as it has, all Earth's offworld stations, factories and satellites will be at risk.'

'Agreed.'

'That damned thing could attack with little or no warning, and we know it now has some lethal weaponry. We certainly have weapons up there that could damage it, but this means they will have to be permanently manned and ready to respond instantly.'

'That is presupposing it uses its weapons,' Calder noted.

'What do you mean?'

'It doesn't even need its weapons,' he explained. 'You saw what happened to the asteroid it struck?'

'I saw.'

'The warp-bubble interface creates tidal forces you would generally only find near to a fast-spinning black hole. If they solve their obvious navigational problems, all they would need to do is plot a course right through any orbital installations, and afterwards there would be nothing left.'

It was at this moment that Serene understood for the first time the meaning of the words 'cold sweat'. That reaction, however, made her tighten her control on herself.

'At present,' she said carefully, 'we have three ships being constructed – I mean the new-design Mars Travellers. They will be redesigned to your specifications so that they can incorporate this drive, and weapons. All your requirements will be met, at once.'

'What do you mean, ma'am?'

'I mean, Professor Calder, I am promoting you to a special position. I am giving you control of all offworld industries, and I am allowing you the power to demand from on-world industries anything you require. I am therefore, in effect, putting all of Earth's resources at your disposal.'

He just stared at her, saying nothing, obviously shaken alert at last.

She continued, 'Aboard Argus Station they managed to build a workable drive during their journey to the Asteroid Belt. With the resources at your disposal I expect you to achieve the same result much more quickly.'

Finally he managed to speak. 'I . . . I can't organize all this by myself.'

'Expert teams are on their way to you right now,' Serene replied. 'You tell them what you want, and they will organize it. Anyone you require is yours.'

'So long as they do what I say,' he risked.

'They will – or they will die. I do not expect you to fail me, Professor Calder.' Enough of the stick, now a bit more carrot. 'And, should you succeed, you will receive anything it is within my power to give, for the rest of your life.'

'Ma'am.' He dipped his head again, this time in serious acknowledgement.

'That's all for now,' she said, and cut the connection.

Threats, she felt, were easy to make and to carry through; promises were equally as easy to make, and as easy to forget. Just like the promises she had made to this character, Rhone, out there on Mars.

Argus

Alex's chances of getting caught had just increased a hundredfold, but if he had stayed a moment longer in that claustrophobic little room he felt sure he would have ended up eating a bullet. There had seemed no point in going on. There he was, again, hiding like a rat in the walls, struggling to get supplies just to keep himself alive. No purpose achievable, reality frustrating him, nothing from the *Scourge* but the instruction to keep his head down and await orders. And then it had seemed as if he was going insane.

The weird vibrations from the surrounding metalwork had registered first. They were horribly unpleasant, imparting to his entire body a feeling like 'restless leg syndrome' – something he had suffered from during one particularly long hospital stay in the past. Then even his surroundings began to distort. The walls seemed to become concave when he looked at them directly but, as he turned away, they stretched in the other direction towards some seemingly infinite point. Odd sounds issued from his suit radio, so that he had to keep turning it off to find some relief, and it was during one of these occasions that the whole room shuddered, as if something had crashed into it or the station itself, and so, finally, he decided to investigate.

The room he had since occupied lay in what had been intended to be a residential section. It was also where Messina's forces first gathered when they had attacked. Here he had found oxygen bottles, a scattering of ammo clips and, best of all, a ration pack before concealing himself away as instructed. The corridor outside his hideaway looked no different, and those distortions were no longer evident, yet, when he reached out and touched the wall, that horrible vibration was still present, if less strong than before. He moved further along, intent on heading out of the end of this section to reach a point where he could get a view into the station, down beside Arcoplex One. But only as he reached his destination and carefully made his way out into the station's framework superstructure did he think to pause and extend his external aerial lead to a nearby beam, and again turn on his suit radio.

A haze of static and a high-pitched whining filled his suit helmet, but out of it, just discernible, came a voice:

'. . . please reply . . . Come on, Alex, we need to talk to you. This is the Sc . . . calling A . . . please rep . . .'

'Alex here,' he said at once.

'We've got . . .'

Alex quickly turned on his visor display and sorted through the various menus to find the one for the radio. Since it was being boosted through that same board from the thruster, he might not be able to do anything, but he was sure there was some facility available for cleaning up signals. Soon he found the relevant menu and discovered he could indeed do something, and the words came clearer, though a sound occurring behind them seemed to keep drilling into his spine.

'This is Captain Scotonis of the *Scourge* here,' said a new voice. 'We're not far away from you but, as you might have gathered, we've got a problem.'

'I've gathered nothing,' said Alex. 'I've been hiding, remember.'

'Ah . . . yes.'

'Why are *you* talking to me?' Alex asked. 'It's normally that Ruger guy.'

'He's a little inconvenienced now,' the captain replied, 'and we're running out of time. Alex, that structure in the

451

outer ring of the station is some sort of space drive. It moved the entire station six hundred thousand kilometres in just eight seconds, but crashed it into an asteroid. There seems to be little damage and, from the readings we're getting, it seems that drive is powering up again. If they use it again we're never going to get to you.'

'What?' Alex could think of nothing else to say.

'We need you to knock it out, Alex. I can't stress enough how important it is that you do so. If they manage to get it running again, Messina will forever be a slave and you'll end up either captured and killed.'

'Space drive?' Alex echoed.

'An inertia-less drive.'

Alex just had to accept it, because this explanation fitted the facts much better than anything he had so far heard from the tactical team. He turned himself round so he was facing out towards the rim, and through the superstructure there he could just about see the newly built ring – this space drive. It somehow looked incredibly substantial now, as if the station structure all around it was made of balsa and the thing itself was fashioned of blued steel.

'Any advice on how I stop it?'

'Do you have explosives?

'Only ceramic ammo.'

'That might be enough if you can put enough bullets into it. You have to try. Alternatively, I'm sure you've been trained to . . . improvise.'

'I'll see what I can do,' said Alex. 'I'll call you when I have some news.'

He pulled the aerial wire away from the beam and wound it back into the pouch containing the booster board. Bullets might well be enough, as Scotonis had suggested. The thing bore some resemblance to a particle accelerator and doubtless numerous holes through the surrounding coils and into the accelerator pipe itself should seriously fuck with whatever it was doing. Then there were also the power-supply cables. The schematic Alexandra had already pulled up showed the main feed running in over by the endcap of Arcoplex One, with control optics leading to both Tech Central and the EM field transformer room – a definite weak spot. But first the bullets. He began to make his way through the superstructure towards the ring itself.

As he started to get a clearer view of the device, Alex did not lose that impression of substantiality, and the image of it hung heavy in his mind, almost too heavy, making his head ache with the load. He decided to get right on top of it before opening fire, since that way he would be able to target whatever aspect looked the most critical. However, even as he drew closer to the thing the sensation he was getting through his handholds grew ever more unpleasant. Upon reaching the base of one of the big beams that supported the device, he paused, just holding himself in position by hooking the sight of his rifle on the metal. Even so, that weird vibration travelled up through the weapon and into his arms, which were now aching as if they had been beaten. His recently healed leg had also begun to smart, and the pain in it there was growing steadily. He couldn't pause, had to move in.

Alex again hung his rifle across his back and scrambled along the beam. The intensity of the pain increased until it felt as if he was being electrocuted through his hands. Abruptly he propelled himself from the beam towards the device, but the pain continued to grow even though he was touching nothing. As he drew closer to the heavy coils and skeins of wiring, his visor display suddenly began flashing a 'systems failure' alert and the smell of burning infiltrated his helmet. In an instant he realized what the problem was: being this close to such a mass of powered-up coils was inducing currents in the wiring of his suit. This could kill him.

He prepared to propel himself away but, when he was a metre from the thing, his descent abruptly slowed as if he was dropping into an invisible marsh. He bent his legs and then shoved hard against . . . nothing. It was enough to send him sailing away again, though slowly. He unstrapped his rifle and turned himself so that he could aim it back towards the device. Smoke now filled his suit helmet and he could hear a sizzling from the vicinity of his chest. He opened fire, spraying a full eighty-round clip along the length of the device, the dampened recoil making little difference to his progress away, then automatically loaded another clip before assessing the damage.

Nothing, no damage at all – but he could see objects bobbing about around the device like disturbed wasps, and realized he was seeing the bullets he had fired. As he watched them, they all lined up along the length of the device, then, led by the bullets at one end of that line, they began spiralling around it. Alex finally caught hold of a beam and drew himself to a halt, snapping his hand away immediately afterwards. This made no sense. Certainly the problems with his suit could be attributed to magnetic fields, and maybe a similar effect had worked on the metal within his suit to prevent him landing on the device itself, but what the hell was doing that with his bullets? They were made of ceramic, so could not be affected by magnetism.

He had to accept this and move on. First he needed to get somewhere he could change out of his present suit and into the VC suit strapped on his back. He kicked off from the nearby beam, sending himself on a course parallel with the device, still holding his rifle in readiness. Just half a kilometre round from his present location lay the cold store supplied by the hydroponics unit in which he had concealed himself for so long. He corrected his course off another beam, kept scanning all around for any activity. Maybe, because he had not actually managed to do any damage, his attempt had not yet been detected.

The cold store soon became visible. It had only two tubular transport feeds running into it: one from his hydroponics unit which lay behind him, and one from further along around the rim. He changed course again, pushing off from yet another beam, and thus came down on the surface of the store, absorbing the shock of impact by bending his legs but only just managing to stop himself from bouncing away by catching hold of a nearby support strut. Next he walked round the surface of the store to the airlock, opened it, and was just about to step inside when the nightmare descended on him.

'We've sustained no damage at all,' Le Roque reported. 'All the asteroid debris was blown outwards.'

'Rhine?' Saul turned towards the man.

'The tidal forces ripped the asteroid apart,' Rhine replied. 'But the impact effectively killed our momentum . . . if it could be described as such.'

Saul would have liked to be able to absorb more data than was being supplied by the hard wiring, but within its vicinity the vortex ring was killing bandwidth and doing some odd things with time. It was also interfering with any equipment out there, which was why Saul had pulled most of the robots back from the rim, for they had started to become a little . . . unreliable.

'That's odd,' said Rhine, 'some debris did get through – I'm reading impacts on the exotic energy shell.'

Saul was on that in a microsecond. Rhine had just said something which, according to the constantly updated theory of his drive, was practically impossible. He tracked the data Rhine was studying, located the part of the vortex ring concerned, but there were no cams available there.

'Paul?' he enquired, and immediately knew he had made a mistake in pulling back his robots. He had been concentrating on the bigger picture, he realized, and, in neglecting the smaller characters in that picture, had thus put them all in imminent danger.

The proctor was descending on a figure in a spacesuit who had been about to enter one of the rim's cold stores. A data packet from Paul, in speeded-up time, showed this same figure opening fire on the vortex generator, failing to do any damage, then moving away. Paul had tracked him, and now intended to take him out.

As the intruder turned, Saul immediately recognized him as Alex, the Messina clone. The proctor reached out to grab his arm and to swing a clenched fist at his face. But Alex jerked aside very fast and raised his rifle protectively. The proctor only managed to close its fingers on the material of Alex's suit, and its fist struck the rifle butt before striking the man's visor. Vapour blew out around the visor, but Saul immediately saw that Alex had just gained an advantage. The blow had turned his rifle so the barrel was pointing straight at Paul's head. Alex did not fail to use that advantage and the image feed filled with blue fire and flying chunks of ceramic ammunition. As the image cleared again, Saul watched Alex entering the airlock, the ripped arm and visor of his suit gushing vapour.

'I'm sorry,' said Paul.

The proctor had received only minor damage, but the fusillade had blown it out into vacuum and it could do nothing until it reached some strut, beam or wall to grab hold of. This would take, at its current trajectory, at least eight minutes.

'How long until we can fly again?' Saul asked Rhine, even while running his own calculations.

'Maybe half an hour,' Rhine replied. 'I can't be more accurate than that.'

Saul acknowledged this news with a nod – he himself had calculated on thirty-three minutes – then immediately headed out of Tech Central. It had been foolish of him to leave this in Langstrom's hands, in effect to dismiss it as just a matter for the station police. Even now, analysing what little data lay available in the station system about these clones, he realized why this one had escaped something as formidable as a proctor.

Apparently, from the moment they stepped out of their amniotic tanks, the clones underwent severe training and indoctrination. They were also the test beds for new improvements in physical enhancements of the kind less detectable than those seen in Committee bodyguards or some of the enforcers: increased muscle density, genetic mods for nerve-impulse acceleration and mental programming for improved performance.

This one needed to be dealt with, and fast.

Saul picked up his pace, meanwhile making his own assessments of the state of Argus and simultaneously checking instrument readings of all the asteroids in the immediate area – he did not want them to go crashing into something when they used the drive again. As he did this, subprograms he had set in motion some time before flagged up items for his attention. One of the flags indicated high importance, so he checked it. What he found momentarily slammed him to a halt.

A transmission had been picked up from Mars, automatically stored by the system, but containing something he had previously ticked as being of interest to him. The fact that it was a radio signal and not a communication via tanglecom had also raised its importance.

Var . . .

The video file had been retransmitted over a period of six hours. This duration meant it had been sent from some low-lying area on Mars, which in itself was curious, and the contents confirmed that.

In his mind he gazed upon his sister's face behind the visor of a Mars EA suit.

'This is Varalia Delex transmitting to Argus Station from Coprates Chasma on Mars. My message is for my brother Alan . . . Alan Saul who, it now seems, is the one you on Argus call the "Owner",' she began. 'Alan, if, by any chance, you survive your encounter with the *Scourge* there is something you need to know. It pains me for more reasons than one,' she grimaced at that, 'to have to tell you that I am no longer the director of Antares Base. Rhone, our director of Mars Science, has seized control and is in communication with the new regime on Earth. Therefore don't expect any help at the base, and be aware that Rhone has an electromagnetic pulse weapon, while other personnel now have numerous hand weapons. I don't know what your response will be to this – whether you will simply ignore the Mars base or whether there are things you want from there. In fact I don't know what your intentions are. Do you intend to remain in the vicinity of Earth? Do you intend to try surviving within the solar system?

How any of us could survive Earth has always been a question I've found difficult to answer.' She paused, seemingly searching for words.

She then continued, 'It seems likely that I will be dead before I know what you intend to do. While inspecting some work being conducted on the edge of Coprates Chasma, I was betrayed by Rhone. He then killed my good friend Lopomac, and attempted to kill me, too, but I threw myself down into the chasma and managed to survive the fall. I am now in one of the last remaining intact buildings of the old trench base. I have about twenty hours of air left and, unless I can find some more, then I will die.'

Again she paused, her expression now turning vicious. 'If you do come here, Alan, I can only hope that you will . . . deal with Rhone. I hope you feel some familial connection, though of course that's never been evident in you before. I should add that not all base personnel are complicit in his betrayal. There are some good people there, like Martinez, Carol and others. Please reply – at least to let me know that you have received this message.'

Saul paused in order to reply, just vocally, just to let her know, 'Var, this is Alan. Your message has been received. Currently we have been delayed because, while running under Jasper Rhine's new space drive, we collided with an asteroid. The station is undamaged, but it is possible we will come under attack before we can get the drive running again. If we survive we will come for you and, if we cannot get to you in time, be assured that Rhone will pay a heavy price.' He knew his words sounded without feeling, but he didn't have the time to deal with that now.

He couldn't think of anything more to add, any comfort to give her. He now broke into a loping run. They had enough problems here as it was and, even if they got to Mars, the chances of him doing anything for Var were minimal. None of the space planes aboard Argus was capable of flying down through the thin Martian atmosphere. Perhaps that wasn't an insuperable problem, given time, but time was the one thing that Var did not have. He began running schematics in his mind, seeing what could be stripped away, making vector and power calculations, redesigning things organically as, merely with a thought, he sent a squad of construction robots out to the space docks.

The lock pressurized even as Alex unclipped and pulled off his helmet. He opened the inner door and pushed himself into the wide space available before the storage racks, fully alert for anyone waiting for him in there. He seemed safe for the moment, but that could not last. If that android had seen him, then so had all of them, and perhaps Alan Saul himself would by now know where he was. Therefore more would be on the way, along with members of the station police force. He had only one option.

Tumbling in zero gravity, Alex quickly stripped off his old suit, unpacked the VC and donned it. He did it much faster than most normal troopers could manage, but then he was much better trained and his reactions a lot quicker. No normal trooper would have been able to survive an encounter like the one he had just gone through. Once he had closed the VC suit, he hooked up the oxygen pack from his old suit as a reserve, connected in the radio booster board, and then pushed himself over to the cylinder transport system. Here he found a cylinder that had come from his own hydroponics unit, still in the process of being unpacked by a pedestal-mounted robot arm. He ducked under the arm and dragged the cylinder from its rack. Only when he had it clear did he consider what could have happened if the robotic arm had been controlled by someone hostile. He emptied the cylinder of its remaining contents, then took it over to the other egress and put it in position. There was no guarantee this would work, but he had to try. He climbed inside and closed the lid.

Nothing happened for a moment, and Alex began to wonder if Saul had reached out to shut down his escape. But then, with a clonk, the thing slid into motion, shortly followed by a surge of acceleration pushing his feet against the base of the cylinder. He closed his eyes. If Saul knew he was in this tube, then the chances were that he would do something about it – such as knocking off the braking at the other end and allowing Alex to arrive at his destination at full speed. So Alex might well be about to die. Then again, another option would be to stop the cylinder halfway along its course and just leave it there until he ran out of air. Certainly he had no way of getting out of this thing while it was in its transport tube. Deceleration ensued . . . a further couple of clonks, and the lid opened.

'What the hell?' said the man looking down at him.

In one motion Alex jerked upright and swung his rifle in a short vicious arc that connected with the man's head. He tumbled back and Alex was past him in a moment, realizing he was now in some sort of automated food-preparation room. As he reached the door, he guessed that this must be the place that supplied the refectories and personal dispensers in Arcoplex One – which meant he was getting close to the power feed to that weird space drive.

Out in the adjacent corridor he turned right and headed straight for a bulkhead door, pausing to study the direction icons and colour-coded map above it, which he memorized.

Heading straight for the airlock, he passed a woman in the corridor but she wasn't armed, so he ignored her. Once through the airlock, he moved out into a cageway running alongside the outer endcap. He abandoned the cageway at once, since it was taking him in the wrong direction, then climbed over the top of the unit he had just left and gazed towards his destination. Through partially constructed floors of the outer ring, he could see part of the space drive and the ducts that ran power and control optics to it, extending towards him then sweeping away to the right to disappear into the endcap itself. He was just about to launch himself towards those ducts when suddenly silver shapes were swarming around them, many of them breaking off to launch themselves towards him.

Alex made microsecond calculations before he threw himself in a flat course over towards the side of the endcap. He stood no chance now of severing the power supply to the space drive, but there was still another potential weakness. The EM field seemed to be an integral part of this new drive and, just beyond the endcap lay the main transformer room. After a few seconds in flight, he hit the curved outer edge of the structure around the arcoplex-bearing housing. As he thumped down a foot to secure himself, he caught a glimpse of someone looking up at him in surprise from a rounded window, before he propelled himself further. As he sailed through vacuum, he turned to survey his surroundings. There was absolutely no doubt now that he had been spotted. There were robots closing in on him from every direction, some of them leaving vapour trails from their use of compressed-air impellers.

At high speed and feet first, Alex hit a section of composite wall. Something cracked in his recently healed leg, but he felt no pain. The composite had dented, absorbing a lot of the force, but he still bounced away from it. Seconds later he snagged a long, tensioned beam strap, managed to hold on, then towed himself down its length. He had pulled himself into a partially walled corridor by the time he felt the vibration of multiple impacts on the structures all around him. The robots had arrived.

Moving as fast as he could in his gecko boots, Alex made it to a manual airlock hatch. He opened it, climbed inside, waited for it to pressurize. The constricted space of the airlock would at least keep some of the bigger robots from following him, and any others would have to come through here just one at a time. Once it had fully pressurized, he opened the lower hatch and dropped through it into an oxygenated corridor. In a slow loping run, he headed for the head of a cageway leading down. He jumped into this and scrambled down through numerous floors to reach a short tubeway. At the end of this lay the door to the transformer room, and Alex couldn't quite believe he had made it this far. However, with air around him to transmit the din of robot movement, he knew he would be going no further. He opened the door on to a platform overlooking a massive collection of transformers.

Packed within a framework extending twenty metres on each side, and rising from floor to ceiling, stood the transformers themselves. These were smoothly rounded-off cubes of laminated metals and graphine composites wrapped in heavy coils of copper and superconductive wire. Quadrate scaffolding filled the rest of the chamber, supporting pan-pipe clusters of heavy ducts that wove away from these transformers and led into the surrounding walls. Alex scanned the scene, remembering how this room had looked the last time he was here, then he focused on the subsequent additions.

Supported amid the scaffolding was a big squat cylinder of hardware with numerous brand-new optic and power feeds leading both in and out of it. Since it was obviously new, this device had to be something to do with the space drive; therefore it had to be crucial. He leaped directly across to catch hold of a scaffolding pole, then began to tow himself towards it. At that moment the door burst open and, one after another, construction robots sped into the room. Hearing sounds from above, he looked up and saw more fast appearing there. Alex halted just a few metres away from the unknown device and trained his rifle on three interconnected translucent boxes that seemed to be packed with electronics. Then he hesitated.

Once he pulled the trigger, it would be the end for him. At the surface of his mind he dismissed the importance of that, but deep down knew this was why he had hesitated. He now rationalized: would destroying this drive increase or decrease Messina's chances of survival? Would those aboard the *Scourge* even care about Messina? Would Messina, who was now probably about as mindless as ex-Committee Delegate Vasiliev, be better off here? These arguments circled in his mind, and his trigger finger remained immobile. Then he looked around to find that all the robots had ceased their approach.

'So where do we go from here, Alex?' asked a calm and horribly reasonable-sounding voice over his suit radio. 'Pull that trigger and I can assure you that Messina will die instantly.'

The words seemed to act like a key turning in his brain, and Alex knew precisely how this must play out. Maybe, in the end, Alexandra had been right about so much. He reached up with a free hand to unclip his VC suit helmet and batted it away from him, then, always ensuring he had a finger on his weapon's trigger, removed each of his VC suit gauntlets in turn.

'Bring him to me,' he said. 'You bring him to me now.'

They were running out of time and Saul did not need the full extent of his abilities to calculate that if Alex caused damage where he was, then it was unlikely to get fixed before the *Scourge* arrived. Everything possible must be done to prevent him doing so. The urgency of that was intensified by the fact that, right at this moment, Saul's sister was running out of her air supply on Mars. Such knowledge had an odd effect on him: his instinctive reaction was to view her as a problem that needed to be solved, damage to reality that needed to repaired. Yet, if he stepped back and coldly analysed the situation, she was an irrelevance. The oddity was that, in this one case, the more human part of him had overridden the greater whole. Perhaps he had been fooling himself about the dehumanizing effect of plugging himself into the machine.

'Langstrom,' Saul instructed, directly through the police commander's fone, 'go to the Arboretum and have Messina secured, but bring him to the EM field transformer room only when I signal. We want to draw this out as long as possible.'

All the while Alex remained in the transformer room doing no damage, the vortex generator was winding up to speed. If Saul could keep him talking for just half an hour, they would then be able to fire up the drive.

'What the hell is he doing?' replied Langstrom. 'Surely he doesn't think he can escape with Messina now?'

The man was clearly watching image feeds and therefore up to date on what was happening, Saul realized. Others were watching too, and he could not help but feel like an idiot whose folly had been exposed before a crowd. Why had it taken him this long to understand how dangerous this Alex was, and why, when he apparently had the man trapped, hadn't he shut down the only possible means of escape?

'He's been programmed to protect Messina,' Saul replied, 'but is now beset by a mass of contradictions that he's not mentally prepared for. Seen in his terms, we are an obvious danger to Messina, so he has been working along with those aboard the *Scourge* to stop us leaving. However, he's not stupid either, and he'll realize that those aboard that ship are not necessarily as concerned about Messina's welfare as they are probably telling him.'

'That still doesn't answer my question,' Langstrom grumped.

'The plain answer is that he doesn't know what he's doing,' Saul replied. 'He just doesn't want Messina to die – or to die himself.'

Saul exited the rim-side endcap of Arcoplex One, entering the train tunnel that led outwards then round the rim towards the docks, but exited it through a personnel access tube heading out to the transformer room. At the same time, he continued watching events through the sensors of the robots currently occupying the transformer room, while also urging a couple of spiderguns over that way. Just a couple of shots from one of those could finish this quickly; however, it was quite evident that Alex had positioned himself very carefully. He would notice if Saul tried to move a spidergun into a position where the shots it fired would not damage the new drive hardware. This situation was sticky, very sticky indeed.

'Alan, what the hell are you doing?' Saul had been ignoring all attempts to contact him, but had now allowed this one through.

'I am going to deal with a bad situation resulting from my lack of attention, Hannah,' he replied.

'And get yourself killed?'

'That was not my intention.'

'He'll probably try using you as a hostage to get both himself and Messina off the station,' she protested. 'Use your robots to deal with him instead.'

'Not feasible at the moment, unfortunately, but the longer I can draw this out, the nearer we get to Rhine firing up the drive again. But if I don't go and negotiate now, this Messina clone could destroy vital hardware and kill our chances of escaping.'

'You're sure this isn't some macho need of yours to step outside your computer world?'

'That was low, Hannah. I'll speak to you soon.'

As Saul finally reached the door into the transformer room he remembered the last time he had entered here, with Malden – and how Malden had died under a hail of bullets from Director Smith's troops. That was not a memory he relished.

He opened the door and stepped inside, two construction robots smoothly sliding out of his way as he walked out on the platform – but not moving too far away. They were ready to interpose themselves between him and Alex should the Messina clone decide that Saul made a better target than the drive hardware.

'So you are Alex,' Saul said.

'Where's Messina?' Alex asked.

This man was a little difficult to read, even though Saul could study in detail every single pore on his face. Certainly he looked scared, and ever so slightly puzzled, but these seemed like a veneer over blankness, like a smile painted on a doll.

'Messina will be brought here only when or if I am ready to bring him here, Alex,' said Saul. 'I'm curious to know what you hope to achieve. I've already told you that the moment you pull that trigger he will die.'

The other man suddenly looked very tired as he shook his head.

'Alexandra was naive, but maybe naivety is a good thing, because it allows you to function without regard for the consequences,' he said.

'I assume Alexandra was your partner – the one killed in Messina's space plane?' Human contact now? Saul reached up, unclipped his suit helmet and removed it, trying thus to bridge the emotional gap.

'She was. She possessed a very black-and-white view of reality that I envy now.'

'Surely this situation is, though with some complications, also black and white?'

Alex just stared at him for a moment, then he said, 'The fact that your robots ceased their approach, and that you yourself are here now, tells me I am pointing this weapon at something vital. So here's what I want: I want you to withdraw all the robots from this room, then I want you to come over here next to me. You will be my hostage, and together we will go to the Chairman's space plane, where you will instruct your staff to bring the Chairman. There we will arrange a hostage exchange, and I will depart with him safely.'

On the face of it, this seemed a viable option for such a thoroughly programmed Messina clone to achieve, but already Saul was beginning to realize that this man was a bit deeper than that. He decided to test him.

'So you can then depart and be picked up by the *Scourge*,' he suggested.

Alex shook his head. 'That would have been Alexandra's expectation. She would have bargained with you similarly. She would have expected to be picked up by the *Scourge*, but found herself ignored.'

'And your own expectation?'

'I will use the cryogenic suspension pods on board,' he said, 'and at some time in the future the plane will be picked up, maybe in better times.'

'So you know about them,' remarked Saul.

'I know about them,' Alex agreed.

'What makes you think I won't destroy that plane the moment it is clear of this station?' Saul asked.

'Because I will release you. Because you gain no advantage by using up energy or projectiles to kill me, especially when such resources might be better employed in getting this drive up to speed or defending this station against the *Scourge*.'

'That seems . . . reasonable.'

'Then send your robots away. Send away that spidergun I see lurking in the corridor behind you.'

Saul glanced back at the spidergun, then, careful to telegraph his moves, gently propelled himself from the platform towards Alex, seeking to get closer. As soon as he caught hold of the scaffolding, he slowly raised a hand in a gesture of dismissal. The robots began to withdraw and the spidergun in the corridor retreated out of sight, as Saul towed himself even closer. Then he spoke out loud, 'Langstrom, bring Messina to his space plane,' though the words never actually reached Langstrom. However this turned out, Saul's main aim was to get that weapon pointed away from the hardware.

'That's close enough,' said Alex.

Absolutely right, had Saul possessed merely human reactions and human speed. Even at that moment he was
consciously controlling every aspect of his body, oxygenating
his blood, ensuring nutrients were in place, increasing his
heart rate and adrenalin levels and calculating the precise
moves he must make. All he needed now was for Alex to turn
that weapon towards him.

'You know that I was made almost incapable of being
disloyal to the Chairman,' said Alex. 'I was indoctrinated to
protect him at all costs, including that of my life. However, I
have been alive a long time for one of our kind, and I have
also been a long time away from reprogramming.'

Why was he saying this?

Alex continued, 'Even when I came here, I was still
functioning on that basis but only now have I understood the
futility of my position. I cannot any longer save the Chairman,
because he no longer exists. He is now no more what he used
to be than that creature that entered my hydroponics unit is
still Delegate Vasiliev. The purpose of my existence is over.'

Something was going badly wrong and just for a second
Saul could not understand what it was. He needed to slow
this down, calm it.

'So what is it you want, Alex?'

'I'm not as trusting as Alexandra was. She would have
been easy for you to manipulate, and would have died the
moment she left this room. I, however, know I will not be
leaving this room alive.'

Saul understood in that instant, and realized he should have
guessed it the moment he saw Alex had removed his space
helmet and gauntlets. The purpose for which Alex had been
shaped was gone, but human motives like vengeance remained.

470

A sheer bloody-minded and suicidal response could therefore not be overruled. Saul launched himself at the man just as the weapon crackled, chunks of plastic, silicon and optics zinging away as its bullets turned the control circuits to ruin.

Forty bullets fired . . .

The rifle swung up towards Saul even as his right hand speared at Alex's throat. Saul pulled back, turned, and clamped his elbow down to trap the weapon's barrel against his body. Alex tried to pull it free but Saul reached down, driving a thumb against the man's trigger finger. The weapon crackled against his side, a searing sensation there, but the bullets impacting somewhere behind. The heel of a hand came up blindingly fast, hammering into Saul's nose. Levering against the rifle he turned completely, bringing his elbow round and smashing it into the side of Alex's head. The man turned away to avoid that, catching only part of the blow and spinning further to bring the rifle down like a club. It struck Saul's upper arm, but without much force since by then Alex had released it, after realizing it was merely a hindrance to close-quarters combat.

Tight, Saul understood. *Very tight.*

Saul was fast, but so was this Alex. Neither of them telegraphed blows and at this range neither of them could get their blocks into place fast enough. Constricted by the surrounding scaffolding, there was also little room for them to separate. They ended up face to face, short powerful karate punches blurring between them as each tried to drive the other into a bad position.

Stop just responding. Calculate.

Time seemed to slow down as Saul's thought processes speeded up. He could see that, though they were both managing to deliver solid blows, they weren't delivering them with maximum effect – the padding and armour in their suits absorbing most of the impact. Saul altered the parameters for himself. *Pull back on next strike, the block will drive it into the upper chest: pause – now.* His next punch hit a floating rib, between bands of armour, and on the one after that, as Alex shifted his head aside to avoid it, Saul opened out a thumb. His fist grazed along Alex's temple, but the thumb went straight into his eye. *Weakening now, and a loss of depth perception.* Saul turned as if evading yet another blow, but raised his leg and slammed his knee into his opponent's thigh, behind the front pad of armour.

Alex's next straight-fingered jab aimed at the point just below Saul's ear missed entirely, and now it was all over. As he drove blow after blow into his opponent's body, Saul also gazed through the senses of a spidergun, now back in range, as it etched out numerous target points. Other robots were returning to the room too. Alex meanwhile lowered his arms and Saul realized the other man was now waiting to die. Surely this was the next logical step: remove this impediment and then try to repair the damage here. But there was an objection partly within himself and partly distributed amidst all of his mind and those things fashioned by it.

Alex drifted backwards with his eyes closed, but as nothing happened he opened them. He spat blood, then snarled, 'You must kill me!'

'*An interesting problem,*' whispered a voice in Saul's mind.

'*What would you suggest?*' Saul asked without speaking.

'*Reprogramming by reality is already underway,*' replied Paul, now actually entering the transformer room. '*I suggest confrontation followed by a naturalistic approach. Direct intervention is not necessary.*'

'Why?' Saul asked out loud.

The proctor sailed across from the platform and landed on the scaffolding. It reached in with one long arm and snared Alex by his spacesuit, dragging him out like a rabbit out of a burrow.

'When it is not necessary to kill,' said Paul, 'it is not necessary to kill.'

'Take him, then,' said Saul dismissively. Then he spoke directly to Langstrom's fone: 'You can forget about Messina now – we've got bigger problems.' Then he turned to inspect the damage.

18

Suffer the Children

Before the twentieth century, increasing mechanization in industry was only seen as a boon by industry chiefs. Less outlay on labour of course meant more profit, and the only ones complaining were Luddites and could be ignored. In the twenty-first century, industries increasingly fell under the control of the state, while continuing mechanization and 'social justice' created an ever-growing underclass of the unemployed and unemployable. This class was generally kept under control by the media bread and circuses of the time, but the problems started with the growth in the number of people being displaced by increasingly 'expert' mechanization – people less easy to control. To manage this, the political classes chose to find employment for them, chose to bring them into the fold by creating a huge and pointless bureaucracy, but even that had its limits. It soon became evident that not all could be thus employed. It soon became evident that, in a population boom, too many educated people were available. The answer was simple: cripple education systems, allow the health and social professionals more of a free hand with the pacifying drugs, start damaging people even when they are children and ensure more of them end up in the more easily controlled underclass. However, even this has proved only a temporary solution, and it is certain that more drastic measures will need to be applied.

Scourge

The background noise aboard the ship had changed, as the preparations being made by the troops transmitted through the metalwork like infernal machines ticking over in a cellar. Clay Ruger reached up, touched his aching head, and couldn't quite believe that he was still alive. Only now, as he hazily recollected events in the bridge, did he realize that the weapon Scotonis had held must have been loaded with taser bullets – the kind that delivered a disabling charge on impact.

He sat upright, then tried to use his fone to get through to Scotonis himself, but heard only a fizzing noise. The taser bullet had obviously taken out his fone too. He carefully climbed out of his bed and went to the door, but it wouldn't open. Next he began walking over to his console, to reach Scotonis that way, but the ship shuddered, a sound like thunder rumbling through it, then came the throaty roar of a side drive, which sent him staggering against a wall.

Clay clung in place until the shuddering ceased, his eyes closed and a cold sweat sticking his ship suit to his back. Distantly he could hear people shouting and a breach klaxon sounding. He took a deep breath, then turned and walked over to his console, sat down and put through a call, to which the captain immediately responded, but with only his image icon appearing on the screen.

'How's your head?' Scotonis asked distractedly.

'It's been better,' Clay replied. 'Why did you do that, anyway, and what the hell's going on now?'

'The point was that you were supposed to be dead,' the captain replied calmly, 'and I couldn't risk you walking out of the bridge and being seen by the staff officers that Commander

Liang had sent up into the executive area. We had you carted out in a body bag to Medical, where Dr Myers checked you out, then we had you moved to your own cabin after Liang's men were gone.'

Clay absorbed that information, but still a big question remained. Why the hell had Scotonis *not* just killed him? In the same position, he himself wouldn't have hesitated. It occurred to him then that maybe Scotonis was a better human being than Clay was, but that wasn't a thought he wanted to examine too closely.

'So Liang had been told that I was supposed to die?' he ventured.

A voice in the background spoke and Clay recognized the gunnery officer, Cookson. 'Glancing hit,' he explained. 'We're low profile right now. Close defences can handle most of it.'

The captain replied, 'That'll change.' Then, 'What was that you said, Ruger?'

'So, now I've got to stay in my cabin?' Clay replied instead.

'No, too risky,' said Scotonis. 'Now you're awake, I want you to move yourself to Messina's quarters. You'll be able to get a good view on the big screens in there.'

'What's happening, Scotonis?'

'We've arrived,' the captain snapped in response. 'Now get moving – because Liang's men might be back at any time.'

'My door is locked.'

'It isn't now. I just unlocked it.'

Clay shut down the console, stood up and surveyed his room, considering what personal belongings he needed from here, but decided not to delay further since Messina's quarters were better protected than the rest of the ship. So he headed for the door. Immediately outside his cabin, the acrid smell of burning plastic hit his nostrils and, looking up, he saw a stratum of smoke across the ceiling. The breach klaxon was still sounding somewhere in the distance and he could hear a robotic voice saying something repetitive but indistinct. The moment he stepped out into the corridor, the ship shuddered once again and another klaxon opened up nearby. Clay stood dumbfounded for a moment, but when, on looking up, he saw the smoke was on the move, he immediately broke into a run. Ten minutes of sweaty panic brought him to Messina's apartments, which were positioned below the bridge. He entered and hit the control closing the airtight door. In here, he was surrounded by impact armour and breach-foam layers within the walls, similar to those located in every essential bulkhead throughout the ship.

He swung his gaze across the partially completed furnishings, and then headed over to a large and comfortable acceleration chair positioned before a multi-screen which looked like a minimalist sculpture fashioned out of one huge curving sheet of black glass. He sat down, strapped himself in, flipped over the chair-arm console and set both the screen and bridge communication running. Images appeared of the views currently available to the bridge crew, and one more showing them all seated and watching the action on their multi-screen.

'What's the situation?' Clay asked.

'Tell him, Cookson,' said Scotonis.

Gunnery Officer Cookson eyed his captain askance, then said, 'We've railed out five test shots, and from them located some of their weaponry, but of course they're not too happy about that.'

Another image now: a close view of Argus Station. Above it streaks of fire appeared, like white contrails, before deforming and fading down to orange, then to red, and finally disappearing. Targeting frames next appeared all over the station like a sudden pox.

'We've precisely located the two railguns Alex detailed, and will shortly be opening fire on them. But first we're going to fuck up their targeting.'

'How?' asked Clay.

'You will see shortly,' said Scotonis. 'Now, if you don't mind, we have work to do.'

Clay grimaced at that, then, using his console, he first opened up the command channels so that he could hear all the exchanges between command staff, then began calling up other views and additional data. In the troops' quarters things had changed drastically. Large areas of the accommodation had been collapsed so as to leave three long hexagonal compartments where now the troops were massing with all their equipment. They were all suited up and carrying weapons, and those behind the primary assault teams were already heading out into a newly connected tube leading to the main exterior airlock, carrying the various sections of vacuum-warfare penetration locks.

'Detonation in five,' Cookson announced. 'Four . . . three . . . two . . . one . . . and *now*.'

The image of Argus Station whited out, then came back with a ball of fire expanding above it. The image fizzed, breaking into squares – the EM radiation pulse delivered by the blast. As this ball of fire inflated, it grew diffuse but even so, when its perimeter hit the station, the effect was visible. The whole massive structure tilted, and debris was blown away like chaff from a plate.

'Reacquiring,' said Scotonis.

Clay did not need to ask what had happened. They'd detonated a nuke close to the station to interfere with electronics and now, since the station had shifted, Cookson was retargeting the station's weapons. Clay tried to sit back and relax, but found he couldn't. Really, he decided, he had too much intelligence and imagination to be a soldier. It was bad enough having to fight in a place where there was air to breathe, but here?

Next a sonorous thrumming that penetrated bone-deep filled the ship. The first time the railguns fired, Clay must have still been unconscious, for he had never heard or felt this sensation before. But he just knew this had to be their sound.

'They're returning fire again,' Cookson noted, 'but their targeting is off.'

Even so, the *Scourge* shuddered again, and somewhere another klaxon started howling. Contrails flared into being all across the top of the station, until it was nearly lost to visibility behind a curiously regular pattern like some epiphyte made of fire, but this only lasted until the next nuclear detonation, which swept it all away before going on to peel hull plates off Argus like a scaling knife. Shortly after this, fire began to glare from inside it, and vapour belched from the newly torn holes.

'That's one of them,' said Cookson and, even as he spoke, another explosion erupted from the station, hurling black chunks of machinery up on a column of fire. 'And that's the other,' he added.

'Trove,' prompted Scotonis.

'Twenty minutes,' she replied.

The surge of the engines shoved Clay deeper into his chair, then tried to throw him out of it sideways.

'Liang,' said Scotonis, 'twenty minutes. Get in position.'

'Already clearing first teams in Section One,' replied Commander Liang.

Troops were crammed into the tube leading to the air-locks. Clay searched for further views, and saw that, even while the tube was full of soldiers, they were still on the move. Soon he found an exterior cam showing them spilling out on the hull of the *Scourge* like ants boiling from their nest. There they had strung out ropes connected to the hull and were using them to secure themselves. They struck Clay as overly exposed out there, but were those inside the ship any safer?

On Argus Station, detonations were still blooming like brief hot stars, and sending chunks of debris tumbling away. Cookson was now destroying their collision lasers, Clay realized, and maybe any other anti-personnel weapons scattered about the surface. It seemed all very easy and going perfectly to plan, which was worrying.

'Nothing more from the railguns,' said Cookson. 'That means they have to be down.'

'As things stand, between the first two strike points looks good,' observed Liang, who must have been studying a head-up display. 'We assault the station internally through them while a third team goes over the hull to take Tech Central.'

The station was now looming huge on the multi-screen as Trove announced, 'Ten minutes, docking anchors primed.'

Next Cookson observed, 'I'm getting an energy spike. There's something—'

All the hardware around Clay blanked and a hot flu-like sensation passed through his body. Immediately on top of this came a numb terror, as he expected the fire he had seen aboard Galahad's aero to descend on him now.

The screen blinked back on, and audio returned.

'Maser! A fucking maser!" Cookson shouted.

'Shut it down!' Scotonis yelled, his voice drowned out by another horrible sound.

Something was happening to some of the troops out on the hull. Some had released their holds and were falling away from the ship, legs and arms waving frantically, spacesuits inflating grotesquely. When some of them began bursting in clouds of vapour and offal, Clay just gaped. The concerted screaming seemed like the feed from a microphone opened into Hell, and it took Clay a moment to grasp that he should not be hearing this at all, for he only had command channels open. Then, belatedly, he realized he was not hearing it over radio, but distantly through the body of the ship. He turned his attention immediately to the troops still aboard.

Two of the hexagonal compartments appeared fine, with all the troops neatly ranked and in the process of filing out, but in the third one a chaotic mass of swiftly moving bodies bounced about like plastic balls in a lottery cylinder. Smoke began to appear too, then some of the bodies that had finally stopped writhing began to sprout fire from their suit seams. Not being out in vacuum, these men were not inflating or bursting, instead being cooked inside their garments.

Again that deep thrumming echoed throughout the ship. Fire exploded out of another part of the station and rose up into Clay's range of view. A series of detonations followed and, as he glimpsed something spearing its way down, trailing cable, he realized that the docking anchors had now been fired. He focused a camera on one of them and watched it hit, driving its hardened talons into hull metal, then begin closing up, tearing up tens of square metres of surface metal until clamping on the firmer structure underneath. The sounds of heavy motors winding in the anchor cables, and the stressing of metal, ensued, followed by stuttering bursts of a side-burner, which took the strain off those motors so they wound up to a scream.

The station loomed steadily closer, then with a crash

Clay's view of it blanked. They were down. He searched for other views, finally seeing surviving troops disembarking onto the plain of the hull and heading out towards where the hull plates were bent upwards around a hole made by a previous explosion inside. Within the *Scourge*, he saw troops exiting even faster. Liang had decompressed the three sections, incidentally extinguishing the flames in one of them, and opened a space door down to the hull to act as a ramp.

Clay felt an odd moment of pride. The troops had come all this way and now they were ready to complete their mission. That he was complicit in the plan to abandon them here didn't seem to have any relevance to this feeling, and in that moment he questioned his earlier notion about Scotonis being a 'better human being'. The feeling died once he saw the silver swarm rising up out of a distant hole.

The robots were coming.

Earth

Serene hadn't realized how tense she had been feeling until the pressure started to ease the moment the *Scourge* was down and anchored. Even if the rebels re-engaged that new drive of theirs, there would be no escape for them, because the *Scourge* now lay within the compass of the drive's warp bubble. They were finished. Despite heavy initial losses on Serene's side, the attack was proceeding to plan, and the remaining fifteen hundred troops would soon take the station. All that mattered now was what might get destroyed in the process. Under slightly less pressure at knowing that he no longer had to plan also for an assault on Antares Base on Mars, Commander Liang had assured her of success, and that the Gene Bank samples and data would be retrieved. He had then been embarrassingly grateful when, in her last message, she had informed him that securing Jasper and an intact drive were no longer important either. Calder was now absolutely certain he could build one – had bet his life on the certainty, and *knew* it.

Serene watched her troops deploying before the approaching horde of robots – a scene she would have to extract the most entertainment from right now, because very shortly such exterior inputs would shut down. Alan Saul's ability to penetrate computer systems made it essential that the assault force left nothing open for him. Liang had pushed for limited-burst transmissions between him and his troops, for delivering only essential instructions, and nothing leading back to the ship. Open video coms originating from helmet cams would have been positively suicidal, since they possessed a bandwidth into which Saul might insert himself. Even the view Serene watched now had its dangers, as became evident when a warning icon began blinking down at one corner of the screen, and then the image froze before blinking out.

Serene gazed in frustration at the blank screen until some words appeared on it: 'Attempted com laser viral insertion'. She flicked the screen to another view, long-range from the Hubble, which was clear enough to show the *Scourge* and the station, but not clear enough to reveal any detail of the action. She sat back, surveyed her garden, noting that some of the plants were dying despite the ministrations of her new expert horticulturalist and the addition of nutrients from the composting of the last one.

'Sack!' she shouted.

He appeared on the other side of the bridge in an instant. 'Ma'am?'

'Bring me a drink,' she commanded. 'The champagne.'

He dipped his head and retreated.

She had intended to have a little celebration as soon as Liang reported success, but why not enjoy that drink now? She could always crack open another bottle later.

Sack shortly returned with a bottle of champagne and a flute glass on a silver tray. He looked a very odd butler indeed. He placed the tray on the table beside her, picked up the bottle and opened it, the cork arcing through the air to land in her fish pond, and poured her a glass. Serene picked it up and took a sip. Once Sack saw that she was satisfied he turned to go. She held up a hand to halt him, then pointed over to a stone bench nearby. He obediently went over and eased his bulk down on it.

'I know so little about you,' she began.

Obviously Sack did not consider this warranted a reply.

'Barring everything in your record, of course,' she added. 'I understand you have family who were taken by the Scour?'

'My father,' he replied.

'Yes,' she said, 'that gun . . .' But the association of the antique weapon Sack carried with the term 'father' raised feelings she did not want to examine too closely. She continued, 'So tell me, Sack, what do you think of what we have achieved so far?'

Despite his lizard skin concealing almost any human expression, he did look uncomfortable. He dipped his head and sat forwards, elbows on knees and hands clenched together.

'You have unified Earth in very difficult circumstances,' he said.

'Is that all you have to say?'

'I would need you to ask a more specific question, ma'am.' He looked up.

'Very well.' She took a sip of her drink and collected her

thoughts. 'Do you think that what I am doing is right? Do you think my methods are just?'

'Right and just for whom?' he enquired.

'I am asking you the question, so you must reply from your point of view.'

'I want for nothing.'

Serene began to feel frustrated with this exchange, and wished she hadn't started it. As she gazed at him, however, she wondered just how others around her might react to his dehumanizing skin . . . how things might be for him on a more personal level, and found herself wanting to continue the exchange.

'What do others feel?' she asked. 'Can you give me a sense of their opinions?'

'They vary,' he said.

'Give me an example.'

After a long pause, he said carefully, 'Those closest to you in Earth's hierarchy are aware that the power and wealth they obtain is directly proportional to the potential danger to themselves of such proximity.'

'Danger from me.'

'Erm . . . yes, ma'am.'

'And those not so close . . . for example those in the upper administration?'

'They have the benefit of employment, they can support themselves and their families, and they know that if they keep their heads down their chances of surviving are good.'

'And what of those we must now describe as the proletariat?'

'They have their fears, of course, but they are distanced from them by the fact that they have absolutely no control over their lives.'

This was going nowhere. 'You've merely stated facts I already know. How am I viewed? What are people's opinions of me?'

'My contact with people outside of your immediate circle is limited, ma'am.'

'But we have travelled widely and you have spoken with others . . .'

'I do not wish to kill myself with my own words, ma'am.'

'Speak your mind without fear, Sack, just this once.'

He continued gazing at her for longer than felt comfortable, and she knew he didn't believe her.

'The world is currently a better place,' he said, 'but not because of the way it is ruled but rather because there are more resources now and fewer people. Many I have spoken to claim to resent their lack of freedom but, because they have been brought up with political officers micromanaging their everyday lives, they are not entirely sure what that lack is. Their resentment is also less because we no longer have the human resources for that same degree of micromanagement. Moreover, they all fear instability more than they resent being ruled autocratically, again because that is simply what they are used to. In their eyes you represent stability and, while they are terrified of you, it is not a human terror. You are remote, unpredictable, almost like fate . . . almost like the Scour.'

It was the longest speech she had ever heard from him and its honesty had a surprising effect, with a tightness in her groin, and she speculated again on how things were for him on a more personal level . . . She shook her head, annoyed that the occasional reactions she felt to this lizard-skinned man might well have been described by her father as an example of perversion, and considered the content of his words. Though he had given her some things to consider, they were not new to her. She was, in the end, the head of state. She *was* the state. Realistically, she had to accept that the old ideologies – on which the Committee's and her own rule had been built – all collapsed under the weight of the reality of human nature. In the end, she was no different from the kings and emperors of old. It was very depressing, and a perfect example of the sentiment that the more things change, the more they remain the same.

'You may go,' she told him, waving her hand with regal dismissiveness, uncomfortable with her reactions to Sack, and deliberately turning her thoughts elsewhere.

Once Earth was organized precisely as she wanted it, she felt it would then be time to turn her attention to something long overdue. The nature of the human race itself needed to be changed. Primitive humanity required alteration.

Argus

With one part of his mind, Saul exerted full control of the robot steadily trying to salvage components from the hardware Alex had wrecked. The thing had all of the detritus now floating in a cloud between its highly complex forelimbs, directly in front of its sensor array, and was sorting through it quickly and methodically. The other two robots assisting the repair team were fully under Judd's control, and they seemed to be working faster, as if the proctor's kinship with them gave it some advantage. The team of eight technicians Le Roque had sent were working to strip back the damage, replacing a coil destroyed by stray shots, and assembling stock chipsets and other components for the high-voltage requirements here.

It would take them at least two hours and twenty minutes to succeed, by the end of which time their common fate aboard this station might well have been decided.

The Saberhagens had done their best but, with the EM pulses from atomic blasts screwing their targeting, it had not been enough to stop the *Scourge*. Saul had known this anyway. Their means of escape had been the Rhine drive, and now things weren't looking so good. If this had been a land battle, the chances of success, as calculated right now, were less than forty per cent, with an error bar of over twenty per cent. But this was no land battle and, in this environment and with the weapons currently being deployed, the chances of mutual destruction stood at over eighty per cent.

With most of the rest of his mind, Saul surveyed the entire station. He calculated that, before it had been destroyed, the maser had killed a quarter of the assault force – waiting until the last moment to deploy it had been the Saberhagens' best move yet. Saul estimated that this left about fifteen hundred troops, which was still more than enough for them to establish a good foothold. Sending the robots out was a good tactic until those invading troops got organized, then they would start deploying their EM radiation pulse weapons and the gains achieved by outright confrontation would be lost. He would pull them inside once that happened, and resort to guerrilla warfare until he found a way to respond with ultimate ruthlessness.

The sight of troops tumbling out into vacuum, generally in pieces, announced the arrival of Saul's spiderguns at the two breaches in the station's hull. Clouds of vapour drifted amid the human wreckage, and returning fire filled the vacuum about the two breaches with splintered ceramic bullets and flinders of metal. Even as the remaining troops were opening fire, the construction robots reached them and began tearing them apart. It was all horribly graphic out there in the utter silence of space. Next, Saul's view, through the sensors of one spidergun, blanked. That happened so fast, Saul only realized why on scanning the hull of the *Scourge*. EM radiation pulse weapons were now being fired from ports in the side of the ship.

Robots began to freeze up, tumble out of control or end up stuck in some kind of loop, which in one case involved a large construction robot perpetually trying to behead a man it had already beheaded. Saul instructed the remaining spider-guns to direct their fire at the ship, while the army of robot foot-soldiers abruptly reversed their progress and headed back for the holes torn in the hull. This was utterly necessary, but it frustrated him that they had done so little damage: a hundred and thirteen enemy troops taken out of the fight but, unfortunately, thirty robots and two spiderguns as well.

The robots began flowing back inside the station and distributing themselves, according to his 'ambush predator' program. They headed past Langstrom's men, secure behind the bullet-proof shields of ten-millimetre machine guns and some hardened glass shields recovered during the last battle to occur aboard this station. In what had now been dubbed Police HQ, some remaining soldiers were distributing weapons to volunteers from among the station staff. Others were spread throughout the station, setting up ambush points and kill zones. Numbers, all numbers: the plain and horrible fact of warfare.

The assault force now began to enter the station, moving along its inner skin, the troops trying to find cover as fast as they could while still attaching safety lines, for they had learned *that* lesson from the fate of Messina's original assault on this station. Saul noticed enemy spiderguns departing the *Scourge* and, using radio and microwave dishes up on the surface, he tried to get a response from them, but they were as utterly indifferent to his blandishments as was the *Scourge* itself. They had also learned not to allow him that opening. Identification of fellows was by sight, since the attacking force wore VC suits of a silvery grey, and had for some reason painted the old Japanese rising-sun symbol on the fronts and backs of them. The attack would adhere to a set plan and communications amidst the assault force would be at a minimum – low-bandwidth radio, audio only, so there would be no chance of invading anything critical via that route. The spiderguns were pre-programmed, probably to kill any humans not wearing those easily identifiable VC suits, and to attack any robot outside their pack. Where was the opening he needed?

Saul continued to watch the invading troops and noted that some were carrying the components of vacuum-warfare penetration locks. He considered the feasibility of spinning up the cylinder worlds again, to make it more difficult to use those things on them, but then considered the power better used to keep accelerating the vortex generator up to speed. Then, outside, he saw the chance he had been waiting for – an opportunity offered by their lack of communication and the way they needed to identify each other.

'Judd,' he said it out loud, 'I presume you do not require me here?'

The proctor, while assembling a chaotic mass of components seemingly at random, swung its blind head towards him.

'You must go,' it said, already knowing his intentions.

'When it is not necessary to kill, it is not necessary to kill,' he said, repeating Paul's words and, of course, their implied opposite.

'Just so,' Judd replied, returning to its work.

Saul propelled himself from the transformer room, giving his instructions to the spidergun lurking in Tech Central and ordering it to withdraw, then he contacted his commander.

'Langstrom, I want fast-response team A heading for Tech Central immediately,' he said. 'I'll meet them on the base level. I'll also be pulling the majority of my robots over there too.'

'That'll weaken us,' protested Langstrom. 'We're having trouble holding them even now.'

'Beat a steady retreat,' Saul instructed. 'Let the invaders do all the work and take all the risks. You're not fighting to win, but fighting to buy time.'

'What are you going to do?' the commander asked.

'Something unpleasant,' Saul replied. 'That's all you need to know.'

'Okay, the team is on its way.'

He moved fast, retracing his route to the transformer room to reach the endcap of Arcoplex One. As he travelled, he watched multiple views of the battle in progress. Langstrom's men had remained in their hides around the rimward penetration, strafing the enemy with ten-bores and rifle fire, then suffering under returned fire as the enemy began to get their own heavy machine guns deployed. Langstrom's teams subsequently began to retreat, squad by squad, taking up well-prepared positions to cover each step of the way. It all began to fall apart as two enemy spiderguns came into play with little to match them – the two Saul had deployed now drifting and twitching, having already been knocked out by pulse weapons. Then the proctors intervened.

Saul saw them approaching fast, six of them having launched themselves at high speed from inside the station.

They were all carrying lengths of ceramic scaffolding like staffs, and were nearly upon the enemy, who were spreading along the inside of the station hull, before they were spotted. A ten-bore spat at them, sending two of them tumbling away with chunks flying off their bodies, then EM radiation pulses hit the others, haloing them with pink fire. In the virtual world, Saul felt their serenity – for even the two that had been so severely hit were calmly reordering their body's resources for survival, each aware of its losses but calculating its trajectory to see how quickly it could get back into the fight.

The remaining four slammed into the inner hull, leaving huge dents – and in one case completely crushing an enemy soldier. Then they were up and into it, thrashing to and fro with their staffs, just about every blow proving a killing one. Why had they chosen to attack with such primitive weapons? Saul did not know and did not try to find out, nor did he try to fathom why they seized two of the heavy machine guns and tried to use them. It was a futile exercise, for the machine guns obviously required some kind of coded link with the gunners operating them.

The wreckage they caused, in both mechanical and human terms, was horrific, but when the two spiderguns turned on them it began to tell. They started to become sluggish, as chunks of their bodies were blown away. One of them managed to snag a spidergun that approached too close, and simply tore it in half. Then, as one, they launched themselves away again, suffering further damage as they escaped. It was enough, though: Langstrom's troops had meanwhile withdrawn to safer positions – safer still when a multiple launch of missiles intersected the remaining spidergun and blew it to pieces.

Elsewhere numerous firefights were in progress, but the

steady retreat was also becoming evident. The assault force was taking heavy casualties, too, and bodies and bits of bodies were spreading out in a steady cloud from the two attack points. The third, and smaller, force of about two hundred men was nearing Tech Central, advancing steadily behind two spiderguns and a line of heavy machine guns motoring across the hull on gecko treads. They were being very cautious, which was good since it gave Saul time to prepare. He exited the asteroid-side endcap of Arcoplex One and began to make his way towards the base of Tech Central, where the fast-response team was waiting, watching robots entering one after another ahead of them.

'I'm going to let the force above enter Tech Central,' Saul declared over suit radio. 'Unless absolutely necessary, you will not engage them.'

'Seems pointless us being here at all,' replied one of the twenty soldiers.

Saul swung towards him. 'I thought you were overseeing the defence, Langstrom.'

'I am,' Langstrom replied, 'but my people are well enough trained and prepared for them to know what to do.'

Saul snorted in apparent annoyance and headed for the nearest airlock, the multi-armed welding robot that had been about to use it scuttling aside. Within the building, he gazed through numerous sensors, and quickly deployed his robots throughout the lower two floors. The main problem here would be the two spiderguns and, once they were out of the way, there would be a slaughter which it was utterly essential that none survived.

He mapped the place in his mind and worked out what would be their most likely mode of attack. The invading force would use the usual methods of urban warfare to secure the place, room by room, working their way steadily downwards. Maybe the spiderguns would be deployed ahead of the troops as they progressed, to take out all readerguns, and that eventuality should be prepared for.

Stepping inside, he sent his orders immediately, in just a microsecond. Construction robots began cutting away sections of cageway, so as to give themselves a wide angle of approach. Other robots with similar cutting gear positioned themselves nearby, because cutting gear was just what was required. It was a simple fact that spiderguns were lethal weapons, but they were also strictly anti-personnel weapons, and as vulnerable to a diamond saw as anything else made of metal. Other robots began concealing themselves for ambush, folding themselves up inside storerooms and cabins, climbing into ceiling spaces or the spaces under floors, behind wall panels or cramming themselves into air ducts, before welding and sealing themselves in.

Saul now issued further instructions. He wanted ten undamaged VC suits, so it would be necessary for ten of the attackers to die very neatly. Robots would have to deploy their ceramo-carbide chisels and drills carefully, for a hole punched into the vertebrae just below the neck ring should paralyse and kill, and not be as messy as, say, a heart puncture. Whereupon the suit should be easy to patch up afterwards.

The crump of an explosion shifted the air of the interior and was immediately followed by the shrieking of a breach alarm. Through cams focused up there, Saul watched a spidergun leap in and take out the two readerguns. It then shot through the door and headed for the nearest cageway. The troops followed the second spidergun in, carting two of the heavy machine guns dismounted and carried ready for use inside. Saul was impressed by the efficient way they progressed, trying to leave nothing to chance as they checked the many niches and hidey-holes. Some robots they did find and, as a precaution, disabled with pulse weapons, but they missed many more.

'Nine of you will come with me,' Saul said to the fast-response team. 'The rest will remain in Tech Central and fire on us.'

'You what?' Langstrom exclaimed.

Saul then explained the plan to him.

Mars

The sun was dropping out of sight and Coprates Chasma sliding back into shadow when Var came across further human remains. But this one would not be supplying her with further oxygen or super-caps. This person must have been inside, and unsuited, when the building had collapsed. The corpse was as dry and brittle as aged kindling but actually came up all in one piece, having been stuck to the bottom of a regolith block like a crushed bug. Moving both block and corpse exposed the floor below, which gave Var something to work to. She cleared compacted dust from this same point back to the wall foundations, then began working along these too, shortly exposing one side of an intact airlock.

Even as she began digging out the airlock, Var wondered what she was hoping to achieve. Would another hour or two of air matter to her? Perhaps now she should really start thinking about how to ease her passing. She paused, almost resentful of this wholly pragmatic part of her mind. Just a moment's thought brought home to her the realities.

Opening her suit directly to the Martian atmosphere was

probably the worst option. Yes, she would die within a few minutes, but it would be a horrible, agonizing death. She should know, since it was how she had killed a number of Ricard's men and she had been there to watch the whole unpleasant process.

The option of just keeping her suit on therefore seemed best. Just let the suit keep scrubbing out the carbon dioxide and, as the oxygen ran out, she would be breathing more and more of the constantly recycled remainder, which would be nitrogen – and nitrogen asphyxiation was fairly painless and quick.

Var returned to her digging. Nitrogen asphyxiation was what awaited her, but she was not prepared to just sit gazing at her head-up display and counting down the remainder of her life. Keeping busy enabled her to hold that reality at a slight remove. Contemplating her demise over any length of time might lead to her broadcasting pleas to the cosmos: begging, praying or something ridiculous like that. She realized that, at that moment, her biggest fear wasn't death itself but the possibility of it being undignified.

'Silly woman,' she muttered to herself.

A further hour of work exposed the outer door of the airlock. She struggled with the manual handle, but it was jammed, so she picked up a rock and hit it with that until it thunked downwards. She heaved the door open, hoping that someone had been trapped inside and still had an air supply. When she turned on her suit light and found the lock empty she questioned her logic. If anyone had been inside they would have used up all their air anyway. She checked the electronic control panel and found it dead, as expected, then stepped back and retrieved a multi-driver from her suit's toolkit. She leaned in with that to open the panel accessing the oxygen-feed pipework. This exposed simple pressure dials, all of them registering zero. Another hour of digging revealed the severed feed-in pipes. But usually, with locks like these, the pipes led to a pressurized air reservoir. She had to find it.

It was dark now and, checking the time, Var saw that in another couple of hours the automatic broadcast to Argus would recommence. She did not have to be there for it to happen, but maybe there had since been a reply. She returned to work, heaving regolith blocks away from the pile around where she had found the severed pipes. In this rubble she found a picture flimsy still displaying its last image – a bull elephant standing at the edge of a waterhole, some odd fragment of someone's life, maybe their fantasies. It was an image that made her feel horribly uneasy and which she instantly skimmed away into the darkness, though she did not know why.

By the time she found the other ends of the pipes, which had been crushed right down to the floor, she was feeling utterly weary. Checking the time, she saw that her broadcast had recommenced as of an hour before, and she decided that now was the time to check for any response. Afterwards she would come back out here, for what was the point in squandering her remaining time on sleep?

Var trudged back over to the building, where, even though she could see the message icon flashing on the screen, she calmly took her time in sitting down. After a long contemplative pause, she finally summoned up the nerve to open the message, but in frustration saw it was an audio file, and she had to run an optic from her suit to the console to hear it. Then her brother spoke to her.

Var listened to it twice, then once more to be sure. Damn, the inertia-less drive had worked. The science of the impossible had been made real and the human dream of starships had just turned into reality. And here she was, dying on Mars. Alan had given her hope, but that lasted only as long as she didn't really apply her mind. Then reality bit in. Even if Argus Station survived the *Scourge*'s attack on it, and shot across at improbable speed to orbit round Mars, the gravity well would still separate it from her, and the Argus Station did not possess Martian-format space planes. Then hope resurged. Maybe they could use something to drop her some oxygen here. All that would be required was some sort of re-entry capsule and a parachute . . .

She shook her head, because it all seemed too implausible. They were probably fighting their own battle for survival out there, so putting together some way of enabling her to survive would be the last thing on their agenda.

Var stared at the screen, contemplating the grim reality of her situation. Nevertheless there was still a little hope, no matter how small. She edited the message she was sending, adding that she had found some extra air, and telling her brother precisely how long she had left. Then she stood up abruptly, headed outside again, fully aware of how hope could be a dangerous thing.

19

Plasma Weapons

It can be argued that that the billions of Euros spent on trying to develop plasma weapons would not have been expended but for these weapons lodging themselves in the public consciousness, first through science-fiction films, then during the boom in computer games of the twenty-first century. The great problems in propelling plasma at a given target have always been air pressure and power. The second of these, for portable devices, was overcome by the development of high-energy density power storage like nano-film batteries and super- and ultra-capacitors, but the first – air pressure – has always remained a problem. Firing plasma through atmosphere to hit a specific target is like firing a jet of water through the sea: it breaks up, loses coherence, and the ratio between distance and energy requirement has always been an exponential one. To some extent this was overcome by laser-guided electric discharges, remote magnetic lenses and tunnelling acoustic shockwaves, all of which resulted in a portable plasma weapon . . . mounted on a tank. But, in the end, one must sometimes go back to the first purpose of the weapon, which is to kill and destroy, and the plasma-firing tank is substantially less effective in this respect than one firing depleted-uranium Hyex shells – and substantially more expensive.

Argus

'Sometimes there's just no other option,' said a voice behind Hannah.

She turned to see that the Saberhagen twins had joined her group, and felt a sudden deep gratitude for their presence. Hannah herself carried a standard Kalashtech assault rifle, but the twins both carried somewhat complicated-looking weapons that they must have fashioned themselves, along with coils of superconducting cable terminating in standard bayonet power plugs. She had seen a lot of this in Arcoplex Two as the defence efforts became more organized, some clever people having been preparing for just such an occasion.

'What's he doing?' Brigitta asked, nodding along the corridor to where Jasper Rhine had a floor plate up and was concealing something underneath.

'Booby traps,' Hannah replied. 'His Casimir batteries have a high-energy density, so inject a little nitric acid and they go off like grenades.'

'How does he intend to detonate them at the right time?' asked Angela, with clinical interest.

By now Rhine had replaced the floor plate. He stood up to press some minuscule object against the wall, before returning towards them with a big bag slung over one shoulder.

'That's the clever bit,' replied Hannah. 'They're not activated now, but they will be after we've all taken our positions. Once activated, they respond to nearby movement.'

'But you have a danger of chain reactions – one goes off and they could all go off?' suggested Brigitta.

'Not so,' said Rhine, pausing beside them. 'All the time

and resources spent in developing the machinery of oppression was not wasted.' He gave a crazy smile and headed off.

'HAD cells,' Hannah explained, pointing towards a small metal button on the wall. 'Human activity detectors were developed to save having readerguns perpetually powered-up. They operate at low power and contain shape-identification software. In a readergun, upon detecting the human shape, they send the signal for the gun to power up. Here the signal is picked up by a micro-relay that opens the acid bottle.'

'Neat,' Brigitta opined. 'But is it enough?'

Hannah didn't want to reply. She had spoken with Saul and he had been quite blunt: they were outnumbered and unless he could find an efficient way to use his own particular talents, they would inevitably lose. And, as he had told Langstrom, the defenders would now be fighting not to win but to buy time. She just hoped Saul had found some way for them to survive this, and was ashamed to admit to herself that she did not care how savage it might be.

'Let's hope so,' she allowed, studying the rest of her group.

Her assistant James was among them, along with four other lab assistants and two robotics engineers. The latter two, and also two of the lab assistants, carried Kalashtechs like herself and James. One of the lab assistants was just a girl, and it would have been nice to tell her to go away and hide herself, but in the end, if they lost here, she would be treated no better by their attackers than any of the adults. The remaining two lab assistants held a sidearm each, while one carried a handheld missile-launcher and the other carried a tube of the ring-shaped magazines this weapon used.

'Okay,' said Hannah, 'Alan managed to take a few seconds

out of his busy schedule to organize our defence here.' They smiled in response; even before Saul had been shot, it had become a standing joke that if he took any more than a few microseconds to think about something, then he was giving it deep and intense thought. 'The area we have to defend extends from the end of that corridor' – she pointed to where Rhine had been laying his booby traps – 'through to the rear of the factory.' She pointed the other way, along the corridor, to where it flared then terminated against a pair of wide concertinaed doors that opened on to the robotics factory. Then she began walking towards them.

Reaching the doors, she stabbed a finger against the panel to one side of them. They began sliding open to reveal the factory floor of Robotics within. All the machines were shut down now, after that mad rush to get as many robots as possible finished ready in time for the attack.

'So what have you brought to the party?' Hannah asked, indicating Brigitta's unusual weapon with a nod.

Brigitta held the object up. 'When we thought they could become a threat, we began making something we thought might be useful against the proctors. These comprise arc-heat helium in a Tesla bottle which is fired with what we've dubbed caps. They maintain the Tesla bottle around the plasma for about twenty metres, but we've only got ten shots each.'

Hannah gaped at the woman. 'What?'

'The bottle caps melt in excess of that range, which tends to make the effect even nastier,' continued Brigitta blithely. 'At twenty metres, the bolt discharge throws molten metal about too.'

'So let me get this straight: in your spare time you've managed to knock together a couple of plasma rifles?' said Hannah sharply. 'As I recollect, the Committee only got as far as reducing them in size so that a tank could carry them, then gave up.'

Brigitta winced. 'They're not plasma rifles as such, because the plasma would dissipate over just a few metres, without the caps.'

'A small point, don't you think?' Hannah observed. She was about to ask further questions, but a sound that had been hitherto just a background hum now rose into complete audibility. Hannah recognized the sound of small-arms fire impacting on the outside of the arcoplex, along with the occasional ominous rumble of explosions. The latter worried her more, because the sound must be transmitting through the station's structure – since vacuum lay outside the arcoplex – and that meant the battle had drawn very close.

'Let's get ourselves in position,' she said.

'Where do we go?' asked James.

Hannah repressed the urge to snap at him while pointing out that she wasn't a soldier, so how did she know? However, none of them was a soldier and she was effectively in charge of this group, therefore it was her responsibility. She needed to think about this with the dry analytical mind of a scientist. The plasma rifles she just could not assess, so decided one should be up here by the doors and one down on the factory floor. The missile-launcher should be up here, too, since the damage it would cause, considering their future survival, would be best wrought outside the factory. Kalashtechs then scattered about the factory, maybe?

'They're inside,' announced one of the robotics engineers, his expression horrified.

Hannah nodded. The sounds had indeed changed, becoming a lot more immediate, the explosions much less muffled and far more vicious.

'Okay, this is where you go,' she began.

It took ten minutes to get them all in position, and she felt she had done her best. Perhaps it would have worked out okay if only the attackers had concentrated their assault through the main corridor. They didn't.

The proctor pulled him from his shoulder and pushed him down. He felt grass underneath his palms, could smell Earth and, unbelievably, he could hear birds tweeting.

'The birds are distressed,' declared a wholly terrifying and unhuman voice, 'they don't like it when their environment changes so drastically. It is noteworthy how simple creatures will become distressed by such changes.'

Alex pushed himself up, his hands still clenching the grass to stop himself drifting off the ground. He then rose to his knees and looked around. He was in the Arboretum, greenery all around him as if he was clinging to the rim of a well full of it. Trees, shrubs and other plants were familiar to him, on some deeper level, even though he had never seen them in such profusion on Earth. The combination of that atavistic familiarity and being enclosed in a cylinder like this completely screwed his perspective. He had been here once before and hadn't liked it then. It apparently took people a long time to get fully used to this place.

'Why am I alive?' he asked.

The proctor was standing just a few metres away, clad in a survival suit specially altered to fit its huge frame. It was leaning on a long staff made from a scaffolding pole, though it seemed evident, by touch controls on the pole's surface, that something had been added to the inside.

'Walk with me,' it said, its voice seeming to reach down to twist something right inside him.

504

Alex just stared at the creature's leathery visored face. The thing spoke perfectly understandable human words, which were yet somehow terrifying. After a moment he managed to summon up the nerve to say, 'Gecko boots don't work so well on grass.'

'Use your toes, foolish man,' the proctor replied.

Alex grimaced and set about removing his VC suit boots. He then carefully stood up, clenching his toes in the grass. The proctor gave him a short nod and strode away, seemingly unaffected by the lack of anything holding it to the ground. Alex followed, tentatively at first but then with growing confidence. Occasionally he caught hold of a shrub to keep him stable, then did that more cautiously after grabbing at the thorny dark green foliage of a wild rootstock lemon shrub. Within a few minutes they reached one of the section dividers within the Arboretum. Here was where equipment and agricultural chemicals were stored. Beyond this lay a section tiered with concentric floors loaded with hydroponics tanks.

The proctor marched across diamond-pattern metal flooring to a door, its feet still sticking firmly. Alex assumed that the gecko soles of its survival suit allowed this, but then remembered his own recent observation. Gecko soles became swiftly clogged with detritus if used on the kind of natural ground they had just crossed. The proctor must be using some other means to keep itself in place – one Alex couldn't fathom. He waited until it opened the door and began to step through before launching himself across the intervening metal, catching the door handle and pulling himself through. The thing didn't even turn round, didn't seem at all concerned that he might be trying to attack it. Alex now pulled his boots back on, then followed the proctor further inside.

'You didn't answer my question,' he probed. 'Why am I

alive?' He meanwhile kept his head dipped, tensing up as if the reply might cause him pain.

'We go this way,' the proctor merely replied, striding for metal stairs that zigged and zagged towards the axis of the Arboretum cylinder.

Alex contained his frustration and considered what he should do next. He wasn't stupid enough to think he had a chance of escaping this creature, but at some point it might well leave him, then he could get involved in the fighting – the sounds of which were rapidly impinging. The proctor led him into a storage room where, in an area cleared amidst towers of plastic crates, an armed group of station residents – most of whom worked here, judging by their dress – were holding some kind of meeting.

A small belligerent-looking woman was currently address-ing a crowd of about fifty. She shot a glance at the proctor and Alex, then returned her attention to her audience.

'We have a heavy machine gun directed at the main en-trance,' she said, 'but that access is not going to be our chief problem. The assault force is using vacuum-warfare penetra-tion locks, so effectively can come in through the endcaps, or wherever the soil is thin enough in the main Arboretum section, or here in the dividing section. So we have to stay mobile – we can't dig in at any one place yet. Hydroponics is as secure as we can make it, because we have closed all the bulkhead doors and we know which way they'll come if they come in through there.'

'Unless they use explosives,' said a tall bald-headed man holding an assault rifle protectively across his stomach.

'Unless they use explosives,' the woman agreed.

'We've got cams covering the outside of the cylinder,' said the same man.

'But they may not last very long,' the woman replied. 'We're now a main target because we have the Gene Bank samples here.'

'And, as a main target,' the man noted, 'we're heavily defended.'

Alex understood the implication. Once the assault force got past the station's troops immediately outside, it was probably all over for them.

'Even so,' said the woman, 'we have to do whatever we can. We all know what surrendering or being captured will lead to.' She paused to survey all the faces around her. 'You all have your particular areas to cover. So keep communications open and be ready to move if or when necessary. Any questions?' None of them seemed inclined to say anything, so she finished with, 'Let's get to our positions.'

The crowd began to break up into groups, and only now did Alex see that there were some more proctors present. The woman picked up a light sniper rifle from where it leaned against the wall behind her, beckoned a stooped and elderly-looking man over to her side, then they approached.

'This is him?' she asked, flicking a worried look at the proctor before she gazed at Alex. He realized he wasn't the only one who felt the sheer impact, the *presence* of this creature.

'It certainly is him, Jenny Task,' the proctor replied.

'I don't see how he's going to be any use to us,' she said. 'Wouldn't it be better just to stick him in a cell.'

Alex glanced at the old man. He was carrying a sniper rifle too, and a pack of ammunition, and was gazing distractedly back towards those currently departing. Alex considered grabbing the rifle and getting out of here. No, the proctor would be on him in a second. He had to bide his time.

'Charlie,' the woman addressed the old man, 'he's with you, apparently.'

The old guy swung round and recognition struck like a blow. Alex gasped and jerked back, both his feet actually coming away from the floor. The proctor reached out with one hand and caught him by the shoulder, dragging him back down.

'I've built a hide in the big walnut tree,' explained Charlie. 'From there we should be able to cover most of the thin-soil areas.'

His face was different, of course, but it was the same one that Alexandra had found. Moreover, Alex recognized him on some deeper visceral level. Here stood Alessandro Messina, or at least what that man had now become. Here in front of him stood the very reason for Alex's existence.

The woman reached out and patted the Chairman's shoulder. 'Charlie here has turned out to be quite useful,' she said. 'Though he's forgotten a lot of his past, his inborn abilities and early training in the Inspectorate military have not been erased. Apparently Charlie once used to be a sniper.'

Alex knew everything it was possible to know about Messina, had treasured that knowledge. The man had indeed been a sniper in the military, eighty years ago, before promotion to command and then promotion out of fatigues into a suit and onto the first rungs of the Executive. A natural ability? Of course, it was one Alex himself possessed.

'But remember, Charlie,' said the woman, 'wait until they are out of the penetration locks. A stray shot inside might result in an atmosphere breach.'

'Sure,' said the erstwhile Messina, looking very serious. 'These bastards are going to be good for my plants – they're not going to kill them.'

'Attaboy,' she said.

'Good for your plants?' Alex repeated numbly.

The mind-wiped Alessandro Messina peered at him carefully. 'Yeah, we turn them into fertilizer.' He reached out a hand to the woman. 'Need to get moving now.'

The woman gazed at the proctor, who gave her a nearly imperceptible nod. She shrugged off the strap of the rifle she was carrying and handed it over. Messina swung it round and held it out to Alex. 'I hear that you should be a good shot, too.'

Alex just stood there dumbfounded. All that was left of his Chairman, his Alessandro Messina, stood before him right now, quite adamantly stating that he would be fighting the *Scourge*'s assault force. Two contrary views were so at war inside Alex that they caused a physical pain in his torso.

'If the assault force soldiers manage to get in,' said the proctor, 'their prime aim will be to get hold of the Gene Bank samples. They will kill anyone who stands in their way.'

It was a statement that Alex could not deny. In the end the answer was quite simple: he would fight beside his Chairman and do everything he could to prevent him being killed. He would obey his Chairman because that was what he had been programmed to do. Nothing outside of these facts was relevant. He took hold of the rifle.

'Yes,' he said, 'I am a good shot.'

Earth

It was time to assess broadly how things stood with Earth and to make some plans for the future. To this end Serene began running a computer model of the entire economy and environment of Earth. This particular model was the best available, with its ability to predict about four days into the future – before a butterfly flapped its wings somewhere and the whole thing went tits-up. However, she wasn't interested in predictions but in the neat and easily digestible way the present and the past were displayed.

Despite everything she was throwing into orbit, and Professor Calder's massive spend, Earth's resources were at a hundred-year high. This was simple mathematics really: production itself was mainly robotized and only limited by materials and energy supply, so it had been little damaged by the massive reduction in population. And while Saul's attack on the Committee had damaged production to a certain extent, it had also benefited it by causing a reduction in political control. Consumption, on the other hand, had been vastly reduced. Running some further calculations, Serene found that Calder's spend accounted for less than ten per cent of the gain made from reduced consumption.

Economically, Earth was looking good. Environmentally it was also better, but the gain was a questionable one. While wilderness areas were on the increase, there didn't seem to be much yet that could grow wild in them. Reviewing extinction and environmental-destruction statistics, and specific stories related to them, Serene began to unearth some disconcerting realities, all expressed in a rather neat little graph.

It seemed that, while the extinction and biosphere destruction rate had been steadily increasing in line with the rise in population, that rise had not been as deadly as was claimed at the start of the previous century. Certainly there had been some big, newsworthy extinctions – like those of the tiger, the lion, the elephant and the grey whale – but they were not the kind that could result in the death of Earth's biosphere. The dangerous stuff had come later; in fact it had ramped up markedly under Committee rule, and one of the stories before her illustrated why.

The North African breadbasket, as it had been called, was a Committee attempt to increase food production. Large portions of North Africa were turned over to agriculture; massive populations were relocated southwards – the whole process wiping out many indigenous species. Desalination plants were built to supply extra water but, due to a cost-based political decision, the resultant salt was dumped in storage bays inland. When, in the middle of the last century, the weather took one of its cyclic turns for the worse, resulting in an upsurge of rain in North Africa, billions of tons of salt had dissolved and run out into the fields, turning them barren. Meanwhile, nitrate and insecticide run-off had caused massive algae blooms and fauna deaths in the Mediterranean, shortly followed by an extension of coastal dead zones, until they met up with those extending out from southern Europe. The North Africa breadbasket had killed a large portion of the Mediterranean Sea.

Serene felt a moment of extreme disgust and annoyance. She had always felt that the Committee was utterly inefficient and this story perfectly illustrated why. Its problem, in the end, was that it had not properly rid itself of its human-centric take on governance. While it understood that humans had to be controlled for their own benefit, it had not grasped that they needed to be controlled for the benefit of more than that. They had to be controlled so as to maintain the ideal that was Earth – something she herself could see plainly but other humans apparently missed. It was the right and proper duty of a ruler to ensure everything in the human world ran at optimum efficiency, while also accepting that the human race was a plague on the face of the planet, an aberration which had its natural-world equivalents but was much more dangerous.

She sat back, scanning her garden, and noticed that some of the shrubs which she had thought were dead had put out new buds. Perhaps the nutrients provided *directly* by her previous horticulturalist were starting to do the trick. A distraction, however, so she returned to her thoughts.

The human race was a problem, and on those terms she must think to the future. While she herself was alive, it was a problem that could be controlled. Though medical research was reporting further breakthroughs in the banishment of senescence, and she could extend her own life, she still might die and whoever took over might not be as resolute.

Senescence . . .

Research into life extension was certainly right and proper for her, and for those she found useful, but perhaps it was time to consider a complete reversal of that concept as regards the bulk of the human race. In the end it came back to her earlier thoughts about modifying humanity.

Serene closed down the feed from the model, did a brief search and opened up some files she had been studying a few months back. The Alexes were an interesting experiment, undoubtedly. Absolute obedience and belief could be inculcated to deep levels – that was evident – but the whole operation was very labour intensive. She needed something better than that, something longer lasting. And in the end, as far as life forms were concerned, that came down to one thing: the immortal genes.

Another search began to render useful results. Telomere repair and extension and other genetic modifications resulted in a limited prolongation of life, but the reverse applied too.

Those who had been seeking out how to make people live longer had, in the process, unearthed how very easy it would be, with some small genetic modifications, also to shorten human lives. This idea had its appeal, but Serene could see problems. Limiting the span of people's lives could result in a loss of useful expertise. Quite obviously you did not want people like Calder dying by the early age of, say, forty. Also, limiting lifespan would not slow down breeding, which primarily needed to be controlled. So what was the answer?

Serene sat back and glanced at the empty bottle of champagne next to her, wondering if now was the best time to consider such things. Next, she turned her gaze up towards the light tubes in the ceiling. No, the sooner she began grappling with these problems the better, and she was starting to get some sense of the shape of a solution.

Truncation of lifespan and control of fertility were essential. The science of eugenics was the answer, and the way of applying that science had been staring her in the face. Wasn't it obvious that the best way of controlling the human race was precisely the method she had already used? She could spread a plague.

Viral recombination of DNA was a proven science, with a history nearly a century long. It should be possible to manufacture a virus capable of modifying DNA so that those infected would have only a short lifespan and would die quickly at the end of it, without senescence, maybe at some convenient age, say at forty or fifty. Perhaps the same virus, or another one, could be made to render everyone thus infected infertile, but in such a way that turning fertility back on would just be a matter of administering drugs. That solution seemed best: the actual ability to have children being state controlled.

As far as expertise was concerned, she could ensure some meritocratic immunization programme, but only against the life-shortening aspect of the modification. Those demonstrating brains and ability would be allowed to live long lives, but their ability to breed would still be utterly controlled. This would result in humanity diverging into two different strands, but even that would not be a permanent state of affairs. As technology continued to advance, and as robots became more capable and more expert computer systems emerged, there would come a point when that shorter-lived version of humanity would no longer be needed.

It would, she realized, work perfectly. Therefore ordering the future lay completely within her grasp. The knowledge made her feel almost euphoric. However, the good feeling quickly passed as she realized that this was all merely a distraction from her immediate concern, which centred on events millions of kilometres away.

Argus

Feeling utterly cold, Saul watched through many sensors as the attackers worked their way down through Tech Central, blowing out the bulkhead doors that had closed to prevent atmosphere escaping. While this was occurring he considered the work of one of Hannah's lab assistants, James Allison. For times when this man wasn't helping her, she had provided him with a research project of his own. She had wanted him to do a comprehensive analysis of the Galahad biochips inside ID implants.

Allison had not been enthusiastic about that at first but, as with all good researchers, he was methodical and precise and soon did become fascinated with the device he was studying. His first report to Hannah concerned the cybernetic virus, shortly followed by the electro-templating method used to produce it from the recipient's own venous system. He then delved deeper into the chip, revealing how its genocidal purpose was concealed within its professed aim of ensuring that no one but the original recipient of an implant could use it. It was interesting to note that when those involved in the implant black market shut down the chip's ostensibly prime process of identification, the chip's real purpose remained untouched.

Allison then detailed for her how the chip was activated. When a microscopic radio receiver within it detected the code of the implant, on the right coded frequency, with the addition of two zeros, it began its work. It was all quite prosaic. Galahad had simply added those two zeros to the implant codes of every zero-asset citizen on Earth, and killed them. Thereafter she had become more selective, still killing at will with two extra digits.

Useful information, if you knew the ID codes of your enemy.

The troops were now nearing the lowest floor, so Saul snapped out of his introspection and set all the robots in motion. The enemy spiderguns had to be dealt with first, because they were the most dangerous. Two construction robots threw themselves at the first spidergun from their place of hiding. It immediately opened fire on them both but, with its firing evenly divided between them, it could not deliver enough of a fusillade to halt their momentum. The two construction robots were almost completely wrecked under fire, but crashed into the spidergun and tangled themselves in among its limbs. Also shuddering under fire, the next two were able to reach it while still functional, if marginally so.

They then set their diamond saws running, and in a business-like manner began hacking it to pieces even while it continued to blow away pieces of their bodies. Other construction robots slammed into the fray until the scene resembled something in a wildlife documentary: ants swarming over a spider and tearing it apart. Eventually the surviving construction robots propelled themselves away, leaving nothing but pieces of the spidergun amid their wrecked fellows.

A similar scenario played out with the second gun, but this time enemy troops were involved, even more so when further robots came out of hiding to attack them. At once, Saul was reminded of when he had first used robots on this station, instructing them to use their integral toolkits against human bodies. Diamond saws sliced through limbs and torsos; drills punched neat, evenly spaced patterns into chests; spacesuited figures shuddered under welding currents; detached heads tumbled; blood beaded the air and splashed against walls. With the spidergun down, the action ceased to be a battle and rapidly turned into a slaughter.

'They're nearly done,' said Saul. 'Let's get moving.'

Even as he led the way in, Saul watched survivors fleeing along corridors, only to be rapidly brought down and dismembered. The machines were bloody and remorseless: efficient killers. He felt no sympathy for those dying, for it was they who had attacked and they were now paying the price. Upon checking, he saw that two construction robots were carting ten cleanly killed corpses up to the top floor. Surveying that same floor through the computer control system, he found only one area not yet decompressed: it was a surgical unit. This was probably because the troops that had searched it could see, through the glass viewing wall, that no one was in hiding inside. He led the way there now.

The corridors were littered with corpses, their blood steaming in vacuum.

'Hell of a mess,' Langstrom observed, kicking a severed head further down the corridor.

'It'll scrape off,' someone else commented briefly.

When they reached the door leading into Medical, the construction robots were already on their way out, a fog trailing after them. Saul entered and gazed at the stack of corpses, then walked over and took hold of one to sling it over his shoulder.

'Follow me through into the surgical area.' He gestured to the viewing window. 'The clean lock is vacuum tested, so it should hold. Bring yourselves a corpse each.'

As he stepped into the clean lock he overrode its hygiene safety warnings, since he only wanted to use it as an airlock. Once inside, he quickly stripped off his suit and was down to his undergarments by the time Langstrom came through.

'Do what I do,' he instructed him.

He stripped the suit off the corpse he'd selected, then stepped over to a dispenser for some disposable towels, which he used to clean away the spill of blood around the neck ring. A repair patch taken from the maintenance kit of his suit sealed the single hole that had killed the wasted-looking soldier. By the time he was donning this second suit, another five of Langstrom's men had entered. Twenty minutes later, they were all filing out, every one of them looking like enemy combatants. Saul remembered to warn the robots, and anyone else defending the station in the vicinity. He wanted only those he had already instructed to shoot at him.

Hannah had once read somewhere how it was the waiting that was the worst part and, though she understood that sentiment, she could not really agree. She would have been quite happy to just wait forever for a fight and never get involved in one. She'd seen quite enough of the results of warfare to be sure of that.

'Why haven't they decompressed the arcoplex?' asked Angela suddenly.

'They've got vacuum-penetration locks, so what would be the point?' replied the lab assistant now sporting a missile-launcher.

'The point would be to kill as many of the enemy as possible, but without putting themselves in danger,' Hannah replied. 'Isn't that always the point of war?' She paused for a second. 'Anyway, the fact that they haven't done so thus far but are certainly inside doesn't mean they won't. So just be ready to close up your suits.' She nodded in acknowledgement to Angela, who simply shrugged in reply.

The sounds of battle had grown closer, but when it finally arrived, Hannah found herself gaping, unable to respond. Two soldiers appeared first at the end of the corridor, and began loping forward. They immediately opened fire, ceramic ammunition slamming into the floor plates ahead of them. Belatedly, Hannah realized they must have already encountered Rhine's explosives and were now attempting to make this corridor safe. She began to raise her weapon . . . just as bright rose light flared beside her, and something like a pink tracer bullet shot towards the two intruders. The thing expanded as it travelled, thus creating the illusion that it wasn't actually moving away, was merely some fault in Hannah's vision. It struck one soldier on the shoulder and there detonated like a firework, flinging him back into the trooper behind. Both of them collapsed, licked by flame and screaming. A missile followed shortly afterwards, exploding against the far wall and tearing it wide open.

'We need to calm . . .'

Gunfire stitched across the wall beside their door. A corridor wall exploded inwards, and the whole area was abruptly filled with smoke from burning plastic. More troops began appearing. Were they mad? Didn't they realize what had just happened to their fellows?

Two more missiles sped into the confusion and silhouettes of dismemberment tumbled out on fireballs. Angela carefully saved her shots until she had a clear target, and with the next two turned three of the enemy soldiers into screaming and burning ruin. Then all at once it just seemed to stop – no one else attacking at the far end, though someone was groaning loudly amid the wreckage. Hannah unclenched her hands from her Kalashtech, realizing she still hadn't fired a single shot.

'What are they doing?' she asked.

'Probably bringing up something heavier,' said the other lab assistant, as he passed over more missiles for the launcher.

'Did you hear that back there?' Hannah called out, glancing back into the factory.

'We heard,' Brigitta replied.

'Seems inevitable,' said James, from where he crouched with his weapon laid across a machine cowling.

Just at that moment a massive explosion shuddered their entire surroundings and the air was filled with shrapnel glass. Hannah ducked her head, her ears ringing, as fragments impacted all around her. When she looked up again, the air inside the factory was filled with lethal glittering flakes, and she quickly slid her visor down. Again she found herself gaping, until gunfire chattered, and James began dancing beside his machine, shedding pieces of his body. She only realized what had happened as she saw the first troops descending through the void where the glass viewing floor above had been. Then she shrieked something wordless, and finally opened fire.

'Over there,' said the man they called Charlie, whom Alex could still only think of as Chairman Messina.

The ground was bulging up alongside some kind of fruit tree scattered with white flowers, one of its roots heaving up as if the tree was getting ready to walk. A huffing sound ensued as the ground broke open and the cylinder of a vacuum-penetration lock abruptly rose into sight. As it rose, breach foam exploded all about it to fill the air like green snow, and the circular lid on its end flipped open.

A soldier rocketed out, his weapon aimed towards the ground while he turned. Messina's rifle cracked sharply, and the top of the man's head disappeared in a spray of brains and skull. The impact sent him cartwheeling backwards into the branches of the fruit tree.

'Not very good positioning,' Messina noted.

'Positioning?' Alex echoed, pride surging in his chest. That had been one hell of a shot from the erstwhile Chairman.

'Out in the open like that,' Messina explained. 'I thought you were a soldier.'

'Yes, of course,' Alex replied, suddenly feeling crestfallen and inadequate.

'Do you want the next one?' Messina asked cheerfully.

'Sure,' Alex replied, gazing up to the point where it appeared the trees were growing down towards him. More foam exploded up there, and shortly afterwards he heard a full clip being fired by one of the more inept snipers covering the area. This should be easy, he felt, like shooting fish in a barrel – a phrase he had never really understood because who would waste bullets to destroy such perfectly good food?

'Oops,' said Messina.

Objects began to rise out of the first lock and, the moment Alex focused his gaze on them, they exploded. Flash grenades! Black after-images chased each other across his vision, almost blotting out the next figure that rose into view. He tried his best but knew he would not be able to manage a single-shot kill, and so he fired a short burst. He glimpsed a man spinning, one leg hanging on by a thread, fired again to send him bleeding into the foliage.

'Messy,' observed Messina.

From behind came the crump of an explosion, and smoke gouted from the doorway into the maintenance building dividing up the Arboretum. The battle had started there too, and it seemed intense – as if that place was the main target. Alex blinked, trying to recover his vision, determined to do better for his Chairman, who seemed singularly unimpressed with his clone's marksmanship.

Another lock cylinder rose into view on a green snow-storm, further objects flying outwards. This time Alex closed his eyes before the detonation, then opened them to see a growing smoke cloud. Beside him Messina fired off a shot, then a second one just after gunfire began snapping through the leaves and branches around them. Alex flicked his scope over to infrared, but the intruders' suits were insulated, so he only picked out his targets in the reflected gleam of the smoke bombs, as they emerged from one of the locks. He calmed his breathing, steadied himself, fired one shot, and saw glowing fragments flying out of his latest target's neck, then swung to aim at the next lock to rise up.

'Messy,' Messina repeated.

Alex knew now that he wasn't referring to Alex's marksmanship, but to how things were about to become – and soon.

Mars

It was morning, but here the weak Martian sun would not limp into view until almost midday. A fog had rolled in again, and a fine layer of ice crystals had frosted the metal of the airlock. Moving with stolid weariness, Var had now exposed three metres of rock-damaged pipes and was idly wondering how many more metres she might be able to expose in the hours remaining to her. In the mere five hours remaining to her.

Fatalism and hope were at war within her, and both of them were losing out to a bone-deep fatigue. After clearing the way to another large regolith block which, when she pulled it out, would bring most of the rubble on the slope above down on the area she had cleared, she stood up and stretched. She couldn't see very far through the fog and imagined shapes emerging out of it: the hidden Martians riding their sand yachts; the red-skinned warriors of Barsoom with swords agleam, the mighty Tars Tarkas looming amid them; the adapted dust farmers or the lurking greys.

'Where are you now, John Carter?' she wondered, her voice sounding cracked and slightly weird to her.

She'd passed similar ironic comments previously to personnel at the base regarding the old stories of Mars, until she

realized they were mostly falling on deaf ears – Lopomac was
the only one to understand. Being the daughter of Committee
executives, Var was one of the few who had once had access
to such fiction and seemingly one of fewer still who had
bothered to read it. In the end the reality of Mars came down
to simple facts: such as dust, unbreathable air and the utter
hostility of a barren world. It was beautiful, in its way, but
then hostile landscapes often were. They were something to
be viewed from the cosy comfort afforded by technology –
take that away and the beauty began to lose its appeal.

Var stooped and was at last able to drag out the big
regolith block, whereupon with depressing predictability the
rubble pile slid down, precisely as she had expected. She stood
back and surveyed the task ahead of her, then decided to
climb up on top of the rubble for a better view towards where
the buried pipes were heading.

The summit of the rubble pile brought her out of the fog,
so that it seemed she was rising up out of some milky river
with islands visible ahead and the banks rising on either side.
Beauty again, she felt; it was a heart-stoppingly glorious scene
that somehow seemed utterly sad. Then she realized that it
wasn't the scene that was sad, but herself, and it wasn't
sadness she was feeling, really, but regret. Acceptance overwhelmed her and she understood that she was really making
her goodbyes, but strong on the tail of that came anger. She
would give up only when her air ran out, and not before. She
peered down through the fog, her gaze tracking along where
she felt the pipes were heading. Then she began to map out
the building in her mind, trying to see what logic had been
followed in its construction.

It made no sense for them to have positioned the
compressed-air cylinder such a long way from the airlock.

Why waste the pipework like that? That it wasn't positioned right next to the airlock probably had something to do with whatever lay nearby. Maybe there had been a suiting room just inside the entrance, with decontamination equipment, something like that. Having to position the cylinder a short distance away, they would have run the pipes along the walls. The fact that she found them a metre and a half in from the wall foundation was probably because they had been positioned that same distance up from the floor when the walls had collapsed inwards. Var gazed at a dip in the rubble on the other side of the heap she stood upon. She would dig there instead, and if she didn't find the pipes, she would work back into the pile, one and a half metres from where the wall had stood. If she did find the pipes there, that meant she would have saved herself a great deal of work and could continue following them.

She scrambled down to a dip in the rubble and began digging, using blocks she unearthed to build a loose barrier in order to prevent further rubble falling in. She worked frenetically, angrily until, just half an hour later, she was stunned to come across the same pipes running perhaps a metre above the floor. It was a victory, a gain, and she allowed a surge of optimism to buoy her, denying her logical pessimism any purchase on it.

20

The Dead Hand on the Helm

Looking back, we can now see how the introverted gaze of the human race resulted in the disasters of the past, and that this began the moment that socialism and social justice were taken up and perverted by the politicians. Ostensibly focusing on the 'greatest good for the greatest number – and right now', while actually gathering more power and wealth for themselves, they failed to learn the lessons of history and failed also to prepare for the future. Had the Committee expended more world resources on building up the space programme rather than on augmenting its leaden bureaucracy and the mechanisms of controlling the growing population, had it not suppressed science that did not directly serve the Committee itself and therefore relegated original thinkers to its cells – effectively bringing technological growth to a halt for over a century – things would have been altogether better. It is contestable that, rather than now looking back on the mass exterminations occurring in the twenty-second century, we would be looking back instead on a flowering of humanity across the solar system, combined with the technological singularity and the beginning of the post-human world. Twenty-twenty hindsight is always too easy, but that's not to say it isn't correct.

Scourge

All of Liang's forces had been deployed inside and were now engaged in shooting up the station.

'So now it's time to go,' said Clay, because he did not like the introspective silence the three on the bridge had fallen into.

Scotonis took a moment to reply, so perhaps he was having second thoughts. Perhaps he, too, had felt that odd sense of pride in seeing the troops they had brought here storming the station.

'Make *him* do it,' murmured Trove. 'Let's see if he has any value at all.'

'Yes, time to go,' Scotonis said, then turned his gaze up to the camera through which Clay was watching him. 'And time for you to make yourself useful.'

A familiar sinking sensation occupied Clay's gut. 'In what way?'

'One of our anchors is failing to disengage,' said Scotonis. 'I want you to suit up, head down to the barracks section and collect a two-kilo demolition charge from there – Liang left plenty behind for resupply. Then place it on the anchor concerned, which is clearly visible just beyond the disembarkation ramp.'

'You what?' Clay exclaimed in dismay.

'You know how to put on a suit and you know how to operate that type of charge,' said Scotonis. 'Which of my instructions are you finding unclear?'

'Send one of your crew,' argued Clay.

'Yes, I could do that.' Scotonis nodded introspectively. 'I could order one of my crew – twelve of whom have already died and eight more of whom are in Medical – to go and risk their lives while you sit there comfortably in Messina's quarters.'

'They would be better at it,' protested Clay desperately. Why was Scotonis doing this? Did he intend to leave Clay behind on Argus, too?

'No, it's a simple task,' said Scotonis. 'All it requires is a little technical knowledge, which you have – and a little bravery, which we have yet to ascertain.'

Trove's words finally hit home and Clay realized what this was all about. He reckoned there must have been some disagreement concerning him. Doubtless Trove – and maybe others – had argued against Scotonis's decision not to kill him. This was therefore in the nature of a test. This was to see if he 'had value'; it was his hazing, his baptism by fire. Obviously Scotonis knew his crew well enough to consider it necessary. And quite likely it was necessary, if Clay was not to end up being murdered in one of the ship's corridors during the return journey to Earth. Clay had to show these people he was one of them.

'Very well,' he said, fighting to keep his voice steady.

He unstrapped himself from his chair and stood up, tried to think of something appropriate to say, but found his mouth had dried out.

'And close up the space door on your way back in,' said Scotonis, offering him something. 'We can't control that from up here – it can only be accessed remotely by Liang or closed by using the panel beside it. That's another divisive allocation of control from Galahad.'

Clay reluctantly turned and headed for the door, and went through it. For a while he walked in a dismal haze, then shook himself out of it as he reached the executive quarters. Here he located a suit storage room, which he quickly entered. He had hoped for a nicely armoured VC suit but his search revealed that only an adapted Martian EA suit remained – offering no protection at all. He began to don it slowly, then mentally pushed himself to hurry up. The quicker he moved, the sooner this nightmare would be over.

Once he had the suit on, he ran diagnostics and found no further excuse for delay. He headed down to the barracks, now open to vacuum, and stepped through the airlock to gain access. Inside the new disembarkation tube, he gazed at the mess all about him: fragments of material drifting through vacuum; equipment abandoned at the last moment, such as packs, magazines for missile-launchers and one or two weapons; and four corpses with suits burned black, hideously mutilated faces gazing through their spattered visors. He moved along the tube, avoiding the entrance into the section where the maser had struck, and entered the next section. Further equipment here, stacked in a more orderly manner.

Clay walked over to a stack of plastic crates whose labels indicated that they contained explosives. Checking the contents lists below the labels, he soon found what he wanted and pulled open that particular crate. Two-kilo demolition charges were stacked inside it like packets of butter. He pulled one out and studied the inset detonator, which was no more difficult to operate than setting up a wristwatch. He stood up, still holding it, and headed for the space door.

The disembarkation tube took him to the open space door, now hinged down to act as a ramp. The vista of Argus Station beyond was nicely lit up by the *Scourge*'s exterior LED lights. He paused at the threshold and gazed across a plain of metal extending to Tech Central, studying the torn-up areas where the station's weapons had been destroyed, but the only movement he could detect there was of corpses drifting amidst wrecked robots and other shattered equipment. The battle was now taking place inside the station, so there was no danger for him here. He had been stupid to be so fearful.

With new confidence Clay strode down the lowered ramp, paused to locate the cable emerging from underneath the ship, and traced it to an anchor embedded in the station's hull just twenty metres away. He headed over there and started to position the charge against it at the joint where the cable connected.

'Ruger, get a damned move on, will you?'

This sudden order from Scotonis made him jump, the demolition charge tumbling away from him until he snagged it out of the air.

'It's not sensible to be too hasty when dealing with explosives,' Clay replied sniffily, securing the charge in place before flicking on the timer of the detonator. He set the countdown to five minutes, which should give him plenty of time to get back inside the ship and see the space door safely closed.

'Are you done?' asked Scotonis.

'Yes, I'm done.' Clay stood up.

'Then perhaps you'd better take a look over at the station's technical control centre.'

Clay glanced that way, and gaped. He could see the flashing of weapons, fragments of metal and the debris of ceramic bullets cutting lines across the station's hull. A number of Liang's troops were now running back towards the ship, under fire from Tech Central, where Clay could now see construction robots scuttling into view.

'Move it, Ruger!' Scotonis bellowed.

Clay moved it, but had to slow down as, in his panic, his gecko boots threatened to detach themselves from the hull.

He concentrated on walking as fast but as safely as possible, which didn't increase his pace much above a stroll. Finally he mounted the sloping ramp of the space door, headed up inside and turned to the console that controlled the door. A glance at the approaching troops made him realize he might already be too late; nevertheless he clicked through the menu to set the motors running, and slowly the door began to rise.

'Use the ship's guns on them,' he urged.

'I was more concerned about the robots,' replied Scotonis. 'A few deserters are hardly a problem to us.'

Clay did not bother pointing out that, though they might not be a problem to Scotonis or his plans, they could certainly be a problem for Clay himself. But Scotonis already knew that, and clearly it didn't much concern him.

Clay watched the figures approaching. The firing from Tech Central had ceased, and one of the two pursuing robots seemed to have been disabled. The other one was still coming, though slowly, and apparently damaged. Two of the men were down, slumped motionless against the hull. One of the soldiers towards the rear turned and opened fire on the surviving robot, just as the first of the men leaped onto the rising door. It must have been accurate shooting because the robot went down like a felled buffalo. That soldier at the rear hurried after the rest, and Clay realized that all of them were going to get aboard.

Time to go.

Clay turned to head up the disembarkation tube. He would proceed through the airlock, and back into executive quarters, then seal the airlock behind him. He managed only two paces before a gloved hand slammed down on his shoulder, pulled him back and thrust him to the floor. He now found himself gazing along the barrel of a Kalashtech towards the face of a black man. He didn't recollect seeing a black man among Liang's soldiers – not that he had necessarily seen them all. Suddenly he began to get a feeling that something was very wrong here. The black man raised a finger to his visor. Shush, be quite now. Clay did not dare speak.

The last of the soldiers had managed to get in by throwing himself through a steadily narrowing gap as the space door closed up. Watching them, Clay did not notice the panic-stricken relief of troops who had just escaped with their lives. They seemed efficient; seemed to know what they were doing. One of them went over to a wall console and began tapping something in. Red lights started flashing as the door fully closed – an indication that the space was now recharging with air. Other men started moving along the tube, checking each of the troop sections in turn, entering them just like soldiers checking buildings during urban warfare. As the lights flashed to amber, one of the troops began disengaging his helmet. That was when Clay realized everything he had witnessed out there had been staged, and that the enemy was aboard.

The lights turned to green, indicating the space was fully pressurized. Clay knew that if he spoke, if he tried to alert Scotonis, he would get a bullet straight in his face. He therefore kept his mouth firmly closed as all the other men removed their helmets, but for the one holding him at gunpoint. The black man then gestured him to his feet and indicated that he should remove his helmet, which he did. As another soldier pressed the barrel of an automatic against Clay's temple, the black man also removed his helmet, and Clay finally recognized him as Commander Langstrom.

'Stinks in here,' observed Langstrom.

'Seems the maser cooked a few of them,' said another, stabbing a thumb back towards the rear troop section. 'Why did you bother to keep him alive?'

'I thought it was a good idea,' said Langstrom, 'as we might need some intel about the ship's interior.' Langstrom turned to another member of this group, who presently stood with his back to the rest as he studied a wall console. 'Do we actually need him, sir?'

That other individual turned round, and Clay felt stark terror as he was examined by those pink eyes in a preternaturally pale face. Alan Saul himself was right here in front of him, just a few metres away from him.

'We'll keep him for the moment,' said Saul. 'If I can't access the ship's systems from here, he can show me a better access point.'

Taking an optic from a pouch at his belt, Saul plugged one end straight into a socket in his skull, then turned and plugged the other into a jack point in the console. He dipped his head, obviously concentrating hard while the others fidgeted nervously.

'That's interesting,' he said contemplatively, then turned his gazed back to Clay. 'So, tell me, Clay Ruger, why did you offline all the ship's inducers?'

'They weren't needed,' Clay replied, the gun barrel pressed against his head feeling as if it was about to bore into his skull.

'I see,' said Saul, his expression turning distant. Then he added, 'I have them.'

Clay risked speaking again. 'What do you have?'

'Sending now,' Saul ignored him, 'though of course it will be a little while before it takes effect.' He then smiled briefly. 'I've also left a little something for Galahad.'

'We need to get out of here, too,' said Langstrom.

'No problem,' Saul explained. 'I've disabled all the ship's armaments, and they just won't have enough time to get them working again.'

'That's it?' said Langstrom disbelievingly.

'That's it,' Saul replied, disconnecting the optic, coiling it up and putting it away again.

The green lights were now back on, flashing before changing back to amber, and Clay could hear the wail of escaping air as all around him began putting their helmets back on.

'What about him?' asked the one who was holding a gun to Clay's head.

'What about him?' Saul shrugged. 'He's as dead as the rest of them and, like them, he just doesn't know it yet.' Saul donned his own helmet.

Escaping air became like a wind as the weapon withdrew from Clay's temple. He quickly put his helmet back on. He could have been shot then for doing so, but he would just as certainly die if he merely stood there. The ramp was now part of the way down again, and one of the soldiers was getting ready to climb out. Clay began backing away from them, and was ignored.

What did he mean by 'dead as the rest of them'?

Just then the charge detonated outside; a bright flash showing through the opening space door, shortly followed by a shower of metal fragments. Clay used this distraction to break away and run for the airlock leading back into the ship's executive section, expecting to receive a bullet at any moment. As he opened the airlock, he saw shots pinging off the metalwork nearby, then his head was jerked sideways by one ricocheting off his helmet. He threw himself beyond the airlock and ran, diving into one of the crew sections, desperately searching for some kind of weapon and finding only a large wrench. He picked it up and waited.

'Are you done there?' asked Scotonis over his suit radio. 'That door is still open.'

Clay peeked out. The intruders were all gone – he could now see them loping towards Tech Central, the two who had apparently fallen out there getting up and rejoining them. He stepped out and headed for the space door control, and set it to close again.

'I'm done,' he replied. 'We need to go now.'

'We *are* going,' replied Scotonis. 'Did you send those troops back out?'

'They left voluntarily,' Clay replied, slightly worried about the tinge of hysteria in his voice.

Argus

A blizzard of hardened breach sealant swirled through the smoky air. The fight in the dividing section of the Arboretum had spilled out into the main Arboretum itself, and the crackle of gunfire was now constant. Alex's main problem was identifying his targets. Someone had told them to put their helmets back on, which rather buggered up infrared detection, especially with the numerous fires and other hot spots created by explosions and tracer bullets.

'It is getting a little fraught up here,' noted Messina.

It certainly was. The crackling of gunfire in the surrounding trees was frequently punctuated by the crump of a grenade going off. Though they were concealed by the surrounding foliage, it in no way protected them. Alex studied the arm of his suit, where the padding had been rucked up and was spattered with blood. It didn't hurt and his mobility was unimpaired so he didn't think there could be much damage. However, he was aware how, in the heat of battle, it was easy not to register quite serious wounds.

Bullets zipped like vicious hornets into the foliage in a nearby tree, leaving severed leaves and twigs drifting away. Alex swung his rifle towards the spot where he suspected the shooter was concealed, but he could see no identifiable target through the smoke.

'They must have some general idea where we are by now,' he said. 'Should we relocate?'

'Is that what a soldier would do?' asked Messina, eyeing him doubtfully.

'Yes, it is, sir.'

'Sir?' said the erstwhile Chairman, his expression flat.

'It's what I always used to call you.'

'You knew me . . . from before?'

The hidden sniper fired into the other tree once again, using up an entire clip to hit the same place as before. Whole branches tumbled away and tracers started a couple of small fires. So much foliage had ended up drifting away after that one fusillade that it must soon be evident that the tree was unoccupied. Someone obviously thought they were concealed there, but it wouldn't take them long to realize their mistake. Similar saturation fire into the tree they were hiding in would kill both himself and Messina very quickly.

'Did you clock that?' said Messina.

'I'm on it,' Alex replied, adjusting his aim to the source of the tracer bullets. Nothing much was identifiable through the murk, but at least he now had a better general idea of the shooter's position. He centred his cross hairs, squeezed the trigger and held it back, emptying a full clip, then he quickly changed clips and waited.

'That seems to—'

A hail of gunfire hit their tree, smacking and cracking all about them, raking up nests of splinters like porcupine spines. Alex reached out, grabbed Messina by the shoulder and shoved him off the edge of the platform. The man didn't need any more impetus before taking himself rapidly down the tree trunk. Alex hurled himself down next, head-first, flipping over at the last moment and landing heavily on his back, before bouncing and then floating up again until Messina grabbed him. The fusillade of fire continued for a while longer, then abruptly cut out.

'So you knew me from before?' said Messina.

'Yes, I knew you from before,' gasped Alex, turning towards him.

Messina nodded contemplatively, then pointed towards a nearby penetration lock. It seemed a sensible place to go, since it offered more cover than anything else nearby. They began to crawl towards it.

They were just ten or so metres from the tree when a grenade exploded behind them. Both hung on to the ground, twigs and leaves storming above them, shortly followed by the whole tree tumbling end over end. Yes, if they'd stayed in it, they would be dead by now.

'What was I like?' Messina asked as they began crawling away again.

The question gave Alex pause for consideration. *What was Messina like?* It having been so long since his last reconditioning, he now found it difficult to form a clear picture of him in his mind.

'You were a leader of men,' he replied.

As they approached the penetration lock, Alex paused by a soldier's corpse. The woman was floating just off the ground, held in place only by a commando knife she had thrust into the soil. There was a bullet hole through her visor and it was full of blood, one eyeball pressing against the glass. He pulled her down and relieved her of her ammunition and her sidearm. Shortly after that, he and Messina reached the penetration lock. After the initial three troops had come through here and died, the attackers had ceased to use it. It could be used again at any moment, but that would be no problem since he and Messina would have plenty of warning. They hunkered down next to it, on either side, Messina covering one direction while Alex covered the other.

The shooting continued all around them, streaks of tracer bullets cutting through smoke and debris. The air quality, Alex noted, was getting quite bad, and he had to keep snorting dirt and splinters out of his nose. This was the problem with fighting in zero gravity: the detritus thrown up by bullets and explosions didn't just settle back to the ground.

'It was confusing at first,' Messina continued. 'There I was, with no memory of my past, doing what I was told while trying to understand the hatred directed at me. I was assaulted frequently, and nearly got killed on the last occasion. But now my confusion is gone.'

'It's gone?' said Alex, noncommittally.

'They tried to keep it from me, of course, but the image of the face I possessed before is not something that can be concealed for long.'

Alex looked round to see him up on his knees now and gazing back, resting his shoulder against the penetration lock.

'I know who I was,' he said – a little sadly, Alex thought.

'You were Chairman Alessandro Messina, ruler of Earth,' Alex stated firmly. Then his gaze strayed to what he assumed was a chunk of debris sailing through the air towards them. It took him half a second further to realize his mistake.

'Grenade!' he shouted, heaving himself to his feet and reaching for Messina.

The erstwhile ruler of Earth stood up, ready to throw himself clear, then took a couple of steps forward, forced by the impact of the bullets hitting his back and blowing chunks of flesh and rib out of his chest. Alex rolled aside, firing at a half-seen figure, coming back up onto his knees as the same figure staggered, then sighting properly and emptying the new clip into it. He saw bits of his target flying away, before the grenade detonated and picked him up in a hot fist.

Screaming somewhere . . . Alex realized it was himself as he was hammered into foliage and finally slammed to a halt against a solid branch. With his ears ringing, he dragged himself back to the ground and then headed over to the penetration lock. But Messina wasn't there. Alex looked up and saw his Chairman's remains revolving in the air above him, like some grotesque expanded sculpture constructed of offal.

Alex went into the trees and found the assailant dead, cut in half. He moved on, no longer concerned now for his own safety; determined to find someone else to kill. When his ammunition ran out, he grabbed up more from the new corpses; when he couldn't find any more ammunition he used a commando knife or his bare hands. Towards the end, his opponents didn't seem to put up much of a fight. He did not know why. How long passed before he realized that the shooting had stopped, he didn't know. He found himself back by the same penetration lock, on his knees, covered in blood, most of which was not his own.

It was over.

Alex reached down to his belt and drew the sidearm he had taken earlier from the corpse here and which, during his madness, he had completely forgotten about. He put the barrel in his mouth, tasted metal and powder residue, and there he paused for a brief eternity, until he realized he had no reason to pull the trigger. He shoved the weapon back into his utility belt and stood up, looking around.

From close beside Hannah, missile after missile sped up into the roof, the blasts tearing out beams and wall panels, filling the air with hot wreckage and creating a burning hollow down through which the soldiers kept throwing themselves. The fires etched them starkly in silhouette, made them easy targets. Hannah hated how obvious the killing was each time she aimed and fired, then watched one of them jerk about like a fish on a line. Plasma shots rose up like ack-ack fire and turned four of them in a row into screaming torches while oily smoke billowed.

Though terrified, Hannah felt a horrified sympathy for the enemy even as she shot them. They possessed no more self-determination than just about anyone on Earth, perhaps even less. They had been directed into this assault with little regard for their lives. To those that had sent them they were just a disposable asset. Taking the station was all that mattered to Serene Galahad; the human cost was irrelevant.

The attack stuttered to a halt amid a snowstorm of fire-retardant foam. Ten minutes passed, though it seemed to be eons. They were probably regrouping, calling in reinforcements, doing whatever it was soldiers did after receiving a bloody nose.

'Is anyone else hit?' Hannah eventually called out.

'James and Tyson are dead,' Brigitta replied. 'I've lost two fingers from my left hand and none of the rest of us is in good shape.'

Wondering which one of them had been Tyson, Hannah suggested, 'Use your suit medical kits while you can.' It would be suicide to venture out of cover now, so they just had to do the best they could.

Brigitta replied. 'Have you got any ice?'

'What for?' Hannah asked.

'My fingers.' It seemed Brigitta had a streak of morbid humour, only just revealed.

'Sorry, no.'

Angela called out to her sister, 'Don't worry, there'll be plenty of spares.' This humour seemed a family trait.

A further twenty minutes dragged past. Gunfire and explosions could still be heard throughout the arcoplex, and somewhere close above them a fierce firefight erupted. This lasted for a good five minutes, until a large blast terminated it abruptly.

'Get ready,' Hannah warned.

Another blast behind spun Hannah round. They were trying the corridor again and had encountered another of Rhine's booby traps. As she opened fire on figures only half seen through the smoke, she heard Angela's grunt beside her and saw her sit back, gazing down at a hole in her thigh.

'Angela?'

The quiet one of the Saberhagen twins grimaced, then raised her plasma weapon again and turned the far end of the corridor into an inferno. A few further missiles converted it into a route no one would be venturing along for a while.

Next the soldiers were again descending from above and the firefight was renewed, the nightmare continued. This fresh battle could only have lasted minutes, yet it seemed ages before the firing from above became only sporadic, then finally ceased. Hannah gazed in perpetually growing horror at the scene before her: the corpses floating through the air, the commingled cloud of body parts and gobbets of flesh, blood and a thousand twinkling stars composed of glass and bits of foam. The two lab assistants, who had been taking it in turns with the missile-launcher, quickly ventured into the factory to snare a floating corpse from the air and relieve it of its weapons and ammo.

'Angela?' Hannah repeated.

'It won't kill me,' she replied, now tightening a tourniquet about her leg.

'Are we all good?' Hannah called.

'No more deaths,' Brigitta replied.

Only then did Hannah notice that her own leg was hurting and look down to see it soaked with blood around an embedded chunk of glass. When had that happened? She had no idea. She reached out and touched the bloody shard, before deciding it would be best to leave it where it was.

'It will take effect quickly,' Saul whispered to her, through her fone. 'High heart rate, adrenalin . . .'

'What was that?' Hannah asked. 'Alan?'

Reception was terrible: a perpetual buzzing broke up his next words, turning them into nonsense. Then he spoke again, clearly. 'They're stopping now,' he told her. 'They know something is wrong.'

'Alan?'

'I've killed them all,' he said. Then her fone made a sound like some small animal dying, and nothing more emerged.

Sudden movement behind them.

Hannah whirled round and raised her weapon. One of the attackers was there, but he wasn't armed. He had just propelled himself into a space amidst the burning wreckage, his arms wrapped tightly around his chest. He seemed to be convulsing.

After another twenty minutes had passed, Hannah finally pushed herself to her feet. She didn't want to think too deeply about what Saul had said. Keeping to cover as best she could, she moved into the factory, first to check on James, who couldn't have been more dead, then to check on the one called Tyson, who, it turned out, was the girl. She too was irrecoverable. Tired and frightened, all of the others just watched.

She finally headed back to the door, calling over her shoulder, 'All of you, with me.'

'Are you sure about that?' Brigitta asked.

Suddenly Hannah was very sure. 'It's over.'

The survivors dragged themselves out of hiding, then moved cautiously out of the factory and joined her.

'We'll head back to my lab . . . if it's still intact,' she decided.

There wasn't one of them without injury. Hannah began assessing whom to treat first, then decided that it should be herself, since she probably had a lot of serious work ahead of her.

'Rhine's explosives,' she said, pausing on the threshold of the wrecked corridor.

With her undamaged hand, Brigitta tapped a palmtop

fastened at her waist. 'He sent their location and disarming codes.' She propped the palmtop on the mass of material she had wrapped round her hand, which was pulled in close to her chest, sorted through menus, then strode ahead.

Once Brigitta had led them out of the wreckage, they came on the first of the invading soldiers, some floating free, but most huddled on the floor, with military equipment scattered all around them. Hannah paused to inspect one of them closely, noted the blood on the lips and one bloody tear below the eye. She knew for sure then what Saul had done – did not need to do an autopsy to know more.

She wanted to cry, but felt arid inside.

Mars

With only three hours to go, three hours of her life remaining, Var had exposed three metres of oxygen pipe, unearthed a lone skull and an old-style laptop . . . but still didn't know if she was any closer to the compressed-air tank. Only after digging for a number of hours had it occurred to her that these pipes might have fed something else. For all she knew, the tank could be under the rubble pile behind her while the pipes she was following terminated at just another airlock.

She paused and stood upright to stretch her back, feeling sore points all over her body where her suit had been rubbing against her. She considered how all the effort she had put in here would result in some unpleasant after-effects, then remembered that if she did suffer sore and aching muscles later, she would be grateful. Funny that – how her mind kept slipping back to its default position of assessing the future. It was as if, on some unconscious level, a part of her kept cautiously approaching the facts of her situation, then skittering nervously away.

On a conscious level she had a problem too. A while ago, when her crunch time lay many hours into the future, she had felt something like acceptance, but now that time was drawing nigh she could feel her desperation increasing. She didn't want to die. It wasn't fair. She had so much yet to do. All the protests of someone on the brink of dying rose up in her mind – all the clichés of an organism never programmed to accept death, and rebelling at the last. She tried not to contemplate this further, ducked down again and continued digging, annoyed by the tears of self-pity filling her eyes.

Another hour of digging excited her inner immortal element as the pipes began rising steeply upwards. This was it; this was where they were not crushed down by the rubble, where they rose up to meet *something else*. She tried to keep calm, but instead found herself hurling rocks away, scooping off dust, frenziedly hacking with her pick. She started to sweat, but worked even harder when she came upon a heavy pipe joint; felt a moment of euphoria on exposing first a power cable, then the side of the small compressor it led to. Further digging revealed the curving perimeter of the compressed-air reservoir. She worked her way up one side of it, tracking along the air pipes, revealed the top of a pressure gauge, tore away the rubble all around it, exposed a broken dial that could no longer give her a reading, began moving away more rubble – and in the process banged a loose rock against the gauge. The gauge itself, pipes and a heavy valve all shifted. She got hold of the entire assembly and pulled it up, until it came away from the bottle below, revealing the hole out of which it had been torn.

Disappointment punched her in the gut, but her internal

organism wouldn't stop. She brushed everything clear of the compressed-air bottle, exposed the top of it completely. The screw-in assembly had been torn out of its thread, leaving the dark eye of a hole. She stared at it, unable to accept what she was seeing. She turned and searched around until she found a length of reinforcing rod she had cast aside earlier, returned to the bottle and inserted it into the hole. It went right down inside the bottle and she rattled it around, a tinny sound carrying to her ears through the thin air. Then she dropped the rod into the bottle and stepped back, reality catching up.

Weariness hit her hard as she climbed out of the excavation. Her head-up display showed that she had maybe two hours left now, and her likelihood of finding anything to extend her time beyond that was minimal. Stepping away from rubble to dusty ground, Var considered going back into the intact building and leaving some message for her brother, but could not see the point. She walked over to a nearby boulder, slumped down and rested her back against it.

Time to die, now.

21

Technology Makes You Free!

The attitude of Committee delegates to technology was always an ambivalent one. They wanted medical technology advanced just as fast as possible so that they could stay healthy and live for as long as possible, but did not want it on general release because that would inevitably exacerbate the world's population problem. They wanted expert computer systems through which to administrate the world, yet artificial intelligence terrified them for it might displace them. They wanted fast and reliable robots operating in their factories and their Inspectorate, but desired utter control over the experts that built and programmed them. They wanted all the benefits that technology could give, because technology is power, and they wanted that power only for themselves. They micromanaged, controlled and suppressed technology so that, in the end, that product of human genius, intended to free people from the exigencies of the world around them, instead enslaved them.

Argus

The shuddering that ran through the station, as if it had been hit by a gigantic club, was slowly diminishing. Gazing up through one of the few intact windows of Tech Central, Saul watched the cause of it: the *Scourge* steadily retreating. Why it had pulled away was debatable, because it began to leave only shortly after he had transmitted the codes to the implants of every soldier and every crewmember of that ship, and it struck him as unlikely that they could so quickly have realized what was about to happen.

'Nearly done,' said Langstrom over radio, 'but it'll take hours to repressurize.'

Langstrom and his soldiers had found replacement windows in a nearby storeroom and were now installing the last of them. This wasn't Saul's greatest concern. If everything worked out as expected, then all those aboard the *Scourge* should be dying or already dead. But the fact that the ship had left so early inclined him to think that maybe something else was going on. He could no longer assume that they were all dead, and it was quite possible that the ship would become a severe danger. For soon it would be able to deploy its weapons again and, quite likely, any survivors aboard it would not be firing merely disabling shots.

'Judd, tell me you're ready,' said Saul, as he turned away, carefully stepping over a corpse, then nudging a second floating carcase out of his path as he came to stand before the newly installed controls.

'Repairs are complete,' the proctor replied.

Saul peered into the transformer room and noted how its occupants were clearing up any free-floating detritus. However, Judd was not among them. Searching further, Saul found the proctor standing, surrounded by corpses, in a nearby corridor. Obviously Judd had found it necessary to deal with an attack occurring there too.

He now surveyed the rest of the station. A lot of damage was evident and, though firing up the Rhine drive did not result in acceleration stresses, once it closed down, the station would be subject to gravitational stresses – he hoped. He checked the drive itself and found it undamaged and completely up to speed, as it had been for an hour or more now. Mentally taking control of the consoles ranged in front of him, he began routing his way round some damage to control optics, inputting his own astrogation calculations and conclusions. Then, with a much smaller part of his mind, he started to check on people he primarily cared about.

'Le Roque,' he said.

Technical Director Le Roque was in what had once been the Political Office. Saul located him crouching over the corpse of Girondel Chang, and felt a twinge of regret. Le Roque looked up, his expression grim. Reviewing cam data, Saul saw what had happened there. Le Roque and others had been defending the place from multiple penetration-lock attacks but had been unsuccessful. Many of them were killed and the remainder taken prisoner. Chang, along with four others, was killed while their guards were dying from the Scour and began firing their weapons in panic.

'What is it?' Le Roque asked.

'I need the station as secure as you can get it, and as fast as you can,' Saul replied. 'Use your secondary control room there to do so.'

'I'll need to assess the damage.'

'We've no time – the *Scourge* has detached itself from the station and could fire on us at any moment. Just do the best you can.' Meanwhile Saul issued instructions to his robots, sending them to cover those places he considered weak. He was ordering them to make repairs even as human blood dried on their metal skins.

Le Roque stood up wearily and began summoning people to help him as he headed off. Saul felt cruel at pressuring him right then, for he knew, from the records, that Chang and some of the others who had died alongside him were Le Roque's friends. But, then, their whole situation was cruel, and spending time being sensitive might get them *all* killed.

Hannah he found in the surgery attached to her laboratory. She was operating on someone who seemed to have been shot an unfeasible number of times to be still alive. Saul decided not to distract her.

In the main laboratory, Brigitta, Angela and others – all of whom appeared to be wounded themselves – were working on the walking wounded or else doing what they could for others more seriously wounded, just to keep them alive until they could go under the knife. Throughout Arcoplex Two, groups were collecting the wounded, but mostly people were just loitering about, looking stunned, or nursing their own wounds. It looked like a slaughterhouse in there, but there were few places on board that did not look similar. The enemy attack had taken a terrible toll.

It took Saul just an instant to count the living and discover exactly what that toll was. Upon its arrival here at the Asteroid Belt, the station had had a population of just over two thousand. Now it contained over three and a half thousand, but nearly two and a half thousand of those were corpses. Nine hundred station personnel had died. Eleven hundred and sixty still remained alive, though how long about fifty of them would survive was debatable.

Even as he finally readied himself to start up the Rhine drive – confident he was doing so faster than any crew could manage, and thus considering how unnecessary any of them was – Saul realized that he did regret the deaths, and he did care. Had the knowledge that his own sister was currently running out of air on Mars restored something of his humanity? That humanity seemed integral to him now, not something he could so easily box off while he made practical decisions.

Time.

Electromagnetic fields played a subtle game with near-light-speed eddies of matter so as to generate exotic energies, and Langstrom leaped back from the newly installed window as reality twisted outside.

'What the fuck!' he bellowed.

Saul reached out to rest gloved fingers on a nearby console, perhaps feeling the need of some physical connection to what he was doing, some human dimension to the way he was twisting up space. And it *felt* like him doing it. He was in it, part of it, suddenly hyper-sensitive everywhere throughout the station, wrapping a warp bubble about himself like someone burrowing into a duvet, shifting as if before the massive exhalation of some god. A jolt ensued as the warp bubble brushed against the *Scourge* on its way out, doubtless sending tidal forces ripping through the ship, which would make little difference to its dead and dying crew. Then came a further jerk as it collided with and destroyed minor debris, and Saul watched streaks of fire tracking across the blackness of the artificial sky outside. He waited, counted seconds and microseconds, then shut it all down.

'The *Scourge* is gone!' exclaimed one of the soldiers.

'We've moved,' said Langstrom, his voice sounding unsteady.

Further than you can imagine, my friend.

Recalculation now and instant understanding of why his earlier calculations were out. The drive nailed reality, but reality still moved at the pace of galactic drift. He input that in his new calculations, and knew it would be right, then started up the drive again, felt the solar system grow small, felt an arrogance of inestimable power, and suppressed it in an instant. The warp took Argus again, as he listened to Le Roque issuing instructions, watched erstwhile killer robots working frenetically to weld up cracks and insert structural members, spraying impact foam, gluing, riveting, tightening bolts. It would have to be enough, because every second counted when it might be one's last breath.

Time passed – a ridiculously small amount of it when divided up over the hundreds of thousands of kilometres involved. The seconds counted away, then the microseconds, and Saul again shut down the drive. Argus groaned as the stars came back. Saul lifted his fingertips from the console, glanced over towards the windows where, bright and clear and disappointingly brown, the so-called red planet Mars hung in void.

He headed for the door.

Earth

Her palmtop opened with a breathy sigh, and just a short search through the menus brought up the program Serene required. It wasn't that she needed to use her palmtop – the programs she was accessing were available to her in the equipment surrounding her – but it seemed somehow right. Using this method reminded her of that first time when she sent out the signals from the communications room in Aldeburgh to extinguish a large and useless portion of the human race. The palmtop updated its lists as it also updated other software. Two options were now provided for her. She clicked on the list labelled '*Scourge*' and gazed at it contemplatively. She could kill with the Scour, or she could send the signal to constrict over two thousand strangulation collars

I am calm. I am very calm.

She tried to ignore the shaking of her hands and the ball of something hot and black that seemed to be growing in her stomach. Transferring her gaze to the main screen that stood amid her garden vegetation – whose condition was now much improved – she contemplated the two scenes it displayed. One showed the *Scourge*, presently under power and on a route taking it out of the Asteroid Belt; the other showed Mars, with Argus Station in orbit about it. Her finger hovered over the send button on her palmtop then she carefully withdrew it.

Why had the *Scourge* separated from the station? Why did they run away?

She was not sure she wanted to take the time necessary to find out why. They had failed out there – they had failed miserably. She returned her gaze to her palmtop, swallowed dryly, and accepted that she wanted to kill someone. Clay Ruger was already history, but plenty of others remained for her to select from: Commander Liang, Captain Scotonis . . .

What?

The list of ID codes was updating again, each steadily acquiring a tick beside it. No, she hadn't pressed send; she hadn't followed through with her instinct for vengeance. What was this? The ticks indicated that those people the codes identified had been sent the signal that would flood their bodies with the Scour, and therefore they would be dying even now. Her immediate thought was that there must have been some sort of software failure; that, as the program opened, it had automatically sent the signal. But that made no sense, since the software she was using was multiply backed-up and mirrored, perpetually ran self-diagnostics, and would close down at any hint of either a hardware or software failure.

Angry and frustrated, she began running checks and it soon became apparent that she had not sent the signal, nor had it been inadvertently sent in any other way. But the status of those ID codes was being updated from the latest transmission from the *Scourge*. She now turned to that and began frantically searching for some explanation, and soon it became clear. Soon everything started to make sense.

Someone had accessed the *Scourge*'s personnel files and downloaded all their ID codes. Someone had done this via a console located in the troop section, after the troops themselves had departed. One of the crew? That seemed entirely possible since now, reviewing the data from the *Scourge*, she saw that there were many gaps in it. Most of the ship cams were offline, so she could not see a recorded view of whoever had accessed that console. It also became apparent that the inducer network had been shut down . . .

Something appeared suddenly on her screen: the blank square indicating a video file. Where had that come from? From the *Scourge* data – meaning something loaded it even as the ID codes were being downloaded. A worm of apprehension crawled up Serene's spine. She quickly ensured that all the latest *Scourge* data had been downloaded to her palmtop, then shut off its modem and put it to one side. She then picked up a console and accessed the hardware all around her, ordering it to ignore any signal from her palmtop – just in case something started up the modem again. Next she focused on the original data download from the *Scourge*. She sent a copy to hard storage, isolated that same storage and deleted the original. To be utterly safe, she cut the power to the hard drive it had been stored on. Then she picked up the palmtop again, and proceeded to play the video file.

'Hello, Serene Galahad,' said Alan Saul, gazing at her with demonic pink eyes. 'I know it is you that is seeing this since, for it to load, you had to open up your Scour initiation software, and I doubt you trust anyone else with even the knowledge that it exists. By now the ID code status of your personnel currently aboard the *Scourge*, and aboard my station, is updating and, even as you listen to this, you will know that they are all either dead or dying.' He paused for a moment, maybe in reflection, though she could read nothing in his expression.

'Perhaps you should now consider how the weapon you created is double-edged,' he continued. 'However, that is not why I am now contacting you. In your arrogance and psychosis, you might find it difficult to accept that I have no interest in you or what you are currently doing on Earth. Your best course now is to ignore me, because I will go away. If you do not take such a course, then I will be forced to take more of an interest in you, and that is something you will definitely not enjoy. That is all.'

His image froze, but it still seemed like he was watching her. After a second, Serene realized she was panting, then with a yell she hurled her palmtop away. It crashed against the low balustrade of the bridge and dropped into the pond.

'Fuck you!' she screamed. Then, when Sack appeared, she snarled, 'Fuck off.'

Sack quickly retreated.

Serene stood up and began pacing. The *Scourge*'s assault had failed and now there was no one left to punish. How dare he kill her people? How dare he take that away from her? She kicked over the nearest plant pot, then reached down and tore a Japanese shrub out of another one and threw it away, tramped over other plants to reach her main screen and kicked it over. She had to do something. She had to do something now.

'Sack!' she shrieked, and went striding over the bridge.

Sack appeared reluctantly and gazed at her in silence. She gestured over her shoulder.

'Get rid of it! Get rid of it all!'

'Ma'am?'

'The garden, you imbecile! Get rid of the fucking garden! Burn the fucking thing!'

She strode for the elevator and climbed inside. Someone was going to pay for this; someone was going to pay for this right away. Saul was the one she wanted most, but he lay too far out of her reach, for now. As the elevator rose she felt slightly better to be doing something at least, even if it was just relocating herself to Messina's old office.

Time for another Madagascar.

She had previously been considering further candidates such as Crete, Indonesia, Sri Lanka . . . No, screw the islands. Something bigger; it was time to think big.

Maybe get continental.

Argus

Hannah clung on to the edge of the surgical table, even though no force actually threatened to dislodge her. When it stopped and that deep sonorous note ceased sounding, and it no longer felt as if some malevolent god was trying to crowbar up reality, there came a short silent pause before the station structure all around her began making worrying complaints.

'Saul's moved us,' she observed.

'Yes, he has,' replied Le Roque tiredly through her fone. 'The *Scourge* separated from us a short while ago, and doubtless he wants us well out of range of its weapons.'

Hannah unclamped her hands from the table and glanced through the viewing window into her laboratory. There were still many patients to be tended, but she could see that her earlier request to Le Roque had been answered and that the military medic Yanis Raiman had arrived to relieve her. She now returned to the subject she and Le Roque had been discussing just before the Rhine drive engaged.

'So you're intending to spin up this arcoplex,' she said. 'What about the damage? What about the potential for breaches around the penetration locks?' As she spoke, she continued sealing the ugly wounds in her latest patient – almost relishing the distraction of this task.

'The robots are all over it,' replied Le Roque. 'The penetration locks should hold but, as a precaution, I've had all adjacent bulkhead doors closed. They shouldn't be a problem.'

Even as he said it, Hannah felt herself shifting to one side as the arcoplex slowly started to spin again. All around, the clonks and groans and the occasional squeals signifying stressed metal increased. Some of the noise would be from equipment or debris in motion – a noise that would intensify as any floating objects began falling to the floor. Doubtless she could hear corpses in motion too, perhaps even globules of blood dropping out of the air. The thought sickened her, but what seemed worse was that there had been no real alternative.

'You're starting them *all* up?' Hannah enquired, with a nod to her new assistants as she stepped away from the patient and began peeling off her surgical gloves, her mind firmly clamping down on her emotions.

'We need to, for air quality,' explained Le Roque. 'Too much debris is floating about and it's blocking the air-filtration systems.

'Well, as long as you're sure,' she said doubtfully.

'I'm as sure as . . . Shit!'

'What's the problem?' Was something going wrong already?

After a long and worrying delay, Le Roque replied, 'I just took a look out through exterior cams. We're in orbit around Mars.'

Weight – or rather a simulacrum of it – began bearing down on her leg and it started to ache. Dumbfounded, Hannah halted her slow progress towards the surgeons' clean lock. She didn't know how to respond to this information, but something inside her did as she felt the familiar surge of a panic attack rising up from her chest. On the one hand, the feeling was horrible but, on the other, she now had sure knowledge that these spasms only assaulted her when she wasn't in any real danger. It was almost a reassurance.

'Mars,' she repeated numbly.

'Which causes further stresses on the station,' said Le Roque. 'I need to get back to work.'

'Okay,' Hannah replied, cutting the connection.

In the clean lock she stripped, stowed her surgical whites and stepped into the shower. Now that most of the emergency cases were at least stable, it was time to start reinstituting cleanliness protocols. As far as she knew there had never been any case of a superbug taking hold here, but that did not mean they would be immune. By the time she walked back out into the laboratory, another patient was being wheeled in through the patient's clean lock, and Raiman was waiting his turn to enter the surgery and take charge.

'All yours,' she said, moving on.

Brigitta was still in the laboratory, carefully examining her hand, sealed in its transparent form cast. Hannah had managed to reattach her fingers temporarily, so they had a blood supply, but some lengthy work remained to repair the tendons, ligaments and nerves.

'Where's Angela?' Hannah asked.

Brigitta waved her other hand jerkily. 'Doing what she can.'

Angela's wound had not actually been from a bullet, but from a fragment of one. It hadn't hit the bone, and it had not been deep so was easily repaired.

'He's all right?' Brigitta asked, indicating Raiman with a nod of her head.

'Probably better than me at this sort of stuff,' Hannah replied. 'He is a military doctor, after all.' Hannah touched Brigitta's shoulder, then made her way to the door, stepping between wounded who had all been provided with analgesic patches and temporary dressings. She had headed fifty metres towards the elevators that led out of the arcoplex before she realized where she was going.

'Just one more thing, Le Roque,' she said through her fone. 'Where is Alan now?'

'Docking Pillar Two,' he replied shortly.

Hannah wanted to ask more, but the technical director sounded busy and hassled. She cut the connection and moved on. Near to the rim-side elevator she stepped into a suiting room, half-expecting to find nothing available there, but surprised to find a full range of suits. This was probably Le Roque's work, too – he certainly knew how to get things organized quickly. She donned a VC suit, headed for the elevator and made her way out of the arcoplex.

Inside the ring-side bearing installation for Arcoplex Two, Hannah entered a building that had probably been intended as some sort of communal area. Absolutely nothing yet marred the spacious bare floor, but its location and the view from the panoramic windows seemed to indicate such future use. She moved over to a window and gazed down, past the rotating curve of the arcoplex into the station itself. The carnage there was horrifying.

The huge volume of space enclosed by the station's new skin was full of floating debris that included corpses and body parts drifting in a vapour haze. The one railgun she could see was now just a twisted turret of blackened metal, with a glimpse of stars through the hole torn in the station's outer skin just above it. Robots were already in full action here, and she watched some of the construction model, clutching huge cable-mesh bags, propelling themselves from beam to beam as they collected debris. It was a familiar scene, little different from ones she had witnessed after Saul had put an end to the attack of Messina's troops on this same station, and she hoped it was one she would never see again. Would the killing end now? Or could it? There was only one person who could answer that question for her.

Hannah exited the bearing installation via a personnel access tube running alongside one of the internal railways, then passed through an airlock into an unpressurized section of the outer ring. She glimpsed the vortex generator over to her right, where walls had been taken out and the station substructure adjusted to accommodate it. Next she entered a pressurized section that took her past a group of three proctors crouching, amidst scattered equipment, around a super-cap power unit. They seemed almost like natives squatting around a campfire, busy at traditional crafts, until Hannah made a closer inspection.

All of them had been severely damaged, but were methodically repairing themselves. It was unnerving to see one of them squatting with its entire torso opened up as it detached its ribs, one at a time, to bend them back into shape or to micro-weld cracks in them. Inside the torso she could see an odd amalgam of dry woody-looking organics and gleaming metal, and something like a big stepper motor where the lungs should be. She shuddered, and moved on.

Back out into vacuum, she followed another railway running around the ring, then turned at a junction to take her out towards the space docks. She only then began considering what precisely she wanted to ask Saul, and in the end realized her questions boiled down to a simple 'What now?' When she entered Docking Pillar Two, however, he was nowhere in sight.

'Alan?' she enquired through her fone, but there was no response.

She began searching the dock, checking dusty storage rooms, sealed offices containing hardware yet to be touched by human hand, the empty acreage of an embarkation lounge, but still there was no sign of him. Perhaps he was outside? Le Roque had not specifically said Saul was *inside* the docking pillar. Hannah went to locate a maintenance airlock giving access to the exterior of the pillar and shortly found herself in an area packed with spares for space-plane fuelling systems. Then she was rising out of the face of the docking pillar, and having to make one of those mental changes of perspective just to stand on it, held in place only by her gecko boots.

Mars . . .

If she was honest, this was her prime reason for coming outside, rather than any real expectation of finding Saul out here. There it was, filling up a large portion of the view, the outer rim of Argus seemingly heading towards it like some steel bridge. She was sure she could even see the inky shadow of Argus Station down on the planet, though that might have been some feature integral to the surface. Hannah spent some minutes absorbing the view, also spotting Phobos poised just beyond the curve of its horizon, then almost reluctantly turned to peer at the nearest space plane.

No sign of activity here, but beyond it, higher up the pillar, she could see a hint of movement. She began walking towards it, and on circumventing the wing of the nearest plane, a second space plane came into view. It had been gutted.

Robots were picking amid the remains of the vehicle like ants in the dismembered corpse of a crow. Its wings had been detached, and the cockpit had been taken apart. Most of the passenger and cargo area lay over to one side, and the pillar itself was strewn with fragments of flame-cut metal, pipes, nuts and bolts and other fixings, and wisps of insulating material like some vacuum-resistant moss. Perhaps this plane had been hit by some kind of weapon during the recent attack?

'Alan is nowhere to be seen either in or on Docking Pillar Two,' Hannah told Le Roque reproachfully, when he finally responded to her call.

'You got that right,' Le Roque replied, sounding irritated.

'What do you mean?'

'It looks like he's gone off to perform a particularly spectacular form of suicide.'

'What?'

Le Roque dryly explained to her how they were about to lose their Owner . . .

Mars

Var's head-up display read zero, but there were always a few more minutes of air remaining after that. She lay against a rock, trying to control her breathing. She didn't want to get into a panic, start panting away her last moments of air and end up trying to tear off her EA suit helmet. She wondered how nitrogen suffocation would feel. Were the contentions that it was a painless way to die just complete bullshit, or would she indeed just drift away? Would it be like sleep with the moment of transition from consciousness to unconsciousness becoming a moment that could never be remembered? Probably. Then afterwards there would be a brief period of unconsciousness before her body started to die.

That hollow roaring in her ears, with a background of irritating tinnitus, was growing steadily. Obviously this was some side effect of oxygen starvation, just like the tightness inside her head, the feeling of growing pressure. She felt warm, too warm, would really have loved to have stripped out of her suit just once more before she died, to feel a cool breeze on her skin—

Cut that out.

Hallucinations now. A Martian wind was blowing dust along the chasma and her mind had connected that to the roaring inside her head. However, she knew the reality: that the winds here, no matter how fast they blew, were wimpish things in such thin air. And they certainly didn't sound like the full-throated blast of a space-plane rocket motor.

Any minute now, she reckoned. Any minute now things would go dark.

Forever.

A shadow was how it started, as it seemingly passed over her. The start of that final darkness? It was a relief that was short-lived, as the shadow passed and a bright light glared through her visor.

Hah! Here come the angels!

A huge shape descended before her, but it had nothing to do with the supernatural. She was hallucinating again, her mind now creating little fictions to escape the inexorable reality of death. A quadrate framework packed with what looked like the main engine of a space plane – cylindrical fuel tanks and one dark figure seated in an acceleration chair – settled out of the sky on a ribbed flame, adjusting as it descended with scalpel blades of steering-thruster blasts. As it finally thumped down, the dust it had stirred up shrouded it from her sight completely.

Var felt she had to congratulate her imagination for that one, but felt rather critical of its engineering credentials and vector calculus. Okay, present her with comfortable fantasies, but at least try to make them believable ones. It quite simply wasn't possible to take the engine from a space plane and turn it into what, centuries ago, had been called a flying bedstead. Such an object would be impossible to control, and that was before she even got into thinking about where it might have come from and how it could have been built in the limited time available.

Ridiculous.

A man clad in a black VC suit strode out of the dust and came to stand over her. He squatted, placing the oxygen bottle he was carrying to one side, then reached in and detached her spent bottle. He inserted the new bottle in place and her head-up display rose to a figure of forty hours. Immediately after that, pumps in her suit started working, blowing a breeze around her face, cool as the one she had imagined she would have felt had she pulled off her suit.

Var began to flirt with the idea of surviving.

'Good, you're alive,' said a familiar voice over her suit radio.

She gazed up through his visor. It was her brother's face; just the eyes were disconcerting. She considered further the impossibility of flying that bedstead contraption still hidden behind a wall of dust. Sure, it was impossible, unless you just happened to be the kind of person capable of stealing space stations and trashing whole planets.

She continued staring at him for long minutes, as reality returned along with its aches, pains and other glorious discomforts.

'What kept you?' she asked.